Fallen Star

A Novel

Edited by ivyinkedits@gmail.com

1st Edition | 01
Paperback ISBN:979-8-218-66937-9
Hardcover ISBN: 979-8-218-66938-6

First published June 2025

Printed in the United States of America   1 2 3 4 5 6 7 8 9

"I looked around in a blood-soaked gown and I saw something they can't take away."

– Taylor Swift

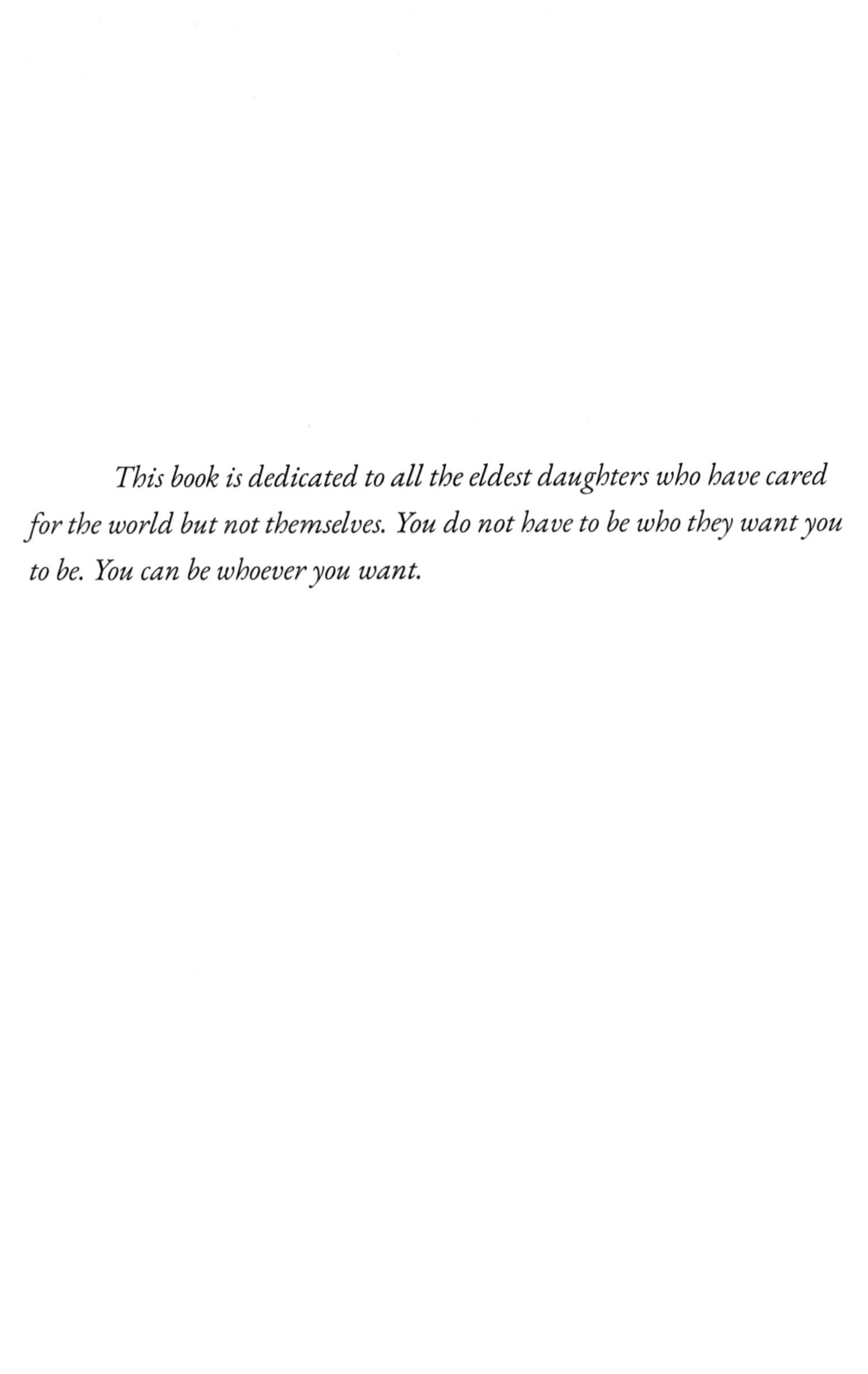

This book is dedicated to all the eldest daughters who have cared for the world but not themselves. You do not have to be who they want you to be. You can be whoever you want.

Chapter One

In my opinion, there is nothing quite like a crisp Florentine October morning. The golden rays of sun painted the underbellies of the lavender clouds a fiery orange-red. I had been up since before the sun, my bags packed since the night before. I was too excited to get home. This scholastic tour was enlightening to say the least, but I truly yearned for the familiar comforts of home and to hear the latest news from my siblings. I had been sad at first to not hear back from them; neither my brother nor my sister returned any individual letter I had written over these past five years. They had added paragraphs in the family letters I received frequently. It would be a relief to see them again.

The tavern we had stayed in sat in one of the busiest streets of Florence. To see the sunrise was rare; once the sun awoke so did the city. Below, through the window, I saw the stable boys lead our horses out to the court yard and begin hitching them to our carriage. I collected my bags and pranced out and down the hallway, knocking loudly on all four of my companions' rooms. Aurora poked her sleepy head out from the first door.

"Really Ma'am. You ought to be behaving more ladylike. We've only one more night before we are back in Inanis," she started groggily, her golden hair tousled from sleep. I shrugged and the other members of our party emerged.

"Our carriages are being prepared. Pack up! See you down in the quarter!" I instructed. Aurora glared at me with her big pale yellow eyes.

"I am a serious m'lady. Your mother will be furious if she hears - or peace forbid, *sees* you acting like this. Please wait for one of the footmen to load your things," she pleaded. I thought for a moment about packing the carriage myself regardless, but her eyes looked like the type of tired sleep would not cure.

"Alright. Only for you," I said before turning to descend the stairs. I waited in the tavern below for the party. A footman, Osbert, practically fell down the stairs a moment later. A smart observer might say he was not used to walking. I waved and the gangly youth straightened, snapping awkwardly to attention as he spotted me at my small table. He approached me, tipping his hat timidly.

"Can I take your things M'Lady?" he asked.

"Have you eaten?"

"What?" he sputtered.

"Have you eaten?" I repeated. The young man glanced around and then back to me. He chewed his lip and avoided my gaze, instead stared longingly at my mug of ale.

"No," he murmured. I smiled triumphantly.

"We cannot have that. Take this and go get something from the barkeep. I think she's got something warm." I placed my coin purse on the table directly in front of him. Osbert stared at the dark purple velvet pouch, his complexion pale. When he looked at the barkeep, it flooded red. She was a grouchy, busty woman. The footman seemed petrified of her.

"Ok, how about you pack my things and I will get you a portion of her hottest meal . How's that sound?" I gingerly took my coin purse back from the table. He nodded furiously and vanished out the door with my bags. I approached the barkeep, who was wiping suds from the inside of recently washed mugs.

"Can I help you?" she croaked.

"Yes!" I smiled brightly. "What've you got that's hot this morning? I would like to purchase two of what you have for my footmen." Her eyes lit up at the mention of my party members. She offered me fried eggs on a chunk of buttered and toasted sourdough bread. I changed my order to three portions, two for the footmen and one for myself. I paid her what she asked, then she scurried off to the kitchen to start the order. I leaned on the bar facing the door and looked around the tavern.

The tavern was mostly empty. A man slept off his drinks in a corner surrounded by empty mugs, his head resting on his folded arms. A pair of younger men laughed and joked towards the front, but otherwise it was quiet. Someone descended the stairs next to the bar wall. I kept my eyes on the doorway, planning a friendly interaction with whoever stepped through. In came Aurora, golden hair brushed back into a low bun covered by a pearled coif from home.

"Seren Astrum! Are those *trousers*?!" She wielded my name like a curse.

"Yes?" I raised an eyebrow. I could not understand how she missed this when I woke her up. She closes the distance between us and looks up into my eyes.

"I know you've got this wild idea that while on this tour you may do as you please, and I have allowed you, but now as we return home you must abide by your mother's rules. Please Ser, if she finds out, I will be her next practice mannequin!" Aurora's hands leapt to her chest and stomach.

"Aurora, it will be ok. When we have disembarked from Ingenium, and dropped off the tutors, I promise I will dress 'appropriately'." Her expression did not ease. She looked at me like I had dropped my glamour and my wings were exposed. My mother, current rule maker and previous breaker, insisted on portraying the family as powerful, proper, and precious. Aurora shook her head wearily.

"Fae tell M'Lady… I see your bags are gone, so why are you waiting inside?" she asked, eyeing the door where both our carriages waited.

"I've ordered morning meals for myself and the footmen," I said.

"You really must stop this. *WE* are hired to care for *you*! I insist you stop now, before we return to Mythénia." Aurora fixed me with a stern matronly stare, brows raised. The barkeep emerged from the kitchens with three meals still steaming on wood plates.

"Here you go. Keep the plates – they're good for the road." She set the dishes on the bar. I smiled and dipped my head to her. She hurried to the next task and I picked up the still warm plates. I handed one to Aurora.

"Since I am not '*supposed*' to do menial labor, you can carry this plate for me," I teased. Aurora rolled her eyes and took it from me. I led the way to the door, kicking it open for me and Aurora. We stepped out into the smoky morning.

Everyone was outside and ready to go. I was last seated. The Royal Tutor and the Human Expert from Ingenium were in the first carriage, pulled by two incognito unicorns, which appeared to all humans as two well-bred white horses, their horns and glamorous coats carefully disguised by a glamour. Aurora and I would be in the last, also pulled by two incognito unicorns. This past year, almost every inquisitive human we spoke to would try to guess their breed, our footment and drivers were exhausted from all the nodding and quiet agreements. Master Wais insisted the best way to study humans would be to live among them. A large part of that was concealing anything supernatural: wings, ears, tails, horns and hooves. That also meant lying a majority of the time. We went to poor taverns that would read us as wealthy Lords or foreign nobility... which was not completely false. Luckily, they did not ask questions and only had eyes for the coins.

The entire year of being in Italy, no one had pushed too hard when we said we were Swedish nobility. They just asked us a thousand never ending questions about Sweden.

Aurora climbed into the carriage and got situated. I gave her a very cheeky '*please don't be mad*' smile as I handed the footmen their breakfast. At first they would not take them, but eventually each man took a plate gratefully. I climbed into my carriage to wait for the final tasks to be finished before leaving.

The footmen came and closed up the first carriage, asking if we wanted a panel open for air or not. I did want air, though I would have preferred flying. Osbert smiled at me as he closed up the carriage, his face no longer that pasty, hungry color. The exact look of the Aurora's complexion now – a pale, internally lit yellow. I turned away from the window and moved myself to the bench where she and the last wooden plate of food sat.

"What now, you insufferable rebel?" she glowered at me.

"You need to eat now." I ripped the sourdough toast in half, offering half to her. She didn't have the heart to refuse me. She took the bread, and I offered the plate of fried eggs. She pulled one off and placed it atop her toasted bread. I did the same.

The human realm was not my favorite that I have seen on this five year tour, but the food made up for it. I had to give Aurora credit too – she always figured out the most delicious combinations.

"Astounding! Where do you conjure these ideas?" I cried after taking a large bite.

"Ha!" she guffawed. "I saw some old man do it a few weeks back, tried it for myself and by Solaris' name if it did not hit the spot. I felt so guilty that I could not share it with my husband." She blushed. We giggled like the young maidens we had been once. She was no longer a maiden, married before we began this five year scholastic tour. Zanos was a nice satyr, but I did take him aside and threaten him with 'human torture' if he ever hurt her. He diligently returned her letters each month.

I took the plate back to my bench and stowed it in my personal bag, which was mostly full of writing material and a spare set of clothes. I pulled dry skin off my lips with my teeth as I pondered the issue behind my sibling's missing letters. I had collected gifts for everyone to make up for missing so much time. I thought of my siblings daily – the times that I would read to them, or practicing my spells with Vesperia. For Vesperia, I found an elegant Unda pearl necklace while visiting the ocean. For Castor, an intricate steel dagger from the Terran King's own armory.

The Italian countryside welcomed us as we departed Florence, heading north towards the forest. Hidden deep within this forest of stone pine, cypress, oak and chestnut trees, there was a clearing surrounded by tiny, secretive mushrooms. This was our hidden fae circle, planted last year when we first came to the Human Realm. Once we passed through the clearing, we would be returned to Mythénia through the West Gate, located on the borders of the Effects Region and Floral Region. After that, we would travel northwest to the city of Ingenium where the tutors would split from the company, and Aurora and I would be bound for home. I began to think of all the things I would want to share with my siblings. Then I remembered – the stars.

"Aurora?" I queried.

"Hmm?" she replied, giving me her full attention.

"Have I yet told you of the newest addition to my abilities?"

"No! You have not! How delightful. What is it you can do now?" Fully engaged, Aurora leaned forward, slightly eyes wide with the wrinkles of a smile underneath.

"A couple months back, I was staring at the sky – sleepless again – and before me I saw a scene, like in the theater, of a noble family walking through the streets proudly. I saw the same scene again when we witnessed the return of the Medici family." I felt a desperate need for her to understand radiate on my face like embarrassment. Aurora's face suddenly looked more concerned than curious. I had lost her.

"Prophecy, Rory. I can see important events in the stars! I look up at the sky and the stars... They *move*! It felt like the first time I flew, so free, so alive! Do you not understand? I can read the stars like you might watch a play. They tell me of things that will come to pass. My mother will be so pleased!" I exclaimed.

"I see, well I do not know about that Ren," she exhaled. Her face wilted like it always did when she had to remind me of my mother's strict rules. "You might not see now just how helpful this is, but I am certain she will. Seeing the future, who would not want that?" Aurora came to my side of the carriage and took my hands in hers.

"Listen Seren. *I am* happy for you, but we both know your mother will not be as excited as you. She was thrilled to learn of the mutated blast spell, but this has no offensive power. She is going to crush your feelings and enthusiasm," she pleaded, desperate for me to understand.

"Rory," I sighed, "I know you are only looking out for me. She and *the Queen* sent me on this tour to show the Regions what a Star Fairy is and what we can do. They wanted this – for me to grow my abilities." I sat firm, holding my position. Aurora deflated. She repeated that she did not want to see me hurt, but would respect my choice.

"You'll do it anyway, so I might as well make my peace with it." She sighed and leaned her head on my shoulder, something we've done since girlhood.

The autumnal forest flew by as we passed deeper into the thicket. I felt a buzz in my chest, and Aurora must have had a similar feeling, because she sat up and moved back to her bench seat. We both leaned on the carriage's right door. The waves of energy increased as we drew nearer. The underbrush scraped the carriage as we rolled over terrain unkind to carriage wheels. Fortunately, we did not need to worry about breaking one, as the footmen and drivers used enchantments to make them sturdy.

The energy field engulfed us, and I watched as the world around us shifted. Now it was every other tree and its friend that participated in autumn. There were coniferous trees mixed in that we could see from the border crossing. The unaffiliated guard nodded his head at each driver as they passed through the West Portal Gate – a large circular stone gate.

No matter where you cross from the Human Realm, you will pass through either the West Gate or East Gate. On occasion, things and beings might wash ashore near the Unda lands. Father would often rant about his conspiracy that the Merkin or water spirits were abducting humans and using a third underwater portal to travel outside of any prying eyes.

A group of humans passed us on our left, heading back to their Realm. I overheard their fairy guide asking them where 'home' was and if they could picture it. I could, and I ached for it.

With their new titles, my parents acquired a parcel of land in the highest point in the Inanis Valley, a manor house, and a small fortune. The manor was a gift and not unlike Hardwick Hall in the English region, home to many English nobility. An architect from Terra or Ingenium must have been inspired. The notable differences between Hardwick Hall and my home is firstly the location; we do not reside in the English countryside. Secondly, I imagine Hardwick Hall is not divided by light and dark. The most important difference is probably the miniature galaxy floating on our ceiling. A living piece of art – something that my parents had made together and maintained since the end of the war.

Our manor came with a name: Twilight Hall. One more thing to commemorate the bloody clan war. Twilight Hall consisted of three floors, ten large rooms, two great bedchambers, a Great Hall, kitchens, servants quarters, a study, two drawing rooms, and a ball room. My mother had claimed the top half of the manor for guests, her reason being it was closer to the sun. The middle floor consisted of the family apartments split clean down the middle. Mother had taken the west wing to look out her window at her home, whereas father took the east for the same reason. The lower portion of the house was relinquished to my father, who did little to nothing with it besides close up all the windows in his study, located just across the hall from the kitchens.

Growing up, I had the second largest room in the east wing. Father would read to me or tell me stories accompanied by little shadow figures that moved at his will. When my sister, Vesperia, was born, our mother chose a room for her in the west wing. Once she and I were old enough, we would feign sleep and wait on the gallery walk above the

Great Hall for one another. We would lay and watch the Galaxy cloud morph and shine until we succumbed to sleep.

The carriage rode northwest to Ingenium now – home of the creation fairies - down a rugged dirt path. Our roads were underdeveloped due to most folk preferring to fly. Something I would love to do myself right now.

"Are you excited to see Zanos?" I disturbed Aurora. Her face lit up and she suddenly did not care for the view of our countryside.

"Yes! Very much so! His last letter, he mentioned wanting to cook me the meal he proposed with! Not only am I yearning for him, but now he's got me salivating at the thought of roast pumpkin, boiled eggs, and lamb. Evil bastard," she laughed contagiously, catching me in her wave of joy.

We fell back into silence; all we had was the passing scenery to draw our focus. I could not stand the staleness. I knocked on the carriage signaling to Nevin, our driver, to stop. A moment later we pulled away from the carriage trail and into the brush.

"What are we doing?" Aurora asked, peering out the left side window, her right.

"Stretching our wings!" I responded. The drivers and footmen let down the step bars and opened the doors for both carriages. Master Wais and Master Rayne complained as they stepped out of theirs. I slipped out of the carriage's right door and onto Mythénian soil.

"Ah. it is so *good* to be home!" I inhaled the crisp, icy autumnal air, laced with a tickle of magic.

"Lady Astrum. What in the name of Solaris is this?" Master Rayne demanded, storming up to me. I turned to face him, seeing his reddened face and wispy hair.

"Master Rayne, Lady Astrum is my mother – I am Lady Seren. I have decided we would stop to remove the weary and burdensome glamours. Lady Aurora and I will stretch our wings – they've been repressed a hearty year. Despite being the highest scholar in the region, you have yet to endure the pain of bound wings. If you detest the Mythénian air so badly, please wait in your carriage." I enunciated our titles. As the Queen's appointed tutor, he had an overwhelming need to wield authority over us all. I was all too excited to be rid of him upon our arrival to Ingenium. Master Rayne stood there in stunned, furious silence, mouth agape as I took Aurora's hand and we released the spell binding our wings we used to hide in the Human Realm.

Aurora's calm yellow wings unfurled and rose from her back. The veins mimicked butterflies and glowed with intense orange light. Mine were an odd shape as the result of mixing bloodlines. I had the tall shape of my mother's wings, with the accompanying glow, but the slim aerodynamic curves of my father's. Revealing them was as easy as removing a coat. I breathed in, found the edge of the glamour and pulled. I heard a gasp from behind me where Osbert and the other footman were waiting as my wings of stardust appeared. I smiled. A unique feature of mine and my siblings' wings were the twinkling lights that emanated and sometimes fell from the formation. We would joke that they were galaxies trapped in a spell. For all we knew, that was the truth.

I smirked at Master Rayne before taking flight, Aurora close behind. We flitted into the sky, sun peaking near mid day above us. The trees below began to shrink as we ascended above the clouds. They looked like they had been painted onto the landscape by the finest brush. Aurora flew above me in a big arching circle - *is her coif staying put by magic?* Her smile was wider than the Effections River.

"Oh, I *needed* this!" she gasped, circling me as I hovered in the air.

"Me too – come up here!" I waved to a spot just above the first layer of clouds. We flew up together, glancing behind us to check that none of the tutors felt like following.

"What is the matter M'Lady?" Aurora asked with a bright smile.

"I hope I did not startle you, I thought it would be fun to find Inanis together. I feel like we've been gone too long."

She shook her head and we both searched the horizon. We knew it was north, but lacking a compass we could only use our wits and our hearts.

"I think I see it just over there." I pointed to our left, hoping it was due north.

"I could not say – do you see Lux?"

"There." I pointed more to my left, laughing. The giant, pulsing orb of light was hard to miss. Lux radiated light so bright that humans thought we had pulled a sun down to land. She giggled back.

"That is Obscurum. Leading me to give my best guess that this," I pointed, "valley is ours!"

"I believe you are right!" Aurora said, and we laughed.

"I wonder if that little glint of light is Mother and The Queen waiting for us!" I added. Aurora's laughter stopped; her body became stiff.

"We should get going," she said, floating back downward. I watched her beautiful wings work elegantly to slowly lower her. Mine would do the same, but I thought that they would not carry me as gracefully. Aurora landed before me and scurried into the carriage before I even touched the ground again. I sighed and decided to check on the unicorns.

With the glamours lifted, the beautiful white horses were now dazzling unicorns with jewel tone coats. The two that had been yoked to our carriage were named Sonipes and Caballus. The two yolked to carry Masters Wais and Rayne were named Equos and Mannus. I landed and strode over to the space between Sonipes and Caballus.

"Hello! Can I get you anything?" I asked.

"You could take this contraption off and fly your lazy asses home," Caballus snorted. His tail flicked, snapping at his team member.

"Watch it!" Sonipes bit back. "Pay no heed to this filly. He is not used to working. The men already gave us our water. Thank you for your consideration, Ma'am."

"Truly my pleasure. I like to help where I can. I really do admire the natural state of everyone. Aurora's wings, your coats," I said. My eyes slid over the stallion's coats, which were shining as though they had just been washed – a fairly common occurrence with unicorn coats. Sonipes had a coat that was a barely discernible pink. His horn, now worn by age, was a spiral of two dusty pink columns with a streak of bright salmon reaching a now dull point. Caballus had a very noticeable cobalt tint to his coat, his single horn twisted, but not yet a pointed weapon. It, too, was blue.

I looked longingly at the team ahead of us, but Master Rayne and Master Wais were climbing back into their carriage. Aurora peeked out of ours, waving me over.

"Thank you for all your hard work. I truly am grateful for your diligent work these past years. I hope you get a long rest when we return," I said to the unicorns as Aurora began urging me back to my seat. The stallions preened and nodded as I stepped away.

"M'Lady!" Aurora called. Osbert was waiting for me to climb back into the carriage before closing up the footsteps.

"Why can we not fly there? The servants have to return with our baggage anyhow. We could simply be a bit early in body!" I asked as I finally climbed in, sitting on my bench.

"You certainly could M'Lady, but you would have to go alone . I am required to return with the rest of the servants. I am, after all, a servant," Aurora said, her tone unsettling me.

"Aurora, I am sorry. I did not mean for you to stay. Truly, I felt you would accompany me. I was unaware of your previous obligation. My sincerest apologies." I attempted an apology, but she was silent the remainder of the ride to Ingenium.

Once our wheels hit the brick and cobblestone road, I watched Master Rayne's carriage pull away and down another street towards their homes. We continued until we reached the 'Tinkers Respite' Inn. Aurora and the footmen unpacked our carriage and carried my bags inside. Aurora stopped me at the Inn's doorway.

"Tomorrow, you will wear proper court attire or you will not have a hand maid anymore. Do you understand?" She was stern and did not move until I conveyed my understanding.

Chapter Two

The morning was a little tense. I imagine it may have gone worse if I had chosen to rebel against Aurora's wishes. I knew she was right– my mother would be livid if I appeared at home in trousers and flew there instead of arriving by carriage.

I thought Aurora would have snapped if I had come down to ask her for help with my gown while wearing trousers. So, I was on my own. I could hardly sleep, so I left my bed before the sun even had a chance to return. By candlelight, I chose a dark blue dress – to match my eyes. I had gotten the undergarments on, but the lacing on this dress was too intricate for me to learn and maneuver behind my back. This is what a lady's maid was for!

I threw my black cloak over my shoulders and entered the hallway with a lit candle on a holder. It was dark and quiet – everyone else was peacefully sleeping. I hoped. Now, it was time to disturb at least one of them. Down the hall to my left was Aurora's door – the closest possible. I knocked seven times with my free hand and waited. After a minute, I knocked seven more times. When I stopped to listen, I heard her loudly get up and approach the door. I stepped back one step. Aurora cracked the door and rubbed the sleep from her eyes.

"Good morning," I whispered with a smile. She does not smile back. I know she is still mostly asleep.

"Morning," she mumbled.

"I need help with the lacing on my gown." I hold open my cloak so she can see the dress underneath.

"Come sit," she yawned, pulling her door open wide for me to enter. I picked up my skirts and followed her in.

Her room lit up with the flickering flame of my candle. Aurora lit one of her own and sat it on the windowsill. She pulled out the chair from the vanity and gestured for me to use it. I removed my cloak, set it on the chair, then stood with my back to her. I could hear her quiet chuckles and realized she wanted me to sit, but she began to lace up the gown regardless.

"My Lady..." Aurora began, "You should sit. Seeing as we will be in a carriage most of the day, you will want the breathing space." She held the back of the chair for me. I felt a flush creep into my cheeks. She pulled my cloak from the chair, laying it on her bed. I sat in the chair and as I rested, I felt her hand pushing my back away from the chair.

Aurora's fingers deftly pulled all the cords into its rightful places and secured it with a fancy knot that was made to look extravagant.

"Thank you," I said, moving to stand up.

"Hold on. We may have a long ride ahead, but I will be styling your hair for your arrival. You have been gone for half a decade – you really should look your absolute best." Aurora seemed fully awake now, refilled on whatever essence that kept her going with a smile on her face. Her hands beckoned me to sit back into the seat. I did – now allowed to rest on the back of the chair. Sitting stiff and straight backed pushed a deep ache into my bones.

I relaxed as she combed and braided my hair. She dug in her trinket box to adorn my hair with a silver string made with Unda Pearls. She handed me a well loved, wooden looking glass. My hair was beautifully piled atop my head in loops of braids. The intricate pearl string was woven into the bouquet.

"Regal," I praised Aurora, handing her looking glass back to her. She glowed with pride.

"Thank you again." I added.

"You are welcome, My Lady, " Aurora replied. She was setting out her clothes for the day. I took my cloak back from her bed so that she might lay out her clothes better. She placed a simple yellow cotton dress and white apron atop the sheets.

"I am sorry to have woken you. Please go back to sleep." I apologized, suddenly feeling horribly rude.

"Oh no! M'lady, you are risen, so I must also! Besides, we have a long day ahead of us. Unless you truly would like to fly..." Her voice trailed off.

"No, no. I only wanted to stretch my wings. I am so sorry for last night. I did not intend to imply that I wanted to travel alone. Only that one whole year banned from soaring or gliding was petty torture, if you were to ask me." I joked. Aurora laughed.

"I understand. I know you did not mean it that way. I am sorry for handling the moment so poorly. I hope you will excuse my rash behavior." She apologized.

"Oh – no. No. This is not what I wanted either. I was terribly rude. I am immensely lucky and grateful to you for being with me all this time. You are my longest friend – who just so happens to be my lady's maid. Even if you were not, I think we would still be friends." I corrected – Aurora had done nothing wrong. I did not want to chase her away with my bad behavior.

"You are my greatest friend. You will not hurt me, even by accident. I know you – I know your heart." She crossed the room to embrace me. She smelled of lavender and sun oil.

"Are you certain you want to get on the road? I asked. " I do not mind returning to my chambers to wait a while so that you might sleep a bit more."

"Yes, Seren. I know. You will sit at your window and watch folks go by, but that is a bit ghoulish, do you not think? The folk from Ingenium are also more outwardly observant than you, dear friend."

"You are right... I will wake Osbert and Nevin?"

"No!" Aurora commanded. I looked at her incredulously. "You need to return to your chambers and await *us* to collect *you*. Please." Her stern tone was laced with an anxious note. I obeyed, collecting my candle and moving to the door. She held it for me and promised to see me soon.

Back in my chambers, I returned the candlestick to the mantle and pulled the vanity chair to the window. Aurora was most likely right. Anyone who saw me looking out the window would probably think I was strange. To mitigate any backlash, I threw on my cloak and flipped up the hood before climbing onto the windowsill, my feet resting on the chair.

I looked down at the fairies below. I felt some peace looking out over Ingenium, knowing that even though we were not back in the valley yet, we were home. Being back in Mythénia was a relief. Below, some folks walked and some flitted – not all fairies have wings you know. My own wings ached to stretch again. Flying was a second nature – denying it for that year gave me a deep resonating pain when the urge to float bubbled up. I assumed it was mostly guilt tinged with fear.

I watched a satyr family shuffle down the street. A father, mother, and a wild, small child wobbled down the street towards town limits. The child was held between the adults, bouncing and bumping into its parents the whole way. A fire spirit strutted from a brick building towards a bakery. She wore a black dress over her live fire skin, specially enchanted, no doubt. Her blue hellfire hair whipped behind her like it was pushed by wind. An adolescent dryad moved out of her way but followed her with his gaze. The lines in his bark were bright, his leaves divided into five segments and light green in color. He was a maple dryad. He shook himself back to his senses and continued onto his destination.

I spied a sprite flitting about the windowsills collecting spider webs. She approached my window; I froze. She was maybe a foot tall if you counted the sharp pointy wings. She had eight eyes and eight appendages, silky black hair, and fuzzy black skin – a spider sprite! What a novel sighting! They rarely leave Fauna. I stayed frozen as she collected the discarded webs from under my window. I was in awe. Her third, fourth, fifth, and sixth arms created a basket for the webs as her first and second grabbed the tendrils and wound them into bundles. She wore a woven dress of white spider silk with long trumpet sleeves and a long flowing skirt.

"Marvelous, " I whispered. The panes of glass must have been deceptively thin. She heard me and while searching frantically for the source, she looked into the window and her eyes caught mine. In a blink she was gone, and a deep set dread took root in my gut. I climbed down off the window and stored my black cloak in my trunk, taking out a second pale sunny yellow cloak with my mother's family crest embroidered on the breast. Just then, a knock came at my door – precisely seven.

"Come in!" I shouted. In came Aurora, followed by Osbert and Nevin. The men took my trunk and a few smaller boxes. Aurora hooked her arm in my arm and led me down the hall to our waiting carriage. The men loaded my boxes while Aurora led me to the open and waiting carriage door.

"Do they need a hand?" I asked, craning my neck to look back.

"No Ma'am! Excuse me ,but get in the carriage already! You are a highborn lady, The First Star and the Heir to Inanis. You are not supposed to handle luggage!" Aurora chided. I instantly felt bad.

"I only want to help. I hate waiting in the carriage. If I help, I am not sitting idly by and we can leave sooner! Is that a bad thing?"

The footman closed up the doors, giving Aurora stronger grounds for her argument.

"No. Your thoughtfulness shows your generous heart, but that does not erase your title. You are a very important fairy Seren. It is not your job to help servants – not even me. Please try to remember that." Aurora's face softened. I could not be angry, though I still felt strongly about helping the others. I responded to her with a nod and looked out the window as we pulled away from the smoky atmosphere of the constantly changing city.

I saw the other driver and footman astride Equos and Mannus now tacked in riding gear. The journey would be most of the day, but we would not need to rest or trade teams. They must be returning with us, though they were employed by Master Rayne.

We left the city behind us and followed the river towards Inanais. I was excited to see my home again. Not just the house I grew up in, but also the town full of all the people I had gotten to know every morning when I snuck out to watch the market, eventually participating. I could still remember the first thing I bought: a sugar cookie with a honeysuckle baked in. A sprinkling of sugar made the soft cookie crunch in a strangely satisfying way.

"Seren?" Aurora burst my day dream, and I returned my gaze to her – she looked concerned.

"Yes?" I fumbled.

"I apologize if I have upset you, M'Lady. I had been trying to get your attention, to ask about breakfast, but you did not answer. Did I overstep?" Her guilt was the first thing I noticed.

"Oh Aurora! No. I am the one who should be apologizing. I must be hungry because I was daydreaming about cookies. What did you have in mind for breakfast?"

"I hope you do not mind. I procured something similar to yesterday. This time the cook made us sandwiches!" She pulled wrapped bundles from her hand basket, handing me one.

"Before you ask, I did make sure the men ate as well. Now you." Aurora added. I tried to hide my amusement, but a snort escaped my nostrils. I took the wrapped bundle and watched as Aurora opened hers by unwrapping the bundle carefully from one side. I mimicked her and revealed my *interesting* breakfast.

I was faced with the fae version of a fried egg on rye toast. Fairies have been 'eating on the go' for most of our existence – we have almost perfected the on-the-go meal. In this case, I saw the distinct orange and red of a cooked phoenix egg, over easy, Calydonian boar meat, and melted yale and taurus cheese with spiced avocado spread. I would have chosen something… simpler, but maybe my pallet was not as refined as hers. I looked up to see Aurora watching me as she chewed a large bite she had taken.

I smiled and prayed my face would not betray me. Biting in, I wished I could unhear the squish of the avocado spread. Aurora seemed pleased and returned to her feast. I continued to eat, but caught myself conjuring ways to remove the wetter elements. I could not continue, so I re-wrapped the sandwich and sat it on the bench beside me.

"Are you full, M'Lady?" Aurora asked around another mouthful. She was folding her wrapper into neat squares now.

"Oh, yes! I am very full!" I started to imagine how to pick at the bread and meat – each plot foiled by the simple fact I was not alone.

"Of course M'Lady. I have been looking forward to our arrival in Mythénia, specifically for this!" She waved the paper wrapping in the air before slipping it into her basket.

"Would you like the rest of mine?" I offered. Her eyes filled with excitement, but then she looked away and down.

"Is your ladyship certain she will not wish to finish it before our lunch stop?"she gently asked. I felt an odd sensation in my heart at her words. I assumed she was feeling guilty for asking.

"I will not eat a bite anymore. Not until we break for lunch. Here." I handed the bundle back to her across the carriage. She hesitated, then took it and ate it more gradually than the one before.

Somehow, we arrived on the topic of Aurora's husband, Zanos. I think it was the food; Zanos is a well loved cook's apprentice at home. He was always asking about ingredients and new recipes, the exact reason my father hired him. As an apprentice, he would get to learn all the famous dishes from across Mythénia. He and Aurora were set for life as long as they kept my mother happy. A heroic feat to be sure.

Aurora was telling me about the Fauna delicacy he had planned for their reunion. Something vegetarian– can you imagine a goat eating any other animal? Humans like to believe that goats will eat anything, in actuality, that would be the pigs.

Jack – the footman from Master Raynes' household – rode beside the carriage and spoke with our driver, Nevin, before pulling back to speak to me through the window.

"Excuse me ma'am?" He tipped his hat to me. "Would now be an agreeable time to break for lunch?"

"Indeed it would be a fine time!" I hollered. I ached to stretch my wings – a year of being bound would take a while to get over. Jack and Equos pulled away, leading our carriage off of the rutted path and near the bank of the river. Nevin followed carefully.

When we came to rest, Osbert was slow to release us from our cabin. He had grabbed the lunch basket before getting off the footman's perch. He let down the footboards and opened the doors for us. I tried not to rush, but the speed I took to the air was enough to rip a gasp from Aurora.

I flitted a couple dozen feet in the air, but Aurora stayed on the ground. I left her and her grounding attitude where they were and soared up to the closest wisp of cloud. My hand passed through the vapor when I reached for it. I hovered and pretended to lay on a cloud, looking down I could see Aurora had set up and was waiting for me. I wanted to stay in the sky but I knew if I lingered I would land and learn that spiced jam was added to my food. Reluctantly, I lowered myself to the ground. Aurora smiled, but it faded fast.

"The innkeeper gave us quite the spread! Would you like me to add pepper jam to your roast?" Aurora asked.

"No!" *That was too quick*. "I apologize. No thank you, but I appreciate the offer." I took the small wooden picnic plate from her. It was loaded with mashed potatoes and pork roast chunks as the 'spread' Aurora was glowing over. There were a few rolls and mini cakes too. Aurora did not seem phased by my indelicate response. She took up her own plate and added a large helping of pepper jam to her roast.

I glanced around, noting that the men and unicorns were not eating with us – again. This was the case during the entire trip. They ate of course, just away from Aurora and I. Occasionally one of the young footmen – usually Osbert – would spend a little time with us. One of the drivers would inevitably pull him back to their herd of males. Aurora passed it off as proper form, but in reality – outside of Effection – there was no reason to adhere to my mother's strict code.

They seemed to be enjoying themselves on the river bank. They had handfuls of food and Nevin was attempting to grab fish from the river, unsuccessfully.

Aurora cleared her throat. I returned to looking at her. We each swallowed the food we had in our mouths.

"I was hoping upon our return, I could request a leave of absence? Zanos and I wanted to return to Fauna to see his parents. I would only require a week's time."

"Oh! Of course! Are you sure a week is enough?" I responded.

"Yes, it shall be plenty of time." She dabbed at the corners of her mouth with a napkin.

"I will notify mother's Lady of The House of your request. I will insist on your behalf – when is your departure date?" I asked.

"We had planned to leave two days post-return to Inanis. If your ladyship agrees, of course." Her demeanor changed to that of a shy soft woman, I could tell that she was worried.

"That is perfectly acceptable. I will borrow a house maid if I am in any need of assistance." Some of her warmth and light returned.

"Thank you M'Lady. We are so grateful to you." Aurora sighed.

We finished our plates and I helped Aurora pack up, but relented when she insisted she carry the basket back to the carriage. Jack bounded over to relieve her of the burden. The stair into the carriage was still down and the doors open, welcoming us to climb back inside. Jack loaded the basket while his companions wrangled the unicorns into their teams.

Equos and Mannus were locked into the yolk and Master Raynes' driver took over. Nevin and Jack rode ahead on Caballus and Sonipes. Aurora got settled and Osbert closed us in. Aurora seemed giddy now, bouncing in her seat and she glanced out the left window. Inanis was growing closer with every turn of our carriage wheels. A lead ball dropped in my gut. I missed home dearly in the sense that I missed the people who made it a home, but I would not cry if I never laid eyes on Twilight Hall again. I only return now out of duty and want to see my siblings again.

Once I had asked Castor and Vesperia what Realm they most wanted to see. Vesperia had longed to visit the Floral Basin, wishing to meet a snapdragon fairy. I wrote to tell her how elegant and regal they are in person, but she did not return my letter. Castor, the miniature rake that he is, jested of visiting the beaches of Unds to meet the mermaidens who were rumored to appear topless. I did write to him to inform him that the results of said beach were varied. Mermasters would on occasion remove a blouse or jacket to add water to their gills, but the most common moisture fix was to soak a compress or scarf in water and wrap it sturdily around their gills. Mermaidens were also some of the most prudent of the elements. They were very thoughtful of the beings they came into contact with. Certainly they would have avoided him.

We continued following the river until we came up on the bend that cut our town from the foothills of Obscurum. Inanis was a quiet, whispering town just outside of the Obscurum Mists. As we approached, I expected there to be a marvelous fair for my return, as was customary for returning nobility. I peered out of the carriage's right window to see... nothing. Not a soul in the road, no banners or decorations.

"What is going on Aurora?" I asked leaning forward even more, sticking my shoulders out the window.

"I do not know M'Lady, but I can find out if you wish."

"I would like to know. This is odd. The town has never been this quiet. Are we making a scene?" I began to worry. I sat back in my seat, Aurora pressed her back and wings flat against her seat back.

We crossed over the first canal bridge and I noticed a huddled crowd staring blankly. I dared not to stick my head out to see what changed as we passed. As we approached the town center where children usually played under a large evergreen, mothers called them back to their sides.

I wonder if the yellow and lilac stallions were glaring at everyone? There was only one way to know. We passed into the shopping district,and I watched as patrons scurried into shops and peered out of the windows. How strange.

Tradition would have dictated a grand homecoming. This was panic and fear. What had gotten into everyone? A few brave or uneducated folks waved, I was too stunned to reciprocate – I hoped the smile I flashed was sufficient.

I could barely hear the whispers and mutters as we passed by, but they all seemed melancholic. I thought I would return to a vibrant valley, ignited into passion to welcome their adventurous soon-to-be Duchess. This was no welcome – it was practically a funeral march. I was surprised they did not throw stones and chase us off.

Aurora was pale, as though she may feint. Master Ranyes' footman and Nevin continued riding ahead, seemingly unbothered. We passed over the last canal bridge and began our mild climb up the hill to Twilight Hall. I caught myself praying for some fanfare as we reached the gate. Nothing. Not a streamer in the trees or a bouquet to be seen. Once the gates closed behind us, Aurora relaxed and began readying herself for the end of our journey.

The laneway was wide enough for two carriages to pass by each other in opposite directions. In front of the manor, it made a circular loop with a preened garden in the center. Twilight Hall rose over the trees and slowly came into focus. The grand entrance was vacant for celebration.

The carriage pulled into the loop and stopped where the paving stones started. No footmen were about – not even the butler could see fit to greet his future mistress. What was more important than the return of the heir?

Osbert barely released the footstep before I burst out of the carriage headed straight for the front door, abandoning all my belongings for the servants.

"M'Lady!" Aurora called to me, but I had flown the distance to the door in a flurry of rage. *What was so important that they forgot about me?*

Chapter Three

I burst through the front door. The Great Hall was empty - not even a servant. I landed hard, my heels stinging. Aurora caught up to me, overburdened with our combined luggage.

"Let me." I reached for two of my bags, but Aurora jumped back.

"You promised you would revert back to proper etiquette upon your return. Ma'am, your mother will have my wings."

I sighed and recollected myself. I closed my eyes and took a deep breath. *Lady like, act ladylike.* I straightened my posture, blinking my eyes open slowly.

"Please take my things to my rooms. I will be up shortly." I commanded with guilt. Aurora bounced a curtsy, then scurried off to her duties.

I set my sights on the east wing, cutting through the pantry into the back hall, then using the back door to check the gardens. I stopped to check the head housekeeper's rooms next to the laundry, but she was absent too. A great metal clang sounded from the back gardens as I was almost to the door.

I pushed through the door to see my mother with her lady's maid – also known as our head housekeeper – Mrs.Sykes, actively stabbing an archery mannequin past its final threads. Straw and stuffing material littered the ground and blew around in the grass.

"Another!" my mother demanded, standing away from the ground where the mannequin lay. Mrs. Sykes saw me before my mother did.

"Ma'am– you have a visitor, " she said before she began cleaning the mess.

"Marjorie, you fool, that is my daughter! Come home from her tour at last." My mother looked up from the remains of the mannequin and released a roaring laugh. "Welcome dear, so glad to have you home." She sauntered over to me and I was able to see her full Lucidus Regalia.

Her golden hair was pulled back in a tight over hand braid down her back, beads of sweat shimmering off her illuminated gold skin. Her war gown was in the bright colors of the Lucidus clan – yellow, white and cream. It fell to her knees where it split to reveal trousers underneath – designed to make riding a horse easier. She was reliving her glory days as a Sun Archer.

She wrapped me in a cold hug, squeezing me tight before she turned to Mrs. Sykes and took up her position again. Another servant and Mrs. Sykes worked to bring in a new mannequin. I walked over to her, thinking carefully, attempting to display my disappointment. She looked over her shoulder at me with a curious stare.

"It is customary for the town and family to receive a returning heir with a celebration. Tell me, mother, what have we done to make the town dislike us?"

"Oh, never you mind. You might consider changing into something more suitable for court. All your gowns are just as you left them. Though, some may be snug. It appears as though you have gained weight." She looked me up and down as if I wore a gown of rags, making me feel so much smaller.

"Of course, mother." I curtsied, bringing a smile to her face. Mrs. Sykes began setting up the new mannequin and having the male servants clean up the shredded remains of the prior one. I turned back to the house, escaping through the garden door.

I used the east servants' stairs to ascend to the second floor where the family apartments were. The Lord's chambers were sealed, the door leading to the Lord's Hallway was also closed. *Father must be in his study again.* No matter. I needed to change my gown. I turned down the north hall and pushed open the door to my bedroom.

I was surprised to see my brother, Castor, lounging on my bed. He was the carbon copy of our mother, but with our father's somber face. His wavy golden locks splayed across the pillows and he lay whittling something with a magic, hovering knife. He looked over. and for a moment, I saw happiness grace his golden eyes, but he killed it with a frown.

"Sister, what are you doing?" he inquired while sitting up.

"I came to exchange my gown. Mother was displeased." I pulled at my skirts.

"Well you are not going to be able to do that here." He chuckled and resumed carving.

"I beg your pardon? Mother said everything was as I left it. Where are my trunks? Will you stop that?!"

"You are pardoned, and excused. Please close the door on your way out, " he sneered.

"*Your* Chambers?" I questioned, then took a look around the room. The same dusty lilac wallpaper, the same furniture, but the items that distinguished this room as mine were all gone.

"Yes. These chambers are mine now, and you need to leave. At once." Castor flung his carving to the bed and rushed me with the small blade. He did not slice me, but prepared to. I took the hint and backed out slowly. The door slammed behind me.

Being removed from my room of one hundred twenty years was disturbing. I had had the second suite in my father's wing my whole life. Where was I to go now?

I returned to the Great Hall down the east grand staircase. Crossing the hall to the west grand staircase, a collection of servants scattered. Climbing the stairs, I heard grunting and the tinkling sound of magic. Curious of the sound, I quickened my steps to the top and was surprised to see Vesperia practicing a dance-like magic.

She pulled nebula clouds from the galactic collection on our ceiling above the Great Hall and began to shape them like our father did to shadows. The nebula figures looked to be like animals; the stars made up the eyes and dusty fragments filled their bodies. Against the lilac walls, they were almost camouflaged.

I hid against the banister in the shadows to watch her more. Vesperia cast another charm and began picking up her small nebula figures. I saw a small bird, a cat, and a rabbit. First, she picked the bird off of the windowsill and launched it back into the galaxy on the ceiling. Then, she tossed the cat onto the bunny, mixing the two. Her hands danced over the figure as it shaped and molded to a combination of both animals. It had large pointed ears and a long cottontail, more like a bobcat's thanks to the amalgamation of the two creatures. When its cat-like face formed, it sniffed the air with a rabbit-like nose and snarled with feline fangs in my direction.

I stood quickly, clapping. Vesperia looked at me first with a sense pride clear for anyone to see, but she quickly hid it with a venomous glare. I stopped clapping and joined her on the landing.

"Magnificent charm! Is this your own creation?" I asked, hoping it might reduce the blazing stare she gave me. It did not – instead her gaze intensified, her nebula companion growling at me.

"Yes, It is. No, I will not teach it to *you,* " she spat. I blinked in surprise. Where was my second star – my right hand maid?

"That is perfectly fine. It is still an impressive spell. Good job. I bet mother is very proud."

"Unlike you, I do not need mother's pride, " Vesperia scoffed, turning her back to me to fling a powerful spell at her creature, bursting it like a supernova. All the fragments of stars returned to their nest on the ceiling.

I kept my mouth shut, as there was nothing left to say. Vesperia left with a 'humph', stomping off to her chambers and slamming the door. I flinched.

There was only one other room I could expect to take – the one connected to mother's drawing room by a hidden door in the wall. They were previously Castors' chambers. I walked quickly past Vesperia's room and towards the door. I knocked cautiously before entering.

Aurora was busy at work with one of the laundry maids, Petunia, putting away my five years' worth of things. They were in the middle of a conversation about their respective significant others.

"Lady Seren!" How wonderful it is to have you back!" Petunia exclaimed. Aurora spun around and smiled brightly at me.

"Indeed. You will never guess what the cook has put together for your return!"

"No, I believe you. I would not be able to guess. Will you be so kind as to tell me?" I tried not to giggle.

"I will not!" Aurora giggled, Petunia could not help herself either. I stepped further into the room, shutting the door behind me. Once I pulled my skirts up enough I was able to sit on the edge of my bed.

"I see." I raised an eyebrow at her. "Mother *insisted* I change into more *appropriate* court attire. When you are finished, will you help me change?"

"Yes M'Lady." Aurora nodded. The two ladies hurried in putting away my clothes. Aurora set out a few of my favorite gowns as well as one that was a gift.

The first dress , my favorite, was a dusty blue velvet gown with bell sleeves that fell to my knees. Not a dinner dress. The second was a deep blue, deeper and more richly dyed than what I wore now. It was made of several varied layers of blue satin with minor gems sewn about the hems, like a deep starry sky. I pulled this dress to me to keep it from being put back in the wardrobe. The last was a light orange-yellow, gifted to me by Queen Solaris on my 120th birthday. The colors matched the Solaris family crest, orange-yellow, white, and pale yellow. Warm colors always clashed with my cool skin.

"I will wear this one. The others can be put back. Thank you, "I announced. Aurora and Petunia each took one of the discarded choices, folding them gently and placing them in the wardrobe. I stood and they helped free me from the first blue dress. Petunia took the discarded dress and left my room through the hidden wall door. Aurora helped me into the blue satin star gown. I hoped my mother would be satisfied.

If not, maybe I will resort to wearing trousers instead.

"Too tight, miss?" Aurora asked me, hands on the corset back.

"No, just praying that my mother will be satisfied."

"I see," Aurora responded, pulling the corset snug.

I walked to the standing mirror in the corner. I loved everything about this gown. I ran my hands across the skirts and bodice. Aurora gestured for me to sit on a chair she procured.

She began to remove the pearled coif from my hair, setting it on the vanity table to my right. I peered around the room – it was almost cream with accents of lilac. The furniture was different from my original chambers, but still had every comfort. There was still a fireplace, a four poster bed, a night stand, a writing desk, a vanity, and a set of chairs for conversation by the fire.

Aurora combed my hair back, twisting the top section into a bun, pinning it to the top of my head. She pulled lightly on the bun, fluffing it to appear more full. Then she moved to the remaining hair, leaving it down but attempting to shape it into loose waves that we both knew they would not stay for long. She added a head piece, an ornate starry headband that matched the gems on my dress. Stepping back she encouraged me to look in the mirror again.

"Immaculate as always, " I said, admiring her beautiful work in the mirror. She looked to me for further instructions.

"You may go. Enjoy your holiday." I grasped her hand, squeezing lightly. She smiled and embraced me.

"Thank you M' Lady." She dipped into a curtsy before running out the door.

I looked at the bed in the mirror. I could almost pretend I was elsewhere. My old bed was a simple four poster with curtains that blacked out any light. This was a carved four poster with the Lucidus family crest in the center of the head and footboard. No curtains.

Facing the room, I found every item of mine that I could remember in my previous chambers. The items from the mantle were moved to this mantle, and the items from my night stand had made their way to this night stand. Even my favorite blanket lay neatly folded on the foot of the bed. Everything was the same, but so very different.

All I could do was speculate, but my suspicion was that the exchange was the result of a nasty argument between my mother and father. I would have to ask.

Though it was nearing the end of the day, the bright light of the capitol Lux shone through the windows. The mountains obscured some of the light, but not all. I walked over to the windows and pulled the drapes shut. At least these provided some shelter from the blinding light. The last thing I needed to do before heading down to dinner was to check my bags. Aurora knew how important the gifts for my siblings were; I was sure she had unpacked them. I looked around and saw the familiar packaging of the presents on my writing desk. I went to collect them to take them down to dinner, but hesitated. My siblings did not welcome me with open arms. I did not want them to discard these gifts out of anger for me. Instead, I placed a light glamour over them to shield them from any prying eyes. No one would be able to find them but me.

With a sigh, I left the room. Descending the kitchen stairs, I landed next to my father's study. Though the west wing was thought of as my mother's side of the house, the Lord's study was already there when the house was gifted to them. I knocked firmly three times and waited.

"Who is it... who's there?" My father's low voice rumbled.

"Your daughter, " I responded, turning the knob.

"No! No, Vesperia. I am too — too busy at present to help you with whatever nonsense – nonsense is daming your head today."

I stopped. That was... odd.

"Uh, Father. It is I, Seren. Your eldest daughter?" I tried again.

"Seren? Wh–when did you get home? Come in! Come in!" His attitude changed. I pushed the door in and saw him coming around from behind his desk to greet me. His purple skin glistened with the sweat of alcohol, black hair tied back in a low ponytail, and his mothy wings curled up behind him. He wore a tunic of dark purple and black trousers. A cup of wine stood half drunk on his desk.

"Just recently. Today, maybe two hours ago, " I informed him as we embraced. I could smell the alcohol on him.

"How l-lovely. Do you happen to know why no one came to collect me for your return cel-celebration?" he slurred.

"Oh, there was not one. When I arrived, everything was gloomy and frightful. Then, when I asked mother, she told me not to worry. I am not sure what it means."

"I see-see. Well, no matter...matter. Sit! Tell me everything!" He jovially gestured to the seating area in the middle of the room. We sat across from each other on opposing sofas.

"Well, I hope you will remember most of what I had sent in my letters. I got to see more of Effect than I had before. We collected the tutors from Ingenium and then came back to start at the capitol. There, I saw where grandmama Idalia grew up, but of course, I was not allowed to leave the carriage as per the treaty. Then we went to Obscurum, where Master Rayne began to lecture me on the war – which I already know all about." I tried to jog his memory. He looked at me with awe and anticipation like it was the first time he had heard this information.

"What about in Obscurum? How long were you there?" he asked.

"We passed by your family home. Grandfather Morris was at the gate. We waved and exchanged greetings."

"Did… he look," he paused looking around the room, " well?"

I hesitated. I did not want to lie, but the truth would be hard for him to hear.

"If I may speak truthfully. No, he did not."

My father's somber expression deepened. A tear fell from his left eye, landing on the back of his hand.

"I promised him – i promised… I would carry out my d-duty to the best of my abilities, but missing the passing of my mother was painful – so painful. Now I must bear – bear the pain of losing my father too. What else must I s-sacrifice for this treaty?"

I had no response. I knew he was angry with my mother and Queen Solaris, but it still hurt that he was angry. He started up his usual tirade about how he missed his home and how the treaty was unfair.

"How is this even close to fair when your mother is *bosom* buddies with the Queen– Queenly Regent! I am sure if her mother's health were to decline, *she* would be allowed to return. The Queen would provide her own personal army to escort her *ladyship*." he spat,

"I guess that is how – that is how the world works when you lose...lose." he complained, walking back to his desk to retrieve his cup. His feet seemed to be against him as he stumbled over level ground.

I nodded and tried to be an attentive listener, but I had this speech practically memorized, aside from the occasional variations like today. I took in the room, admiring the new additions to his collections. He had solidified two more figures on his shelf. Now he had a cockatrice, unicorn, griffin, and narwhal proudly displayed. The fireplace was walled off to keep the room cool and dark. The drapes had been nailed over the windows to block out the sun. The only light was a few candles in strategic places.

"You know, your– your mother would have been be-beheaded for her role in the war. The children of leaders were not s-supposed to participate – to preserve the lines of succession. She disobeyed that order. Directly from her elders! In Obscurum, that is punishable by death... death!" My attention was brought back to my irate father.

"Yes, I do know." I responded blankly. Forcing a neutral tone. My father sighed and summoned a decanter of red wine. A shadowy figure materialized and brought it to him.

"I am sorry, sorry... my starling. I know you have no s-say over the past." He poured a large helping for himself and drank deeply. Refilling the cup a second time. "What are you all – you all dressed up for?"

"Nothing. Mother thought the gown I arrived in was not befitting the court. I would hate to upset her on my first day home."

"That woman! What a fiend!" He slammed his cup on the table in front of us as he sat down again. Wine sloshed over the edge splashing on the table.

I had nothing to say again. He has whipped himself into a frenzy over one shred of information. *I knew I should not have said anything.*

My father guzzled more wine as if he were a merkin running out of water. He continued his somber trip down memory lane. I felt compelled to stay by the tension in my heart, but my nerves were on fire, wishing me to leave.

An aggressive fourteen count knock startled us both. Father jumped hard enough to spill the entirety of his wine.

"Ah! W-What now?" he bellowed.

"Mrs. Sykes, your grace! Dinner is prepared and the table is set!" she yelled through the door.

"We will be there in a moment, a moment" he replied.

"We? Is Lady Seren in there with you? I have not found her or her lady's maid yet."

"Yes Marjorie! We sh-shall be out shortly! Out ... shortly." he responded with a snap. Father set down his empty cup and gestured for us to go to the door. He opened it for me and allowed me to pass through first.

"Come along, we must not keep *her grace* waiting." He used my mothers title as a jab. I led the way to the dining hall.

Chapter Four

The fourteen-seat table was set for five, with the place settings arranged at one end – one seat at the head of the table surrounded by the other four. My mother was already seated at the head of the table. *Oh dear.*

"What in S-Solaris?!" my father screamed from behind me. My mother toyed with her fork.

"I guess you lose Kyrinn. I wish you success in your future endeavors," she said with a smug smile. Father flew over me and landed hard enough to rattle the dishes.

"Why do you– you get to decide which customs we follow?" he spat. She did not look at him or even acknowledge his presence.

"I s-speak to you, woman!" He smashed a fist down on the table. "You deny our daughter her home-homecoming celebration and now you insist on *pissing* on the head of house traditions? *Why tonight?*" Her head snapped back and she cackled.

"You proclaim this injustice, yet I do not know who you think made *you* head of this family. It is not your name we carry! You have no right to assume any power over me. I am the –"

"Eldest daughter... of the chief Cyrus Lucidus... The bravest clan to fight with Solaris. *We know,*" my father finished slurring his words.

"And I do not have to listen to some drunken fool who *lost.*"

They stared at each other, neither moving, for quite some time before Castor and Vesperia's entrance snapped them out of it. Father took the plate from in front of mother and walked over to the opposing head of the table. Vesperia and Castor sat on either side of our mother, Vesperia replacing mother's plate. I took my plate and utensils to the middle of the table. A servant brought father new utensils and a full decanter of blood-red wine.

Wine was poured and the dishes were served. Mrs. Sykes called for the cook staff, who brought a parade of five items: The entre, a roast goose, followed by a vegetable stew, sweet bread rolls, and blood pudding. Dessert was a plate of the cook's special chocolate cake. Mrs. Sykes instructed the servants to fill our plates. I watched anxiously as they started with my mother and siblings, then me, and lastly my father. His expression grew darker and a shadowy dust began to fall from his wings, collecting in pools on the floor.

"Dinner is served, " Mrs. Sykes announced, and staff evacuated the room. Mother speared her serving of the roast goose and used her knife to slice a bite off. Father stared at his plate. My siblings cut into their food, Vesperia giving me a nasty look when we caught each other's eyes. I glanced at my father only to witness him conjure a hideous spider dripping in darkness. I held my breath as he flung it across the table.

The scream was ear-shattering. Castor flung his hands over his ears and dove under the table. Our mother had flown from her chair and was now angrily hovering above the table. The shadow spider jumped and tried biting at her slippered feet. The first time it caught her was its last. She shot it with a sun blast and it dispersed back into inanimate shadows.

"How *dare* you attack me!" mother roared.

"*Me* attack *you*? W-who in Mythénia would believe that?" He spat. I turned my attention to the plate of food before me. This was my homecoming dinner. I ripped a piece of the goose away and ate it. I hoped Aurora would sincerely thank Zanos for me. This was delicious. Our cook Bartholomew, or Barty, was always delivering the very best.

"This is all your fault!" My sister's voice came from – my soup? I peered over the lip of the bowl and sure enough, there she was. Her miniature face, in my soup, telling me that I am responsible for this turmoil.

"What? I have no idea what you mean," I whispered to my soup.

"Yes you do. I heard you tell father that mother forgot your homecoming. It was not *her* duty to attend to you. *That is for your lady's maid.*" The last sentence came out as a hiss.

"I know Aurora sent home all my letters and made arrangements for my homecoming in advance. Whatever you are implying is an incorrect and incomplete version of facts."

"Ha!" she scoffed. I saw her begin to formulate an insult then I quickly splashed my soup on top of my roast goose to interrupt her spell. The sudden, strange action ceased the bickering above me.

I looked up to see that both were hovering above their respective seats, hurling charms and dishes at one another. I cringed and offered a meek smile. My father returned his attention to my mother as she shot me a disappointed glare. He formed a petal pixie from the shadows in the eaves and flung it towards my mother. She shrieked and shot it with a finger. It exploded into shreds of shadow, slowly seeping back to the weaves. Vesperia glowered at me as she ate. Castor's plate had been removed from its setting; he was no longer in his seat.

I peered under the table to see him stuffing his face like a feral animal. Mrs. Sykes harshly enforced mother's 'no private meals' rule. She did not want us eating in our chambers because it would "cause a rift in the family". As if there was not one already. Castor also glared at me before turning away. He crawled away with his ravaged plate, returning to his seat. When he appeared from under the table, our mother ceased bickering with our father.

"Did you get enough to eat, my dear?" she cooed. Vesperia and I both looked at Castor.

"Yes. And I am done. May I be excused, mother?" He was quiet but polite, if a bit curt.

"Yes of course, darling! Do not forget about tomorrow, alright pet?" She waved to him as he exited the dining hall. Vesperia rolled her eyes, and I kept mine on our mother. She quickly returned to her skirmish. With a quick glance, she caught father's thought just as he was manifesting a true shadow weapon. He was shaping and hardening the shadows into a physical blade. Horror struck my heart. What would I do if he succeeded in slaying my mother?I had no time to react, but she did.

My mother recited an elder charm calling forth the power of the sun. Our dining hall was quickly filled with the growing brightness of mother's inner light, disbursing all shadows, including the blade father had made.

"Enough Kyrinn. You should follow your son's example. Leave, before I make up my mind between life and death," she spat in a deep unnatural tone. He looked down at my sister and I with deep sadness. His eyes gave way to the feeling of powerlessness, dropping one tear as he slowly floated out the door. I turned back to the table to see Vesperia had plastered on the facade of someone who could not be bothered. After the way she treated me, something had to be amiss, but at this pace she was never going to tell me.

"Will you stop looking at me like that! You are disturbing me!" Vesperia shouted. This drew mother's attention as she returned to her chair.

"*What* is the matter?" she interrogated.

"Nothing. A misunderstanding," I replied quickly.

"Oh no. There is *no* misunderstanding. Ever since I arrived here, you have been giving me this ghastly stare!" Vesperia scoffed. Mother reached over and patted her hand.

"You look plenty fed, darling. You are excused. Be ready for tomorrow." Mother gently tapped the table. Vesperia smiled, then gave a quick curtsy before dashing out the door.

The door shut with a resounding bang, leaving me alone with my mother. Her stare made me feel trapped. I could tell she was forming a statement. My mind began to wonder, imagining what I could have possibly done to incur her wrath so soon. Besides just now with Vesperia. She took up her fork and continued eating, periodically spearing me with a look of intention. She worked through most of her roast goose before ripping me from my spiral.

"Did you mean to cause that spat at dinner?" She started playing with her blood pudding. I set my spoon down and thought back to the start of dinner. *She fixated on father's outburst at the start, but surely she did not think I had an ounce of influence over his actions?*

"No, but I am sorry if I did. That was not my intention."

"If? Do we need to call to Cruor for a healer of eyes? Did you somehow miss the skirmish above you?"

"No ma'am. I did not intend to cause any issue."

"Well you certainly did. You seem to have upset your brother and sister too. You will have to keep those emotions of yours in check from now on. Hmm?" She snapped her fingers, releasing the bright sun charm.

"Yes Ma'am." She nodded with glee once and threw her napkin on her plate.

"Now that that is settled, we have serious business to discuss. In five days we will be hosting a ball. The Queen has an announcement, and it includes us hosting a visitor from Obscurum at Twilight Hall for some time. I need to know, for certain, that you will *mind your manners and emotions.*"

"I will."

"Good girl. Tomorrow you will chaperone your siblings and go to your father's family tailor on the edge of Obscurum. They are each to receive a formal outfit in Tenebrae colors. Do you understand?"

"Yes Ma'am. I do have one question–"

"Insolent girl! You have no right to question me. You want to know about the ball and the announcement, your outfit, and our guest, but *I refuse!* You were an insufferable inquisitor and now you have become a nuisance false sage. How ungrateful you are, even after your education tour. You will be wearing a gown that I have chosen from my own personal collection." She stood and glared down at me. I had nothing left to see. She had ripped out any words I had wanted to say, making it clear that I should not ask any more.

"We are in agreement then. Mrs. Sykes informed me you have given your lady-in-waiting leave of absence. She will not dress you, but has agreed to wake you tomorrow in preparation for the journey. If you desire assistance, you will be responsible for the procurement of a replacement. Had you gone through me, this would not have been an issue. You are excused." She took her leave and I was left alone in the dining hall.

My legs took a moment to catch up with my thoughts, but once they did, I was able to get up from the table. I pushed in my chair and exited through the kitchen. I looked at nothing, but instead raced up the stairs. On the second floor, I went directly to my door, but I stopped when I heard the latch of a door. Vesperia had been waiting and listening.

I chose to ignore it,, pushing into my chambers and locking the door behind me. A night gown and hair bonnet were set out by the wash basin in the corner near the standing mirror, on a stool. I pulled lacings and used a basic levitation charm to wiggle away from my gown. I folded it neatly and left it on the vanity chair for the laundry maids. The nightgown was solid black satin, matching the bonnet next to it. I slid into both and prepared for bed by washing my face.

My thoughts raced, wondering what announcement would pull the Queen Regent from her Luxurious castle. Especially to host an event through us. *Maybe mother and the Queen were going to announce the annulment of the treaty, and thus mother and father's marriage. Allowing them both to return home. Not likely.*

I brushed my hair as the final act of my nightly ritual, braiding it loosely and slipping the bonnet over my head. I pulled the covers back and wiggled into bed. Lying in the crisp clean sheets was a long missed comfort. I had not realized my exhaustion, but the moment my head hit the down pillow, I fought to keep my eyes open.

Chapter Five

The morning snuck up on me. I awoke feeling groggy and slow, but my eternal curse was to never sleep in. Once I wake, I just rise. I cannot relax until my duties for the day are done. I shuffled to my vanity, hair bonnet in hand as it had fallen off in the night. In the mirror, I saw a melancholic hag blinking crusty sleep from her eyes. Mocking me. Slowly, my wits returned to me and I collected my energy to begin my morning routine. All of which I could accomplish alone if I abandoned proper court attire. That would not serve me well today, so I planned to call down for a maid before getting dressed.

I laid the bonnet on the vanity top and picked up my brush. Starting from the bottom, I worked out all the knots and tangles. When my hair was shiny and manageable, I replaced my brush on the vanity table. I began to split my hair into three sections to braid. Once I had twisted the strands into braids, I secured it with a ribbon and began to curl the braid into a flat bun against my head. Using the mirror, I carefully pulled a few strands of hair loose to frame my face.

Obscurum was a dark and gloomy place – residents usually chose darker colors to compliment their complexions of cool colors. I had only two courtly gowns remaining that would match the tones of the town.

I had a choice between a dark green walking dress and a dull yellow-orange silk gown. Given my destination, I chose the dark green. I had no desire to stick out or draw attention to myself. Thankfully this gown was easy to dress in. I laid it and a clean chemise on the bed before heading for the door. I had my hand on the bolt when a hardy knock came from the other side. I stopped. I had learned Mrs. Sykes' secret on my scholarly tour. Aer fairies could use a type of magic to listen into other rooms – all by the breath of another. I held mine.

She knocked again and tried the knob. When she found it bolted, she snapped her fingers and a precise gust of wind came in and shoved the locking bolt aside. I flew back from the door as it swung open with another strong gust.

"Ah, you are awake. I trust you have arrangements for your dressing this morning?" Mrs. Sykes pried. I did not judge her for not wanting to dress the fully grown woman she had dressed since birth.

"I was waiting for you to see if you would send a maid up to help me tie into my day gown." I gestured to the gown on the bed. She gave it a cursory glance but had no gentle feelings about it if her face was to be believed.

"Of course Miss. Will you be needing anything else?" she inquired coldly. I began to shake my head *no* but stopped.

"How long of a wait should I expect for my siblings?" Mrs. Sykes' face gave away her displeasure, the tone in her voice bored and entirely uninterested in queries as she answered.

"I am afraid that is not knowledge I have the pleasure of having, Lady Seren."

"Alright. That is all, you may go." I dismissed her with a shaky tone of authority. Mrs. Sykes looked as though she may burst from containing her laughter. I waited for her polite retreat before sighing and throwing myself on the bed. Though it was not my old four-poster bed, it was far more comforting than the bedrolls and cots we slept on while traveling.

Moments later, I sat up and began to re-dress. It had taken years to become comfortable enough to dress myself in Auros's presence. I thought it was silly to have another person in the room watching me dress when I could handle slipping on the gowns and undergarments – I only needed assistance with the ties. I changed quickly enough that the laundry maid that had been sent up truly only had to tie the back ties for me. She took yesterday's dress with her as she left.

We both descended the servant stairs into the kitchens. She moved onward to the laundry while I stayed and bothered the kitchen staff over ways I might be of use. Étienne, the head chef, put me to work peeling purple potatoes for breakfast.

I had gotten through a bucket's worth when I heard the chiming sound of Mrs. Sykes searching for me, her house keys clanging against each other. I set the knife I had been given down and crept around the kitchen to the scullery, where I ran into and out of the battery, across the Great Hall and raced up the east stairs. I used my wings sparingly; her super magical hearing would have caught the full beat of my wings if I flew up the stairs. On the landing, I turned towards my former door and reached out to knock. I lightly rapped on the door, and a groan and indistinguishable mutter replied. I gently pushed the door open and threw my voice inside.

"Cas? Are you awake?"

"Mhmm." I strained to hear his reply. I stepped in further, asking again.

"Just a moment longer, please," he groaned, not even trying to open his eyes.

"Ok, but if Marjorie gets in here, you know she is going to use the North Wind to throw you out of bed. I am being gentler," I joked. He did not respond, as was usual.

Quietly, I removed myself from the room and started back down the stairs. There was no other way, besides the lovers' walk, a balcony that connected my parents' apartments. I descended the stairs quickly and crossed the Great Hall again to the west servant stair, where I could ascend to my sister and I's chambers. I stopped in front of her door.

The door of the chambers belonging to her maid, Mystine Oscuro, was ajar. I leaned my head against Vesperia's door and heard the two speaking, but could not identify what exactly they were saying. The conversation stopped and I heard the soft clacking of the lady's maids' shoes approaching the door. I flew to my door and made it appear as though I was just now leaving my quarters by pulling the door open and closed. I caught Mystine's eyes as she exited the darkness of my sister's chambers.

"Is she still asleep?" I pointed to her door. Mystine's dark grey eyes darted to the door behind her and then back to me. She nodded.

"Do you need assistance in getting her to wake?" I offered. She looked hesitant but nodded. I smiled and approached the task.

Vesperia's room was dark and quiet. I pushed farther into the room past the door.

"Vesperia?" I called softly in a sing-song voice.

"Mmmm…" she responded sleepily. I knew this was a faux answer. She had been doing this since she began to sleep in her own chambers.

"Ves. Hello… Vesperia…?" I tried again, this time summoning a handful of glitter, a charm similar to light fairies but not as bright. I threw the mystical glitter in the air, watching as it hovered in a cloud, casting a blueish candle-like twinkle across the room.

"A few more moments please, " Vesperia muttered, rolling over.

"Of course, but if Marjorie gets in here before then, you know she's going to blow you out of bed. How about we sit up and wait for Mystine to return with your morning tea?" I stepped closer to her sitting area; her writing desk was clean except for several candles melted on the surface. Vesperia rustled in her sheets and I assumed she was waking.

"Mystine? What do you mean?" she said more clearly. "She will be back soon, with your tea. We are trying to save you the torment of a windy morning. Where are your match sticks, sister? My charm will go out soon." I tried lifting the top of the desk to look for matches, but it was latched.

"Sister?" Vesperia's confusion caught me off guard.

"Yes, it is I. Your sister. Are you well?" I tried to comfort her but instead, a guttural scream erupted from her bed.

"No! I am not well! A stranger is in my bed chamber insisting I get up!" Vesperia shot at me.

"A stranger? *No*, I am your –" My response was interrupted by a pillow smacking me in the face, hard. My starry glitter charm fell apart and we were submerged into partial daylight darkness. Vesperia's chambers became a dark dusty sun-blocked fighting ring.

"Ow!" I yelped.

"Get out!" she screamed, throwing another pillow towards my voice.

"I was only trying to –" Another pillow hit my head.

"Get out! Get out!" she continued as she threw the last of her pillows. I took to the air to avoid the last two but learned quickly that was a mistake.

Vesperia must have heard the pillows miss their mark because she gathered energy in her hand in a light purple glow and began rapidly releasing small-scale shooting stars at the ceiling. A few came close to truly hitting me. I re-directed the others to hit the stone outer walls.

"Fine! I will go! I do not understand your outbursts. I am sorry for bothering you!" I lowered myself to the floor and walked towards the door. Vesperia screamed wordlessly until I closed the door behind me. Mystine was flying up the stairs as I crossed the landing to my door. I looked at her sadly. She was going to have to listen to a rant the whole morning. At least she would get some respite while we were in Obscurum.

I leaned back against the door. I tried not to think about how gut-wrenching those screams felt to me. Or why she made them. We had been good friends before my tour, but now I did not know what we were. Maybe she was right to declare us strangers. We have barely spoken in five years. I stared at the gifts I had chosen and my heart withered a little more. The box containing the oceanic Unda pearls, naturally and without cruelty harvested by the local Unda tribes, sat unopened beside the sheathed dagger of Terra forged steel.

Gifts are not meant to be held onto until the receiver is worthy – they are already worthy the moment the gift is thought of – but I knew I needed to wait until they were ready to receive anything from me. I pushed off the door and added more power to the enchantment, hiding them from the view of anyone else in the room besides me. I could not cry every time I saw them. I was going to need to make up five years' worth of bonding and support. Somehow.

I searched my new room for my cloak, finding it on a hook in a closet. I would not be getting fitted for a new gown, but that did not mean I could not purchase more dress pieces for later. I snuck my coin purse into my skirt, hoping my cloak would conceal the added lump and potential clinking of the coins. I checked myself over again in the full-length mirror. My almost black mahogany hair was tied up to show my face, and my blue-grey eyes, framed by sleepy bags, wandered the fabric of my skirts to find no suspicious signs of a concealed pouch. Perfect. As I could not find any issues, I turned to the door. Opening it, I caught Mrs. Sykes on her way up.

"Mystine and I have gotten her day started already!" I called to her cheerily, placing a smile on my face. Hers screwed up in displeasure.

"I stopped waking your siblings when you left, miss. Besides, everyone heard you wake your sister. I have come all this way to notify you that the family is waiting for *you* to join them for breakfast." I nodded and walked silently past her in the stairwell.

In the dining hall, my parents had taken up the opposing head of table seats. My brother patiently waited in the middle.

"At last, you join us. Where is your sister?" my mother snapped.

"I saw her leaving her room as I came down," I lied. She huffed but took a moment to speak, almost as if she had to think of something to get mad about.

"I had to send Majorie up to rouse you two. Were you two gossiping?"

"No, mother. I was not speaking to Vesperia. I was in my room getting my cloak." I pulled at one side for emphasis. This invited her scrutinizing gaze. I watched as her eyes raked through my hair, over my gown, and to my shoes. She could not hide her displeasure, but her eyes caught something of more value – Vesperia. She was walking in from behind me, closely followed by Mrs. Sykes. I was saved by the changing of the atmosphere. Mrs. Sykes called the servants to begin filling our plates, and I took a seat in the middle and pulled over a plate from the nearby place setting. Vesperia sat on mother's right side.

"Shredded purple potatoes, over-easy quail eggs, and your choice of sausage, bacon, or grilled honey ham. There is a light wine, dark brandy, and fresh water. Please ring if you require anything, ” Mrs. Sykes said with a deep bow to mother. The servants were dismissed and they all filed back into the kitchen. Before anyone had the chance to touch their food, our father cleared his throat.

“Excuse me, everyone. I would like us to take the time now to indulge in one of my family customs. Lawrence!” he called for the butler, Mr. Huich, who came running into the dining hall immediately. He had with him a worn, small book clutched to his breast.

“You cannot be serious.” Vesperia sighed.

“I do not know what you mean, daughter. Everyone! Listen, please. I have here an old book of prayers to the Darkness. I would like us to read one at every meal. We can skip some meals of course, but I will start us today, ” he began, but was cut off by a scratch of laughter from mother’s throat.

“Kyrinn, you *dunce*. Solarisian law forbids Void worship – your book will need to be confiscated.” Mrs. Sykes approached Mr. Huich to take the book, but he kept it out of her reach.

“Eleanor,” his voice dripped her name in disgust, “you are too presumptuous. The *book*, nor *reading its contents* aloud is illegal by Solarisian law. The congregations were forced to close and *worship* was outlawed. The children are still allowed to *learn* their heritage.”

“Then why, fae tell, have you kept it from them all this time?” mother started.

“I am not the one suppressing heritage here, Eleanor. You require a new looking glass, for surely yours is broken.” He reached for the book and Mr. Huich relinquished it. Father flipped through the pages, looking for a passage he was happy with. Finally, he selected a page near the middle, opened the book more, and held onto the back pages with his left hand while he used his right-hand pointer finger as a guide.

"This passage I feel applies across many storylines and can be applied broadly." He cleared his throat, and mother sighed as he began again.

"*The absence of light is not the absence of meaning. In the darkness, the void shows us the value of all we once knew and all we hope to know. Because in nothing– we find everything.*" He closed up the book and returned it to Mr. Huich's care. The table was silent – no one had eaten.

"Uh – sir?" Castor began.

"Yes son?" our father replied with enthusiasm.

"May we eat now? I mean no disrespect, only that we have a long journey ahead of us."

"Yes! Yes, of course!" I watched as our father deflated. Vesperia and our mother joked to themselves over their plates. All I could hear was the tink and clink of dishware and their occasional cackles. The rest of us ate in what little silence was left.

Father seemed content with his victory, regardless of the childish snickering that came from the other end of the table. Castor flinched every time someone reached for something too quickly. It broke my heart. He inhaled his servings, ignored his wine, and excused himself from the table while mumbling something about meeting at the carriage. I was now left alone with my more offensive family. Vesperia and Mother began to taunt father and me for our dark clothing. When father had enough of the teasing, he gave me a sorrowful half-smile and dissolved into a pool of shadows, dissipating into the corners of the room. I was now less than half a plate away from escape; the others seemed to have hunkered down with more wine and second servings.

Now that the men had left, Vesperia was not under any pretext to remain docile. Mother whispered in her ear and a wicked grin split my sister's face. She gathered energy from around her, glowing a soft purple, and formed the illusion of miniature me, followed by a regularly sized black spider. I watched her little puppet show out of curiosity, even though I had an inkling of what was to come. I had prepared a full bite on my fork when she made the spider jump on miniature me and eat her face. The movement startled me more than the actual illusion. My mother gave me the matriarchal eyebrow raise of serious inquisition.

"What startled you? Was it arachnids you grew scared of over these past five years? Surely a small house spider does not frighten you," mother joked. I saw the look on my sister's face and knew she had meant it. Vesperia shook out her hands, clearing the illusion. I looked down at my plate. I no longer had an appetite, so I pushed it away and stood.

"No, mother. I am not afraid of spiders. I was startled, that is all. Thank you for the conversation over breakfast. I beg you to excuse me to mind the carriages before our long journey today." I tried to keep my tone as even as possible, then exited the door behind me. I strode outside and flung my cloak into the carriage before kicking off the ground to fly on my own two wings.

Mother had strict rules about flying indoors – they were suffocating. Almost as bad as being in the human realm. Carriages were wonderful for long distances or for fae without wings, but my own mother restricting flight felt incomprehensibly strange.

The early autumn air of the late morning was crisp and felt dewey on my face and hands. I flew on, above the lowest layer of clouds. I could see below, but not hear. This proved to be a good strategy. Vesperia came out of the front door pulling Castor by his wings. I watched them struggle and argue but waited for them to separate before coming back down.

"Look who decided to join us," Vesperia snapped as I touched the ground. I politely ignored her snide remark. Osbert and Nevin came around the side of the house the stables were on. Osbert opened the door for us and procured the footstep.

"Apologies for the delay, Masters. Your Carriage." Osbert bowed. He held the door for Vesperia and me, then handed the door off to Castor, who shut it. Osbert climbed up front with Nevin and then we were off. Vesperia and Castor shared the backward-facing bench, and I was alone on the forward-facing bench. They agreed to not touch each other. Castor was scrunched into the left corner and Vesperia the right. I thought back to my writing desk, where the gifts were still hidden beneath the illusion of glamour. I began to wonder what they might say about the gifts.

I was truly at a loss for imagination. All attempts I made were thwarted by the overwhelming anxious feeling that cursed me with the worst-case scenarios. Like Vesperia snapping the necklace and stomping on the pearls, or Castor using the knife to attack me.

I was reminded of the first trip we had taken to Obscurum. Vesperia and I went to the same tailor, with our governess, to be fitted for our first court gowns. We giggled and joked the whole way, while our governess was all too happy to release us into the care of our paternal grandparents' tailor. We spent the whole first part of that trip picking fabrics and styles, then being measured for the dresses and sent home. Castor had been too young for court then – he had cried as we left without him and rejoiced at our return. How vastly different this trip was.

"Are you going to do that the *entire* time?" Vesperia cut through my daydream.

"Do what?"

"Make that strange face and stare off into the void."

"No, I am sorry. I did not realize I was making any faces."

"She is one to talk with a face like that!" Castor shot.

"Says the *face sucker* I had to peel off of a *laundry maid*!" Vesperia shot back. I gasped.

"*Why* do you gasp like a *child*? Oh right, you would not know. Our little brother has become quite the philanderer." Castor's face turned red and my mouth fell open.

"I am not so loose and libertine that I do not know her name! I may not be courting her *properly*, but I am no lecher. Her name is Elspeth and she is very smart!"

"Oh ho ho! Well! Now we know. Did you meet while trying to hide some nasty bedding? Is that why you are ashamed then?"

"No! Now stop talking about her. Please," he begged. I nodded in agreement – there was no gain or loss in keeping or divulging this secret for me. Vesperia, on the other hand, had a nefarious glint in her eyes.

"Ok, ok! Do not *burst* a vein. What do I get in return for keeping this secret to myself?" Castor became unable to sit still in his seat. He moved positions multiple times before he had a reply.

"Uh, I will give you my pin money for a whole season. All winter," he offered.

"Two – Winter and Spring."

"Are you *serious*?" Castor pleaded. Vesperia kept her mouth shut firmly, sticking her right hand between them. Waiting for the shake of acceptance. I watched as he shook away the next two seasons' worth of pin money.

"Thank you, brother, for your faith in me." She flashed an evil grin and pushed herself back into the corner.

We sat in silence for some time, over a decently appealing landscape, but once we reached the dry plain , my imagination died and

I craved interaction. The Obscurum mist, a black fog, crept up to meet us and I caught the flash of our driver's light spells.

"Have either of you visited the city in the last four years?" I felt no subject was safe, but this could be if I presented it correctly. Castor looked at Vesperia and she waved her hand at him.

"Yes, sister. Once or twice since your departure. The Tenebrae tailor *is* the best," Vesperia stated. She threw a teasing look at Castor, who relented and began thinking of how to answer the question.

"I – at first – came to learn of our heritage. I returned a while later to visit an acquaintance." Castor tried to continue but began to cough. "I, uh, well. You see. We became friends and then *courted*. It did not work out – obviously."

"What... what an adventure," I replied. There was a moment of silence between us, while the carriage team was almost too loud. I could hear Nevin and Osbert speaking, but could not hear the words.

"She was not a prostitute if that is what you are thinking, sister! Vesperia thinks the same, but it is untrue! She was the baron's fourth daughter. Our house would not have been so bad." He defended so aggressively that I could not help but laugh. It must have been contagious because Vesperia began sputtering too.

"It is not funny! Many a young lady finds herself in such a situation!" he continued, thus adding to our laughter. My sides began to hurt and my eyes watered. This was normal, this was right.

What had I done to ruin this bond?

Chapter Six

Our carriage stopped, and Vesperia took that as the moment to recollect herself. All her laughter died away and an important, very serious expression appeared. Osbert released the footstep and we all filed out, starting with Castor, and ending with me.

Castor flit ahead to hold open the shop door for us. As soon as I had snatched my cloak, he commanded Nevin to drive on and park off of the street. Vesperia did not concern herself with the direction of the carriage. She stepped into the shop and was immediately greeted by Mr. Vestor himself. A short wingless man, he had the darker complexion of Ingenium fae but dyed his hair dark to fit in Obscurum. He wore a green, tailored vest over a white shirt, slim brown trousers, and polished leather shoes.

"Hello, little stars! Come in! Come in!" the little old man called. He gestured to a collection of blue overstuffed furniture by a fireplace: A chair, a couch, and a chaise lounge. Vesperia took the chair, and I perched on the edge of the couch, leaving Castor and Mr. Vestor to choose a seat next to me or the chaise lounge. Thankfully, Castor chose the couch.

Mr. Vestor sat on the chaise lounge very carefully. He was getting to the age where fairies must prepare to perish. His hands were cracked and withered, he wore thick glasses, and his skin was beginning to show every wrinkle. He removed his eyeglasses and cleaned them thoughtfully with a cloth from his shirt pocket.

"Your father wrote to me a week or so ago. He notified me of your needs and implored my assistance, which I could not deny. Though, he only mentioned two. I thought you were still on your scholars tour, my dear?"

"No sir. I arrived home yesterday. Just before dinner. I will not need a gown – it seems mother has chosen one for me," I responded politely. He hummed in thought, a lilt indicative of wisdom clear in the sound.

"What fashions do you fancy these days? These will be my last ensembles. I am afraid my time has come," Mr. Vestor announced. Castor looked unbothered, but Vesperia exchanged a look of grief with Mr. Vestor.

"Oh, Mr. Vestor. How generous of you. We can find another tailor; you should spend your last days on a grand adventure! Doing something you love." I stared at her, stunned. She truly was only mad at me.

"Call me Sey, dear. Seymour, but my friends call me Sey. I *am* going on the grandest adventure and will *love it*. Sewing is my adventure – the adventure will be bringing your inspirations to life. They are my last pieces. I will go out in the most elegant, gossip-inducing, dramatic way possible. How better than with two final ensembles for my *second* favorite family?" They laughed sadly together, leaving Castor and I to exchange twin looks of awkward confusion.

"In that case, Sey, make me something marvelous! Big puffed sleeves and velvet cuffs. An overskirt with velvet trim to match the cuffs. Buttons down the back. A faux square neckline, trimmed in velvet again, just to be conservative. Oh! And a double skirt!" Vesperia began to wish away while Castor and I stayed quiet. I noticed a tiny pencil scribbling in the background as they spoke. When they finished, the pencil paused and waited while Mr. Vestor addressed Castor.

"And you son? What fashions do you fancy?" The pencil was poised to write. Castor thought to himself for a while, the pencil hovered touching down on the pad and coming back up a couple of times.

"I like the look of the Frenchmen's tights. For a tunic though..." he pondered, "...mother would probably appreciate it if I added something from the region. What have you got with feathers, Mr. Vestor?"

"Please, all of you call me Sey, or Seymour. Mr. Vestor is so formal. I can whip up something with feathers, but – and excuse an old man for his assumptions– I thought you said you wanted to add elements of the region, m'Lord?"

"You are quite alright. Please call me Cas – and I did. Though I *specifically* said 'my mother' would enjoy it. She has reservations about 'human' anything. To appease her, I will ask for a Mythénian touch, but that is why we came to you. If these are truly to be your last pieces, I shall like to wear mine as often as possible. Feathers if you please!" He was joyful. Seymour had the touched look of a deeply loved father. The pencil had spun around with every word, taking note of my sibling's specifications.

Seymour guided us into a new room with a small, one-person platform. He held out his hand to Vesperia, offering to help her up onto the platform.

"Vesperia my dear, you first." She took his hand, stepping up with delight. Castor and I found seats on stools, though we had to move some bolts of fabric. We watched Seymour measure every dimension of our sister while the pencil scribbled each centimeter. He used his magic to resize a mannequin to Vesperia's shape and then pinned the slip of paper with her requests to its neck before placing it in the hallway.

"Now for fabrics!" He waved a wrinkled hand and bolts of fabric floated to them. A little spool of purple velvet ribbon followed behind.

"Stay there so that we may compare the fabrics against your complexion. Here is your velvet ribbon." Seymour handed Vesperia the purple velvet ribbon.

"Oh! I love the swirls. It reminds me of fathers wings," she cooed. Castor grew a nasty expression until Vesperia caught it in the mirror. He stopped after she turned around to scold him.

Seymour draped two fabrics over my sister's shoulder. A pale violet and a dusty lavender. He made a decisive hum and took away the violet. He snapped his fingers and the bolts of blue and purple crushed velvet engulfed her forearms.

"House colors would dictate the purple over the blue, but the choice is purely yours, " he mused.

"Purple of course," Vesperia answered. Seymour pinned the two fabrics to the mannequin and began measuring secondary colors against the first and then Vesperia's skin.

"What color ornaments?" he asked.

"I will be wearing a silver necklace and rings to match." Vesperia stepped down from the platform and threw herself on a pile of fabrics.

"Ah! This will be lovely, " Seymour said, adding two more grey and silver translucent fabrics.

"My Lord Cas! You are next, come on over!" Seymour called. Castor left his stool and stood on the platform, doing his best to stay still during his measurements. Castor feigned being ticklish when Seymour began measuring Castor's chest, having to slip the measuring tape under his armpits. Seymour caught on though, and administered a wet finger to Castor's left ear. That got him to jump off the platform and laugh from his gut.

Vesperia admired the material selected for her gown. I felt a tinge of envy in my stomach when Vesperia caught my eyes.

"Are you jealous that we will receive new ensembles and you will not?" she mocked. I drew in a deep breath through my nose.

"No," I lied, "I am simply admiring the choice fabrics you will get to wear. I cannot wait to see what Mr. Vestor creates for you."

"Hmph," she responded, unable to force an argument.

"Splendid idea! This ensemble really will be the best of my work! I will use this French pattern for a bell sleeve tunic with fringe and add those elements!" I caught the tail end of the conversation, missing Castor's design choice.

"Thank you," Castor responded. Seymour pulled a spool of wide ribbon from a cabinet.

"You will have to pick the fabric, but what do you think of this ribbon?" Seymour handed Castor a roll of inky black ribbon and we all watched as white stars came in and out of focus. "An encased enchantment – no better time to use it!"

"Only if you are positive you will not want to put it on some other piece."

"No. These truly are my last works, my Lord. There is no greater use than the first son of the stars. Take the gift, " Seymour insisted. Castor blinked away tears and nodded.

"Of course. Where was this made?"Castor asked.

"Ingenium, of course, by two fairies. One of light and one of dark, just like your parents. They worked together to weave light into the darkness to make this ribbon. It was inspired by your sister's birth. I am sure they would want you to have it."

They compared the Tenebrae house colors against the twinkling star ribbon. Eventually, they came to a tie between two types of dark grey-purple silk.

"I prefer this one." Castor chose.

"Then this is the one you shall have!" Seymour proclaimed, "I imagine this would look spectacular as a transition between your lavender skin and the garment. I have the most elegant embroidered cloth." He pulled out a deep vivid purple silk that was embroidered in ribbons from left to right.

"Sey! You know me so well!" Castor exclaimed.

"I thought you would enjoy the elemental embroidery."

My attention caught *elemental* and before I could stop, I blurted out some nonsense about my travels.

"Castor does indeed adore the elements – Especially the Unda! Do you remember the notions you used to have of them, Castor? I sure do. I hope my letters straightened that out." I laughed nervously.

Everything around me ceased. Even Mr. Vestor's floating fabrics and pencils.

"Excuse me?" Castor faced me. I felt my cheeks grow red with heat.

"I – uh – well...you know. I meant no disrespect, I was only hoping to tell you about my travels and the things I have –"

Vesperia cut me off with a loud, incredulous scoff.

"Castor? Do you recall inquiring after our sister's recent adventures?"

"No I do not, Vesperia."

"Then it is settled. Seren, no one implored you to share. If you could refrain from embarrassing us in front of our dear friend, Seymour."

I nodded, my face still flushed. Tears pricked at my eyes.

"My sincerest apologies, Castor, Mr. Vestor, and you, Vesperia. I will strive to do better in the future. I am sorry to have disturbed you." I stood and excused myself, letting myself out of the shop.

On the street, I searched for the carriage, but Nevin must have moved it away from traffic. I spotted a narrow walkable space between the tailor shop and its neighbor. I dashed in and let myself release the tears I had held back.

Crying felt good, but I did not dare continue for long. Being alone and abandoning my duties as a chaperone was not something that would help. Mother would learn of it and I would never hear the end of it. I wiped my face and threw a minor glamour over my face to appear clean-faced and unfazed. I returned to the shop and heard the group still merrily conversing in the fabric room.

"I apologize, but I am closed!" Mr. Vestor called from the back.

"It is I, Lady Seren of Astrum House. I have returned to chaperone."

"Oh do come back in!" Mr. Vestor responded. I followed his voice back to the fabric room. The fabric was no longer floating about the room. Instead, swatches were pinned to mannequins shaped exactly like my siblings.

"We were just ending our conversation," Mr. Vestor said before turning back to my siblings, "Your parents will settle the tab when I send them the invoice. If everyone is happy, then you are released!"

"Of course we are!" Vesperia exclaimed.

"Indeed!" Castor joined.

"Very good!" Seymour chuckled, "Then I pray, leave me to my work while I still can!" He waved his frail hands dismissively.

So much for some extra everyday dresses.

Vesperia led the way, exiting the shop. Castor called out to Nevin for the carriage, and it did appear from around the corner. I sighed as quietly as I could muster. Osbert hopped down from his spot next to Nevin to release the footstep and held the door. Castor waited as Vesperia and I climbed in – we sat opposite like before – then he joined by slamming the door shut.

Castor situated himself to look at me directly.

"Seren. I can appreciate that you had taken an interest in my life the last time you were home. However, that does not mean you know me now. I request that you refrain from mentioning my childish notions from before your tour. Furthermore, I think it best you keep the tales of your journey to yourself. Save it for the Queen's ball." He was firm, and I wanted to argue and defend myself but what sort of position was I in to do that?

"Of course. My apologies to both of you. I see I disrespected you and will work to change that." Vesperia and Castor looked at each other and I wondered if he, too, learned telepathic communication. They seemed to converse through thought.

"We accept your apology," Vesperia announced after a long, silent break. I nodded and kept thinking of ways to win them back again. The return carriage ride was much quieter – almost silent except for the unicorn team hoof beats and Castor's snoring. Vesperia entertained herself by creating small illusions that burst when the carriage jolted. I watched as she grew frustrated, but I held back my suggestion to keep them solid.

After an insufferable long ride, I could feel our return to Twilight Hall. The Queen's security barrier danced over and past us. Nevin pulled the carriage around the front of the house where the lance curved. Osbert released the footstep and held the door that faced the house. Vesperia shook Castor awake – or tried to. I watched her lightly pinch him on the leg as she slid out the door. He woke with a start and did not connect the painful pinch with Vesperia, as she was halfway to the door now.

I let him exit the carriage ahead of me. He stretched and yawned obnoxiously. Vesperia had stopped on the walkway just before the front patio, where Mrs. Sykes and Mr. Huich were loudly bickering. Mrs. Sykes was waving her finger at Mr. Huich, who had his hands on his hips, rolling his eyes. I slipped past Vesperia and approached them.

"What is the matter?" I demanded from them. They stopped their bickering and greeted me.

"Nothing M'Lady. *His* Master," Mrs. Sykes shot daggers at Mr. Huich, "set *my* Lady Astrum into a bad mood pre-dinner, and now they are having it out."

"I object!" Mr. Huich exclaimed, "He did no such thing! I merely asked which seat her Ladyship preferred for the meal."

"It is not your duty to inquire about *my* lady's place setting!"

"I *am* the head of house staff! It *is* my duty!"

"I beg your pardon sir, but-"

"You are excused."

"What?" Mrs. Sykes stumbled.

"I am excusing your behavior. Consider your apology accepted," Mr. Huich started smugly.

"You arrogant little prick!" She hurled a gust of cold north wind at him, resuming the skirmish.

"Ok!" I yelled, guiding my siblings past the two servants and into the house. The glamour on my face faded, but I did not need to replace it.

Inside, our parents were indeed arguing and breaking things. I guided my siblings to the staircases while carefully assessing the location of the storm. I concluded they must be in the dining hall because of the direction and resonance of the noise.

"Go to your rooms quickly and quietly," I instructed. Vesperia and Castor were stunned, only able to nod before flying off. I stayed in the entryway, making my way to the dining hall through the kitchens. I wanted to follow them and listen in on the specific problems they mentioned, just like I had always done.

Chapter Seven

The current battleground, the dining room, was at the base of the west wing. Vesperia would surely hear every smashed dish and scream, but I hoped that Castor would be safe in his room in the East wing. I hid in the kitchens to listen to every word. Once I knew what the issue was, I could fix this and my family would be fine again.

"You are one of the most hot-headed and irrational individuals I have ever had the displeasure of meeting!" my father yelled.

"You are one to speak! You are the worst insufferable know-it-all that will *never cease* speaking!"

"That is *rich*!"

"At least *I can* say that I *am*! You have nothing without my father's support!"

"Ha! His *support*? You mean *compensation* for my daily *hell* with you!" my father laughed. "Which you have also taken from me!"

She stormed from the dining hall towards the kitchens. I hid behind a large wooden table. They entered the kitchens, my father turning towards his study.

"You are incompetent at the least, irresponsible at best! If I let you manage this house's finances, it would go bankrupt in a fortnight!" my mother hissed, throwing a sunbeam at the door, stopping my father from leaving.

"Foul woman! You should catch your tongue before the divine smite you!" father bellowed, changing directions to the Great Hall. I used the servant stairs from the kitchens to the second-floor landing, where I snuck through my mother's room onto the lovers' gallery above the Great Hall.

From above in the gallery I knew I would be visible in the light from the nebula floating around the ceiling. I used a simple charm to disguise my figure from below, being careful to replicate the nebula's glare on the wall behind me. I watched my parents fling minor spells at each other. Father would erect a shadow figure and mother would shoot it down.

"Even if the divine *were* here, they surely would *not* smite *me*! *We* won the war, WE are the chosen! If anyone in this house is 'enlightened' it is I!" she hurled the verbal jab while delivering a furious blow with a sunbeam.

"Ha! Blasphemy! You and your traitorous kin ripped this land apart and now we are forced to abide by your customs and *your* will. Even the Queen is one of you!"

"Now who waves a traitorous tongue Kyrinn? Speaking ill of our Divine Ruler?" I watched from between the rail posts on the banister as they overcame each other's enchantments, steadily growing more powerful as they tried to overpower each other.

"She is not *my* Divine Ruler. I respect her position, but the way her husband's family came into power disturbs me, to say the least. The way of Obscurum is to let The Void choose a leader," he said.

"Well, there you go! The realm was void of a leader. The absence of a true leader showed the Great Solaris' the way!" mother yelled.

"You speak too freely of times you do not know of. Your palace walls were too high to see the suffering of others. The Solaris clan devastated the region," father stated. I felt a heavy weight in my heart remembering another spat similar in topic from my earlier days.

"Be aware, Kyrinn. You know the Queen is a girlhood friend of mine. I would not wish for you to have married a traitor."

"To be found guilty of treason and marked unseelie would be less problematic than living with you daily." Father rounded on mother and they spared again with more powerful charms.

I had enough. I released my charm, spread my wings, and descended from the gallery. They had moved into the ballroom to hurl spells around. I landed hard, creating a loud *slap* when my shoes hit the floor. I heard them both gasp and cease casting. I walked into the ballroom with the best confused face that I could muster.

"I do not know if you may have forgotten that sound travels a great distance through the air in a stone house or if you two have purposefully projected your graces' voices across the house, but I can hear you from upstairs."

"Do *you* challenge *me*?" Mother advanced on me, a sunburst in her hand. Father intercepted it with a wall of thick darkness.

"Eleanor! Cease this as *once*!" he commanded with a great booming voice. Mother spun to face him and threw the sunburst at him. He dodged it, but became enraged.

"What are the dinner arrangements? We have returned and I am sure Castor and Vesperia would love to tell you all about their beautiful ensembles." I tried to redirect the conversation. Mother scoffed and stormed out of the ballroom through a side door. Father and I remained, but the agitation in his aura did not dissipate. Instead, it found me.

"Seren. I understand you feel an obligation to speak for your siblings, but you need to learn when and where your opinions are allowed." He then huffed and retreated up to his room through the servant stairs. I stood dumbfounded in the empty, now-dark ballroom. The glow from my wings was all I had, and they were not bright enough to illuminate my way. I summoned a part of the Nebula from the ceiling outside of the door in the Great Hall. I watched the cloud of tiny stars bob towards me, bringing me light.

I used the light of the stars to move out of the ballroom and into the Great Hall without incident. After having done their job, I released them back to the nebula cloud.

I floated into the dining hall through the kitchens. The table had been set, but not served. Plates, cups, and bowls lay in remains on the floor. Paint or material were left behind on the stone walls where someone threw a dish. I attempted to tidy the mess manually, but cut my thumb on a sharp edge. I pondered leaving the mess for Mrs. Sykes and Mr. Huich but decided against it.

I called the broom and mop from the closet and began sweeping the broken dishware and debris from the floors. Not only did I refuse to track down the two bickering Aer fairies, but I felt no need to intervene in their skirmishes. Aer fairies were some cold fighters. They would remove the air from around you, suffocating you. So instead, I collected the debris into a pile that I could levitate into a bucket. I began mopping the floor with only water; I had no desire to find soap and make a proper mop bucket.

When I finished, I set the broom and mop gently back in the closet. I heard the front door open and the quick-paced clack of Mrs. Sykes' shoes. She scurried up the grand staircase to mother's room, where another door slammed.

"This will be a lovely dinner," I muttered to myself before taking my seat at the table. Mother insisted we all eat together or not at all. I heard the front door open again and assumed it was Mr. Huich. There were no footsteps that affirmed my suspicions. Lawrence would flit about the grounds anytime he could potentially get away with it. After all, flying was first nature to a fairy, and denying an Aer fairy flight was cruel.

I waited in the dining room for what felt like an hour. Then pushed away from the table to pillage the kitchen. When I pushed the door in, I caught Mrs. Sykes directing the kitchen staff to create well-balanced plates of food.

"Oh, I apologize. I will return to the dining hall." I bowed my head and turned to retreat.

"No. No. No one is eating in the dining hall tonight. Your parents are too cross to leave their chambers, " she responded.

"Oh? I was under the impression that Mother's rule was still in place. The one forbidding *anyone* from eating in private?" I inquired. Mrs. Sykes let her hands fall and now turned to face me.

"Yes. That *was* the rule. The rules have changed since you have been gone. Do you wish to have dinner in the dining hall then?" she asked cooly.

"I would take it in my room, but if there is someplace else I can take dinner to make it less stressful for you then that is where I would like it." I willed my embarrassment to stay hidden. She returned to her conducting and I was relieved she was no longer staring me down.

"Your bedchamber is fine. Expect us within the next few minutes." Her response was harsh, but not mean. I closed the door and flew, unbothered by the idea of my mother catching me, closing the door behind me. I looked around my room and still did not feel at home in this new chamber. I saw my books and was uninterested, I dared not look at the thin glamour of my siblings' gifts. So all that remained was the window. I climbed onto the window seat and stared at the blinding metropolis. Lux.

I used to peer out my window down at Inanis and imagine the lives of the people we looked over. Was there a mother who had exactly the amount of children she wanted? Was everyone fed? Did our community support artisans and performers? I wanted the best for them all. I knew my readings would help in the future. *I just knew they would.*

One good thing about living on the outskirts of town was the easy access to the living stars above. I did not dare venture outside before dinner came, but I did swing the pane of glass out into the night so that I might lean out and peer up at the sky. It was hard with the illumination from Lux, but there they were, twinkling above.

I took in a deep breath and concentrated on the sky, willing my mind to forget the house and the glowing city. They danced for me, illuminating the sky into patterns and lines that I would read like a book. The stars shifted into new positions slowly showing me a scene.

What would become of my family? I thought up at them, praying they heard me. I watched as the stars repeated their dance above me. Two constellations collided into a new one. Several stars escaped the previously separate constellations to be on their own. Some stars outshone their neighbors. The new constellation looked like a mother, holding her child, wings gently fluttering behind her.

A knock came at my door jarring me from my vision. I blinked and the stars returned to their original spots.

"Come in," I called, pulling the window closed. Mrs. Sykes entered with two men from the kitchens. They each carried armfuls of food on trays and drinks. She pointed to them to make up the table by my fireplace. There was not enough room to make a proper place setting, but for only me, Mrs.Sykes made the chair and small table work.

The servants set up two fully served plates. A quail paired with vegetables. And bread. A garden salad sporting all the very best from our eternally blossoming gardens. They left a chalice and decanter of dark wine, plus a jug of water. A selection of cakes and cookies was added to the final setup.

"The interim maid will collect the dishes in the morning with your laundry. Do try not to break anything," Mrs. Sykes sighed. I had no idea how to respond without evoking some modicum of rage. So I nodded in affirmation of her request. I stood by the window until everyone else left, and flung it open once the door was closed behind them. The stars did not dance for me again. I left the window open for the crisp autumnal air and sat down to my dinner.

I finished all that I could, but had to leave some of the cakes and the salad. Any other time I would have shared with Aurora, but she was hopefully eating even more delicious meals than I. I pulled my feet up onto the chair and stared into the fire. When we arrived at Mount Ignis, one thing immediately caught my attention – the flame seers. They traveled in large groups with each other, always carrying an oversized candle with a bright blue hellfire flame. The candle was their way of seeing into the future. I approached them to inquire about their practices and methods.

So many flame seers came to the local Lord's house to meet my summons. It was not wasteful though, I believe they did encourage the growth and cultivation of my unique prophetic experiences. Once they had described the feeling of their visions, I was ready. They taught me everything I could possibly need to know about prophecy – even if I was only a curious noblewoman to them. I carried their teachings with me through the Floral region and the Human Realm where I had my first real prophetic vision.

Chapter Eight

Sleep evaded me. I watched the moon disappear and the sun peek up to take its place in the back gardens. When I felt the hour was not too early, I dressed myself in a tunic, trousers, and cloak and disappeared into the morning before mother, Vesperia, or either of their gossipy maids could see me.

The road to Inanis curved down the hill and into town over a canal bridge. My only real obstacle was the gate. Queen Solaris had placed a powerful enchantment around our grounds to protect us from any backlash from the war, but once I crossed the canal bridge I was free to pretend I was any random fairy. I landed near the shrubbery of an outbuilding and began walking towards the gate.

I pulled my hood over my head, concealing my face, and walked quickly down the laneway to the gate entrance. As I approached, I saw that the gate was closed and only one Royal guard stood watch. The royal guard was dispatched from Lux to all of Effect on Queen Solaris' orders. I watched as he paced back and forth before deciding the best course of action.

When the Solaris guard turned to return to the opposite side of the gate I took off from the ground, pushing myself as hard as I could. I watched carefully to make sure I was out of sight before the guard turned to face my direction again. I was no Aer fairy, so I could not manipulate the wind to make me fly faster. Instead, I used my surroundings to keep me hidden. The minor wood between our hillside and Inanis was the perfect place to land and rest.

I descended on the Inanis side of the estate, aiming for the body of a tall thick tree that I could hide behind while I landed. Once I was on the ground, I had to lie down and catch my breath. *Maybe I should have stretched. That year bound in the Human Realm sapped my stamina.*

I used the cover of the woods to gingerly work my way to Inanis. I used landmarks I knew and the sun to point myself in the right direction – southeast. The woods were familiar to me, from my girlhood – before the strict rules were imposed. Vesperia, and Castor (later on), and myself would stroll these woods imagining all sorts of enthralling stories. Like the time Castor insisted on being a knight. Vesperia obliged his wish for us to be scared, helpless princesses. I, however, insisted that princesses could not be scared of some imaginary beast, and that *I* must play the beast. Castor had complained when I chose to be a basilisk and would turn him to stone. After a few tantrums, I agreed to be a wyvern so he could slice my draconic wings and immobilize me to save Vesperia, the princess.

I found the road and peered at the sun through my fingers to verify my direction. I turned to follow the road south to Inanis. The road was packed with dirt and stone pathways carved by the decree of the four realm rulers. One being our Queen and the late king. It was empty – no early morning merchants joined me, or they had beaten me into town. Occasionally non-residents would come to the town market to sell goods or to trade. I was looking forward to finding something local.

After crossing the canal bridge I set my sights on the Brilliant Nest. I had to pass Inanis Loop Street and turn right at the well. The

Brilliant Nest was the second building on the street. A two-story building, the first floor was dedicated to their inventory – mainly books. The second floor was a manageable living space.

As I approached I looked for signs that the proprietors were awake and preparing for the day. If they were not ready for customers, I would return after the market. I rejoiced when I saw two figures meandering about the lower level. I walked up the short path, avoided some debris, and pushed the door inward.

The old brass bell chimed as I passed through, alerting Nydia and Clara that someone had arrived. I did not call out, knowing my voice would give me away. I wove through the shelves of books, scrolls, ink, and quills hoping to catch either of them before they caught me. Nydia was quick to find me. She squealed with surprise and cooed gentle compliments while enveloping me in her winged embrace.

"It has been so long!" she chirped. I took note of the grey in the feathers around her face and the light glaze over her dark brown eyes.

"I have only been gone for five years. So yes, a very long time," I replied. A scoff took me off guard, I looked to my left and saw Clara leaning against a wall. She held a steaming cup with one hand, the other rooted in the pocket of her trousers.

"Clara! It is so nice to finally see you again!" I exclaimed, She snarled and turned away, retreating into the next room. Nydia looked at me with her dark eyes as if to apologize for her wife. I gave her an understanding smile while watching the glow from Clara's wings fade. Nydia used her stout blue wings to usher me into the next room. We entered together and joined the annoyed Clara in the central sitting area.

I studied Clara and noticed more wrinkles in her glowing yellow skin. Her blonde hair was fading to white and losing its shine. Her internal light was dimming too. Nydia did not look half her age, but bluebirds did not age as people might. Her feathers were losing their luster, and some their color, but the blue of her top feathers was ever brilliant. They sat together on a chaise lounge and looked at me.

"So what was it like out there?" Clara asked gruffly.

"Riveting! I learned so much. I cannot wait to apply it all here in Inanis! There is a system of governance that Flora uses and I think adapting our system to resemble it might ease some tensions. I observed more of course, but I am sure you would rather assist me in finding a book than listen to me prattle on about a half-decade-long trip."

"Nonsense! We asked!" Nydia sprang into the conversation. I nodded and allowed my lips to curl into a smile.

I continued, beguiling them of all the adventures I had on my trip through Mythénia and then the Human Realm. Clara seemed the most fascinated by the descriptions of other realms, as she had never left Effect. When she had met Nydia, she had just moved to Inanis from Lux as a transplant by the Queen. Once she met Nydia, all her dreams of moving away ceased.

"Which region was your favorite?" Nydia asked.

"I enjoyed them all, but Effect will always be my favorite."

Clara played with her empty mug, her face creased in agitation. She abruptly got up and exited the room, taking her mug upstairs.

Nydia sighed and resettled herself on the chaise lounge. I fiddled with my nails, ripping off the broken ends.

"Did I say something wrong?" I asked Nydia. She hummed and took a moment to answer.

"No. You did not say anything wrong. Clara missed you and I think she's a tad grumpy about your leaving. She will not tell you so – I think it best you do not mention this conversation. I will go retrieve her and you can peruse the stacks." She pushed off the couch and flapped her wings once to catch her balance. She trotted after her wife up the stairs. I heard her claws clack across the floor above.

I found a shelf of books nearest to me and began my joyful perusement. The spines were all so colorful and each title called out to me. I felt guilt start to grow in my gut for wanting to read every tome. I did not think I would finish reading the entire store, but maybe I could try.

The shelves were evenly spaced for winged folk to feel comfortable shopping. I moved to a new shelf searching for a book that called to me, one that demanded I read it. This is how I have always chosen my reading material. I could hear Clara and Nydia speaking about friends – me. I ran my fingers along the spines of a few books, their titles interesting, but not enough for me to pry them from their shelves.

'The First Gathering', 'Hollow Bones', and 'Tinker Finger; A Remedy'. They were interesting to be sure, but not *my* interest. I would prefer something useful for a change. I looked around for sections or markers or anything, but as usual, the stacks were to be searched by

intuition. I continued my search as I wondered what my perfect book would be. I thought of the books I had at home, so many unread, and yet I would purchase another today.

A clattering of talons and boots marched down the stairs. Anxiety shot through my system, but I had no reason for it. They returned to the sitting area and I heard them settle in again.

"Seren?" Nydia called. I poked my head out from the shelf I was browsing – Clara waved me back over.

"I have to apologize. Nydia is right – about quite a lot – that I was cross because you had been gone so long. It may be out of line for me to say, your ladyship, but we have looked out for you like the daughter we did not have. I was worried you may like someplace more than here..." she trailed off.

My eyes watered, but I cried internally. Nydia and Clara both became worried and fussed over my comfort.

"I am alright. I think I am relieved most of all. I missed you as well. Mother would not allow me to send letters other than to the family. I am so sorry." I felt a pang of regret in my chest.

"Relieved?"

"Yes! It has been an *age* since anyone has been truly happy to see me! I thank you for letting me tell you of my adventure. It was akin to a long and intriguing book!" I laughed.

"No one has asked you to regale them with stories of your travels?" Nydia looked appalled. Clara patted her blue wing.

"Unfortunately, no. Everyone at home seems to be in a cross mood – every day." I tried to be polite.

"Not even your siblings? I thought they loved it when you told them stories?" Nydia asked.

"They too have been in a cross mood. I have not the faintest idea why."

"Well... how about we help you find the right book? Maybe that will cheer you up." Clara offered. Nydia looked to me to verify that was something I would participate in. I nodded.

"Earlier I was looking for something that might help me figure out why everyone is so wound up. Maybe you know which books would be helpful."

"Certainly!" Nydia lifted herself from her seat and trotted to a bookshelf in the farthest northeast corner. I got up and followed her. She was mumbling to herself about light when Clara came up beside her. Clara's glow was dimming with age, but she was still brighter than a candle flame. Nydia chirped happily and ran a feather over the spines like I had with my finger. She stopped on a red bound, medium-thick spine. She pulled it from the shelf and handed it to me. '*The Guide for Lost Souls: Finding Yourself*' I read silently.

"Oh! This is perfect!" I breathed. Nydia wrapped me in a feathery embrace.

We all walked back to the central seating area. I had a hand in my pocket to leave payment for the book. I knew all too well after this emotional visit they would not ask for payment, but it was the right thing to do. I would set it somewhere they could find it later. Clara and Nydia sat on the couch again and initiated our old ritual.

"There is this woman– I want to say a peony – but all flowers look the same to me. This flower fairy came in asking for books on pollination, and Nydia offered to help." Clara chuckled.

"How helpful!" I said. The curious looks from Nydia and Clara clued me into wondering what alternative meanings there might be. I thought for a moment and understood. "Oh."

They laughed and continued to tell me of the five years' worth of patron mishaps that I had missed. The flower woman, an elk Lord, who was looking for Panthera fae books. Hemlock was looking for a tome on self-sacrifice and so many other stories of what I had missed. I began to feel a deep grief of losing out on these moments with them.

The front door's old brass bell chimed and I took it as my chance to leave before I started crying.

"Just a moment!" Nydia called.

"Ok!" the patron replied.

"Thank you so much for your help. This will be just what I need." I smiled. Clara and Nydia both hugged me.

"Of course! Thank you for stopping by! Will we see you again soon?"

"Sure!" I lied. I was not sure if I would be able to sneak out of the manor again. Not until after the ball, surely. I gestured to the back door with a questioning look. Clara understood my meaning and nodded, waving it off as nothing. Nydia went to assist their customer and I slowly walked to the back door. I waited for Clara to turn her back before placing a stack of five gold coins on the merchant counter, then slipped out the back door.

This time I was smart, stretching my wings out before taking a deep breath before lifting off the ground. Turning left, I headed west, following the river street until I got to West Street where I turned left again, heading east now, towards the town. I picked out a seat on the low stone wall that made the town center.

I watched a couple of carts to go by with goods from Lux headed towards Obscurum, but then there were no more. I turned to my book and pulled it open. I read the author's note: '*For those who feel lost in the sea of others ~ take this raft and float to freedom*', then turned to chapter one. The chapter began by telling me how unique and special I was.

You are the only one of you we have. True, but also false. True because I am the First Star, there are no other First Stars. False because others could easily replace me. I wanted to continue reading, but a gaggle of children ran into the square screaming – playing.

They scattered across the center of the square around the tree. I looked around for a collection of parents but found none standing idly by. Unaccompanied minors. I knew better than to interact with a group of children on their own. So I took it as a sign to take my leave and find amusement elsewhere. I pushed off my perch on the wall and walked to my right where the Market House was.

When Inanis was founded, the town held a market around the evergreen tree, but with the addition of carts to merchants' traveling gear, the town had to imagine a new way to hold a market. An inventive fairy transplanted from Ingenium suggested a special meeting house for the market and other town needs.

The Market House was shaped like the letter 'L' and made from fired bricks from Elemental Terra. It was one story with a traditional thatched roof. The front and back doors were each a set of double doors so that merchants could bring in their wares. Inside, I took my time examining the tables as I passed by the first time. I returned to purchase things that caught my eye. A cotton fairy was selling linen garments and I was drawn to a delightful blue blouse and a matching skirt. I waited patiently as she helped the gentleman in front of me.

"Hello, Hello! How can I help you?" She greeted me. Her head was covered in the fluffy cotton she wove into the material. She had lanky arms and a thin frame, her skin a pale green like a plant stalk.

"I am in love with this blouse and these skirts, can I get them both?" I asked.

"Certainly! I happen to have two skirts out – which would you prefer?"

"Both, please! If that's alright?" She happily pulled the three articles off her table and folded them into a neat bundle that she wrapped with paper and tied with string.

"Two silvers or one gold." She asked before handing over the package. I passed her two gold pieces carefully so the other patrons did not see.

"Please keep the extra! This is exquisite craftsmanship," I said, before walking out of the Market House.

When I got outside, the cool autumn morning my stomach gave me a warning gurgle that it needed to be fed. I knew just the thing. Across the street was the baker's building, smoke puffing out from the chimney, alerting Inanis villagers that goods were being made and ready for eating! I flit over the street, above the pedestrians, landing on the empty bakery steps. I pushed open the door and was met with an outpouring of flavorful aromas.

Inside, a fire spirit floated behind the counter. She wore a chainmail apron and a dark, flame-resistant dress, her body made entirely of red hot flames. She smiled to greet me as I came in.

"What may I serve you today?" she asked, her voice like the crackling and popping of a campfire.

"I am undecided! The whole place smells delicious. What would you recommend if I told you I had no favorite?"

"Hmm…" she thought, holding her chin with a hand. I waited patiently. The building was full of lovely smells for me to imagine eating. The flame spirit made a single sound of knowing before darting to her oven and retrieving a small hot cake.

"A breakfast cake! Blueberry!" She wrapped the cake in bakery paper, leaving the fluffy dome exposed, before handing it to me.

"Thank you." I took the small package. "May I ask you something?" I laid a gold piece on the counter.

"Yes!" She took the coin and added it to her revenue box.

"I do not mean any offense, but why is it that a flame spirit is up north in Inanis? Do you not miss Mount Ignis?"

"No offense taken!" She was joyful, "If I am correct, you are either Seren or Vesperia Astrum, correct?"

I nodded.

"Then you are the reason I moved here! So many regions are attempting to mix bloodlines, and yours is the first success! I wanted to be close for any of the soon-to-be momentous occasions! You all are history in the making!"

"Yes, you are correct."

"The First Star! Oh, what an honor!" She curtsied.

"Thank you, but there is no need for that. I am merely here to support the community today. Though, if you are in search of a momentous occasion, there will be one in five days. Many dignitaries from the regions will be in attendance right here in Inanis. I hope that helps business," I said with a smile before turning back to the street.

I decided a walk would be the best way to enjoy this *breakfast cake*. I turned right to head west, towards the center of town again. I admired the golden top and baked berries. Taking a gentle bite, I was surprised at the tart burst of berry and I found myself continuing to marvel at the look of the cake and its delicious flavor while walking.

As I entered the square, I looked up just in time to see a team of black horses galloping towards me. I pressed my bundle of clothes tight to my chest and took to the sky, barely missing the dark blue carriage.

"Hey!" I yelled at the driver as he barreled past. I shook my head and landed back on the street only to discover I had dropped my breakfast cake. I followed the carriage with my eyes until it disappeared past the canal bridge. *Reckless dark Lords. Always in a hurry to go hide away in the dark mists again.*

With a deep sigh, I decided it was time to return home. Someone would be sent to wake and dress me soon. I walked to the edge of town where I then jumped and took off flying north towards Twilight Hall. Once I had passed over the woods, I saw the dark carriage again, rolling up to the gates of the estate!

What in the...?

Adjusting my course, I flew down to meet the aggressive driver at my gate. The crest on the door was not my father's family – this was a combination of dark abyssal blues and the Obscurum black. I landed in front of the gate, between it and the carriage. The guard came out from his post wielding a sword.

"Halt! Who are you? This is a noble house under the protection of Queen Helia Solaris!" He yelled. The guard was short, pudgy, barely able to fit into his own uniform. He looked like a Terra fairy, from the square harsh features on his face. I pulled my hair away from my face and looked him in the eye.

"Seren Astrum. This is *my* house, and *this man* attempted to run me over in town just moments ago." I pointed at the driver, who blanched.

"I- I am so sorry miss - uh- M'Lady," He stuttered.

"Are you delivering the Lord, sir?" The guard spoke over me. I had half a mind to smack him right there.

"Yessir!" the driver yelped. The guard waved his arm and the gates opened, the Queen's barrier allowing them entrance. I thought I saw the curtains of the carriage move, but it could have been a tousle from the movement of the carriage.

Chapter Nine

I passed through the gate behind the dark Lords carriage and noticed the brilliant sun carriage with the Solaris crest shining on the side parked in the lane. The yellow-gold carriage was pulled by a team of six Aethon horses. Their bodies burned brightly in shimmers of hot white and bright orange. The fire steeds shook their heads, throwing embers across the ground. They had flaming coals for eyes and their hooves mimicked the look of volcanic glass. *The Queen was here.*

The mysterious guest parked beside the Queen's carriage, and the driver acted as a footman, opening the door for the passenger. A tall, slender, grey-skinned dark fairy stepped out. He stretched his moth-like wings and tightened the grey ribbon holding back his curly raven-black hair. I stopped and hid behind the shrubbery in the laneway, watching him until he was inside. *That must be the Queen's guest.*

I collected myself and squeezed my parcel tight, approaching the front door. Mr. Huich was nearby to welcome me inside.

"Do you require assistance, miss?"

"Yes, thank you." I handed him the package. He unwrapped a corner to peek inside. Once he noticed it was clothing, he headed for the laundry suite.

I quietly snuck past the ballroom and kitchens, mother's favorite places to receive guests. Once on the stairs, I felt more at ease escaping to my chambers. When I reached the landing, my mother's eyes locked with mine as she held the door to her withdrawing room.

"Good morning, Lady Seren. Have you eaten?" Her tone was sharp. My stomach clenched.

"No, I have not. I was in town for a new book." I held up the evidence. Her face was a solid mask of fake content as she crossed the hall to me.

"You must join us then." she covered her words in sweetness, but spoke again, this time very quietly. "That is, after you change out of this peasant garb. You are a *lady*. I swear, somedays I wish – ugh – get dressed." She turned in a flurry of fabric and marched back into her withdrawing room. I scurried away to my room where I slipped out of my blouse and trousers then into a clean chemise. Frantically, I searched for a worthy gown for breakfast with the Queen. A knock came at the door before Mrs. Sykes entered.

"Miss, do you need assistance? Your mother has stalled breakfast for you."

I could feel the shame burning into my skin. I nodded and sat in my vanity chair and watched her rummage through my wardrobe. She pulled a bodice and kirtle set from the back, as well as the pale, yellow-beaded monstrosity.

"Is *that* necessary?" Mrs. Sykes gave me 'the look'.

"Where are the sleeves?" she asked. I pointed to a drawer on the left side of the wardrobe. She pulled out the matching, over-beaded sleeves and gestured for me to stand.

"Her Majesty the Queen is here. Your mother would not see you in anything but the finest." Mrs. Sykes tied me into the gown piece by piece. I understood what she meant. *We must always show our gratitude or she will think us ungrateful.* Mrs. Sykes tied the final tether and lightly pushed me towards the door. I looked back to see her gathering my discarded clothing. I was most likely never going to see those 'peasant clothes' again.

The walk to the drawing room was short, but getting there felt like it took forever. The door was propped open by a brass sun the size of a baby. I skimmed the room with my eyes as I entered. Mother sat on a couch next to the Queen's chair, wearing a white gown with gold trim. Vesperia wore a light grey, satin gown, sat across from them on the opposing couch and Castor was not there. The mysterious stranger sat in the other singular chair across from the Queen.

"Come in," The Queen demanded. She wore a gold dress with many ornaments sewn on the skin-tight sleeves, making her dark, golden skin look wrapped in gold dust. Her golden hair was wrapped into a braided top bun and ornamented with chains of white metal. I came into the room as she commanded.

"Sit." She directed me to sit next to my sister. I sat carefully after bowing deeply to the Queen. Vesperia gave me a quick – possibly illusionary – glare, then returned to fluttering her eyelashes and smiling at our guest.

"Have you been introduced to your guest of honor?" the Queen asked.

"No, not yet, Your Majesty," I responded.

"This is the Lord Umbriel Caligo, third son of the late Earl Caligo. He, too, was on a scholarly tour, but instead of riding through each region, he joined a lesser Ineritus clan." She waved a white-gloved hand at the Lord, who stood and bowed.

"It is a pleasure to be meeting you all this lovely morning." His voice was surprisingly sonorous.

"We are so very pleased to have you," my mother interjected. "Why do we not start our meal and we can discuss more over our morning tea?" The room was silent; we all deferred to the Queen.

"Yes, what a fine solution," the Queen announced, and the servants began to make up plates for each of us. Today looked to be an egg, over easy, with fruit and toast kind of day. Hot grey tea was poured into all our cups. The Queen was served first, followed by the guest, and then the family. As per custom, no one touched their plate until the Queen began to eat. We all waited as she had her plate inspected by a flower fairy for poisons. When her poison tester was finished, she still did not eat.

"Before we begin, I would like our young people to hear me. I am here for one purpose and one purpose only. To drive Effection into the future. Think of what I have said while you eat and then we shall continue." She raised her tea cup and drank, starting the meal. As I ate, I pondered the Queen's statement, drawing up all the ideas I had had over the course of my scholar's tour. We ate in relative silence, the cups and forks clinking against plates as everyone gingerly cut into their food or sipped their tea.

I contemplated my ideas from the past five years – some were not befitting a Queen's ears, as they were just silly little dreams. I settled on the idea of integrating the Ineritus clans into society – the idea of using my prophetic dreams to aid the realm and implement a new ruling system. I knew the Queen would not like a couple of the ideas, but at least she would want to know the progress of my abilities. That was one of the primary reasons for sending me on the tour in the first place.

I finished my breakfast and set my plate on the small table between us. The Queen also finished her place and cleared her throat with authority for a silent room – all sound ceased.

"I should like your attention, please. It is time we take a moment to gaze upon the future of Affection. Seren –"

"Yes, My Queen! Thank you! I want to say first, thank you for the astounding tutors. I feel I worked hard and enjoyed myself, which provided me the opportunity to learn so much that I can apply to Effects and then Mythénia as a whole. The Realm would have *us* to thank for the kick into the future. The first thing is –"

"ENOUGH!" The Queen stood, blazing. I froze, stunned. I looked at my mother and then my sister. Both wore looks of horror and embarrassment. I shut my mouth hard, shame burning my face. "Brazen child. *Silence*. As *I* was saying… We must now gaze upon the future of our region. My late, revered husband planned your bloodline with his blood and sweat. The future must be secured. Lady Seren, I formally present you to your *betrothed*, Lord Unbriel Caligo. Third of Caligo House, Scholar of Forgotten Cultures, Hero of Lux, and so much more. So please, Lord Caligo, tell us more about your accomplishments."

"I was sent to live with cousins as they traveled around Effection, though they are not Ineritus, but instead wealthy merchant ship owners. I was delighted to travel with them. My time with them was short. They soon began to grow their family and could not attend to my tutoring, so I passed on to another relative who took me to stay with a dear family friend on the edge of the region, near the coast. That is where I had my first encounter with an Ineritus woman. She was anxious, and was insistent that I did not touch her hands." He regaled the room with his experience.

I listened, but could hear less than what would have helped me participate in the conversation. I was usually more polite, but my faux pas with the Queen had rendered me useless. I looked up to try and watch Lord Caligo, but caught my mother's wicked glare instead. This jolted me into focusing singularly on every word Lord Caligo said – a choice I would soon regret.

"I was still quite young. At barely ninety, I could tell she had lived many more years than I. She removed her metal gloves and simply brushed the stone beside me. I watched as it crumbled to ash," he continued and I began to realize, by the cadence in his voice, that he was just as arrogant as many other noble sons I had met.

"This is how I came to learn of their immense power."

Or you could have simply listened *to her.*

"This is when I sent the Queen a short but descriptive letter telling her of my findings and how, with her support of course, I could study–" *Why do we need to study an established culture?* "– them and help them assimilate into society." He seemed quite pleased with himself. *I could have done that so much better and on my own.*

"Yes! How very enlightened of you, Lord Caligo. I think we would like to hear your more personal accomplishments. Something that the lady might find … attractive?" the Queen redirected.

"Ah! Yes! Quite right!" he started again, stopping to sip his tea. He drank and finished by smacking his lips and uttering a sigh before continuing. "As was stated before by Her Majesty, I am the third son of the late Lord Caligo. My brother has yet to marry, but titles shall not befall me in this lifetime from my own family." *Oh, that must be it, he is looking for a title marriage. How honeyed the pot is for him. I wonder how much of this is orchestrated?*

"Do not mistake me – I do adore my family. I should like a family of my own, of at least five children." He sipped his tea again. I glanced about the room, and to my chagrin, everyone was enamored with his tale. Vesperia looked especially flushed. *She must have caught his meaning also.*

"Learning is a passion of mine, so I would strive for my whole house to be of educated minds. I do so abhor the drabble of the uneducated." *Perhaps you should educate them?*

"Other than those pillars of my personality, I am but a simple faeman, searching the Greater World for all its intellectual treasures!" he proclaimed. Vesperia was quick to clap for him; I was far less amused.

"Brava, I say! Well, I will be leaving to arouse the rabble in your meager village for the festivities! A wedding of the First Star is sure to be of *some* fanfare," the Queen laughed. I disliked the way she spoke about our people, but held my tongue, as I had made one mistake too many already. She stood and so we bowed, as was customary, until she left the room. I scurried out soon after through the adjoining door hidden in the wall.

Inside my chambers, I tore off the beaded gown in a rage. Beads scattered everywhere. These people had no regard for me or my desires. They expected me to marry this random man just because he comes from one-half of my bloodline? Ridiculous!

Chapter Ten

I stared at the floor where the gown shreds and beads lay. Surely, my trousers were gone for good. I looked around the room that was mine but also was not mine. The gifts for my siblings were still covered by the minor glamour – good. The laundress had not stopped by yet, so I felt stuck in my chemise, not wanting to be stuffed into another gown.

Suddenly and without warning, my door burst open and the white yellow glow of my mother was there.

"How *dare* you speak out of turn, in the Queen's presence no less. Interrupting a Queen! You should be grateful that Mythénia is a far more civilized realm than that of the humans. Do they not execute their disobedient?!" she screamed.

"Not that I know of." I partially lied. Her hand, hot with anger, struck me across the face. I could feel the scorch mark appear. I stood frozen in place, my neck snapped to my right.

"*Insolent child*. I *know* you abandoned your duties to galavant about the town. You *will* afford Lord Caligo your time and *find your place* in this betrothal or *else*," she hissed, before stalking out of my chambers through the adjoining door.

My arms and legs began to shake. I put my hand up to my face and traced my mother's singed handprint across my cheek. I turned to the mirror – it did not look good. The hand print was clearly visible in a puffy red hand shape across my left cheek. I saw where the blisters would form within the next couple of days. I threw a small glamour over the patch and turned towards my wardrobe.

Tears ran down my face, aggravating the second-degree burn. I sifted through my clothes until I found a simple skirt and a front-tying bodice. I slipped on the green, everyday linen and carefully tied the front corset while sniffling back tears. I threw a random pair of slipper flats to the floor, slipped them on, and left, quietly shutting my door behind me. I glanced around the hall and saw no one. I hurried down the stairs and through the kitchens, then out the front door.

The Queen's carriage still waited outside. Lord Caligos' had been put away. I sprung into the air and flew straight for the patch of woods separating our estate from the village. Among oak, beech, and ash trees, I felt less like an invader. *Maybe I feel more at home here because I have spent five years sleeping under them and traveling through them.*

Under other circumstances, this would have been a beautiful autumn day. I kicked a rock mildly when I landed. It flew maybe three feet before landing on the soft dirt again. I checked my surroundings, and even took the extra steps to search my landing area. When I was sure that I was alone, I released the deep scream I had held back before. My eyes turned to springs as I sobbed. The mark on my face burned and enraged me more.

I began to fling shooting stars at trees, imagining my mother's hand coming down on me over and over again. This was not the first time either – I dredged up every past event where her hand met my skin. The scorch would fade within the next few days and clear up before the ball, but the burn on my heart might never. My eyes turned from springs to cascading waterfalls. I took off jogging, throwing stars this way and that. Trees released their leaves after my glittering stars exploded on their bark. The trees were much sturdier than my weak starlight attacks. If I were not so emotional, I could summon a powerful blast.

Like Vesperia, my thoughts attacked me, forcing me to stop. Could Vesperia fell a tree with her abilities? Had she grown so much without me? The tears continued. I fluttered my wings and hovered, only to feel so heavy that I needed to land again. I walked aimlessly, kicking rocks and shooting branches off of the path I took. My thoughts took a miserable turn towards Lord Caligo.

Self-absorbed Caligo. If he did 'study' the Ineritus, he would have learned that they choose to be alone. Their abilities are quite literally to destroy things. Everyone knows that! I shot an ash tree with a more powerful star– it lost most of its leaves. *The only thing worse than a sunblind light fairy is a dark fairy with his head in a bag. Everything outside of his bag is 'new'.* I threw another rough star, hitting an oak with a hard thud. I angrily yelled and threw a few more into the forest. *This could have been a beautiful day!* I did not see where my shooting stars landed.

"How does it make any sense that *he* gets to spend the better part of two hours prattling on about his lush life between his family homes in his first century? Castor had the *same* offer, but declined. Lord Umbriel is not special because he *chose* to go!" I sent a star flying at an ash that dropped a hefty amount of leaves.

"I, on the other hand, had no choice. Just one day, mother pulls me out of my rooms and notifies me that my studies will be abroad now. When I spoke 'out of turn', she slapped me! That was the last time we spoke in person before I left. I still applied myself and took in as much as I could! I might have acquired something of use, and they silence me to hear this spoiled brat's trade of houses? Every son that is not the eldest was *expected* to do so!" I yelled to the forest.

"I bet he is still doing so now! He has no title to look forward to, thus he is preying on *my* house to receive one! How brazen he is to send the post directly to the Queen!" I screamed, throwing a star at a beech tree. *How arrogant of him to do so.* I watched the leaves fall. *I wonder if he directly asked the Queen for a bride, or if some magnificent blessing has found him. I would have found a multitude of ways to honor the Ineritus clans in society, things that would make them feel welcomed into society. Has he even learned that each clan has its own source? There is a clan whose hands destroy all they touch and another where saliva is the source of decay. Does he know of the obscure clan that cuts off their ears to avoid hair loss?* I flung a handful of stars at a cluster of aspens, but only two hit a trunk.

"Ugh!" *I could not be forced to marry this prick right? Father would never agree.* My mind sifted through Lord Caligos's monologue to find something unworthy. I thought back to his remark about wanting at least five children and shuddered. Throwing a larger star at an oak, I watched as it exploded into multiple tiny stars that shimmered as they fell to the ground.

"Disgusting," I spat. I jumped and flew way deeper into the forest, away from any path that someone may come upon. Away from

Twilight Hall and Inanis. *I have full faith that he would assume all credit for anything I suggested for the region. I would be reduced to a shining statue of a wife. No purpose or life of my own. I would fade away to nothing.* Overcome by this darkness, I landed in an overshadowed glade and pondered this arranged marriage more seriously.

"If I go through with this, then my five years of study travels will be for literally nothing. They told me it was to train me to lead one day... well how am I to do that with a fool as a husband?" I kicked a stone, sending it flying across into the sun-brightened grass. I continued to lurk in the shadows. Facing a row of trees, I shot my stars at them one at a time. The darkness of each shadow momentarily disappeared. A mischievous smile cracked its way through my gloom. I took off on foot deeper into the forest.

I imagined in my head the face of Lord Caligo in every dark shadow I spotted. The foliage above grew dense, providing me with many targets. I loosed one, two, and three medium, silver-tailed shooting stars in the dense shadow of Caligo. They exploded in a burst of smaller stars for just moments before fading into nothing.

Take that, you arrogant, self-centered dolcop! You will never dull the radiant light that I am! I ran deeper into the forest, sure that I was heading west, the darkness closing in around me. I saw Caligo everywhere, and I stopped. *I will extinguish your dark influence before you can extinguish my light!* I screamed in my head as I summoned the largest shooting star I could and charged the darkest patch I saw. I imagined his real face exploding and released the large star, only to watch it disappear. I felt my slipper tangle in a root and flung my hands out to catch myself. My face landed before my palms in the soft, squishy mud with a wet slap.

"Ew," I said – a mistake. I never imagined mud to be so foul in taste. I coughed it up and slipped once more into the mud. I rolled onto my back and shook my head. *I cannot believe that just happened.* I laughed and tried looking for the evidence of my star. Above me to my right, wedged in an oak tree, was a silver nebula of miniature stars.

"Woah." I carefully stood and walked to the oak with the nebula embedded in the bark. I tried to touch it, but my hand passed through like a cloud. A few of the tiny stars moved away from my fingers like tadpoles in water. I giggled and then wiggled my fingers slowly. Invisible waves moved the tiny stars, but nothing else. *How do I clean this up?* I looked at the nebula – it was so beautiful that I almost did not want to.

Maybe I could leave it? No – there are only three of us. It would certainly cause an issue. I took in a deep breath, in my gut, and envisioned taking the nebula into my hands and releasing it back to the ether. Releasing the breath in a slow controlled stream, I tried recalling the nebula. I could feel the tenuous pull, but it did not budge. I tried once more with a deep breath and eyes wide open, releasing my breath slowly. Nothing.

"I guess this is a special tree now," I said to the forest. If I was going to leave magic stars embedded in a forest tree, I needed to protect it. I looked around and found a fallen branch. I pulled a twig from it and scrawled a circle of Mythenian magic in the mud. With a whisper, it shone a silver lilac and locked in place, solidifying the words I wrote into the ground.

I prayed the tree would survive and stay where it grew – that my magic would not damage its growth and ability to be a great tree. I began to feel immense guilt for scarring it. I decided to sit with it and tell it about myself so that maybe its spirit would not feel burdened by the magic it now held.

When I finished regaling the oak tree with my life story, I had to admit I felt so much better. I stood, said a formal goodbye, then jumped into the air. I flitted through the dense forest until I lost my patience and burst through the canopy. I had been correct in assuming I was traveling west. Twilight Hall was in front of me, facing away. I pushed farther and began the flight home, aiming for the back gardens.

I will make the best of this.

Chapter Eleven

Thankfully, night came quickly. I had excused myself, properly, the first moment I possibly could. I read peacefully in my room from *The Guide for Lost Souls; Finding Yourself*. The author was very neutral on any divisive topic, which bored me, except for their natural tendency to note hard evidence that certainly changed my mind. For instance, this author wrote *'you cannot reach into the cranium of another – though you may wish to – and change their ideas of you they are intangible things'* which was something I had not considered before. By true nightfall, where the sky is void of all color, I could read no more. I laid the book softly on my nightstand, then blew out my bedside candle, enveloping me in darkness. My eyelids left heavy and my mind was muddled, but sleep avoided me. It felt intentional. I tried to ignore the single drop of alertness lingering in my body but my mind scooped it up and used it all to fuel the most anxiety-inducing thoughts possible. Each one left Vesperia and Castor deceased. The only way to ease my anxiety was, unfortunately, to rise.

I put on my soft lavender robe and lit a single-star spell for silver light. Leaving my chamber, I easily snuck over to Vesperia's chambers. Quietly, I pushed her door open to peek inside. I willed the silver star to float into the room for my benefit. It hovered over my sister's limp body. I held my breath. She slept on her stomach; her arms and legs were contorted in various directions. I could not hear her usual snoring. Watching, I finally saw her breathe. When I was sure she was breathing, I recalled my starlight.

I closed the door to Vesperia's chambers and stood as quietly as possible. Listening very carefully, I tried to discern if mother was awake or not. Taking a few light steps forward, I could hear no tell-tale signs of mother being awake. I launched into the air and flitted quickly across the house, down and around the Great Hall, then up the east stairs. Stopping at the landing, I touched down and tip-toed to Castor's chambers – my previous chambers. The star still glittered above my hand. I pressed my ear to the door and heard the loud, asphyxiating snores. I sighed with relief.

Turning, my eyes caught a flicker of candlelight in the spare bachelor suite. I picked my way over to the hallway and extinguished my starlight, folding my wings down into my robe to hide their glow. I walked closer to the mysterious candlelight, then looked out into the hallway, towards the flickering candlelight. A dark figure was outlined in the glow of the small fire. I saw the weak outline of Lord Caligos' face. I strode forward, wanting to see why he was also awake. Normally, a maiden of marrying age being alone – at night – with a strange man could be cause to doubt my virtue. Though, considering we were betrothed, I decided it should be fine.

"Lord Caligo," I called to him quietly. He turned but did not seem surprised.

"Evading sleep?" he questioned me with a sly smile, and I bristled at his words and expression.

"No. It is the opposite. I would love to sleep," I retorted. "What are you doing awake so late?"

"I *am* avoiding sleep. I am afraid it is hard to sleep away from the comforts of home," he stated pitifully. I willed my eyes to only look at his face, for I may roll my eyes. His face portrayed a sad little boy, but I was no fool. He had all the luxuries being the son of a Baron could afford him. Also, I happened to know the guest room was quite lavishly furnished. The guest room was a small apartment on the third floor on my mother's side of Twilight Hall, the West. The Queen's apartment was on the East side of the third floor and was even more lavishly decorated.

"I am forlorn to hear this, my Lord. How might we, as your hosts, accommodate you better?" I tried to be polite. I wanted him to tell me that the furniture on loan from the Queen was tasteless or something equally damning.

"There is nothing, my Lady. I simply miss home. Like you, I have been gone for too long."

"And exactly how long were you away?"

"Most of my first century, and now these past thirty years. Why do you ask?" he seemed to glow with pride.

"Well, and I could be out of line here, if you are over one hundred thirty years of age, and have spent the better part of your first century abroad traveling between family homes, then you must not have many memories of your true home. Do you?" He said nothing in return, so I assumed my victory.

"Please notify Mr. Huich if there is anything we can do to improve your stay. If that is all that is keeping you, I must bid you goodnight and I leave you with this advice: Do not let Mrs. Sykes find you haunting the halls. She will blow that candle out as she blows you out a window. She is very superstitious." I smiled demurely and left him in the spare suite.

The escape to my rooms was dark, except for the ethereal glow of the nebula on the Great Hall floor. I scurried down the east stairs, across the Great Hall, and up the west staircase on foot, all while clutching my hidden wings through my robe. I carefully snuck back into my chambers, leaning against the door, and only then did I realise how out of breath I was. After I was able to calm myself, I hung my robe on the back of my chair, then climbed back into bed.

My mind wandered back to the quips I had made to Lord Caligo, making my face feel hot. *Would he tell mother about any of our conversations? Would he have reason to bring it up?* Rolling over to my left side I looked out my bedroom window. I missed the moon. Sadly with lux illuminating this side of the valley, I may never see it from my bedroom window again. *I wonder if I could create an illusion of the moon*. After my last thought, sleep finally took me.

When I awoke, the sun rose and indicated to me that it was mid-morning. Surely, breakfast was ready by now. Mrs. Sykes had not been sent to retrieve me, so there must not be a rush. I swept my feet out of bed and lazily chose a gown for the day. I found an easily self-dressing one that I could button myself – a light blue gossamer gown. Once I had gotten it on, I braided my hair into one large braid that fell to my elbows. I tied the weave with a ribbon, light blue to match the gossamer fabric. In the mirror, I could still see the scorch mark on my face, so I threw a new glamour over it, then left my room. While leaving my chambers, I was immediately caught by my mother.

"Seren. Come here, she demanded. I joined her at the door to her bedchamber at the very end of the hall.

"Can I trust that you have chosen to find your place?"

"Yes," I answered, forcing little to no tone to sit in my voice.

"Splendid. I am delighted to hear you say so. I am of the mind that, should you come to accept what is good for this family is good for you, that you will truly be happy. Now, breakfast will soon be served – you are to go and entertain Lord Caligo." She forcibly turned me around and shoved me towards the stairs.

"Yes, mother," I replied. She seemed satisfied, but I swore I could hear her mumble *"I wish she would learn how to dress without a maid already"* under her breath .

How am I supposed to magically learn how to prepare outfits when I have had a maid my whole life? Is there some magical spell that befalls me when I turn one hundred and twenty-seven that should allow me to accomplish this task?

Ignoring whatever I may have heard, I continued down the stairs. My wings ached to fly, which would have been much faster.

The dining room had been decorated in the dark colors of the Caligo Crest: dark blue, black, slate grey, and an ashy purple similar to the base color of the Tenebrae Crest. Our silver dishware was set out on the dark blue tablecloth, paired with dusty purple cloth napkins. Throughout the room were bouquets of dried flowers all in Caligo colors.

My father sat happily at the head of the table; Lord Caligo sat to my father's left. The seat to his right was unclaimed. If I sat anywhere else, my mother would be furious. When I stepped into the dining room, my father called out to me.

"I reserved this chair for you, my star!" Lord Caligo seemed… *relieved* to see me. I sat and placed the napkin on my lap – like a lady.

"Has Umbriel told you of his connections to *our* family?" My father cheerily burst into conversation.

"No, he did not." I managed to suppress my immediate suspicions of Lord Caligo.

"How delightful! Do tell her!"

"I learned while speaking with your father that I–"

"He is your second cousin, once removed! His mother had him quite late, but she is *my* third cousin!" My father beamed with delight. Lord Caligo held a look of contempt for my father. *Serves you right.*

Mrs. Sykes accompanied my mother, Vesperia, and Castor into the dining room where she then waited for them to be seated before calling for the meal to be served. Castor sat next to me, while Vesperia looked conflicted at having to choose between the seat closest to our mother or the open seat next to Lord Caligo. She turned to take the seat next to Caligo and mother's face dropped. Vesperia sat with a glare towards me.

"Children! You too shall like to hear that Umbriel is a close relation of ours!" My father dove into the conversation, embarrassing Lord Caligo yet again with the retelling of our distant kinship. Vesperia was the only one who seemed to care. Umbriel was speaking to Castor by mouthing words to him under his father's monologue.

"What is that?" mother interjected.

"Oh, uhm, well I was explaining the division of the original–"

"No, you dim whit. Lord Caligo. You said something to my son just now – what was it?" She was sharp and father fell silent with a deepening frown.

"Oh – I was inquiring about a stroll through the village. I hear Inanis is littered with hidden treasures." He seemed to throw his voice down at the table. Mother appeared to brighten at this.

"Mmmm, yes. I do believe Seren would be the *expert* on the village sights and shops. She will take you to see the sights after breakfast." She forked a heap of eggs into her mouth.

"I – erm – I was not intending to visit the village today, my lady. My sincere apologies for the implication."

"No, you did not. I did. You and my daughter are betrothed now. The town will learn of their new Lord before the end of the week," she commanded between bites. Lord Caligo looked at me, but I knew better than to argue with my mother once her mind was made up. I focused on my plate and said nothing. The matter was settled in silence.

Our father did not resume his monologue. Instead, he began to gnaw off Lord Caligos' ears with an outpouring of information about the villagers. His discomfort made me want to giggle, which Vesperia heard, earning me a mean look. I was surprised when she did not use an illusion to spook me. I cleared my plate, but stayed to witness the burden of Lord Caligo by my father. I was enjoying his continued suffering – my mother did not.

"Ugh!" she groaned. Throwing her utensils on the table and storming from the table. Vesperias's glare deepened before she, too, left in a huff.

"Excuse me, father." I laid a hand on his arm. He paused his ramblings for a moment to look at me.

"Yes, my star?"

"I need to ask Lord Caligo something." I smiled at my father and looked to Lord Caligo, attempting to hide my glee. "Will you be ready to leave for the village soon?"

"I should only need my cloak and walking shoes," he responded with a nod.

"Lovely. I am going to excuse myself and I will meet you by the front door soon. Then I shall show you all Inanis has to offer." I stated, then stood. Lord Caligo nodded in agreement as I turned to leave. I heard my father pick up once again with the long history of his family in Obscurum.

I climbed the stairs again to collect my cloak, my new book, and my pocket money for the trip. On my way back out, I caught Vesperia lingering in her doorway.

"Would you like to join us?" I asked, but was met with an exasperated sigh and the slam of her door.

Chapter Twelve

When I arrived outside, I found that I was alone. This gave me just the right reason to lean against one of the pillars and leaf through my book more. I was beginning to lose myself in the pages when the front door slammed, jolting me back to reality. I looked back to see Lord Caligo wearing knee-high polished black boots and a black fur half-cloak chained across his shoulder.

"Where is the carriage?" he inquired. I snapped my book shut.

"Do your mighty wings not carry you?" I prodded. He gave me a stern look, not unlike my mother's. It made me furious.

"My wings *do* carry me. And well. That is not the point. Commoners fly, and commoners walk. Noblemen *ride*. Surely you know this by now, my lady, ." he scoffed.

"I do, but I find some customs to be arbitrary and well... distancing. Are *we* not meant to oversee this town, however small?" I pushed off the pillar to face him. He would not face me; he was looking for a servant to fetch a carriage.

"You are right, but how should they take our lead if we are not at the frontmost part of history?" he replied.

"I think you mistake leadership with notability. Many lords have already fallen away from history. You cannot rely on a status to solidify your contribution to history. Notable action – or inaction – will do that." His face was still with an unreadable expression. I was unsure if he was angry or thinking. I did not have to wonder for long.

"Sir? My Lady?" Mr. Huich called.

"Ah! My good fellow. Would you please send the carriage to us? We will be going to town."

"As you desire. Will that be all?"

"Yes." Lord Caligo dismissed Mr. Huich, who nodded and scurried off to rouse the stablemen to ready a carriage. I walked to the edge of the gravel path and sat on the brick edge of our house, balancing my book on my knee to read while I waited.

Quite a while later, the carriage did arrive. It was our carriage, with Nevin and Osbert aboard. They nodded to me as they pulled up. Osbert gave me a short bow and held the door open for us. I climbed in first, taking the front-facing bench. Lord Caligo was forced to sit on the rear-facing bench.

"I also happen to agree with your mother. Flying is undignified for a lady. Someone could peek up your gown and then your virtue would be spoiled!" he resurrected our earlier conversation.

"My opinion remains unchanged. I advise you not to speak of my virtue any further."

"I beg your pardon, my lady. I meant no offense. I am only expressing my admiration for the rule your mother holds." I pried my book open again. He huffed and remained silent for the duration of our ride into the village.

When we crossed over the canal bridge I closed my book and stowed it in the crevice between the bench and the back cushion nailed to the carriage wall. Lord Caligo understood why and prepared to leave the carriage as soon as it stopped. Osbert had barely gotten the door open when Lord Caligo burst through. I followed behind, taking note that we had stopped at the Inn – Dusk 'Till Dawn. The unicorns could relax here, and I had a suspicion Nevin craved a warm beer away from the buzz of the house.

"Lord Caligo. If we are to be *married*, you should know all there is of the place you shall be caretaker of. Are you ready to listen?" I asked. He looked taken aback, but nodded solemnly.

"Good. Follow me." I waved him towards the tree in the center of town. "This live oak was deemed sacred after King Solaris and my maternal grandfather's armies drove back the darkness. I do regret that the town's history is so against the Obscurum Clans." I turned to him. He was busy admiring the tree, looking up in awe of its large branches.

"You said this is a *live* oak – are the others dead?"

"Oh! No! This is simply a type of oak."

"I see. Do not fret about my personal feelings on the lore of your home. Obscurum lore is quite *literally* darker."

"I will not, as you suggest. I would like to tell you I have studied the dark and bloody history of our region. I am of the belief that light cannot exist without darkness and darkness cannot exist without light. Without each other, they would both be meaningless." I began walking north, hoping Lord Caligo would understand my intentions and follow. I stopped at the community well, placing my hand on the cool, old stone, steadily growing a little bit of moss.

"This was the first thing the earliest settlers built. After this, the meeting hall." I pointed south to the large building made of Terra brick. Umbriel glanced over his shoulder at the building then returned his focus to me. He approached *hmm*ing and *ahh*ing as he bent over to study the well. I flicked my gaze to the Brilliant Nest, praying for once that I might skip the shop. I looked back only to realize it was too late – Lord Caligo had seen my stare.

"What is over there?" he asked, standing and beginning to walk in the direction of the shop.

"Nothing!" I blurted, stepping in front of him, only to instantly regret it.

"Oh? Is that so? You wish for me to avoid which shop?" He craned his neck around me to read the sign above the door. "The cobbler? Why must I ignore the cobbler?"

"No – no reason. Unless you should need new soles." Lord Caligo studied my face for a long time. I began to worry that he saw the scorch mark on my face under the glamour. His charcoal eyes dug into mine.

"You are keeping the truth from me. Lying is unladylike. Why must I avoid this shop? Do you have a secret lover?" He began to toss accusations out. "I see now why you have no issues with flying above the rabble – your virtue is already spoiled." he began to whine.

Without thinking, my hand shot up, as if on its own crusade, slapping Lord Caligo firmly across the face. His head snapped to my left and a large red welt appeared. He glowered down at me. I stared back at him with determination.

"How dare you–" he started.

"No! How dare *you*!" I interrupted, "To speak on a lady's virtue when she's naught but a stranger to you. For *shame*! I warned you earlier not to speak of my virtue again. Not that I should have to dignify your pryings with a response, but as for my virtue, I shall tell you *once* – I have no lover!" I spat, turning and walking away in the direction of The Brilliant Nest. I stopped and inadvertently allowed Umbriel to catch up. I had not realized that he had been following me. I ignored him, stoic, facing forward and praying that Cara and Nydia did not see me on the road with him.

"I– I would like to extend my regrets at offending you. That was arrogant of me."

"You call that an apology?" I snapped. He balked, fists balling at his sides, then relaxing.

"In Obscurum, this is how we apologize. I am sorry to not meet your standards," he replied.

"That was closer. I will accept a thoughtful apology, however it is delivered. I was forced to be here, but I do not have to be a part of your subjugation." I jumped into the sky and lingered above town, maybe twenty feet up. Lord Caligo looked up, squinting against the sunlight. I watched from above as he sighed with his whole body and jumped up to join me. He glided up to me with a couple strokes of his mothy wings.

"I really must protest; this is against the rules." He scowled.

"That is also not an apology. When you are ready – so am I."

"I *apologize* for speaking out of turn about your virtue." He was grouchy.

"Thank you." I turned to him. "Now, would you like the rest of the tour?" I asked. He nodded. I offered him my hand, and with some apprehension, he took it. I gently pulled him along the north-south road that went right through town until we were at the southernmost entrance. I hovered in place, and he followed my lead.

"We face north now. There is Twilight Hall," I pointed. "He followed my hand, seeing the manor peek through the woods. Pulling my hand down the road and taking my hand from Caligo, I used both to indicate the southern portions of town. "The housing district." He followed my hands, curiously studying the streets before looking back at me.

"Some look larger than others. Why?" he inquired.

"These are the more wealthy homes." I pointed to the east side, by the farm fields. "Those are the apartments." I pointed west to the taller structures.

"Oh, you mean Lord's apartments, for bachelors."

"No. For the townsfolk... we have no other lords here. All the lords in Inanis reside at Twilight Hall." I could feel my face contort into a quizzical look. I have never been able to keep my face from expressing my innermost thoughts.

"I see."

I moved forward, flying closer as I directed him to look down on one building in particular – A mid-sized apartment building on the fringes of West Street.

"That one with the blue-tinged roof is where my lady's maid lives with her husband," I remarked.

"A maid with a husband… how strange."

"Why is that strange?"

"Well, she cannot have two duties. She is surely lacking if your attire is any proof of her ability."

"I may slap you yet again." His eyes grew wide and his attention sharp.

"I only mean – that is to say – oh, just hit me." Silence fell around us as I clasped my hands together. Lord Caligo looked at me with surprise.

"You are not offended?" he whimpered.

"Oh, no. I am, but I cannot strike you for that. I know that I am poorly dressed. That is because I gave my maid a week of leave to celebrate a five-year belated honeymoon." My eyes became misty. "They married the night before our departure. I wanted them to have ample time to rekindle their romance."

"That is most kind of you, my Lady."

"It is, maybe, but I also don't do it for praise. I do it out of love. No one on this continent could love her more than me. I am lost without her – as you can see." I implied my dresses by flicking the skirts of my current drapery back and forth. More silence followed.

"You are not dressed. I am sorry for the offense I gave. Your gowns are lovely and befitting of you." Lord Caligo gracefully dipped into a bow mid-air. I smiled and nodded in approval of his apology.

"You did not know. There *is* something you may know actually!" I brightened up. Lord Caligo seemed to cheer up as I did.

"There – do you see where the east road connects to the square?" I pointed.

"Yes."

"That is the place your carriage tried to flatten me yesterday." His face paled to a strange lavender. He opened his mouth, but words did not follow. I smiled.

"I-I am so *incredibly* sorry. I will speak to my driver a-at once!" I nodded, and he shut his quivering mouth.

"Now that is an apology. I believe you mean it." I slowly lowered myself to the ground, Lord Caligo falling behind me. We walked in silence towards the town church. It had a bell tower rising to touch the sky we had just abandoned. The building was a dusty white, almost – but not quite, grey. The roof and doors were plain, natural wood.

"This is the third building erected by the community." I gestured gently at the church.

"Marvelous! So everyone here is of the same faith? There are so many places that have a divided populace. I think it would be nice to see unity."

"If unity is what you are after, you have settled in the wrong place. The only Effection clan to be close to 'unity' is the Lux, but you dark fae would have a hard time obeying and loving a god of pure light, would you not?" giving him a blank stare. He returned it, and so we sat, staring for a minute too long.

"My Lord, do I offend thee?"

"No. No, I am only thinking. You are right, even in the smaller communities around Lux, there is a divide."

"I did not mean to force your mental strain."

"You did not. Something else caught my attention."

"What was it?"

"Come over here." He waved me over, and I looked over at him, affronted. He sighed and continued to urge me to come over. I relented and closed the distance between us with a few paces. He gently turned me by my waist and pointed to a mother with her small children. My heart sank.

"Look at them! So carefree and wonderful. The world is so bright and new to them. What do you think?" I could not remove my eyes from the mother all on her own, balancing mank baskets and attempting to purchase more food, all while wrangling a baby that needed to be held and a toddler that wanted to hold everything. *Is this to be my life?*

"Depressing," I whispered. Lord Caligo stepped back away from me.

"I beg your pardon, but how are children depressing?" he shot. I focused on him in order to ignore the cries of the little ones as they were shepherded home.

"You are forgiven. Our lives are not the same, Lord Caligo. A man may ask for a baby, but it is the mother who must make the child. Parenthood is not evenly yoked," I responded, maybe too harshly. Lord Caligo's features hardened as he came to understand.

"You will not have my children then?" he asked, astounded by my statement. I stared at him incredulously.

"No. I never claimed to be for or against the task, but I have better intentions for my time than to raise children." I was as level as I could bear.

"A betrothal contract denotes the strive for heirs. To carry on the family name, which is what the Queen wants. Are you against the Queen? Are you saying you wish to doom the future of the Astrum name?" his voice was raised now, the volume attracting the attention of a few passersby.

"No! I just told you I have the intention to use my time as Heir Apparent to enhance the futures of my family, my village, and maybe even my region!" I picked up my skirts and flew off, back towards the

Dusk 'till Dawn Inn. I could hear Lord Caligo say something, but I decided it was not worth the air to challenge him to repeat himself.

I landed at the entrance to the dirt lot. The Inn was built and connected to a pen and barn. I walked across the crunchy dirt to the entrance of the Inn. The door creaked as I pushed in, but no one looked up from their drinks. My eyes needed a moment to adjust to the dimmer atmosphere. I spied Osbert in the corner with a man doubled over a bucket. As I approached, I saw the man was Nevin.

"What happened?" I asked Osbert. He looked up, surprised as he saw me.

"My lady! Where is your fiance? You should not be alone!"

"Shush, Osbert. Tell me what happened here." He swallowed his pride and admitted that Nevin had lost himself in mug after mug of beer. Together, we gently lifted him and slowly got him to the carriage after Osbert ceased his protests about what Highborn ladies should or should not do. Lord Caligo trotted up as we maneuvered him into the carriage.

"What is this?" he yelled.

"Shh! Help us, and I can explain sooner." I threw my voice over my shoulder as I held Nevin's left side. Osbert navigated opening the carriage door. A line of drool dripped from Nevin's mouth.

"No, thank you. I want nothing to do with this mischief!" He leaned against the fence while Osbert and I fought the liquidated man into the carriage. He refused to remain seated, so the floor became his resting place. I rolled up my cloak as a pillow for his head. When we had gotten Nevin situated, Osbert climbed into the driver's seat. I heard a loud sigh from Lord Caligo – he still leaned on the fence away from the carriage. Osbert and I exchanged looks of irritation. He had a reason not to communicate with Lord Caligo – he had to ready the carriage.

I, on the other hand, did not. I approached Lord Caligo to explain the situation, only to be greeted with a massive eye roll that could be seen from the heavens.

"Nevin overindulged, but there is nothing to fret over – Osbert is a capable driver."

"How delightful," he muttered before climbing into the carriage at last. The return to Twilight Hall was anything but 'delightful.'

Chapter Thirteen

We argued the entire trip back. He adamantly defended that child rearing is the noblest duty a woman could have while I was vehemently denying myself that role, but not scorning other women for wishing to have the opportunity. All while Nevin snored from the floorboards.

Finally, after what felt like ages, we arrived at the gates. I attempted to rouse Nevin with a few gentle taps to his cheeks, but he was out like a spent candle. Osbert pulled the carriage to a halt, but before he could get down himself, much less release the footsteps, Lord Caligo slammed the doors open, bringing the footsteps down with it, and stomped off into the house. Osbert joined me and, again, we struggled with the heavy drunken man. Mr. Huich, undoubtedly drawn out by the commotion, arrived to assist by taking my part of the burden.

I returned to the carriage for my cloak and book before turning back towards the house, walking to the front door. Then, unexpectedly, Castor burst through the door, quickly followed by Vesperia.

"Get back here! Mother will hear of this!" Vesperia shouted as he leaped into the air, soaring up over the manor into the back gardens. Vesperia groaned, then saw me and stopped.

"What are you looking at?" she snapped.

"My rude sister, chasing our brother as it happened before me. Why are you attempting to detain him, is that not his governess' responsibility?" She scoffed, then faced me directly.

"Not that you would know, but she has been ill, so he is sitting in on *my* lessons on the basics of hospitality."

"Oh, well do not let me keep you." I backed away. "Please go after him."

"You know mother's rule! Flying is undignified rabble rushing. We have no such haste. You and our brother both *love* to bend and break that rule."

"Do you not enjoy flying?" She looked at me as if I had asked her what flavor toad she enjoyed most.

"No, of course I do not. I am concerned about who may see up my skirts, sister."

"Then maybe a set of trousers would help you to engage your wings. Flying is a delight– so freeing." I almost laughed. Her face tensed, and she collected herself before speaking.

"Sister. You may be able to bring yourself to break mother's rules. I, on the other hand, do not."

"We are born to fly, Vesperia. Why would that be a bad thing?"

"It is not *bad*," she repeated, "it is about respect and about proper decorum. We have to mind our virtue."

"If one more person speaks to me about virtue today, I swear I will burn all my gowns in the kitchen hearth this night! Someone accidentally looking up while I fly overhead is just that – an *accident*. Pure coincidence. It will not taint my character," I groaned. Vesperia mocked me with a groan of her own. Hers came with a pulse of her inner light like our mother.

"How are you this dense? If your character is *anything* but pure as fallen snow, you will cost us *everything*." She threw a burning star and it exploded behind me.

"Hey! Watch it!"

"I will do as I please! You are not my caretaker!" she snarled, manifesting yet another flaming star. I lifted my hands in defense, dropping my cloak and book.

"Then go back to your tutor and I will retrieve Castor." In response, she launched the star and it exploded at my feet, just barely missing my possessions. I yelped.

"No! You are meant to be entertaining Lord Caligo – where is he?"

"He too was overly concerned with my virtue and has most likely retired to his chambers for the day." I waved my hand in the direction of the third-floor guest suite, rolling my eyes. A star exploded on my side. It burned into my gown singing my skin.

"You are going to ruin us!" Vesperia screamed, throwing more stars haphazardly. Some came very close to hitting me if I had not moved out of the way.

"I seriously doubt that. A betrothal cannot be so easily undone. If he cannot stand my company, I just might survive it. I did not travel Mythénia for all those years only to return a broodmare for a 'choice' stallion." I continued to dodge her emotional spell-casting. Mother and our gardener would be cross with us both very soon.

"Ah! Of course, not you vulgar woman!" She shot at me more. "You could not wait to be rid of your family – *that* is why you left."

"What are you talking about? You know the King and Queen paid for and requested that scholarly tour. It was to show the fruits of their labor – the union of light and dark." I'd had enough. I pulled a large star from the ether and launched it at the ground near my sister's feet. She shrieked in response.

"Liar!" she accused. We exchanged shooting stars, the explosions damaging our pristine hedges and the garden in the center of our, now cratered, laneway. Vesperia's stars were powerful, but her aim was guided by emotions. I matched her shot for shot – only mine hit their marks. I never aimed to hurt her, though.

This dance was growing exhausting, I searched for an end to it without hurting her. I threw a large star at her, hitting the pathway beneath her. It exploded into a mist of a thousand tiny stars. No moment was more perfect for me to jump into the air than when she held her arms up to shield her face. I made a bold swoop for my book and cloak before rising to the sky, narrowly missing her last attempt at violence.

I felt guilty about the trick, but maybe she would calm down alone. I attempted to follow the direction Castor had flown, over the manor and down, but had no way of knowing if he stopped in the gardens or continued into the north forest between us and Obscurum. Mid-ascension, I felt a severe and fast-spreading pain in my arms. I looked back to see that Vesperia had summoned our mother's Sun Archer bow and was using it to lose flaming star-tipped arrows at me, more accurately than before. I began to twist and roll through the air to make as little a pattern as possible, dropping and rising randomly like a silly, lazy butterfly.

She ripped a rage-filled scream through the air once I was out of her range. I continued for a little while longer – just to be sure – then landed in the fringes of the north forest, just before the long tendrils of Obscurum's mists began to mix in with the trees. The return would be long, but it would grant me enough time to be away from Vesperia's rage. I began the journey home, walking southeast for a while until the urge to kick rocks violently diminished, and then I took to the sky again. *No one is out here with me, no one to ruin my virtue.*

The noise of the forest and my wings was calming – I was coming to find the company of others too obnoxious. I soon became glaringly aware of forgetting to eat lunch. Thankfully, flying was faster than walking and Twilight Hall appeared before me quickly. As I approached, I heard yelling. I landed, crept up to the property line, and peered over the chest-high garden wall. Mother and Vesperia were exchanging the bow and taking turns sticking the wooden mannequin with flaming arrows. I watched Vesperia take her turn and with the release of a flaming star-tipped arrow, she let out a cry of anger and pain.

I waited through our mother's turn and jumped the small wall – with a little assistance from the flutter of my wings – to make a smooth, soundless landing. Then, I carefully and quietly made my way around the garden and towards the back door. I waited until the bow was back in Vesperia's hands to turn the knob and open the door. Once inside the house, I walked quickly down the hall to the kitchens. I poked my head in to see who was in the large, hot room. With no Mrs. Sykes in sight, I snuck in and interrupted the first person I saw: an assistant with pastries for tea time.

"May I steal one?" I begged. The assistant I had cornered was not familiar to me, but he dipped the plate in a mute gesture of allowance. I took a small jam-filled, flaky crusted tart and placed it on a linen napkin from the counter. I smiled at him as I wrapped the napkin around my meager lunch before returning to the door. I stopped to listen before running across the hall to the smaller hallway that led to my father's study and small library.

The library was seldom used, overflowing with old and new books. The collection began with my father's few books from home and then our school books, to eventually the titles my father and I purchased through the years. There were not enough shelves for all the tomes we had now, so the newest ones began to pile on every flat surface that was left unused – which was all of them. The furniture had been covered by dust sheets in my absence. I chose my usual chair and pulled off the dust cover, grateful my tart was bundled safely in a napkin as the dust scattered into the air again. I settled into the familiar chair and set down my bundle of cloak, book, and now tart on the arm of the chair. I looked around and picked up the nearest volume – anything to distract myself—as I ate my mid-afternoon snack. The book was one from, I assumed, my father's collection. It was written in Italian, which was very close to Mythénian. I could read every other word and guess the ones in between. The text seemed to be on the intrigue of numbers and *the stars.*

Reading in silence was bliss. I could occasionally hear the screams of my sister, but they subsided soon enough. The ideas represented in this book here are hilariously off-target. Whoever introduced the author to the heavens of Italy had only been guessing.

The tart was long since devoured, and my mouth now dry. I craved water. My eyes grew weary, which led me to set the book beside the used napkin, now folded neatly, and stretch my legs that had been curled under me. I rolled my ankles gently until they popped, staying in the chair not wanting to get up yet. I finally felt at ease.

Something moved in the corner of my left field of vision. I turned my head towards the shadows between two large bookcases. They began to waver and dance like my father's magic. I braced for his incoming, because once he saw me. I would be trapped here until dinner. *I should clean up and leave before he materializes.* Without hesitation or grace, I snatched the linen napkin from the table and hastily replaced the chair's dust cover when the body of a dark fairy appeared from the shadows. Those charcoal eyes were not my father's. I collected my things and turned towards the door.

"Oh, it is just you," I mumbled. He looked directly at me. *Oops, he heard me.*

"Am I interrupting something?" I faced him.

"No. I had assumed you were my father."

"Do you often run from your father?"

"No! I am simply finished with the room. I took the change of lighting as my cue to leave."

"I see." He smirked at me. "Well you are welcome to join me. I had no plans to disturb anyone." He came further into the room and I saw he had changed into a loose embroidered tunic of a deep, almost black, blue and grey legging trousers that came down to his feet in a mild point off of the toe. He inspected several bookcases, but moved on to the stacks once he realized they were newer. Compelled by his curiosity, I stayed to see which volume would pique his interest enough to pick up. He glanced up a few times to watch me, but seemed unbothered by my presence.

We both stopped when we heard the door to my father's study open and close, followed by face paced footsteps. Lord Caligo looked past me to the door with wild eyes of worry. The footsteps came closer and he dove behind a linen-covered sofa. The door to the library swung open. My father examined the room, stopping when he saw me.

"Oh! Good evening, my star. Have you seen Lord Umbriel?" I looked around me in a mock search, careful to avoid the couch, then shook my head.

"Very well. He seems to have disappeared while we were speaking of our homeland." he sighed, shutting the door. Lord Caligo peeked over the couch, looking to me for reassurance. I gave him a nod to come out. He came out of hiding and threw himself bodily onto the covered couch. A cloud of dust displaced into the air.

"So you *are* avoiding my father?" I could not hide the tone of my voice.

"Yes. I beg your pardon, but he grows more wearisome the more he talks and asks of Obscurum. It is the same as always, enveloped in the dark mists. Besides, I have not seen its streets for half a decade – I know none of the answers to his questions." He pressed two fingers to the bridge of his nose. He rolled to now sit on the couch, placing his feet on the rug. I perched on the opposite couch's arm.

"My family is truly aware of this. We beg your forgiveness for the exposure," I replied. He caught my meaning and looked up.

"I am not attempting to end our betrothal contract if that is what you are thinking."

"I was not, but I confess: I would like to." We stared at each other in silence for quite some time. His expression growing firm and *painful*..? He began to chew his lower lip in what I could only assume was thought. I, too, was thinking – thinking about how to disappear without seeming rude.

We were both startled into jumping to our feet when a knock came at the door, before creaking open. I waved my hands at Lord Caligo to hide once again. He dove behind the couch once more. Mrs. Sykes poked her head through the opening, giving me an eerie, uncommon smile.

"I thought I would find you here. Dinner is ready." She was quick. The door creaked shut, signaling to Caligo that he could come out of hiding. He stood and adjusted his shirt and vest, brushing off the dust he had landed in. We both headed for the door at the same time, then stopped. Like a rehearsed waltz, we continued to approach the door and stop a few more times.

"Ok! Ok! This is ridiculous! One of us *must* go first," Caligo hissed, reaching for the door. I stared egregiously at him. He seemed to be asserting that he should go first.

"Why, fae tell, is that?"

"Well, because of your..." my expression broke his thought process, "...family," he finished weakly.

"Yes. *My* family. They would be concerned about two betrothed folk relaxing in the library. I see your ruse. They are not going to mind. In fact, it would please them."

"But it is not proper!"

"Fine. Have it your way. We will enter separately." He nodded and pulled the door open. I dashed through before he could turn his body to face the doorway. The bitter look on his face would bring me endless joy for years to come.

Chapter Fourteen

When I entered the dining room, there was already a massive amount of tension in the air. My father and mother were at odds, at opposing ends of the table. Castor seemed to have chosen our mother tonight, as did Vesperia. The spots nearest to father were set with only plates, the utensils forgotten next to my siblings' place settings. I approached carefully, walking to the side of the table opposite of Vesperia, next to Castor. I smiled at them both as I retrieved the utensils. Castor politely smiled back, but Vesperia gave me a nasty look – her hands had burns and blisters.

As I sat, Lord Caligo appeared through the second doorway. *At least he could use his brain for something.* He took the plate from beside my father and replaced it next to Vesperia. Vesperia's inner glow shone brighter for a moment. I could tell she was thrilled to be near Lord Caligo.

"Umbriel! Where did you fly off to? We were discussing hunting in the North Eastern forest, between Obscurum and the Cuor lands, if one should like to challenge some vampires." Father feigned a wobbly voice like he used to do when he made his puppets tremble before the evil troll or malicious dragon. No one was amused now. He took the silence hard and slouched into his chair. Lord Caligo looked around the room and came to the realization that he was the center of attention.

"I certainly hope you were not flying in my home, Lord Caligo. The rules are clear and our decor is priceless – and on loan from Her Majesty's collection," my mother warned.

"No, Ma'am! I would never disobey a house rule! You have my word!" he assured her. Vesperia practically sparkled with joy before sending me a sneer.

"Dinner is served!" Mrs. Sykes burst through the kitchen door, halting all previous conversations with the long list of dishes prepared for us. A seven-course meal was brought in, each item added to our plates, but before we could begin to eat, father cleared his throat, displaying his ratty copy of *Devotions of The Void*.

"Tonight I will read my second passage, from chapter two!" He cleared his throat again and began. "*The faithful shall gather under the empty sky in prayer to the Unseen. Through rituals of Darkness, we may yet see the True Essence of The Universe. Let Darkness fill you, for it is the source of all creation. In the silence of the Night, the faithful shall find their voice. A Hymn of shadows echoes through The Void to you.*" He sniffled back a tear, closing his book. Tensions at the table snapped. Mother's inner glow blazed white with rage. Vesperia and Castor shrank away. Vesperia almost hid behind Lord Caligo, who exchanged a look of terror with my father. He sat frozen in his seat, reduced to an observer of what would happen next.

Mother threw a burning ball of light across the table. It leaped from her hand like a ray from the sun, instantly singeing my father's coat. He yelped in pain and doused the fire with his wine. Lord Caligo looked as though he had witnessed the front lines of battle and would faint.

"You know *better* than to recite such passages! If the Solaris guards or even Helia were to hear of this, your whole family would be marked unseelie and tossed from their homes!" Mother stood, sending her chair flying backwards. My father, now soaked, glared at her with malice I had not seen in more than a decade.

"I *do* know, Eleanor. Please be seated so our guests may eat. You are being *inhospitable*. Which may be the true *unseelie* act." He speared a roasted potato wedge with a fork and ate it with a cruel smile.

"Kyrinn – you are more foul than I thought. Do you believe that a guest from Obscurum would permit you to blaspheme the crown? Solarisian Law is for *all* regions. As for being hospitable, let us ask *him* who has made him feel the most welcome." She turned to Lord Caligo, fixing him with a stare I knew all too well.

"Go on Umbriel – tell her." Father leaned on his arm which rested on the table. Lord Caligo looked back and forth between my mother and father. His face seemed to change from surprisingly pale, like that of a faint observer, to instead embarrassed, cheeks dark as if blotted with ink. I could tell he wished to evaporate into the shadows because I wished it, too. We all watched as he collected his thoughts and courage.

"My *generous* hosts... I do not wish to be an instrument for your torment of one another. Lord Astrum, I do respect Solarisian Law. Though the devotionals are a harmless tradition," he added, "I think it best to abide by the ruling set before us. I am no king, nor do I wish to be. Why should I change anything? I have learned through all my stays at homes that are not mine that you follow the rules you are given."

Any sliver of attraction I felt towards Lord Caligo died on his last statement. I felt the feelings wither away like speedily dying flowers wilting into dust. *If I were in his position I would be doing exactly as father is now – insisting we preserve a dying culture.*

"See!" mother shouted. We all flinched when she thrust her finger at our father. My father rolled his eyes and called for more wine. Mother assumed the debate was over and claimed victory as she sat down. My siblings and I resumed our meal, quietly moving on from the events that had transpired. Lord Caligo seemed put off from his meal by the argument, or maybe the devotionals. I allowed my mind to wander as I ate my vegetables.

"I think we ought to hear more of our guests' precious thoughts. Tell us – what else fills your head during the day, besides Solarisian Law?" Vesperia urged. Mother had her mouth full but nodded encouragingly. He obliged, still not touching his plate.

"I think of my family, of my future, of the places I have yet to visit, just like everyone else I suppose." Vesperia looked deflated at his response.

"I do not think of my family – I am too busy with lessons to think of them more often," Vesperia started, but quickly read Caligo's face as displeased. "That is, I mean to say, I wish I would think of them more often." Her cheeks flushed a dusty rose and she looked away.

"Surely when you are married you will have all the time in the world to give to your family – especially the new one you will make with your husband." He comforted her by setting a hand lightly on her shoulder. She looked back quickly at his hand, then up at me. I could not tell if she was scared or elated, her face became unreadable until I noticed the sparkle of glamour on her face. She was hiding her red cheeks and Lord Caligo must not see it. If looking at just the right angle, I could see the shimmery seam of her mask right along her jaw and hair lines. I could tell Vesperia was drowning in bliss and was suppressing her inner glow as much as she possibly could. Her exterior expression now displayed the deeply interested, flirtatious young woman.

"One can only hope," she breathed. They stared at each other for a moment too long before Lord Caligo returned to his dinner. My mother cleared her throat and set her goblet down hard.

"Speaking of family, tell us…why five children? Surely less would suffice in continuing the family line?" Lord Caligos' face deepened in color with embarrassment. He coughed and gulped water from his goblet.

"I do not wish to be crass, so I will resign my answer to this over dinner: I desire more than just a couple of children. I believe that more is better so that they might all enjoy the company of one another. All of the large families that I have visited are quite harmonious." He quickly stuffed a boiled carrot in his mouth. My mother seemed satisfied and did not explore further. I was sure she understood his true meaning as well.

The doors from the kitchens opened quickly. Everyone turned their heads to look; this type of interruption was unusual. Mrs. Sykes and Mr. Huich came in together, matching step for step. Mrs. Sykes handed mother a large letter sealed with golden wax across the front. Mother picked up her dinner knife and broke the seal. She unfolded the paper and mumbled to herself as she read. When she reached the end, a slight smile graced her lips while she refolded the letter.

"What is it, mother?" Vesperia inquired. Our mother shot her a warning look and she shrank into her chair, hiding her hands. Mother tossed the letter onto the table.

"The Queen is returning to Lux. We will see her for the ball but not before. She would, however, see you two," she pointed to Lord Caligo and I, "in her box at the theater. Tomorrow."

"How delightful!" Lord Caligo exclaimed before my thoughts could comprehend the request. An invitation to Lux for the theater was almost a day's journey. There was no way to politely decline the invitation either – practically making it an order.

"You will take Lord Caligo's carriage and Marjorie will accompany you. As much as I would love to return home, it is improper and against Royal Law." Mother was pointed about the last part. Father, seemingly having had enough, downed his wine and exited the dining room. Mr. Huich followed close behind after retrieving the devotional book of darkness.

Mrs. Sykes called for a dessert course – bread pudding – to be served in celebration of the invitation. I was not keen on the idea of bread pudding *or* celebrating. Mrs. Sykes directed the staff to prepare bowls and more libations. This was my opportunity to excuse myself.

"I beg pardon. I am feeling full, so I shall refrain from the pudding. The rest of you please enjoy – excuse me." I stood and maneuvered around the table. I looked back as I reached the door to find Mother and Lord Caligo watching me go. Lord Caligo had stood – as was proper. Vesperia watched him with awe.

Enclosing myself in my Lux-facing room felt more like a cage than a place of solace. I chose to linger in the rear gardens. At night it was peaceful. No one roaring over target practice, no snide remarks about my choice of dress. Thinking of gowns made me miss Aurora. *I hope she is enjoying her well-deserved time off.* I was going to need assistance shortly though, to meet the expectations of everyone for The First Star.

I sauntered through the grass to the stone benches that overlooked our kitchen garden. With the hold of a few Floral fairies, we had every vegetable and fruit we could want year-round. I especially liked the pumpkins. Something about them was so intriguing. I loved the way their vines twisted, and how the flowers looked like little golden stars for a while before they closed up to become pumpkins. I sat on the bench closest to the pumpkin patch, looking at the many gourds in various stages of growth.

The silence of the cool night was peaceful. Distantly, I could hear the birds calling out from the forest beyond the garden wall. An owl gave a few short hoots to a friend far away. I heard no reply – if there was one. The flowers and bushes rustled gently in a lazy breeze. I breathed in the clean cool air and tried to emulate the laissez-faire feeling it gave me for the moment. If only I could tack my worries to the wind.

I heard footsteps, heavy and uncoordinated. I looked around me and saw the outline of a man stumbling towards me. After a moment, I realized it was my father, drunkenly walking the grounds with a decanter of dark wine in hand. He swayed towards me like a moth to a flame, my inner glow like a beacon. He landed hard as he sat next to me, almost toppling backward, dropping the decanter into the grass. Thankfully, it did not break. He leaned his head on my shoulder and sighed.

"Oh, what a pity we dark fae did not prevail against *them*," he mumbled.

"It is?" I shook him off my shoulder. He did not respond, so I elbowed him in the ribs. He responded by sitting straight up for a moment before slouching over and resting his elbows on his knees.

"Yess, it *iss*," he slurred. "The rites of The Void are quite un-un burdening-ing. The light is-is so *picky*. It requires *perfection*. The darkness takes you – you as you are. *Hup*," he hiccuped, then looked for his drink.

"Well it is not up to us, now is it? I do not wish to challenge Her Majesty on the use of Void worship. Father, why is this so important to you?" I knew I should not be asking such serious questions, but I could not help myself.

"Be-because, daughter. It is *dying* like my family in-in the war." He sloshed his words like a glass of wine.

"I see," I started. "I think you best cease, Father. For the love of your children, do not have us marked unseelie and lose the Queen's favor."

"Oh no! Never! That can never happen," he insisted as he continued to look for his decanter.

"Are you saying that it is impossible to happen or we should never let it?"

"We cannot – cannot let her kill us off."

"No father, the Queen's *favor*. You said we can never lose it. Do I take this to mean we cannot possibly lose it?"

"My s-sister. You will not know of her. S-she challenged the King and was sent away…" he trailed off, leaning dangerously forward. Before he could fall, I grabbed his arm to steady him.

"Let me take you inside, father – help you to bed. I think this is enough for tonight." I pulled him to his feet and pulled his right arm over my shoulders, then steered us inside. I was able to maneuver us both in through the garden door. Once inside the house, I was disturbed to hear the screams of an argument in full swing.

"It is unfair mother! She has been on multiple occasions and I have yet to go once! I am tired of the dark gloomy Obscurum trips. I want to experience our Queen's illustrious capital – your home!" I heard Vesperia screech. I climbed the stairs with my father, taking the servant stairs one at a time.

"The invitation does not mention you, darling. You must follow the prerequisites the Queen sets forth. There is an alternate purpose for the trip. This is final," mother scolded. I carried Father into the hallway where his door was the first on the right. I could no longer hear the argument.

"Lawrence! Lawrence!" I called. The air fairy popped his head from his room next to my father's and took in the sight. He came and took my lush of a father into his room, slinging one of father's arms over his shoulders to carry his weight. I turned to head down the stairs, but not before a glance at my old room. I could not see a glow inside from my brother. I did, however, see Lord Caligo lurking in the shadowed staircase leading to the third floor. I looked away quickly and raced down the east staircase and then into my room.

Chapter Fifteen

My attempt at sleep was poor. I was shaken awake by one of the laundry maids. She urged me to rise so she could help me dress. I think it took her a few tries to truly rouse me. Stretching, I sat up in bed. I looked around my chambers – the light suggested it was mid-morning, most likely breakfast time or after.

"Has everyone called for breakfast yet?" I yawned.

"No my lady, they are all gathered in the dining hall awaiting yourself," she meekly responded. She did not meet my eyes or look at me directly.

"Very well. Fetch a gown and let us get to it." I slapped my knees and slid from my bed. My bare feet touched the cool wooden planks. The maid nodded and hurried to the wardrobe. She was selective and picked an ensemble that was much heavier than I had anticipated for a morning meal and a day-long carriage ride.

"Is everyone else so formal this morning? Has Her Majesty come to join us?" She looked up at me finally with tears welling in her golden eyes.

"No, my lady," she whimpered and went to replace the gown in the the wardrobe.

"Wait – I apologize. I only meant it in jest. My mother would be pleased to see me wear more than the average gown. You chose well. Please help me put it on." I attempted to amend my bad choice in words. The maid returned and set the pieces of the gown on my unmade bed. She handed me a fresh shift and turned her back to allow me some privacy to change.

"What is your name, maiden?" I worked to pull her into conversation once again. She faced me and took my discarded shift, placing it on the bed away from the clean gown.

"Galena, my lady." She curtsied quickly before making the bodice of the gown ready for me to step into.

"From where do you hail from, Galena?" I continued. She avoided my eyes again and did not answer. I asked again as she assisted me into the skirts. "Where do you come from, Galena?"

"I beg your pardon, my lady. I am aware my heritage may be a shock, but I assure you I am safe. I would never harm anyone under this roof." I stared at her. It was not that serious. I simply meant to have idle conversation, not a hefty unburdening of some well-kept secret.

"Go on," I urged. She took one of the sleeves from the bed and brought it to me to slip my hand into.

"My family resides in the village Hirudo – it is half the size of Inanis between Obscurum and Cruor in the dark mists," she said as she tied the sleeves to the bodice. I moved my head to catch her eyes, the teary golden eyes she would not look at me with. Her pinkish skin and red hair hardly looked Vampiric. She avoided my gaze by retrieving the last sleeve.

"Why are you so ashamed?" I asked, harsher than I had intended.

"Folk tend to assume I am a vampire or worse. I am not! And I am not dangerous," she declared, meeting my eyes.

"Okay, you are not dangerous. What are you?"

"A healer," Galena proclaimed. "My family has been Blood Weavers since inception. We can mend any ailment or injury without the use of herbs or medicines." She tied the ribbons of the sleeve to the bodice. I nodded silently, thinking.

"Any injury?" I asked. Galena looked up at me for the first time. Her eyes held their own question.

"No – not all. Some injuries require a joint effort. Usually a bone fairy and a skilled blood fairy, if the customer wanted to heal in such a way. It is less painful to heal naturally, of course," Galena explained. She gestured to the chair at my vanity table and picked up my brush. I sat as Galena pulled my hair back with her hands and brushed it gently until all the knots were worked out. She tied and pinned it in a low-hanging bun and styled it with a coiffure of pearls, matching the cream gown she had chosen.

"This is lovely, thank you." I smiled at her through the mirror. She smiled back then turned to collect the old shift. I turned in my chair to face her.

"May I ask a favor of you?" I felt less sure of myself, but my heart said it would be a good thing.

"Of course my lady. If it is within my power, I will do anything you ask." She waited, patiently holding the shift.

"Can you heal burns?" She responded with a simple nod of her head.

"Would you visit my sister and offer her lady's maid your services? My sister has burned her hands. It looks painful, and I do not like to think of her suffering." My gaze flicked to the glamour hidden gifts for a short minute. Galena gave me a pitiful look of understanding.

"Yes, my lady. I am acquainted with Mystine!" She dipped into a quick curtsey and looked to me for dismissal.

"Thank you, you may go. That is all." I dismissed her with a smile. She left quickly after flashing a small smile back. My mother, and by extension, Mrs. Sykes, was very nasty to all who displeased her. If she was low enough to be assigned to assist me, she must be on my mother's last nerve. Mother demanded perfection.

Thinking of perfection made me want to examine my ensemble in the full-length mirror before leaving. The cream gown and white shift gave me the faint idea of a radiating star in the sky. If not for my dark hair, I might be the ideal star. I traced my cheek and chin with a light finger; the scorch mark was fading. Soon I would be able to leave without any glamour, but not today. I reapplied a fresh glamour to hide the burn.

I straightened my back, fluttered my wings out for display, and examined the room. The glamour on the gifts was still holding – I did not reapply that one. The room was as tidy as I could manage with everyone waiting on me. I hurried out my door and resisted, with pain, the urge to fly down the staircase. With my luck, Mrs. Sykes or one of her spies would see and I would be in for an excruciating punishment.

As fast as I could, I raced down the steps to the first floor and then trotted to the dining hall. Everyone was gathered and divided. The seat with a place setting left open was next to my *lovely* sister.

"Thank you all for waiting, I apologize for my tardiness." I bowed to my mother and father respectively. "Lord Caligo– I must apologize to you directly as well – I should not have kept our guest waiting." I bowed to him also. A quick glance at Mother through my eyelashes told me I had snuffed the flame of anger in her for the moment.

"Quite alright. I find that a reliable sleep schedule is the key to punctuality. Maybe that is what you need," he responded. I had no idea how to reply to him so I straightened from my bow and took the open seat beside Vesperia, who shrank away.

Across from me, Castor waited for his meal. I tried to get his attention, but he would not look up from his plate. He only looked up when Mrs. Sykes called for breakfast to be served. His eyes tried to follow each dish as they entered but soon became engrossed with the portions he had been served.

"I would have liked to have taken our morning meal together with a passage from my *valuable family heirloom*," my father started, "but it has mysteriously gone missing. Lawrence is beside himself with grief!" I watched Castor flip through emotions– discontentment, fury, and then a mischievous grin took over his lips. My gut told me Castor had hidden the book – or worse.

"Ha! Serves you right!" mother laughed from the other side of Vesperia. When I turned to look at her I caught Vesperia using an illusion of a conservative listening face, but her true face stuck its tongue out at me before returning to ogling at Lord Caligo in front of her. If only he knew.

We were served porridge with sides of crushed nuts, pitted fruits, and honey. I watched as everyone took heaping servings of fruit and nuts – I could not stand the mix of each texture. I opted for a light drizzle of honey and a spoonful of sugar that I mixed in completely. Mother engaged Lord Caligo in a vibrant discussion of all his travels – his favorite and least favorite places to have stayed.

"My favorite would have been my uncle in Ingenium. Always so orderly and efficient. My least favorite will forever be this quaint friend of the family. A woman raising two children on her own. She had once been highborn, but married low. Her husband squandered her dowry, gave her two mouths to feed, and died brawling with the debt collectors. Her home was always a wreck – always. Her children would always return from wherever it was they went dirty and smelling of manure, ruining any progress I had made in tidying up! I gave up assisting them and wrote to my eldest brother to send me anywhere else."He prattled on about two more, no doubt kind, families that he felt did not meet his standard of cleanliness.

Castor pushed away from the table, leaving suddenly. I had eaten maybe five spoonfuls of my porridge, but when I looked up, he was already gone. I leaped up, starling Vesperia into dropping her glamour, who was temporarily glaring at Lord Caligo before turning to me. Excusing myself, I followed Castor, hoping to catch him before he locked himself away or ran off. Thankfully, he was just walking down the hall. Against Mother's rule, I flew down the corridor to him.

"Brother, wait!" I called to him. He jumped and turned. His face read as melancholic and furious. Anger held back his tears.

"What do you want?" he spat. I recoiled, landing further away than I had intended.

"I, well, wanted to give you a gift – from my travels." I tried to offer a smile. He did not return it. Castor crossed his arms over his chest.

"Is that so? What might that be sister? The mud off your shoes?"

"What? No, I would never! How could you think this of me? I thought you knew me better." I sighed. His hard exterior melted slightly.

"I too thought I knew you better than I do now. You have changed, sister," he shot. It pained me to hide my reaction. I kept a carefully painted mask of my own features as my face. He would spot a glamour if I tried to use one, and would take great insult to it.

"I apologize for any slight I have done to offend you. Would you still accept my gift?"

"Pah! You do not even know what you must apologize for! Yes, I will see the gift, but I do not promise to keep it." He was blunt.

"Understood. I have it in my room. Would you wait in mother's drawing room or another place you choose?"

"The upper withdrawing room, between the guest suites." He huffed and spun on his heels, walking away. Following his lead, I turned and walked back to the staircase toward my rooms.

Lord Caligo came around the corner and I slipped into the servant stairs before he could see me. The stairs took me to my mother's withdrawing room, which I incorrectly assumed was vacant. Mother and Mrs. Sykes were engaged in a silent study of ball gowns. They looked up at the same time like they themselves were the eyes of a larger beast.

"Come to change into a more appropriate theater gown, my dear?" mother cooed.

"Yes mother, and to beg Marjorie's assistance, if you can spare her." I fell into the deep curtsey again, hoping to please her.

"Yes, you may, but do hurry. Marjorie, you should choose a darker gown. The theater should be a darker setting. Oh, and Seren, your sister will be joining you, I cannot afford to send Marjorie. Behave." She waved a dismissive hand at me – a signal to leave.

I had no way of knowing how long Castor might wait, or when he would get to the withdrawing room, but I knew he would be cross about my outfit change. I stood and made my way quickly to the passage door between this room and my chambers.

"Thank you." I bowed again then slipped through the door. I began peeling off the sections of the dress I was wearing, like an orange. The skirt, the sleeves, and then the bodice fell heavily on the floor. Mrs. Sykes came into my room to see me standing in my shift, awaiting a gown. She blew an exasperated sigh and crossed the room to my wardrobe. She knew exactly where to go to find the sleek purple velvet gown gifted to me by my paternal grandmother.

"This should do." She pulled the bundle of velvet from the wardrobe and laid it out on the bed. I began to twitch with anticipation, anxious that I would miss Castor. I reached over and took the skirt from the bed and hurriedly put it on myself. I tied it on while Mrs. Sykes stared with a confused expression. She placed the bodice around me and laced the strings, then moved onto the sleeves. With one arm free, I removed the pearled coiffure from my hair.

"My lady!" Mrs. Sykes yelled.

"Everything is well. I will manage my hair without you," I insisted. She took my remaining arm and encased it in velvet too.

"Fine, but if your mother is unsatisfied, I will relish in the punishment." She patted the neat bows on my shoulders where the sleeves met the bodice.

"Thank you," I said loudly, emphasizing that I no longer needed her help. She left with another huff, slamming the door. I pulled my hair back and wove it into a braid with a slender purple ribbon woven in, then curled it into a bun at the nape of my neck. Using copious amounts of pins, I fastened it in place.

Finally, as I walked to the door, I reached into the glamour and retrieved the Terran blade. I took it with me, along with my black cloak. I closed my door as quietly as possible, wincing as it clicked shut. Ascending the west stairs near Vesperia's bedroom, I prayed Castor was still here and not waiting long. At the top of the stairs, I could hear jovial laughing from the drawing room. Two male voices – I assumed Lord Caligo and my brother. I stuck my head into the drawing room to find that I was correct. Lord Caligo and my brother were laughing heartily until Lord Caligo spotted me.

"Your appointment, my lord, " Lord Caligo said with a strange lilt in his voice. Castor snorted a laugh and they bid each other goodbye.

"I will see you soon, " Lord Caligo said as he passed me. I used my cloak to shield the dagger from him; he might have gotten the wrong idea.

"Come in – sit. Let us see this gift." Castor gestured to the tea table beside a set of chairs. I nodded and set the dagger on the table with a metallic clatter. I sat in the chair facing him.

"I waited until the right item found me, but I hope this is to your liking." I watched as he admired the dagger, his eyes sweeping over the hilt and sheath.

"This is exquisite – may I?" He held his hand above the dagger, wanting to pick it up. I nodded and he took it firmly in his hand, unsheathing the blade. His eyes lit up with excitement as he examined the blade.

"I am so happy you are pleased with it. I was gifted one item from The Terran King's armory. This is what I chose. Maybe I do know my brother after all?" His face dropped the broad smile, shame overtaking the joy in his eyes. Sheathing the blade, he laid the dagger on the table between us.

"I am sincerely sorry, sister. It is only that you were gone for so long and never wrote to us. We began to think you had forgotten us, and believed it, " he sniffled. I opened my arms, and he came around the table and knelt by my chair, embracing me. He looked up at me from the floor – the tears had returned.

"I have no idea what you mean. I *did* write to you, as often as I wrote to mother and father. Did you not receive any of my letters?"

"No, we only heard of your travels over dinner, if they did not fight. Which was not often. We came to assume you did not care. How could we blame you?" he cried. I stopped a tear with my finger and wiped his face with a fold of my dress.

"I will figure out where they are. Perhaps someone still has them. I drew you pictures of the Merkin. Before you ask, no, they do not wonder about naked!" We laughed. Castor's were strained at first. He picked up the knife, turning it over in his hands and fingering the delicate carvings on the hilt.

"I am so sorry," he said again. We shared a silent look of understanding – it was healing.

Chapter Sixteen

When Castor and I finished making up, I excused myself to return downstairs to wait for the carriage. The journey would put us there at the proper time for the showing. I was nervous about using the Royal viewing box without the Queen in attendance with us. My descent of the west stairs was interrupted by Lord Caligo in the hallway outside my door.

"Oh!" The sound escaped me as I almost ran directly into him. He looked just as surprised as I was.

"Shh, shh!" He held a finger to his lips. I held my breath and heard it – my father was calling for Lord Caligo as he ascended the stairs. There was no place to go but up, I began to pull Lord Caligo back to the stairs. He pulled back, stopping me.

"What is below us?" he asked. My mind stalled – I could not think properly, there was too much going on. "*Hurry*," he hissed. I heard my father's steps coming closer.

"The library," I whispered. Lord Caligo pulled me into his arms, wrapping both arms around me as a pool of swirling shadows opened up below us. The floor disappeared and I felt us fall, but not a true fall, more like sliding down a steep hill. Lord Caligo's arms held me up as he firmly planted his feet on the library carpet. The shadows dissipated and no longer held us. Lord Caligo gently set me down, and when my feet touched the rug, I was amazed. I looked up at the ceiling to watch the last of the shadows disappear. Lord Caligo released me and stepped away. I stood, gazing at the ceiling in amazement. I had never heard of any fairies being able to move through solid objects.

"I hope you will accept my deepest and most sincere apologies. I was unbecomingly rude and short with you," Lord Caligo started.

"Of course, of course – *how did you do that*?" I rushed to ask. He stuttered and could not form the words, ironically.

"That is the main focus of my family's abilities – shadow manipulation. I learned how to slip through the shadows on accident one day. Once I told my family, we decided to call it Shadow Slipping."

"I must say, it – your Shadow Slipping – is astounding! I adored learning the major abilities associated with each clan. Is this a minor ability?" Now I was the one prattling on. He looked down at me with a familiar look of confusion, the kind everyone gave me when I was curious about something strange.

"Yes, it is a specific ability of the Caligo family. I have not found another Obscrum clan that can do so."

"How interesting. I would love to have you tell me more, but my sister will be accompanying us and I am not sure that will be of interest to her," I admitted. He did not look as surprised as I had been. Though, maybe in a way, I had known he did not wish to talk about it.

"We should be going then. I will let you use the door. I will – you know– slip out." He nodded towards the dark corner of the library, away from the windows. I nodded in agreement and strode purposefully to the door. When I reached the handle, I stopped to ask Lord Caligo if he would just come with me, but I watched him slip through the shadow. With a sigh, I pulled the door towards me and left the library, heading for the front doors.

Everyone, and I truly mean everyone, was waiting for us at the front of the house. Lord Caligos' blue and black carriage was ready to take all three of us to the theater. A team of beautiful black and grey unicorns were pulling the carriage, one stomping its foot impatiently. I looked around but could not find Lord Caligo. Vesperia was ready to leave at that moment. She was dressed in a silvery gown that looked to have stardust on it, one of our specific abilities.

Our father had Castor captive with his drunken ramblings of the history of our family line. Castor looked to me for escape, but I could not offer a solution. I would be leaving any moment. Our mother gasped and we all turned to see what had disarmed her. We followed her gaze to the side of the house where Lord Caligo was strutting towards us in a different outfit than the one from earlier. At breakfast, he wore a black tunic and trousers. Now, he wore what I would consider his best outfit thus far. He wore a black caplet across his shoulders, a dark blue quilted vest, and tailored skin-tight trousers that tapered to a point for his shoe. The points of his shoes were laid back with black ribbon. His long, raven-black hair was tied back with a silver ribbon.

"After you two." Lord Caligo held back the carriage door for us. Vesperia took the lead, swaying elegantly up to the stairs where she took Lord Caligo's hand and climbed in. I follow behind, opting not to take Lord Caligos' hand. My mother scoffed behind me. I took the seat next to my sister. A long journey next to Vesperia was something I knew I could handle. Sitting next to Caligo was a gambit I was not willing to try. At least with company, Vesperia would not elbow me in the side.

Lord Caligo climbed in after me, taking the open bench across from us. He pulled the carriage door shut and knocked on the wall between him and his driver. Lord Caligo and I leaned forward to wave goodbye through the window. I caught Castor's eye and waved to him – he seemed to brighten a little. I could feel Vesperia shifting in her seat to wave also but the carriage window was too small and she was too far away.

Immediately after passing our gates, the carriage increased speed and we practically flew down to the village. I looked to Lord Caligo to maybe say something to his driver, but he and Vesperia were long lost in a conversation regarding the beautiful work of Seymour Vestor. I allowed myself to inspect the interior of the carriage. There were two upholstered bench seats, done in a plush blue fabric to match the emblem on the doors. The seats had drawer handles – three to be exact – making a smaller version of a dresser under the seats. Very clever.

We sped through Inanis, thankfully not hitting anyone along the way. Residents from our village seemed to know to stay out of the way of any dark carriage. They all ran so much faster than the rest of the region as if they left a candle burning at home. At this pace, we would reach Lux with time to spare.

The countryside flew by in a blur of flora and other travelers. Vesperia and Lord Caligo became animated and loud over the specifics of their ensembles. Vesperia wore an older piece, but she left that part out when he complimented the stitching around the sleeves – a Vestor specialty.

"Here, feel this!" Lord Caligo knelt on the carriage floor so that my sister could feel the soft interior fabric of his vest. While he rubbed it between her thumb and forefinger, he glanced at me. He nodded with his head that I, too, should check the feel of the fabric. I held my hand up to decline with a polite smile. He returned his full attention to my sister.

They continued their fashion conversation as we flew through the even smaller village of Bright Vale. This was a junction that would lead you straight south to Ingenium, or if you headed west like us, you would arrive at Lux. I became easily bored with the carriage ride. The scenery had changed to a drab desert framed by mountains in drought. Our side of the mountain was lush and green – this side was sun-baked.

Mother, Marjorie, and the Queen all speak of the plain's luminous beauty, but in my opinion, it was no more than a box of glittering sand. The views of the ocean might change my mind, but the sea was too far off to glimpse now. If I was lucky – and I am usually not – I might see it bathed in moonlight. The open plan encouraged a full view of the domed palace. Even in the distance, you could see it – just look for the grounded sun that never sets.

The true sun was setting gracefully across the western sky, dragging blankets of color behind it. A few bright stars became visible from my window, as the sun set, in Vesperia's window. There were only three stars in the sky at this time, ironically like my siblings and I. More would come with the setting of the sun. I clasped my hands in my lap and begged these stars to watch over us. Vesperia and I were on the road, far from home. Castor, who was home alone, was likely forced to be in the middle of whatever quarrel our parents would have that night.

"Are you well, my lady?" Lord Caligo asked. I jolted at the sound of his voice.

"Yes! My apologies for looking unwell. I am only thinking," I replied, trying to smooth over any issues I may have caused.

"There is no need. I was only curious. I have been entertaining your sister on this journey. You should have my apology," he said. Vesperia shrank back and he noticed. "My young lady, please do not take offense. I only mean she is my betrothed and I should have given her my time first."

"I am not offended. I know what is proper. I feel my own regrets at robbing you two of a long conversation. Surely you have plans to arrange for your wedding?" Vesperia suggested. Lord Caligo seemed put off by the suggestion.

"I am a bit road weary. Perhaps another time?" I redirected. Lord Caligo looked relieved.

"Yes, of course. The window, my lady. The air and natural view should ease your discomfort." With that, he and Vesperia fell into conversation once again. Only now, they went on about their aspirations for parenthood. I quickly found a quiet place in my mind to escape and ignore them for the remainder of the trip.

☆

When we arrived in Lux, the carriage slowed significantly to a normal pace for an inhabited area. Maybe it was the city that changed the driver's mind, or maybe there were simply too many pedestrians and other carriages to out maneuver. We bounced down the main road for quite a while – I recognized some of the landmarks and shops. I found myself squinting at the residents – their collective glow was impeding my vision like person-sized fireflies. The carriage pulled onto a side street where the emanating glow of citizens dissipated a little. There were still pedestrians, just not in large groups.

The theater was a large and round building with two main entrances. One was for the upper seating, reserved for anyone with the coin to purchase tickets. A second was the floor, the space in front of the stage. The floor space was open to anyone of the lower class who could not afford seats. It was standing room only. We pulled up to a line of other carriages waiting to unload passengers.

One by one, the drivers and footmen released their charges until it was finally our turn. Lord Caligo sprang to action the moment the door was open. He offered his hand to assist me – I took it. Then, I stepped gingerly down and onto the ground. He released my hand and took my sister's, also helping her down. The driver climbed back on his perch and snapped the reins, driving the team away. Lord Caligo offered an arm for both myself and my sister. Vesperia took his left arm quickly. I hesitated, but decided that taking his arm would be better than following behind like a chaperone.

We walked together in the queue to be seated in the upper desks. When it was our turn to enter, Lord Caligo released our arms with a quick apology and approached the host. He withdrew the letter we had been sent, the wax seal hanging precariously off a shred of paper, handing it to the host – a tall, thin, grey-moustached man.

"We are the guests of Her Majesty, the Queen." The host examined the letter and the seal before handing it back to Lord Caligo.

"Of course, my lord. You must be the Lord Caligo and these must be the Astrum Ladies. Welcome to our establishment, please follow this lad to your box." The host directed us to a young floral fairy – a pansy. He was a short, young-looking man, about Castor's age. He ushered us up a flight of stairs.

The Queen's box was up three flights of solid, enclosed stairs and set alone in the direct line of the center stage. There were no better seats. Inside the box were many regular chairs – all overstuffed armchairs with plush footstools in the Queen's crest colors of white and cream set up in two rows of seven. One chair for each recognized clan. For delegates most likely. Two ornate large chairs were placed on a raised platform behind the fourteen armchairs. These throne-like seats had a long, velvet upholstered, shared footrest.

"Sit anywhere you like, except, of course, the Queen's seat," the usher said before closing the door behind him. Lord Caligo walked forward and inspected the view. He made a grunt of approval and then meandered back to where Vesperia and I stood.

"Shall we sit?" I encouraged, looking longingly at the seat I wished to sit in.

"No, no. We have been sitting for too long. I will stand." Lord Caligo proclaimed. He stretched, and Vesperia watched like a wonderstruck child.

We were interrupted by a Harold's trumpet and a crier yelling for the respect of the Queen. *She is here.*

"All rise for her Royal Highness, Helia Solaris – Queen of Effection," he yelled. The entire theater stood with a sound like rolling thunder.

Ascending from the stairs like the sun from the sky, her inner glow approached us like an impending sunrise. As she entered, Lord Caligo, Vesperia and I bowed as low as we could. She passed by us without a word and addressed the crowd. They cheered and clapped, giving me the mental image of a lightning clap. Queen Helia waved and smiled at her people. When she lowered her hand, they all sat with another roll of thunder. Then she turned to us as we continued to bow and approached.

"Rise, you three. Tell me why it is you, little Vesperia, who comes as *chaperone* instead of your mother's lady servant?" now that I stood, I saw she had raised a brow. I glanced at the seat in the middle of the front row, longing to sit again, but my sister being under inspection made me want to stand with her. I chose to stand next to Vesperia for the moment as she explained herself to the Queen. I, too, wanted an explanation for her attendance, though I was sure it was a result of her tantrum last night.

"Mother could not spare Mrs. Sykes. She declared a need for her to direct the decoration of the ballroom. They both wanted to make your ball illustrious for you, Your Majesty." Vesperia bowed again, lower than before. The queen's radiant glow danced off the stardust on Vesperia's gown.

"Very well. Take your seat then." The Queen looked displeased, but with a heavy sigh, she shot me a look of dismissal and I followed Vesperia to the seats. Lord Caligo had chosen a seat very close to the one I had mentally picked. I winced as Vesperia aimed to take it, but instead, she sat to his right. The seat to his left was mine. As I passed, a shimmer of light from Vesperia's dress caught me in the eye, painfully.

"Ah. Sister? Could you withdraw your stardust glamour, please? The theater is supposed to be dim and you are iridescent." I tried to be nice. She dropped her jaw and began turning a deep shade of reddish purple before throwing up a facial glamour to hide the shame I saw.

"Do not instruct me, sister. I am *your* guardian tonight," she chided.

"You most certainly are not," I responded, keeping my voice low.

"Fine. Yet still, do not tell me how to act. You are not our mother. Your authority over me died the day you left." she glared at me over Lord Caligo. He caught her eye and she gave him a delicate, apologetic smile.

"You should listen, my young lady. The theater requires a certain ambiance. Even the beloved Queen is using a spell to dim her magnificent glow for the atmosphere," Lord Caligo chided in return. To this, from him, she listened. Her stardust glamour faded, alleviating my eyes of the irritant.

Below, the acting troupe collected props and set pieces. Everyone was looking for their seats when Lord Caligo stood up, looked to the Queen, and knelt to one knee. He produced a dazzling emerald-cut, single-carat sapphire set between two mirror half-carat obsidian gems on an intricately carved silver band with some type of dark metal woven in.

"Lady Seren Astrum, will you marry me and join our houses in blessed matrimony?" he declared loudly. I blushed deeply as the crowd collectively gasped. I looked at my sister, whose mask portrayed a proper amount of excitement.

Lord Caligo smiled at me from the floor, though I could tell he was eager to get his scene over with. I would love nothing more than to fade into the shadows if I was him. I scarcely wanted to be here myself. The crowd seemed to wait with still breath. Lord Caligo's eyes pleaded with me to say my line and let us move on with the night. I could feel the Queen's eyes boring into my back with the heat of her power.

"Yes," I responded with the most manufactured enthusiasm I could muster. The crowd erupted in cheers and whistles. The Queen laughed as she quieted the masses, though the whispers continued below. The stage crew clapped and thanked the Queen for a night to remember, then began their performance. The whispers in the crowd continued into the second act.

Chapter Seventeen

After a tenuous carriage ride home in the wee hours of the night, I assumed – incorrectly– that I might be able to drift into dreamless sleep. Instead, my mind kept me awake by haunting me with the scenes of what I had endured after the performance. At the conclusion of the performance the Queen was addressed again, but our descent was even more outstanding. The audience at large stayed behind to congratulate us on our engagement and blessing from the Queen. Many ladies told me their specific joy in my upcoming nuptials. I caught many indecent comments made to Lord Caligo about me by some men.

The only public opinion that bothered me was my sister's. When he had dropped to his knee, her face had tightened into a deep, angry frown. At first, she had tried to stifle it, then attempted to utilize her glamour to cover it, but her emotions were too strong – her glamour had fallen and she spent the remainder of the night with a scowl on her face. For the duration of the play, I sat mesmerized by the deep blue sapphire or cautiously eyeing Vesperia. On the other side of Lord Caligo, she seethed, never looking towards me.

When we arrived home, she took off running inside the house all the way to her chambers, where she promptly slammed the door. Later, I heard her yelling at Mystine over the whole ordeal. I had been held back by Lord Caligo. He announced that he had one more gift for me to pair with the Caligo family ring. His name.

"You must call me Umbriel now. We are, in all capacities, betrothed. I will use your given name also." I was shocked, but it did little to upset my nerves. I was already in quite an uneasy state after the public proposal and subsequent congratulations.

I nodded and excused myself to bed, where I lay across the end. The sapphire looked foreign on my hand, clashing with the purple tones of my skin. I took the band of the ring in my fingers, pulling it free. The gems were beautifully cut with but a few dings from previous wearers and an inscription that was worn down illegibly. I set the ring next to my sister's hidden gift on my writing desk and lay there staring at them for what felt like the whole night.

I must have dozed off, because I woke up lying across the foot of my bed, facing the ring. The sun was slowly rising, turning the sky outside my window a light pink. I swung my legs off the bed and onto the cold hardwood. The sensation sent a wave of instant energy through me. I felt wide awake.

Padding over to my wardrobe, I pulled a clean shift out and a yellow-orange beaded day gown – one that I could put on myself. *This beading should keep Mother off my neck for the day.* I tossed it onto the bed with the shift. A quick look in the mirror told me to apply some rouge to my cheeks, I was too pale today. Thankfully, the scorch mark on my face was faded and I did not need a glamour to hide it any longer.

I pulled the old, dirty shift off and put the clean one on. I carefully and slowly assembled the gown onto myself. A couple of times I felt stuck, but eventually I figured out how to lace up the back on my own with a little help from my mirror and a levitation spell. Before anyone else could wake up, I left my chambers and began walking quietly down to the kitchens when a feeling of shame flooded over me. I stopped and examined my person – I could not feel any mislaid fabric, but then it dawned on me. I had forgotten the ring. Carefully, I crept back up to my chambers, snatching the ring from its place beside Vesperia's pearly gift hidden beneath the glamour.

The kitchen was a mass of chaos. Servants ran from either end of the kitchen out either door and back empty-handed. The chef and all his apprentices were scurrying between several cooking pots and several large pans. I assumed they were preparing for the ball tomorrow. Our Great Hall would host hundreds of locals, aristocrats, and nobility.

"May I help at all?" I displayed my empty, workable hands. Chef Etienne approached me. His burly body took up most of the kitchen walkway to face me, effectively blocking the servants' routes through. He shook his head and took my left hand.

"No. This is meant to be your engagement breakfast – a feast of happiness. Traditionally we would have held a dinner, but the proposal was not here. This must do. You are instructed to wait, M'Lady. No labor for you today." He patted my hand and returned to work. I was quickly pushed out of the kitchen and into the hallway.

Unable to return to bed, I ascended the stairs to retrieve my book. Once I held my copy of *The Guide for Lost Souls*, I returned downstairs but instead of going to the kitchen, I turned to the library.

The library was still packed up because no one else was using it, but my chair remained uncovered. I shut the door behind me and walked to my favorite chair; it beckoned to me. Curling up, I opened my book to the page I last read. Time passed me by as I ate up every word the author wrote. They only used their last name so I could not picture them as a man or woman. They were simply an author.

While nose deep in the book, a servant was sent to track me down. She knocked quietly at the door – so quietly that I almost did not notice – but it came again and again until I responded.

"Come in!" I yelled. I closed up my book and left it on the nearby table. The small servant girl came in quietly and bowed.

"Breakfast is ready. The Lady Astrum requests you, Lady Seren, to be in attendance shortly," she said in the sweetest voice before darting out the doors again. I followed her out and saw she was not in the hallway. I concluded she must have run back to the kitchens the moment she was out of sight. When I walked into the dining room, I saw that everyone else was waiting on me. Another table had been brought in to hold the overflow of food for this engagement breakfast.

"Finally! Now sit down," my mother ordered. I moved to take my usual spot, but my mother cleared her throat and looked at the empty seat next to Lord Caligo. Withholding my sigh, I sat and was greeted by a menacing scowl from Vesperia. Mrs. Sykes gave us a tour of the table and assigned a servant to each member of the table to build their plates for them. My attendant was baffled at my request for the smallest, most plain arrangement. Toasted bread, butter – no jam. Any plain egg that was fully cooked and ham. No sauces, no gravy, nothing extra.

"My Lady, you eat breakfast like a fasting nun. Are you well?" the servant who filled my plate asked.

"Yes. This is my everyday appetite. Thank you though." I unfurled my napkin, placing it on my lap. Lord Caligo and my mother were engaged in stories of adventure and heroism. Lord Caligo could only repeat the stories he had heard. My mother's proud battle victory was not one of the tales he had heard. He listened intently, missing his mouth several times with a forkload of food. Vesperia watched their interaction the way she used to watch me master new spells.

Across the table, my father and Castor appeared gloomy. Father had an air of dejected withdrawal, while Castor looked more like a forlorn prisoner. I made the assumption that father was saddened by his missing book and being forced to endure breakfast the way we all had before. They were slumped in their chairs and frowning down at their breakfasts. Castor ate slowly and our father nursed a goblet of wine while he shuffled food across his plate.

Breakfast felt more like a wake – the chatty mourners and gloomy ghosts. I fit in neither group. The ring on my finger drew my attention, the way it caught the light. I admired it silently, turning my hand over in the sunlight. It was a beautiful piece that looked strange and unreal on my hand to my eyes – like someone had stolen it and asked me to hold onto it. I looked to my left at Lord Caligo. He and my mother were still engrossed with story-swapping. He was at ease, in his element. The look my mother gave him made me jealous.

I finished my breakfast in silence. Personal silence, as no one spoke to me. I became focused on every part of the Caligo ring. The sapphire had damage that matched the band. I imagined what activities a lady of the high court might have done to blemish the piece so deeply. The possibilities had limits, just as the wearer once did. *Is marriage only meant to limit women?* The obsidian cuttings absorbed all the light from around them. I began to imagine the jewels siphoning away my light and my heart began to race. I had to set my utensils down and flatten my palm against the cool tabletop. I had forgotten the table was full of others, but when I looked up all I saw was my sister quizzically investigating my behavior change.

Her attention turned to our father, I too looked at him – out of curiosity. He had guzzled down his goblet of wine and dropped it back onto the table with a clatter, but it did not break.

"Kyrinn!" Mother shouted, interrupting Lord Caligo mid-story. Father turned his bloodshot gaze down the table, I felt a chill as he glared at her.

"Eleanor," he mocked her, pushing back his chair with a loud scrape against the tiles. He walked out of the dining hall without another word. Mother and Vesperia looked at each other, sharing looks of derision. Castor looked ejected and even more worn down. I needed any excuse to leave – this was it. I mumbled an excuse and withdrew myself from the dining hall swiftly. I knew where my father had gone. I made my way quietly to his study across the hall. Passing the library, I felt my book and cozy chair call to me, but I pushed on. His study door was closed, I rapped on the wood firmly.

"More wine!" my father called from within.

"It is I, father – Seren. And I do not have wine."

"Come back with wine! Red!" he yelled. Exasperated, I looked around for a servant. They buzzed through the house in various stages of preparations for the ball. I spotted one heading in the direction of the kitchen.

"Excuse me? Could you retrieve a decanter or bottle of red wine for my father?" I stopped the passing male Terra fairy.

"Yes, M'Lady. Red it will be."

"He is in his study. Thank you," I replied before turning back. This time I let myself in without knocking.

My father had his head on his arms resting on his desk. He groaned, but if there were words, I could not decipher them. Anxiously, I twisted the Caligo ring on my finger as I waited for him to speak to me. He did not.

"Father?" I asked timidly. He jerked up and fixed his glazed eyes on me.

"Yesss, little itty-bitty star?" he slurred. I sat on a chair across from the desk. I could not push the words from my lips. I chewed my bottom lip and tried forcing the words out.

"Do I have to marry Lord Caligo?" I whispered. He groaned and leaned closer.

"Hmm?" he mumbled back. The servant I had asked to bring wine entered then, drawing his attention. His brow creased with curiosity, then relaxed upon noticing the bottle of dark red wine.

"Thank you, my good fellow." My father held the sentence tensely. The young servant placed the decanter and a clean glass on my father's desk near him.

"Thank you, thank you. Now go on – go. I wass speak-ing with my dau-ght-er." he enunciated, shaking his hand at the lad. He shakily poured himself another drink and flapped his free hand at me to continue.

"I said, father… Do I have to marry Lord Caligo?" I blurted. My father looked at me, I could tell he slowly processed the information I had just thrust upon him.

"Umbriel?" he asked. I nodded. "Why should you not? He is Perfect-perfectly accept-acceptable." He took a long gulp from his glass before attempting to refill it.

"Yes father, I know, but … marriage… It is just not what I had in mind."

He looked at me like I was a ghost. He sipped his wine and his eyes fluttered closed as he drank more deeply. He emptied the glass and slammed it down hard on his desk. I jumped.

"Well, it i-is on the Queen's mind. And let me – let me tell you, my dear-dear, sweet girl. What the Solarices want, they get. You go-got it?" He leveled his gaze to mine, almost soberly.

"Could you not intervene? As my father?" I asked after a long pause of silence. His head drooped as he turned to face the boarded-up window.

"No, my sstar. I cannot. The war is won and they will get what th-they want. With blood, with magic, and with numbers. Child it iss time you learn-learned that not all-all your heart's desires iss yourss to h-have." He began to refill the glass, but his unsteady hand dropped it.

The glass shattered on the stone floor the way my heart's hope broke in my chest.

"That, my dear, iss what may very well ha-happen to you if the Queen is dis-displeased," he muttered, before taking a long drink from the decanter.

Chapter Eighteen

Father only ever spoke of the war or its consequences when fully in his cups, usually right before he would pass out. This ensured I never received the full story. The most I could authenticate was that the Obscurum clans lost – horribly. The Solaris' troops were known for their fury, and my paternal aunt Kerrell was 'sent away' to the devastation of the Tenebraes.

I had abandoned my father to his wine and misery, but could not find the courage to step farther into the hall than the few paces I had gotten from the door. My feet felt heavy, my wings felt bound. I stood stupidly in the hallway between the door to my father's study and the doors to the library. The ring on my finger burned into my bones, but I dared not take it off. Instead, I turned it over and over around my finger.

If I do not do this, what will become of my family? Would Vesperia or Castor be sent away to appease the Queen for my insolence? The thought made my heart race like I had run the entire acreage of the estate. I had promised myself I would try. There was nothing more to do but keep my word. I resolved to continue the attempt, though I did not know how. Shaking my head to loosen my nerves I forced myself forward to ascend the stairs. I wished I could fly, it would have been more swift, but the idea of a lecture and possible slap from my mother stopped me.

My chamber door brought me a strange comfort. I pushed inward and breathed in the clean mid to late-morning air that breezed through the drafty windows. I walked over and secured the curtains to the walls with the ropes fixed to the wall then pushed the windows open all the way. The strong, unhindered breeze was wonderful on my flushed face. I breathed in the fresh air deeply and tried to collect my thoughts, but when I did, the singular thought was *why me?* It repeated over and over in my head until I broke. I dropped to my knees in front of the window, unable to contain my sorrow for one more second. Tears spilled from my eyes onto the floor.

I looked at my left hand through blurry tears. It glared back at me as tears splashed onto the back of my hand. The sobs stole my breath and I began to have trouble taking more in. I used my right hand to rub my sternum gently, praying I might soothe the panic. I sniffled a breath – it was not enough air, I began to sputter, hyperventilating. Forcefully, I drew in a hiccupy breath, held it, and released it slowly. My sobs were reduced to hiccups and I felt exhausted. The bed called to me like wine called to my father. On my knees, I crawled to my bed and pulled myself into the covers with a few more sobbing gasps.

The pillows were cool and my blankets warm. It was not long before I succumbed to a sorrowful sleep.

Soft, gentle hands stirred me from my slumber.

"Seren – Seren. It is time to rise," a voice sang to me, light and melodic. Groggily, I pried open my eyes to be rewarded with the sight of Aurora smiling down on me. The afternoon sun hit her golden hair, illuminating it and her lovely face. Her inner glow bathed me in a golden light. The sight of my friend electrified me. I sprang up in bed, hugging her close. She laughed loudly and embraced me back.

"Oh, how I have missed you," I said, pulling away to see her face again. "But wait! You are not supposed to return so soon. Is everything well with you?"

"Yes! Yes, very fine indeed!" she replied with a smile.

"Why have you returned so soon?"

"Stop playing coy with me. Do you think I would miss my only friend's engagement ball?" I felt the joy leak out of me and into an abyss growing in my stomach. My feelings appeared on my face – I could tell by the concern growing on Aurora's face.

"You heard about that?" I asked, avoiding her perceptive gaze. She tilted her head to her right.

"Everyone has heard the news. I was surprised you did not tell me yourself!" She sounded hurt.

"I am sorry. I did not know until last night when he gave me this." I watched her as I pulled my left hand free of the covers to reveal the Caligo heirloom. Her jaw dropped and her eyes widened to encompass the moon.

"Oh, how divine!" she gushed over the piece. I pulled it free and relinquished it to her. Aurora accepted it and began inspecting it with wonder.

"Marvelous! What does this inscription say?" she asked me.

"I do not know – he did not say," I responded with a shrug. She studied it closer but gave up easily and returned it to me.

"So?" She looked to me for more answers. I held the ring in my palm.

"What do you think of him?" she continued like I was being intentionally dense. My mouth twisted into a frown and I began to chew on the inside of my cheek. Aurora did not move her eyes – she let them bore into mine. I tried to look away but they held fast.

"I think he is a prick," I spat. Aurora erupted into laughter once more. I did not join her. Instead, I watched her with a look of annoyance pinned to my face.

"It is not funny! I have to spend the rest of my life with him! That would be another one hundred and fifty years of him speaking over me and flouting his minor accomplishments. He makes every single conversation about him! Aurora, I cannot stand him!" Her laughter stopped abruptly, She looked at me with pity for longer than I could bear. I looked away, to the spot where Vesperia's gift was hidden.

"Seren. I –" she hesitated, "I am so deeply sorry for you." She picked up my hands with hers and held them. Her eyes portrayed her understanding. I felt the stinging pain of new tears prick my eyes and threw myself into her arms and cried. She let me weep until I had run my eyes dry, and then she helped me sit up and prepare for dinner.

"Your mother gave me strict instructions to dress you in 'House Colors', so that means you will have to wear that awful lilac gown. The good news is it will only be for dinner!" she attempted a cheery tone. I was all out of energy to put on a charade. For now, at least. I may have to muster some energy for dinner. I pushed off the bed and went to my vanity where Aurora applied the perfect makeup. She brushed my dark hair out before knotting it in a high woven bun. When she finished, she laid a hand on my shoulder while holding the wrenched lilac dress draped over her other arm.

I stood and followed her guidance on where to stand while she laced me into the dress. Even with a clean shift, it still scratched me. This lilac monstrosity devoured me and tormented me with coarse stitches and embroidery. The embroidery spanned the entire sleeve length and around the collar. Aurora gently pried the ring from my hand and replaced it on my finger. I stared at the foreign object, unwelcome in its new home. I could feel the resentment building.

"You are all done up, my lady. Is there anything else I can do for you?" She waited patiently.

"Walk me down to dinner?" I asked. She smiled brightly at me through the mirror.

"Of course!" She gestured for me to lead the way. I picked up my skirt and made my way to the door. On the landing, she offered me her arm. I took it.

"Why must I dress so elegantly for dinner, dear friend?" I asked as we descended. Aurora would not meet my eyes – hers were trained on each coming stair.

"Aurora?" Finally, she looked at me, fear blooming in her glowing amber eyes.

"The Queen has come and will be here until the ball tomorrow evening," she whispered, turning her head back towards the stairs. We reached the base of the stairs in silence. Being a light fairy, she should have adored and admired our King and Queen, but ever since I met her, she had been fervently against their grotesque displays of power.

"I see." I released her arm, though I wished I could bring her with me into the dining hall. I turned to face her, pulling her gently to face me. In a whisper, I gave her a direct order.

"Go home. Quickly. Before she sees you, and demands that you stay." Her eyes focused, understanding. The Queen was famous for demanding other light fairies stay to enhance the glow; she always liked to brighten the room. Aurora and I embraced, and then she turned to leave.

"Will I see you tomorrow?" I lightly caught her hand. She looked at me over her shoulder, eyes burning with tension.

"Of course. You will need to look your best." She squeezed my hand and dashed to the garden door, where I knew she would fly into the forest and navigate home under the cover of the trees.

Alone, I faced the dining hall door and steeled myself for what was next. With a deep breath, I advanced through the door, entering the candle-lit room. Inside, I saw another lavish feast. The secondary table was set on the left of the room. It was filled with steaming pots and plates of vegetables, poultry, and fish. Dishes were still being brought out and arranged, forcing my family and Lord Caligo to wait, hovering in the right corners of the room in two groups. My mother and sister were attentively listening to Umbriel tell them of an exotic adventure.

Castor hung back from them with a growing look of boredom. My father hovered behind Castor with an almost sober demeanor. I glided over to my brother and attempted to remove his solemn attitude.

"How do you fair this night, brother?" I dipped my head to him. If the Queen was here, I needed to be as proper as possible at all times. He dipped his head to me automatically, then blinked to refocus. He came back from his mental wanderings. He wore a matching lilac ensemble of trousers and vest, as well as a sparkly, tailored jacket.

"I shall be well once we may finally eat." He watched the servants arrange a roast boar on a large round table on its very own platform – perpendicular to our long family table. It had one singular ornate chair with a matching place setting. The Queen's chair.

"Have you been waiting long?" I asked, rocking on my feet. Castor looked at me with heavy irritation. I stopped moving, and he nodded.

"Seems Mrs. Sykes retrieved me first," he pouted, leaning against the wall. Servants scurried to and fro with dishes going into the dining room, or empty arms rushing back to the kitchens. Mrs. Sykes was nowhere to be found in the buzz, leading me to believe she was in the kitchen directing the masses. I saw a delicious platter of carved turkey only to have my stomach pinch. Turkey is one of my favorites.

A commotion at the front door drew the attention of many in the dining hall. Vesperia and Umbriel began to preen like a pair of stuffy birds. Mother readied herself by standing in front of everyone, near the Queen's chair. She fluffed her skirts and adjusted her sleeves. My father looked to the ceiling, whispering silent goodbyes to the shadows in the rafters, then joined Castor and I's smaller group.

"The Queen is here," he whispered conspiratorially. Castor and I looked at each other and rolled our eyes together. Mrs. Sykes and Mr. Huich entered the dining hall, holding the doors open for a trio of Queens Guards followed by The Queen Herself and her lady in waiting – a young light fairy with one of the dimmest glows I had ever seen. Castor threw off our father and dipped into a low bow. My father and I followed his lead.

"Rise and be bright," Queen Helia declared. She was escorted to the platformed chair and table. She waved her hand for us to sit. We all hurried to our seats, carefully avoiding one another until every chair was claimed. My mother claimed the seat closest to the Queen, the same head of the table she always sat at. My father sat at his usual opposite end. My sister chose my mother's right side, Umbriel to her left. Castor took a moment to think and chose to sit next to Umbriel, the seat I knew I was supposed to take, but now I felt the need to sit next to Vesperia to collect around the Queen.

There was a pit of guilt in my heart for not sitting with my father, but the Queen would make a mockery of it if I tried. I settled into my seat and began unwrapping my utensils from their napkin cocoon when a clatter came from the direction of the Queen. We all snapped to attention, looking towards the Queen's Table. Queen Helia was standing, analyzing us.

"Lady Seren," she said slowly, "why are you avoiding your betrothed?" I looked around and realized she was right – we were not next to or across from one another. To her, it would look like I was avoiding him. I felt Queen Helia's gaze upon my hot cheeks. I met her eyes.

"I did not realize, my Queen. We were more concerned about sitting down. I do not wish to avoid Lord – Umbriel." I corrected it too late.

"Do not address your betrothed with his title. That is improper. You wear his ring. Are you not happy? Umbriel?" she addressed him now. "Have you not invited your betrothed to use your given name?"

"I have, my Queen!" he responded firmly. The Queen's gaze rested on me again.

"Then it is settled. The ladies Vesperia and Seren will trade seats so that the lovers may gaze into each other's eyes over this delightful feast. You, Lady Seren, will address Lord Caligo with his given name. Am I understood?" Her gaze was unflinching. Against my better judgment, I glanced around the room to my family.

My mother gave me a warning look backed with fire. My sister scowled uncontrollably. Lord Caligo – Umbriel– blinked at me repeatedly like we were in dire need of assistance. My father was shakily pouring another glass of wine ,unperturbed by the Queen's presence.

"Yes, my Queen. Right away, my Queen," I said with as much emotion I could muster. Vesperia continued to stay in her seat until our mother burned her with a menacing glare. She stood fast, almost toppling the chairs. I held mine out for her and attempted to push in hers for her, but she brushed me off.

I looked back at the Queen as I sat down in my new seat next to my mother and across from Umbriel. Satisfied, the Queen smoothed her skirts and sat back down in her ornate seat above us all. She wore a smirk of victory. I returned my attention to my place setting – unwrapping the utensils from the neatly folded napkin and laying the cloth napkin across my lap. Mrs. Sykes began reciting the long list of dishes prepared for the night. I followed her with my eyes as she walked until she passed behind someone's head. First, it was Vesperia to my left, who attempted another venomous glare but was zapped with a ray of light by our mother. No one acknowledged that she had been hurt; they all stared at their plates in hopes they would not incur the wrath of Eleanor.

Then it was my father, who was too drunk to offer any support besides a slosh of wine. Briefly, I had a mind to look upon my brother as she slid behind Castor to announce the roast turkey and its origins. Then she stood behind Umbriel, who blew three kisses and winked. I assumed this was for the Queen's benefit. It made my stomach roll. Finally, she reached her dessert menu, standing behind the Queen and my mother, near the kitchen doors.

Mrs. Sykes assigned an attendant to everyone – the Queen declined a server from our house and instructed her lady's maid to carve her turkey and serve her plate. She demanded a helping of each dish. This was then duplicated by my mother, then my siblings, and Umbriel. Umbriel asked for two more dishes in response to the Queen's choice. My father and I were the only ones to not follow suit. He stayed to his cup of wine and I continued my normal habits of the most plain items. I only wanted vegetables and slices of the roast turkey.

We were invited to eat by Mrs. Sykes, who then relinquished the speaking floor to the Queen once more and dashed back into the kitchens. The Queen raised her golden chalice in a toast as her lady's maid tested all her food for poison. We all raised our cups towards the queen.

"A toast of happiness, love, and grace for the young lovers as they open their lives, hearts, and minds to the bountiful world around us." She fixed me with her molten golden eyes, boring holes deep in my stomach that would not leave for the entire night.

Chapter Nineteen

Dinner dissolved into a tea party with ale between my mother and the Queen. Queen Helia called for a musician, and mother granted permission for everyone to fly for as long as the ale was warm. A troupe was summoned from the village and brought in as soon as they arrived. The Queen was still in control of herself – my mother, not so much. I left when her jokes became serious jabs, which only increased as I left on foot.

Either the tear-induced nap or my still unsettled nerves forced me to remain awake when I laid down for bed. I could not sleep, not well. Dawn came, regardless, when a soft knock came at my door at sunrise.

"Come in," I called from my bed. Aurora popped her head in, but her expression told me it was not a good morning.

"My lady." She dipped into a curtsey. I threw off the covers and twisted in bed to face her.

"What has happened?"

"Your mother has requested to see you as soon as you are able." She had dark lines under her eyes and trembled slightly.

"Sit." I moved over, patting the bed beside me. She hurried over and obliged me. I clasped her hands and gave her a look of sincere worry. She dipped her head to avoid my eyes.

"Tell me," I urged. She hesitated, but eventually spoke.

"Your mother... After the Queen retired, your mother must have become enraged at your early leaving. She called me back to the estate in the early hours to berate me about leaving you unattended for the Queen's night. She commented that your sister had outlasted you at your own engagement banquet." The strain in her eyes told me she had been working all night.

"I am so sorry." I drew her into a hug. Her body was so light that I imagined her falling asleep while standing and being dramatically punished for doing so. She relaxed into me and I ran my hand across her back, the way I imagined different mothers might have done for me.

"Ser, I am exhausted," she whimpered.

"I can see. Stay here and rest. I will be back." I released her and moved off the bed, helping her to lie down. I covered her with my blankets and caressed her cheek. She smiled weakly, eyes closing. I was half sure she was already drifting to sleep.

I picked a reasonable blue gown with light beading and an embroidered corset. The lacing was hard to do by myself, but the peace on Aurora's face kept me from waking her. My hair was easier, though it was beginning to look oily. I knew mother would have a fit about that too. I added some powder to my hair to absorb some of the oils. All that was left was to review myself in the mirror before entering my mother's withdrawing room. I double-checked that the Caligo ring was still on my hand and had not fallen off in the night.

I fluffed my skirts and pinched my cheeks to bring the blood into them. My eyes were puffy, but she would see through any glamour if I tried to use one. I approached the door between my chambers and her withdrawing room, laying my right ear against the cool wood. I heard my mother's loud voice directing people, but not what she said to them. The door squeaked a little as I opened it – I looked back to ensure that Aurora stayed asleep. With a last thought, I threw a glamour over my bed to make it appear empty, so that she might sleep longer.

Stepping into the drawing room, I became involved in a strange scene. My mother lay disheveled in her nightgown and robe on her overstuffed couch, holding a cloth wrapped ice chunk against her eyes as she commanded servants to do specific tasks. They all scurried around with their eyes down. Marjorie stood behind my mother, braiding her hair, watching the room like a hawk. I stepped carefully through the servants and waited in front of my mother's table.

"Mother, you requested to see me?" I fell into a curtsey, holding it as she removed the ice to look at me. Her gaze burned through her bloodshot eyes, scorching my skin with judgement.

"Yes. Did you choose your gown or did your maid?" she asked. Her nose wrinkled at my gown.

"I insisted on this one, ma'am," I said, still facing the floor in a curtsey.

"Fine. You may stand already." She waved her hands at me, returning the ice block to her eyes and tilting her head back to rest on the arm of the couch. I stood, relieved. Mother pat Marjorie's hand in what must have been a silent command. Mrs. Sykes turned and retrieved a hefty wooden box from under my mother's bed. She set it down on the table between mother and I.

"This is my Lucidus court gown. I wore it on *my* wedding day and now you shall have it," mother declared without moving. Marjorie pulled open the box to reveal a pale yellow – almost white – silk dress with a square neckline full of sparkling beads.

"May I?" I gestured towards picking the dress up while addressing Mrs. Sykes. *This is the gown that was planned for me, a wedding dress? This could only mean one thing. They intended to marry me off tonight.*

"Yes," mother snapped. I approached the box and carefully pulled the gown from inside. I had not seen it before, but now I saw the millions of tiny sparkles affixed to the dress. It was no glamour – the fine crystals were manually fixed to the dress with white thread, making the whole gown shimmer as I moved it. The skirts were metallic gold and underneath, at the bottom of the box, were three silver ornaments with the Lucidus family crest stamped into the metal. There was a round silver pendant on a long chain, a chained belt with an oval pendant that hung down, and lastly, a tiara with a thin, translucent veil attached.

"Must I wear it all?" I asked meekly. My mother sat up abruptly and hurled her ice chunk at me. I was quick enough to avoid it, but it shattering against the wall only enraged her more.

"Yes, you pretentious child. All of it. It is an *ensemble* and holds direct meaning to your family. You will wear it all. You will behave and you will not embarrass me! Do you understand?" she growled as she stood, approaching me. She leaned over the table and box to make direct eye-contact with me. Her hazel-gold, bloodshot eyes burned into me more and more the longer that she did not blink.

"Yes, mother," I finally said. This released her hard stare and allowed her to return to the couch.

"ICE!" she barked. Mrs. Sykes scurried off to fetch the ice and a fresh cloth. I watched her go, wishing I, too, could be dismissed.

"You should be so lucky, " she muttered, throwing an arm over her eyes.

"Yes, mother." I carefully closed the lid after replacing the garment.

"After your major disgrace last night, the Queen almost rethought your engagement. Are you trying to ruin us?" she snapped.

"No, mother. I apologize for leaving so early."

"As you should be. To keep you from any more chances of inappropriate behavior or outbursts like last night, you are confined to your room until our guests arrive. Upon that time, Marjorie will retrieve you. You are not permitted to leave until then. Am I understood?" She removed her arm long enough to glare at me from the couch.

"Yes, mother," I said, lowering my head. I could still feel her burning gaze on me, chiseling away at my forehead.

"Leave, now. I am weary." She relaxed into the couch, replacing her arm over her face. I collected the wooden box and returned to the door between this room and mine.

In my bed chamber, I set the box on the foot of the bed, but did so quietly so that I did not disturb Aurora, who was still soundly asleep. I felt remorse at what I would do next, but soothed my mind with the knowledge that it was necessary. With a gentle shake to her shoulder, I woke her.

"Huh?" She jolted awake, twisting from sleeping to sitting up and looking around.

"I am sorry dear friend – I tried to be gentle. I am so very sorry to wake you for this, but can I implore you to attempt a few errands for me?" I sat on the bed between Aurora and the gown box.

"Yes of course, Seren. What is it?" She rubbed her eyes and yawned.

"I have been ordered to be confined to my room. I could get a more serious punishment if I leave and am spotted. Could you retrieve my book from the library? It is called '*The Guide for Lost Souls*'. Then, if possible, could you sneak me a bit of food?" I clutched my stomach before it could grumble.

"Of course. I shall return soon. Pray I do not get caught by Mrs. Sykes and be put to work," she jested, flinging back the covers and fully disturbing my glamour. She quickly passed through the door, leaving me alone.

The air was still and quiet – except for the faint buzzing of my mother's orders in the next room. Facing the gown box, I steeled myself and re-opened the lid. Away from my mother's perceptive eye, I could explore the gown better. I took out the single-piece top of the dress. Fixed sleeves, but not the type that needed laced together like my normal dresses. The miniscule crystals affixed to the gown felt coarse like a cat's tongue as I ran my hand down the sleeve. The silk trim was a comforting addition. I found it continued inward as a lining. When I pulled the full length from the box, the hem of the skirts fell on the floor and then some. My mother was a few inches taller than me.

And because this is a surprise, there is no time for a tailor or to find tall enough shoes. I will be tripping in this ocean all night. After admiring the shimmer of the crystals in my full-length mirror, I set the upper part of the gown across my bed like I was putting another body into the covers. Next, I drew out the massive full metallic gold skirt, its hem still resting on the ground. It had so many pleats and drapes that it reflected the sunlight like a steady river. Inspecting the fabric, I was relieved to find it was smooth like silk, but not as fine. It was heavier and thicker than silk.

I laid it on top of the bodice and returned to the box for the ornaments. The belt and necklace were made of white gold, not silver like I had first thought. It reflected the sunlight just as the skirt piece did, but in a more solid fashion.

With care, I pulled the tiara and ornaments out, laying them on the next piece of fabric to inspect them. The tiara was also white gold and the veil weighed nothing, but sparkled just as the bodice did. I was comparing the engraved crests on the belt and necklace when my chamber door flew open and slammed shut. I stood, bracing for the inevitable, but I saw it was only Aurora and relaxed.

"I apologize! I bring you gifts!" she said quickly, out of breath. Then, she revealed a tea tray with little treats on napkins and my book.

"Oh!"

"Zanos came to work too – he swiped a few tea snacks from the guest platters." She smirked, but not for long. Once she saw the gown and ornaments laid out on the bed, she filled my hands with the tray and ogled over the exuberant fabrics.

"My word! Oh! Seren, this gown! When will you wear it?" She ran her hands over the smooth, metallic skirt.

"Tonight," I responded, paying more attention to the scones and fruit spears on the tea tray.

"Oh, Seren. You did not say this was to be your wedding night!" Her inner glow grew brighter with joy. I felt myself shrink.

"Oh… I see," she said, her light suddenly dimming. We held the somber moment in the room until Aurora crossed the floor to me and embraced me. I could not keep the tears at bay any longer. I wept into her again – scared for my future.

We cleared the bed of the gown, storing it back in the wooden box then sliding it under the bed. We both climbed into my large bed and succumbed to the cool sheets. Aurora began to snore lightly, while I attempted to drift off to sleep. I could not get past the sliver of information I had gleaned from Aurora just then. This ball was to be a wedding, and they did not even tell the soon-to-be bride. What sort of tricks were they playing at? *You may be able to force me to marry him, but you will not surprise me with my own wedding.*

My heart began to race my thoughts as they ran wild, plotting to run away or fight my mother. Rationally, I knew neither was plausible, but the beating in my chest did not cease for some time. To pass the time, I curled up in the window to read in the sun, but the words floated away into the abyss of my imagination while I continued to stew over the impending wedding.

I stared out the window in thought, watching birds soar by in beautiful, swooping arcs. I envied their wistfulness, their freedom to do as nature bid them. From my window perch, I was able to see when our guests began to arrive – about an hour before dinner. I walked with urgency to the bedside to shake Aurora awake and pull out the dress. Kicking the box over to my vanity table I began to shed my clothes with haste.

"Guests are arriving! You need to make yourself available to Mrs. Sykes so that she may send you up to dress me!" I roused her from sleep, just in time, because a servant was sent to collect me in the absence of Aurora. A soft knock began to rap at my door, a gravelly voice calling to me. I made Aurora hide on the other side of the bed while I allowed the young maid in. She stepped in gracefully and announced that my mother requested I be dressed in a high court gown. I showed her to my wardrobe where she picked a new gown and assisted me in dressing. It was a stuffy light silvery-grey with slim sleeves and massive skirts. As the flower maid helped me to lace up the bodice, I snuck a glance at Aurora behind the bed. She still looked so incredibly tired.

I was quickly ushered out the door and down the stairs with no time to look at my appearance in the mirror. Downstairs, everyone was lined up in the Great Hall to receive our guests. On the right of the staircase were the family, Umbriel, and the Queen. To the left of the stairs was our battalion of servants. I watched as the little flower maid found a spot to stand. I descended the stairs in my new silvery dress.

Mother watched me and wiped the look of sickness from her face, replacing it with the solid visage of a strong leader. Father stood stoically sober next to her, eyes fixed ahead of him. Castor was beside him, and Vesperia next to Castor, happily smiling up at Umbriel, who stood at the end of the family line. The Queen stood alone a few paces from Umbriel, and I realized that was where I was meant to stand. Fear gripped my insides, sending a chill through my bones. When I was finally noticed by the Queen, she snapped and pointed to the spot between her and Umbriel.

I obeyed with a quick bow to Her Majesty before taking my place in the line. Our first guest was the barons of Cruor, the Carmines. They wore elegant void-black, dripping with red ornaments like a blood crystal necklace and blood crystal brooches. They moved down the line, introducing themselves and accepting our family's welcome. When they came to Umbriel and I, they bowed low and Baron Carmine addressed us.

"This is my darling wife Sabine, and you may call me Darick. It is a pleasure to join you this evening." He shook Umbriel's hand and offered me a curt nod. The Baroness was much more courteous to me. She made eye contact with me and offered a real smile that met her eyes. When they moved on they were faced with the Queen and bowed deeply in unison. When they were released, they wandered to a refreshment table at the end of the hall.

The ballroom was sealed with ceremonial ribbons, but the tea tray feast had been laid out already. The guests trickled in behind the Cruor Barons. Each gave us the honors required of our titles and measured against tonight's festivities. I held strong doubts that in any other event, I would not be afforded half this attention.

Everyone had arrived and we were finally allowed to mingle. I was pulled into an uncomfortable conversation with a High Lord and Lady of the Occeus clans.

"Children are precious! I could not have survived my two-hundreds without them!" the lady Spina laughed.

"Yes, I am in agreement!" Umbriel used an arm to pull me close to him. "I would love to see five, or more, little void stars running about the manor." The Lord and Lady nodded happily, and Lord Spina chuckled. They looked to me for my opinion; I could not help myself.

"I have thought of children, but in truth, I think my energy is better spent elsewhere. For instance, influencing my village and region. I learned so much from my travels." They looked at me as if I had four too many eyes or fire in my hair. I could feel the blush creep into my cheeks and prayed it would go unnoticed.

"Well, that will all be up to your husband now, dear." My mother laid a gentle hand on my shoulder, so light that I almost flinched. A chill ran through my skin. At least I could not blush while frightened. Umbriel turned towards my mother, offering her a smile. This smile held a lie behind it, but what that lie was, I could not tell.

"Indeed you are right, mother." I patted her hand hoping she would remove it. She did not. Instead, she tightened her grip.

"You must excuse us, your lordships. I have need of my daughter." She pulled on me, her fingertips hot on my skin, even through the dress. I turned and let her lead me to the end of the staircase, where she turned so quickly I thought she might strike me again. It took all my composure not to flinch. She did not, however, strike me. Instead, she fixed her eyes on me sternly with a burning intensity.

"You will march up those stairs and wear the gown selected for you! Your siblings can behave, why can you not? Do not answer – I do not care for your opinions, as I am sure no one else does. Come down and behave like the star you are, or else," she commanded. I obeyed, walking up the stairs as gracefully as I could while shaking.

Chapter Twenty

Waking Aurora was the easy part; she and I both almost cut our hands on the minuscule crystals on the dress as we slid it over my head. The metallic skirts were much easier to put on. Once I had been laced into the gown, Aurora fixed the white gold ornaments to their places. The belt was lightweight, as was the necklace. The tiara on the other hand weighed like a castle brick. The veil I knew was weightless, but it too felt like it might pull my head off with the heft of the tiara. Aurora hugged me close before exiting through the hidden door to my mother's withdrawing room.

Alone, I studied myself in the mirror. I knew that image was me, but she did not look like me. *It is only for a few hours.* I ran my fingers over the silk trim; it was cool like water under my fingers. The Caligo ring stood out against the bright Lucidus regalia like a dark spot on the sun. I inhaled sharply, then forced myself to leave and return to the ball below.

As I descended the stairs, the crowd of nobility and high houses looked up at me one by one, everyone watching me take every step. I was the focal point of the evening now. Umbriel met me at the base of the stairs offering his hand to me. I took it and he swung me around to make my dress flutter, eliciting awe-inspired murmurs from the crowd. He turned me, and I tried to recognize faces, but the only person I could see was my sister. Her countenance was solemn as her eyes followed us. I could not help but think she wished to be in my place – if only we *could* trade places. Flying sparks drew everyone's attention to the doors of the ballroom. Umbriel ceased spinning me, stopping me with a hand on my elbow. The Queen was standing by the ballroom doors, waiting by the ceremonial ribbons. She beckoned to us to join her. Umbriel, hand still on my elbow, led us to the ballroom doors to stand next to the Queen.

"Attention all!" the Queen addressed the room with a loud, carrying voice. The crowd ceased their conversations and turned towards us. I could feel their eyes staring like thousands of little holes being burned into my back through the thin cloth.

"As we begin tonight's festivities, do keep in mind that most of you are guests to this house and to this region. Please abide by the laws and house rules. The chief rule to follow tonight is 'no flying'. To those of you with the ability to fly, we would greatly appreciate your compliance with walking and dancing along the floor with the rest of us. Let us keep the court high, Seelie, and jovial! Thank you to our gracious hosts, the Lady and Lord Astrum," she gestured to my parents who bowed and waved to the crowd. "and, of course, to the lovely couple that gave us a reason to gather!"

"Hear, hear!" chanted the crowd. With a bit of fanfare and flourish, the Queen used a beam of light to sever the lavender ribbons from the door. A cheer rang through the Great Hall as the servants pushed the doors open, revealing all their hard work from the past few days.

The ballroom had been repainted a dusty purple-blue that was ornamented with glittering light spells as the paint faded to the floor. Obscurum Mist rolled in on the floor in deep black and grey wisps. The floor was relaid in an obsidian and pearl checkered pattern like a chess board. The sides of the room where tables and seating were arranged was solid obsidian flooring – separating the dance space from the resting space. Every table was adorned with small lanterns of fairy light wrapped in black, transparent tulle ribbon.

"Shall we?" Lord Caligo offered me his arm. I took it and allowed myself to be led into the stunning new ballroom. Upon the entry of the Queen, a lively band began to play from above. A balcony was installed to provide a separate floor space for the guests. I saw in front of us a table on a raised platform — for the Queen – and just below it, a heavily decorated couple's table made up for only us. The Queen was ushered to her seat above everyone, and our other guests filed in after Umbriel and me. He led us to our table by arcing around to the right. I looked at him questioningly, but his response was a mysterious smirk.

As the table drew nearer, Umbriel took my hand to lead me. Swiftly and without warning, he spun me around and began a short dance in front of our seats. He concluded by dipping me backward. The crowd was awash with glee, thunderous applause rang throughout the room and I swore that I heard a few women swoon. I looked up expecting to see Umbriel looking at me, but instead, he and the Queen locked eyes – sharing a silent conversation. As he raised me, the applause grew to a deafening level. Umbriel led me to the table and pulled out my chair for me. I was grateful to finally sit. The Queen's face was glowing, and Umbriel swelled with pride as he sat in his seat beside me.

The Queen raised her hands for quiet. The band ceased playing and the audience slowly came to a quiet.

"It is with great honor that I announce: Let this ball begin!" She beamed her brilliant inner light through the whole ballroom, then dispersed it into millions of particles of glittering dust that showered the crowd. The crowd released a cheer of joy and surprise while the band took up playing again. Several guests began to wander onto the dance floor, and those who did not dance would take turns admiring the decor and praising my mother for it. Some came to visit us at our couple's table, and most only praised Lord Caligo for his 'exquisite catch'. I was a mere statue, something to be admired but never spoken to. I had not felt this way since the birth of my brother, the true heir as the only son.

I watched the door that led out to the Great Hall. No one else came in, but I watched as the kitchen staff replenished the dinner spread at Mrs. Sykes' behest. A sharp smack on the table drew my attention back to the people before me. It was only Umbriel – his expression was sour and stern.

"I have been speaking to you. Why do you never pay attention?" he asked. I felt my temper rise and prayed for it to remain hidden.

"I do not know what you mean. I am not mishearing you on purpose. It is quite loud in here."

"Your excuses are irrelevant. Now that you and I are publicly betrothed, you must appear somewhat amused by me. Pay attention. It is time for us to take to the floor." Umbriel stood, offering me his right hand.

"I–" I stopped, taking his hand. There was no use in continuing this argument, not with the Queen directly behind me and my mother lurking heavens knows where. The music lulled to a stop, the end of a song, then began a new one with a slow, romantic melody. Umbriel led us in the newest dance from the human realm, called an Almain, which was a very bouncy, spinning dance that turned us all around the room. My dress glittered and sparkled as we spun past the sitting crowd. I began to feel self-conscious about my internal light radiating through the dress, illuminating it too much. The tiara pulled on my hair like an angry child.

I could feel everyone's eyes on me and had nowhere to look but Lord Caligo. He kept smirking like some plan had been perfectly hatched. It made me uneasy how often he looked at Vesperia and the Queen. Thankfully, the song came to an end and I pried myself from Umbriel's grasp, forgetting the customary bow to one's partner afterward. I practically ran to the table, eager to take my seat. I quickly sat down, hoping to make it look as though I needed to catch my breath.

Lord Caligo stalked over to our table and looked directly at the Queen. Some unspoken words passed between them. She sent up a sunbeam into the ceiling that exploded into dust, and everyone responded with awe. Their attention was drawn to our table where Umbriel was using his shadow magic to build an archway with clear spaces for embellishment – spaces which were soon filled with glittering star clusters by my sister. The Queen descended her pedestal and approached us, materializing an ornate book with a gold ribbon marking a page. It was eerily like a holy book; my heart began to race.

"We apologize, everyone, this will take but a moment. You are free to stay and join us in uniting these two noble houses forevermore," she announced. Joyful whispers erupted around me. Lord Caligo offered me a hand up. I took it, only to notice that I was shaking. I stood carefully as he led me to the altar of shadows and stars. The Queen met us and I realized I could not feel my feet. My siblings approached the altar, which felt sacrificial, with matrimonial items. Vesperia carried a bouquet of Caligo blue roses, and Castor bore a ceremonial goblet that we were both to drink from after we said the vows. Castor stood behind Umbriel , stone-faced and avoiding eye contact. Vesperia, however, was all too pleased to have caught my wandering eye. She gifted me a sneer of great displeasure.

Lord Caligo took both my hands in his, making us both face each other. Everything was coming together the way it should, but not the way I wanted it to. The Queen drew in a deep breath, opening her text, then running a finger down the page until she found the passage she sought. As she read the passage aloud, I caught none of the words. Everything passed by and through me with little to no effect. The only thing that I could feel was the needle-like pain in my head from the weight of the tiara and the burning stare of my mother behind me. For a fleeting moment, I thought of running, making a break for the garden door, flying away, and never coming back.

No. Stop. You must stay, you promised you would make the best of this. I took in Lord Caligo in his blue and black regalia, a tunic and trousers that blended him into the shadows. His mothy wings carefully folded down and behind him like a cape. He was smiling at me with the most ingenuine smile I had ever seen from a fae. I looked at Castor one more time, but he stared at the floor.

"Will you, Lord Umbriel Caligo, join into this family, The Astrums, to strengthen its numbers and carry on its generations, forsaking your own clan – the house of Caligo – to become Lord Astrum the Third?" the Queen addressed Umbriel. My eyes snapped back to his face; he exuded joy.

"I will!" he said enthusiastically, projecting his voice for the whole room to hear above all the whispers.

"Will you, Lady Seren of Twilight Hall, The First Star, heir to the Astrum house, allow this humble realm servant to join you as your beloved always?" the Queen asked me. Now I began to feel the eyes of the room shift to me. I looked around to verify and wished that I had not.

The room seemed to wait on bated breath. Not a breeze, sneeze, or cough flew through the air. I could not bring myself to speak. Castor saw me, and finally, I pled with my eyes for him to do something – anything. He stared back, confused. I felt my arms go numb.

"Lady Seren?" the Queen asked with the tiniest twinge of annoyance that was barely perceptible. I looked at her and allowed my fear to show – my uncertainty. Her expression was hot and blinding. I felt tears well in my eyes, so I turned back to Umbriel, who was glaring furiously.

"I-I…" I stammered. They all looked at me with growing frustration, the room anticipating an answer. "No. I cannot."

A gasp ripped through the room from all the guests. The Queen began to burn more brightly with rage. Umbriel was maintaining his false cool face, though his eyes swirled with malice. He held onto my hands tightly.

"I am so sorry," I cried, the tears falling as I pulled my hands free from Lord Caligo's grasp. Then, I pried the heirloom from my finger. I pressed it into his hand while he gaped at me.

"I am sorry," I said again, then turned and ran towards the door of the ballroom. The crowd parted for me. I saw the open hallway as my saving escape. Through the open ballroom doors, I saw the front door, wide open and welcoming. Jumping into the air and spreading my wings, I flew to the door, only to feel an immense and burning pain spread across my back and down my spine. I fell to the ground, my gown engulfed in flames, my body in agony. The last thing I heard was a glass-shattering shriek I could not place, then it was all dark.

Chapter Twenty-One

The floor was hard, gritty, and cold. Opening my eyes made my head hurt so I kept them shut. I slowly collected my bearings. I was on the floor, my back burned in agony, and my head throbbed. Shakily, I was able to get on my hands and knees. They hurt like they were scraped or bruised. I crawled forward, bumping into a stone wall with my knuckles after crawling a few feet. I followed the wall with my hand, crawling along the floor until I came to a door. My eyes tried to peek open again, but there was too much light, so I shut them again.

Passing by the door, I was stung with the cruel bite of iron. I jerked my hand away, stifling a cry. My back ached, but I continued forward until my head smacked into a new wall, ringing erupting in my ears. I followed this wall until I came to a piece of furniture. I did not dare open my eyes again for fear that the light would burn. I used my hands to explore the item and found it was a box of straw for a bed with a threadbare blanket. On the other side of the box was another wall running perpendicular to the one I had left to explore the box. I felt a cool breeze and assumed this was the exterior wall. I used my right hand to explore the wall while I leaned on my left, my back screaming in pain. I found a small round window with no glass. The air was freely flowing in.

The pain was too great. I dropped down to the floor again, crying out in pain. I wanted to lay on my back, to rest, but the pain was excruciating. With all my effort, I pulled my body into a sitting position, biting my lip to keep from crying out. I moved so that the window, the source of light, was at my back. I felt more confident in opening my eyes now that my face was away from the light, so I slowly opened my eyes. It hurt, but after a few blinks, I began to adjust to the intense light.

The room I was in was a small stone cell with an iron door, which had a small rectangular slot in the middle. The box I had found was a wooden box filled with straw and a white threadbare blanket with many holes. In the middle of the room was an overturned chamber pot. I prayed it was empty. The grit on the stone was crumbling moss and stone mixed in with dirt and straw. I wiped my hands on my gown and discovered I had been redressed. Someone had removed my mother's gown and replaced it with a basic tunic dress-like chemise of grey linen. I felt violated. I pulled my legs under me and curled into the fetal position, careful to keep my back from touching the wall.

I stayed that way, huddled over until my calves burned, wondering. *Who had done this to me? Who had dressed me? Why am I here?* The more I thought about it the more my head hurt. *I remember the ball... and leaving... wait – no. I attempted to leave, but someone stopped me.* I continued to decode my memory loss. My back and calves now burned with the same intensity, eating at my nerves. I fought the urge to lay back down because I had to figure out why my back was in so much pain. I knelt forward on the gritty stone and twisted my right arm over my head to reach between my shoulder blades. Where there should have been the familiar threads of my wings, there was nothing – panic set in.

I reached my left arm under and around to feel the remaining space across my back – still nothing. Instead of glossy wings, I felt the dry sticky mess of a fresh scab, quite a large one. Tears flooded my eyes and I began to sob. Each shaky breath heaved through my body eliciting more pain from my back. I mourned the loss of my wings, and with each sob, I felt my heart harden to lead. I cried, clawing at my clothing until it came off. I saw the stain from a large pool of blood that had spread and dripped down the back. I held the dress to my chest, my nails digging into the fabric. The sobs devolved into a hyperventilating coughing fit filled with tears. Now my chest and back ached in pain from each cough.

"HEY! Shut up!" someone yelled, banging on the door. I gasped and held the dress to my face, smothering the sound, attempting to catch my breath. I shuddered and swallowed each sob.

"Wait! What am I doing here?" I choked out. I waited, but no answer came. I returned to sobbing, only this time quietly. After a time, I began to shiver from the breeze. Though it was wet from my tears, I pulled the dress back on. I crawled into the straw bed, pulling the threadbare blanket over me, and then with the knowledge that my wings were gone and I was a prisoner somewhere, I cried myself to sleep.

☆

The menacing sun was falling when I opened my eyes next. I peeled off the blanket and stopped at the sight of my fingers. I held my left hand in front of my face and examined the blackening of my fingers. *Is this the plague? Is this why I have been locked away?* My hands ran over my face, not finding any boils or pustules. I also did not feel the way humans had described the plague as feeling. I would be the first fae to contract a human virus, which led me to believe that was not why my fingers were black.

The lead in my heart grew heavier when I connected the evidence. This was all a side effect of wing removal. *Inertirus magic? Was I turning to ash?* My heartbeat quickened. I wondered how long I had when the rectangle on the door slid open with a loud clang. A tray was set on the ledge, balancing precariously. I scurried over on my hands and knees to grab the large wooden tray. Once I had my hands on it, a hand shoved it off the ledge and slammed the small rectangular slot closed followed by the heavy metal sound of a lock being bolted.

My dinner consisted of a roll, some grey sludge, and a pile of peas. A wax-sealed note was hiding under my roll, the first item I had picked to eat. *I guess I should be glad it was not hidden under...whatever this grey stuff is.* I picked it up and saw that it was sealed with my mother's family crest, the Lucidus spark in scarlet wax. Using my left thumb, I ripped the seal opening the letter. I read the letter penned in a quick scratchy hand.

My dearest sister Seren,

I have not long to write this to you, but I fear they will not tell you and will keep you blind as part of your punishment.

After the Queen hit you wish a sun ray, mother's gown went up in flames and you fell to the floor. Against orders, several servants splashed you with water to douse the flames, but the damage had been done.

You did not wake for some time. Both the Queen and our mother attempted to reanimate you, but you remained unresponsive until father summoned your lady's maid. He and she were able to rouse you enough to call a physician, but again, the damage was done.

Your wings can never be restored.

I am deeply sorry for you, though there is more. Because of the nature of your departure the question arose: Is wing stripping the new protocol for the unseelie?. The Queen left soon after, but the rumors persist. The counsel of four will be convening soon to decide your fate. Father has sobered enough to put in a few good words and insist you get a trial.

In a couple days, you will have a trial to determine if you are Unseelie or something else entirely

I wish you luck and swift healing.

forever your loyal brother,

Castor Astrum

I traced his signature with a black-tipped finger. They had stripped me of my wings and had no real reason with which to defend themselves. Hot angry tears splashed from my face onto the letter as more sobs wracked my body. Someone banged on the door, telling me to be quiet again. I cried silently and tried to eat my peas with my hands. The roll I tore into pieces, at first to try the sludge, but it was terrible, so I continued eating the roll by pulling pieces off. The small metal slot opened again with a clatter.

"Tray!" a man commanded. I set it down on the ledge, and meaty hands ripped it off and the metal door closed again. Turning back to the cell, I took in the serious state of things. Castor had put himself at considerable risk writing to me and somehow getting it to me.

I have to prepare for this trial, I stood up. Pacing around the cell with a cold stone floor kept my mind turning, but the dimming light was counteracting all the energy I was building to scheme. After looking out the window, I judged that I had about thirty minutes of daylight left. The thought gave me a start. *Would they bring me a candle?* I doubted they would. I stopped pacing to retrieve the letter and look over it again. Reading the lines 'after the Queen hit you with a sun ray'... 'your wings can never be restored' brought back all the aches and burns I had forgotten.

The trial mattered, but not enough. My flight would never return; I would become like the wingless. To add insult to injury, I might be labeled Unseelie for the rest of my life. One hundred seventy years would be a long time to be seen as selfish and opportunistic. I continued pacing, letter in hand, contemplating my next move. How was I going to win a trial? I could show off my wounds and suggest that maiming one's subject is cruel, but that could lead to more trouble later – and easily mark me as Unseelie for rebellious acts. I turned and walked from the door to the window, watching the sunset behind the mountain range. Leaning on the short windowsill, I admired the pinks and oranges painting the sky.

"I must be in Lux. The Obscurum mists are not visible, " I said aloud to myself. I could see a handful of hazy stars poking through the last of the sunlight. My cell rapidly lost light, driving me to panic. I faced the door and waited for what seemed like too long. The room became shadow-shrouded as the sky turned darker and darker blues. Still, they did not bring a candle. I stepped forward, away from the window, and began to summon the energy for my spell. I felt the essence of magic gather around me, and I held it until it was the consistency of a ball of light and willed it alive. Nothing happened, not unusual after trauma. I started again, this time imagining three spheres of light coming into existence. The essence gathered but a strange tingling sensation erupted from my extremities.

"Ah!" I yelped as the pain intensified with my spell, shooting through my body like lightning. I fell to the floor, my feet feeling like standing on hot coals. All the light in the room was gone now. I sat on the cold stone floor, watching the distant flicker of torches filter under the iron door. The cool stone felt saintly on my burning feet. I felt them on the underside of my forearm and found that they were truly hot. My fingertips also gave off a radiating heat that only calmed when pressed to the cool stone.

I waited in the cold dark for what seemed like an hour before my feet felt ok enough for me to move. A light sting greeted me when I put weight on my feet, standing. I used the dim flickering torchlight from under the door to guide me as I shuffled towards the straw box. Walking was not as painful and my hand did not hurt when I gingerly picked up the threadbare blanket. I pulled it around my shoulders like a cloak. It did little to trap my minimal body heat, but it did give me a false sense of security that I accepted eagerly. I shuffled back to the window, leaned on the thin strip of windowsill, and looked out.

A dull glow from below signaled to me that I was above the Lux castle. The spherical building was like a grounded sun, always burning bright. The glow did not dull the glimmer of the distant stars above. They shone against the black, velvet sky in defiance of the luminous fair folk below. I gazed longingly at the sky and then my heart broke for the hundredth time. Never again would I soar through the sky, hoping to touch those stars. Tears in my eyes made the sky blurry, obstructing my view. Suddenly, a warm hug-like feeling blossomed in my gut. I sniffled and fought the tears back, then looked around, only to be drawn back to the sky.

Above me, against the black sky, the white stars danced. There was no way for me to know if anyone else could see what I saw, but I knew I was not imagining things. First, they twisted from left to right. Some flew beside others, awakening them to the festival above. Shapes began to form like clouds did on breezy summer days. The stars formed new bodies outside of the mapped constellations, stepping ever closer to one another. I wiped away my heartache tears and gave all my attention to the sky. Four figures appeared in a row, like a wall. A fifth figure approached them, smaller. The four figures did not move. Instead, as the fifth figure approached, one by one, each of the four pointed an accusatory finger at the fifth. The lone figure stood taller, facing the accusers, back straight. The accusers advanced, hands raised in attack, enveloping the fifth. The stars became jumbled and shapeless, I could not decipher where one figure ended and the next began. I watched and waited until the figures separated and revealed the fifth figure swaying unsteadily on the ground. The four victors laughed and pointed back in the direction the fifth had come from, banishing them.

The stars burst from their temporary places back to their normal high homes. I blinked, confused, but instead of tearing apart what I had just witnessed, I calmed my heart and mind by finding all the Mythénian constellations. The Big and Little Bears were both to my right but cut off by the view from my small window. I could just make out the back half of the Little Bear's hindquarters as he followed his mother, the Big Bear, across the sky each night. The Bovine was grazing peacefully in the leftmost part of the sky I could see. The Fighting Rams clashed below The Bovine – eternally locked in a power struggle. To their right was a larger constellation: Pegasus. Pegasus flew against the current of the sky; she roamed wherever she pleased. Her story resonated with the free spirit of all equine folk. My last identifiable constellation was Draconia, well the left wing of Draconia.

Now with some fresh peace of mind, I began to mull over the vision I was granted. I mused to myself how strange it was for me to be unable to conjure a simple light spell without intense pain, but still be able to see visions in the sky. Regardless, I had been shown something and now had to ascertain the meaning. I gave the stars one more longing stare before settling into the straw sleeping box. It was cold and scratchy, the blanket not big enough to cover myself and the box, so I submitted to the torment of the scratchy straw while I covered myself with the blanket, ruminating over the message. Sleep or exhaustion, I could not tell, came for me swiftly. I barely had the chance to form my thoughts before I was nodding off. The faint idea that the vision was warning me of my impending fate lingered at the forefront of my imagination, training my dream to torment me with the idea of being executed over and over again. My sleep was restless and full of nightmares.

Chapter Twenty-Two

I awoke with a start, light stinging my eyes. The slot in the iron door was open and a tray waited. I scrambled over as fast as I could, only to watch the tray fall to the stone floor as I was close enough to touch it. The tray clattered against the stone, scattering the elements of my meager breakfast. I had been given a serving of hot porridge and a stale bread heel. The porridge was unsalvageable, so I picked up the bread off the floor and brushed off the grime. I did my best to clean the mess up and placed the tray neatly by the door. The bread was not filling, but it chased away the pangs of hunger tormenting my stomach.

While I gnawed on the stale heel of a loaf, I thought back to the vision I had last night. Four figures worked together to banish the fifth, a new arrival, who was smaller than the first four. *Perhaps it means that the four leaders of the regions will reprimand me? Or maybe mother?* The figures had no distinguishing features, making it harder to distinguish who they were. *Perhaps it is my family banishing Lord Caligo.* I mused that thought, swallowing the last bite of bread.

The sun shone brightly through the small window, illuminating the cell and casting a bright pool of light against the wall. It was early morning, I assumed. I crawled back into my sleeping box, covering my eyes to pass through the rays of the sun. I retrieved Castor's letter and re-read it for any clues, but found none. Left with more questions than answers, I tucked the letter away again into the straw.

Three concise bangs erupted from the other side of the door, but the slot in the door did not open, so I remained seated in the straw. I assumed they were accosting someone else nearby. I was sorely mistaken when I heard the locking mechanism open with a solid clank. Three fully armored men rushed in. My heart leapt into my throat as horrible thoughts flooded my mind. All I could utter was a choked scream as they grabbed me. Two of the men pulled my arms and legs away from my body – one held my wrists and the other held my ankles. The third slapped metal cuffs to my wrists connected by a short chain, then another set on my feet. Then they lifted me up and set me on my shackled feet.

"Go," one of my captors commanded. The shackles on my ankles allowed me to take short shuffling steps rather than the longer strides I was used to. I obeyed the command and marched out the door of my cell. The hallway was a short stone corridor with no other cells; mine was the only one. At the end of the corridor, I found a descending staircase of stone that curved tightly from right to left. I had to step forward carefully with one foot before the second could join. I moved slowly down the steps with my captors close behind me.

"Where are you taking me?" I mustered the courage to ask. They gave no reply – only silence. I continued down the stairs. The tension in the stairwell was tangible. I could tell they wanted me to go faster, but short of throwing myself down the stairs, this was the fastest I could go. Finally, I reached the bottom of the tower, exhausted, only to find a heavy wooden door reinforced with vertical metal bars. One of the guards shoved past me roughly to pound on the door.

"Door! Prisoner in chains!" he called. Someone answered on the other side, followed by the heavy sound of large locks being turned. The door swung open away from us and into the new room. The next room was obviously the main dungeon. Cells lined the corridors, of which there were two: a right and a left, identical.

"That way." The guard shoved me to the left corridor. I tried not to peek into the cells of the other prisoners, but I could not stop myself. Something in my mind told me that someone I loved was there. Each prisoner I did see would glare or snarl in my direction. I never saw anyone that I knew. I waddled down the corridor barefoot and embarrassed until we reached a set of ornate wooden doors, reinforced with metal in a swirling floral pattern – like vines. Two guards worked together to muscle open the large doors once the large cylindrical lock was removed. The remaining guard took my elbow and led me through the doors into an open entrance hall.

This hall was a large room made of pillars supporting the overhead, domed roof. The guards walked me across this Great Hall and into a very formal, made-up courtroom. It was painted in pale yellow floor to ceiling. To my left was a gallery of benches separated from the larger floor by a waist-high wall. There was a singular table by itself a few paces from the short wall, and then opposing the singular table was a row of four tables sitting next to each other in a row. Lit candelabras were set at the ends of each table. I was led to the singular table in the middle. My ankle shackles were then attached to a long chain affixed to the ground.

"Do not move. You are to wait here until your trial begins. Do you understand?" the guard spoke down to me as I sat down on the wooden chair.

"Yes," I answered, forcing a monotone voice. The guard huffed and walked away to stand at the doors we had just come through. I twisted in my seat to survey the room. The gallery of benches guarded a second doorway, also fixed with double doors.

"Face forward!" the guard yelled at me. I turned back quickly, facing the row of high tables. I waited on my seat for what felt like hours, and the chair began to make my butt go numb. Then, a loud creak from behind me signaled that the double doors were opening. I dared not look for fear of being reprimanded again. I became self-conscious about the blood stain on my back and worried who would see it and what they would think. *Would they think it is my fault?* From what I could discern, the gallery behind me was filling. A herald appeared in my field of vision from the doors to my right. He walked toward the middle of the room, in front of the high tables. He turned sharply like a soldier to face the room. He did not look at me, or anyone, it seemed. His face remained blank and uninterested. A guard stood to my right, not speaking to me either. The gallery began to sound full of murmurs and whispers that coagulated into one loud buzz of conversation. The guard next to me roughly grasped my arm and yanked me to my feet the moment the herald called for attention.

"All rise for the honourable lords and ladies of the high court!" he yelled, his voice carrying through the courtroom, silencing the gallery. The gallery stood, and I was nudged to turn left, facing the gallery. My mother and father entered the room stiffly, followed closely by my siblings. They sat on the empty bench directly behind me. I was suddenly morbidly embarrassed to appear so disheveled in front of them. Only Castor spared a glance for me; it read like an obituary.

"Welcome our esteemed guests, King and Queen Alces, of our neighbor, Fauna!" the herald announced. A pair of beautiful and heavily decorated deerfolk walked through the gallery doors. They took their time walking down the aisle towards the high tables. They wore matching outfits of deep, forest green silk tunics. Queen Alces wore a dress tunic and King Alces wore a traditional tunic with trousers. The green highlighted their dark ruddy brown fur and gold accessories. The King's antlers shone with tiny chains looped around each prong with dangling gemstones at the end of each chain. Both had long, straight black hair pulled back into low heavily-braided styles. They took their seats at the first of the high tables at the far left, the King pulling out his Queen's chair for her before sitting himself.

"Welcome, our esteemed guests, the King and Queen Crystallus, of our adjacent neighbor, Element," the herald called. I recognized these two; I had stayed with them for a few months while on my tour. The large blocky man with deep, red skin marred by granite-like veins running across his body and face was escorting his beautiful crystalline wife, who looked like a living piece of emerald. The King's red hair could easily be mistaken for rocks the way it was shaped, pointed out from his forehead and down to his shoulders. The Queen's hair was sleek black, matching the large stones set on her dress. The King wore a robe of muddy brown, while the Queen wore a blood-red dress adorned with large chunky black crystals around the neckline and hem. They walked with purpose, the Queen leading and the King following, to the second table from the left – next to the Alces. King Crystallus pulled out his Queen's chair, as well.

"Welcome our esteemed guest, King Sequoia, of our neighbor, Flora!" the herald bellowed. The doorway was eclipsed by the largest of dryads. I had not stayed with the King during my travels; he was a sight to behold. His branches brushed the ceiling and he had to duck to avoid the rafters.

The Great Redwood....Hyperion...

Once he stood up straight, his crown flattened against the ceiling. King Sequoia lurched slowly forward down the aisle to take the first table on the right, directly in front of me. He wore no clothing, as his bark was like thick fur, but he did wear an ornamental crown of flowers arranged near his face. He attempted to sit, but the furniture was not to his size, he crushed the chair with a loud crack. Shrugging, he sat cross-legged on the floor behind the small table. He looked like a very tall father playing dolls with his children.

"Queen Helia Solaris welcomes you all to the trial of The First Star of Inanis, " the herald announced, quickly moving to stand next to the doors I came in on the right.

"Bow," the guard behind me ordered, pushing on my shoulder. I bowed my head and bent my knees as much as I could without losing my balance. The Queen sauntered in and the doors were shut behind her. She paraded herself down the aisle until she stood where the herald had been. She faced the gallery and addressed them with open arms.

"Hello, my faithful servants. You are all here to witness and report what you see here today. Today, you will witness the trial of Seren Astrum. You will hear from the lords and ladies of the high court – our decision will be final. I have already removed my vote, as it is believed by some that I may be unable to remain impartial. Do not fear, gentle folk, our perpetrator is restrained." She gestured to me and the entire gallery shuffled to look at me. I was grateful that I was turned to the side and that they all could not see my gruesome back. "Let us begin!"

Queen Helia took her seat at the remaining table, and the guard turned me and forced me down into the chair again.

"Seren Astrum, you are brought here to answer for the crime of insubordination and rebellion. If this court were not called for you, my choice would have been execution. Due to the nature of your injuries, you have been granted this one chance to convince this panel that you are worthy of living. This will be your chance to speak before the gallery of your peers and your accusers. Tell us, why did you disobey a direct order from your Queen?" Queen Solaris questioned. She waved her hand for me to stand and address the panel. I stood and bowed over my table to each of the highnesses.

"Hello, everyone," my voice trembled. " I am grateful for the opportunity to explain." I could feel the eyes of the gallery glued to my back, on the bloodstain. I straightened my spine, set my jaw to a mild smile, and faced the Kings and Queens of Mythénia.

"If I may," I looked at each one, "I would like to start from a place farther from the incident." I had to think on my feet – I had not had enough time to prepare a good defense.

"Go on, " King Sequoia's rumbling voice answered as he waved a hand for me to continue.

"Thank you. I will start with my diligent participation in my Scholastic Tour, where I spent at least one night in each of your realms. I was, by our gracious Queen Solaris, to experience the realms and advance my abilities – which I have done. This scholastic tour lasted five years. Five years away from my family and home. I am grateful for the experience to be sure, but upon my return, I was immediately instructed that I was to wed a man I had never met. This is not uncommon, I know, but so quickly after my homecoming? I was taken aback, and yes, a bit cross. I believe that the abilities I grew while on my tour could be used to help my region and the realm, if permitted," I stated. Queen Solaris was not amused. However, King and Queen Crystallus urged me on despite the whispers in the gallery.

"I came home after my tour hoping to assist my region and community with my gifts, not by changing my marital status."

"Enough! Sit," Queen Solaris snapped. A murmur from the gallery erupted, silencing any more orders from the Kings and Queens. I returned to sitting as comfortably as I possibly could. The numb feeling in my buttocks returned swiftly. The room was half full of whispers and low voices. The Kings and Queens talked amongst themselves, except for Queen Solaris, who remained silent. Queen Crsytallus stood, addressing the room. Silence fell in the gallery.

"We remember your stay with us at Crystal Palace. We were awestruck by your abilities and the rate at which you had developed with no formal teacher. Though, you cannot seriously believe that you would lead your community alone?" she asked me, her gem-like eyes cutting into me.

"Yes, Your Majesty. I worked very hard to become a powerful First Star. I was under the impression that that was what the Queen Solaris wanted," I replied softly. Her eyes, and those of the gallery, bored into me.

"I see," Queen Crystallus said as she returned to her seat.

"I would like to see these abilities," King Sequoia's voice boomed. The other Kings and Queens nodded in agreement. Queen Helia beckoned to the people behind me – my family. My siblings approached the high tables and then walked to a spot on the floor that she pointed to. They stood against the wall to my left, awaiting further instruction.

"Stand," she barked at me. I stood, and with the snap of her fingers, the guard beside me unlocked my shackled feet, allowing me to stand near the rightmost wall, with the door I had come in from.

"The younger Astrums will demonstrate their abilities, and then the eldest will be judged on her ability to duplicate the spells," she announced. A rumble erupted from the gallery. "I promise you no harm will come to you gentlefolk. Observe." She flourished her hand in my siblings' direction. Vesperia glanced at our mother in the gallery before stepping forward. With a wry smile, she took up her casting pose and began to draw power. She manifested the energy into a small hovering light that radiated like a closely burning star. The white light bounced off the floor and her face painting her angelically. The Queen gestured for me to make my own attempt. I already knew what would happen, but I could not disobey the Queen right now. Everyone waited for me, their eyes stuck to me like the scab on my back.

Against my feelings of fear, I drew all the energy that I could withstand. Pain burned through my toes and fingertips. I watched as the blackened tips crept further up my fingers, reaching my second knuckles. I could not form any shape. Biting my lip to keep from crying out, I lost control of the energy and it dissipated. My eyes met my sister's bewildered stare. She stepped back after disassembling her spell. The Queen held a triumphant smirk across her face.

"Can you not perform even the simplest of light enchantments?" she almost giggled.

"No, Your Majesty," I murmured.

"Speak up when speaking to your Queen!" she demanded. I flinch at her raised voice.

"No your majesty," I projected my voice. "But I–"

"Silence!" Queen Solaris roared, her inner glow growing to a blinding height. We all squinted, and some of the gallery and high court shielded their eyes. I wished I could do the same, but my hands were still shackled together. A guard led me back to my seat after the Queen dimmed her light, then snapped at Castor and Vesperia to sit back down. They scurried off and returned to our parents. Castor shot me a quick, heartbroken look.

"Queen Helia, if I may, allow me to inspect the prisoner?" King Alces asked, standing. He and his Queen's black deer eyes absorbed all the light that shone on them.

"You may," she answered the King, then turned to me, ordering me to stand with a snap of her fingers. I stood quickly before the guard had any chance to grab me. I padded to a spot she indicated and stood as tall as I could bear. He approached me, inspecting me like Aurora inspected foreign beds. He pulled the collar of my gown away from my back, then leaned in to peer down my back. The cold chains from his antlers brushed my bare shoulder. I fought the urge to shiver and back away.

Next, he lifted each of my hands and squeezed each finger one at a time, making a small hum of thought every time I winced or flinched. He glanced at my bare feet, but did not inspect them in the same way. He faced Queen Solaris.

"I think she has been fully separated from the essence, Your Grace." He bowed. I bit the inside of my cheek, fighting back tears.

"She will not wield any magic, and any attempt will increase this rot on her body. We can call a Cruor healer if you wish to learn more. To put it bluntly – she is barely a fae now." A single tear escaped my eye.

King Alces returned to his seat, and the handsy guard came and led me back to my chair. King Alces spoke with his Queen and then addressed us again.

"We pose a question. What is to become of her? Surely she cannot be Seelie. Her actions are clearly selfish, but if we mark her Unseelie, does that mean we will maim all Unseelie in the future?" he flung an accusatory tone towards Queen Solaris. She stiffened in her seat. The gallery erupted into chatter, and the Kings and Queens followed suit.

Chapter Twenty-Three

Many attempts were made to quiet the masses in the gallery. Eventually, the gallery was hushed by the herald and Queen Solaris. King Alces and Queen Solaris stood facing each other. He had accused her of an Unseelie act – if she were to face repercussions, I could leave and be free again.

"You were not in attendance, Oisín! You know not what you speak of! She defied a direct order from her Queen and her parents. I am not the one on trial!" she screeched. All my hopes were violently dashed to dust.

"Your grace, let us keep our composure! We simply must know what is to happen to her," King Alces insisted.

"What do you propose then? Do you wish to take her to your realm?"

"No!" Queen Alces yelped, her doe eyes wide. King Alces returned to reassure his wife. A pit opened in my stomach, sucking in my heart slowly. The Alces spoke to each other in hushed tones while glancing around the room. I followed their eyes, flicking my gaze to each corner they looked at. King Sequoia had retreated into himself, pulling leaves and petals off of his flower crown and the sides. Queen Crystallus was eyeing Queen Solaris with envy, the King staring off into the gallery.

"We cannot agree to take on a risk like her without marking her Unseelie and sowing chaos in our region," King Alces finally announced. He gave a nod of finality and sat in his chair without another word, lightly wrapping an arm around his Queen.

Queen Solaris composed herself with a deep sigh. She paced the floor in front of the high tables, her burning eyes locking onto mine when she turned to face the other direction. She stopped in front of me.

"We shall all cast a vote. Let us decide what the options are before us." She started to pace again, her wings shining brightly with every step. "Seelie or Unseelie for sure, but shall we add another?"

The room was relatively silent – there were only a few murmurs from the gallery. I turned my head to the left slowly, like I was watching the Queen as she paced, but I strained my eyes to look back at my family. Mother sat on the end nearest the aisle, then father next to her, Vesperia next to him, and Castor on the far end. At least, I assumed. I could not see him.

"We will not support execution, Helia." King Crystallus stood abruptly. Queen Crystallus stared past me at my family, giving me an uneasy feeling.

"Fine, Jasper. What else do you recommend?" Queen Solaris spat.

"Exile. Never to return," King Sequoia spoke up. Everyone's head spun to look at the dryad King.

"Please elaborate," Queen Alces requested with a dainty raised hand, her soft voice carrying through the quiet room.

"Exile," he continued, a chill piercing my bones as he spoke. "She may never return, and if she does, the punishment is death," King Sequoia declared, continuing to pick at the leaves in his flower crown. Queen Alces turned to her husband. Queen Solaris looked properly intrigued. She approached the herald, speaking a quiet command to him that immediately sent him fleeing from the courtroom through the gallery doors behind me. Leisurely, the Queen walked so that she was in front of my table. Maybe I was seeing things, or overly sensitive, but her inner glow seemed to pulse brighter as she glowered down at me. When she spoke, it felt as though she was speaking directly to me, but her voice carried through the entire room.

"While we await my servant's return, I would like Lord Umbriel the Third and Lady Astrum to approach. We have a broken treaty to mend before another war ravages my region." Her hot eyes raked over me. Shuffling from behind me, my mother appeared next to my table, though she did not look at me. My now ex-fiance approached as well, standing on the other side of my mother. They bowed low to the Queen until she tapped them lightly to rise.

"Honorable Lady Astrum, your house bears a heavy burden today. You must reconcile with the crown. What do you have to say of your daughter's treason?" Queen Solaris asked.

"My daughter has committed no treason, Your Majesty." Mother fell into a curtsey and I almost felt relieved. *She is defending me!*

"Excuse me? You are at the trial of your daughter, Seren Astrum, and yet you say she has committed no crime?" the Queen looked incredulously at my mother as she remained head down in a bow.

"Excuse me, your highness. I do not have a daughter named Seren. My only daughter's name is Vesperia." Mother's words blew apart all my carefully constructed composure. I felt my heart shatter and be sucked into the pit of my stomach. I felt dizzy and nauseous, the floor an inviting respite from this cruel trial. I used all my remaining strength to sit up and hide any emotion that I could.

"I see. That does make sense. How, then, do you, Lord Caligo, feel about a continued engagement to the Astrum Daughter?" Queen Solaris asked. Lord Caligo stepped forward one step and knelt on one knee.

"I would be honored to wed whomever my wise and generous Queen declares. Lady Astrum's daughter is a lovely choice, should I be so fortunate." His words made me feel hollow and cold. The Queen grew a bright toothy smile, twisted in wicked delight.

"Very good. Lady Astrum, call your daughter and let us ask her if she agrees to this betrothal."

My mother called my sister to her side, and they embraced so lovingly that my vision began to blur with tears. They queried her about her wishes and plans to enhance the Inanis Valley. Her answers must have been satisfactory, but I could not hear through the rushing blood in my ears. The floor still looked like a kind of relief.

Lord Caligo knelt in front of my sister, producing the Caligo heirloom ring. She nodded and he slid it onto her ring finger. The gallery applauded and the newly engaged couple was excused. Mother was then pardoned by the Queen and allowed to return to her seat. She spared no glances towards; she had disowned me.

Blood rushed into my head, the wind pulling through the hole where my heart had been. It was all so consuming. I felt nothing, saw nothing, heard nothing. My thoughts spun like a falling leaf with no real direction. *Vesperia, Umbriel, mother – they all betrayed me. What if this whole thing was a plot from the start?* That thought took root in my mind as the only plausible scenario. Anger boiled in my veins. *How could they?* My mind ran away from me. The anger hardened to a stone face when the herald returned with a handful of parchment. The space in my chest still oozed with pain, but I resolved that no one would see any more of my tears.

"– a piece of paper," Queen Solaris' voice broke through my mental fog. "Write Seelie, Unseelie, or exile. We will tally the results and the majority will be the deciding punishment. Whatever we decide now will also decide the next line of discussion. If, for instance, she were to be deemed Unseelie, we would then need to cast a vote to see where she will live out the remainder of her days.

"As long as she never returns to Effect, there will be no issue with me. We would also need to discuss how to address the Unseelie after this, should we all vote Unseelie, that is. So take your parchment and cast your vote." The herald passed out pieces of parchment to each King and Queen along with a quill and inkwell for each table. Everyone except Queen Solaris began to cast their vote.

"You expect us to cast a vote for the future of Mythénia?" King Sequoia bellowed. Queen Solaris faced him with what I imagined was a ruthless glare. He blanched and could not offer any more contradictions.

"As I thought." She faced the other Kings and Queens. "King Hyperion is not wrong – this is a very serious matter. Do not take it lightly. I am not. I have removed myself from the voting pool to ensure that this treacherous fae gets a fair trial." She walked over to her table and sat while everyone else made their decision.

A low, quiet hum filled the room as the gallery and high court began to talk amongst themselves. Internally, I fought the urge to turn my head and look around the room, especially at my family. I could feel eyes crawl over my back and the blood stain, and I wanted to see who was gawking.

Green, vine-like strings of essence flowed from King Sequoia's fingertip, drawing my attention. He used it to pick up the quill that was too small for his hands and guided it to write on his slip of parchment. I quickly looked down the tables at King and Queen Alces, who had not come to a decision, it seemed. They talked with their hands wildly flicking this way and that. I looked at King and Queen Crystallus only to see that King Jasper looked horrified while Queen Beryl had a cool resolve wrapped around her while she stared at the gallery. Each of their slips was neatly folded at the front of their table. My eyes slid back to the Alces – they had finished their private discussion and were writing on their slips of parchment. I forced myself to take a deep breath. It was shaky and I prayed no one saw the shudder that shook my whole body. While breathing in and out, quietly, I prayed the shaking would stop. *They will not see me cry. They will NOT see me cry.* I repeated in my head as I watched Queen Solaris collect each slip. When she had every slip in her hands she cupped her hands together, shaking them.

"I will read aloud the votes, and if there are any outbursts there will be severe consequences." The gallery went dead silent. The high court sat, stoically waiting. She took one slip and cleared her throat to read aloud.

"Exile." A gasp ran out from the gallery. The Queen glared at the gallery and a hush fell over them again. She set the read slip of parchment on her table. Pulling out the next slip, she unfolded it to read.

"Exile," she repeated, placing this slip on top of the first.

"Unseelie – Transfer," the Queen sighed, dropping this slip into a new pile. A glimmer of hope in the dark. I stared at the slip of parchment with the last slivers of hope I had in my broken heart.

"Exile," she continued, and the word began to sting. She placed that slip on the pile of other exile votes.

"Exile," she read again. It was the last slip. She placed it on her table with the rest with what looked like a hint of true joy upon her face. My whole body went cold, and I began to anxiously assume what would happen next. The Queen wiped the paper from her table, and I watched the slips fall to the floor like snow as she lifted herself up to sit on the table.

"Seren Astrum, for the crime of treason, you are banished. Banished from Effection, banished from Mythénia, and if you ever return, you will be put to death. You are no longer Seren Astrum, the First Star of Inanis. Your name was a gift from the parents who have now disowned you. From now on, you will not call yourself by either of those names." Her command struck like a flaming arrow, piercing deep into my flesh, hitting bone. I was overwhelmed by feelings. I was cold, but I was also burning. I was dizzy, but I was overly conscious. I felt empty, but so unbelievably full.

The guards yanked me to my feet, and I gasped, letting out a small yelp. I saw my father lurch for me, but a hot hand from my mother stopped him. Castor's eyes pleaded with me. *'Do not fight them, I cannot watch you be hurt again'.* Vesperia's face betrayed her entirely. She wore no glamour to hide the champion-like grin of someone who had won a historic battle or slain a mighty beast. The guards pulled me to the dungeon door. I struggled against them, but my miniscule strength was no match for both guards. I tugged my arm away, but being shackled it did nothing but earned me a swift kick to my stomach from the guard to my right. I let out a wounded grunt and then I fell to the ground. A guard throwing me over his shoulder was the last thing I remembered before blacking out from the pain.

When I woke next, I was unbound and rolling around in a jail cart that was bumping its way along the dirt road towards Ingenium. The light outside was dim, early morning, and from what I could see, I was locked in. The jail cart was like a cage on wheels, but with bigger bars like the ones used for transporting dangerous animals. *Is that what I am now, a dangerous animal?* Through the bars, I could see Lux slowly fading into the distance. I must have been out for half a day.

Soon, we would be at Ingenium and I imagined the driver would want a break. I gave them no indication that I was awake, slowly sitting up listening to the mindless chatter between the guard and driver. There were two male voices. I was easily able to tell that they were tired. One started a conversation about food.

"Ah, why'd ya have ta do that?" the other guard replied.

"We will be done soon enough. You can get some of Aspen's lovely cookin' eh?" the first voice joked. They continued talking, but I became lost in my mind by plotting my escape. The cart rattled over the rocky dirt road until it met cobblestone again. We turned several times until we came to a stop in a dark courtyard.

This is my chance! They will have to take me inside for the night. I can stay awake and slip away when they nod off.

I pulled my feet under me and kept myself ready for what was next.

Through the bars, I saw a black unicorn with a darkly dressed rider join us in the courtyard. *A shadow guard, maybe sent by the Queen?* I made myself focus on the two men that drove my cart. They had hopped off and were headed inside, without me! A moment later, a Solarisian guard came out of the inn and exchanged words with the dark rider. The unicorn added his own opinion with a snort, but was urged to the cart.

Without a word to me, the men unhooked the beast that had been pulling the cart and hooked up the black unicorn. The dark rider took up the driver's seat and the Solarisian guard joined him. My plans of escape were thwarted. I curled up and began to cry silently. I still did not want them to know I was awake.

Daylight chased us as we left Ingenium and climbed the mountain towards the west portal. We were on the exact path I had taken home, but in reverse. I began to shake as my energy sapped with the cold. Watching every tree pass by ached like it was being ripped away from my physical body. Half of me wanted to close my eyes to shield myself from this strange pain, but the other half wanted the trees to be burned into my mind. I would never again see my home, so this was the next best thing. To remember the trees.

Odd that only a few weeks ago, I was in the human realm eager to return, melancholic because I could not bring the images of this exact forest to my mind. Now I could lose this image forever if I did not etch every tree, shrub, and stump into my memory. Tears filled my eyes as the wave of energy from the portal washed over me.

Please, no! I am not ready! Please! No! I screamed in my head, panicking. The tears spilled and sobs threatened to escape as we crossed through the West Gate and into the human realm.

Chapter Twenty-Four

Passing through the portal did not hurt. What hurt was leaving behind everything I had ever known – again. Except this time, for good. The cart stopped in a grove of trees where the Solarisian guard jumped down from his seat and opened the door to my cage.

"Come on." He reached his hand in for me to take it. I would not let him touch me. He grabbed for me, but I moved too quickly for him in his leather armor. "Stop it!" he yelled.

"Take me back!" I begged.

"Oh no. The Queen was firm on that. Get out before I make you. Or worse – kill you." His orange-gold eyes should have been warm, but they stung like ice. He gave me a very serious look that bid me to crawl to the door. He held his hand out for me to take it and I did. He then helped me out of the cart and shut the door.

"Now, my instructions are to leave you. That is what I will do. Do not try to follow us back through the portal, because if you do, our orders are to kill you. If you go that way," he pointed behind me, "you will find a small village where someone will help you." I looked in the direction he pointed and saw smoke wafting up from between the treetops. The trees here were preparing for winter, losing most of their leaves and showing only bare branches. The fallen leaves painted the ground gold.

The guard jumped back onto the cart and they drove away, leaving me there barefoot and alone. I sniffled back tears and turned towards the village, picking through the underbrush. Without shoes, every rock and twig were daggers. My soles became sore but I pressed on. Looking behind me I saw I was still alone. The path I was on became blocked by thick shrubs; I had to find another way. I looked for a wildlife trail and found a thin deer trail that curved around the large collection of thick shrubs.

The deer trail led me to a small brook. Crossing it felt heavenly on my feet as I stepped in. I stayed by the brook for a while, allowing my feet to soak and splashing my hands through the running water. I looked at the progression of the decay on my hands. The blackness had reached my last knuckles and my entire foot, but not yet my ankles. I was grateful that the ripples in the water distorted my reflection, as I did not want to see what I looked like after all that torment. The sun rose above me, slowly working its way towards its peak in the sky.

I hope everyone is happy now. Vesperia can have the lovely Lord Caligo – I know that will please her. Mother will have a perfect daughter. I hope they do not learn of the letter from Castor. If they do, I hope they will go easy on him for being the only male heir. I continued to play in the water as my thoughts grew darker. *What will they do to Aurora? Have they already done something*? I had no way to verify with what or if Aurora had been punished. Tears threatened my eyes as my only childhood friend lingered in my mind. I would never see her smile nor hear her musical laughter again. The tears escaped and ran down my cheeks. They dripped off my chin, splashing into the brook.

I pulled my knees to my chest and let myself sob fully. Hot tears flowed from my eyes, wetting my arms and creating a wet spot on my dress. Each sob hurt as it struck my lungs, so much so that I could not inhale without a spike of pain. Gasping, I clung to my curled legs and rode the waves of sorrow until there were no more tears left to cry. My sobs turned to wheezes as I calmed myself down. I doubted this would be the last time. Sniffles and hiccups followed. I wiped my eyes and splashed some water on my face. It helped smother the burning on my cheeks. I had had enough of the dirt and water. I stood up and brushed off my dress and hands. The grey smoke still plumed gently over the tops of the trees.

No trail was visible from where I stood. My path forward was through the underbrush or around. For fear of deadly vipers or vicious predators lurking in the shadows, I opted to circumvent the thick bushes impeding my direct route forward. Going around took longer, but I was able to find an animal trail that looped back toward the column of smoke.

Finally, after some distance, I found a path that led into the village. Walking on the rocky dirt path was uncomfortable but manageable. I began to approach the village but then decided better. Throwing myself back into the woods, I hid next to the path and waited. *This road could be guarded against outsiders – I cannot just walk in.* I carefully followed the road through the trees, walking alongside the path, but far enough away that the trees hid me from view.

The road widened to a messy, rut-worn town center. This village sat on a crossroads, it seemed. Cart trails came and went from multiple directions, all intersecting in the town just a few feet from where I stood.

Children ran across the road, headed straight for me. I whipped my head around frantically, looking for a place to hide. My only option was the bush I had been avoiding. Carefully, I pulled a few branches to the side and stepped in-between two closely grown prickly bushes, crouching low to hide myself.

The children burst through the tree line with serious force. Several leaves became dislodged, falling to the ground below. The gaggle of children consisted of four boys and one little girl. The boys ran ahead with the little girl following behind as best she could. They looked like they were trying to outrun her, but she was determined not to be left behind. Two of the boys picked up sticks and faced the girl.

"Halt!" one said in a stern falsetto. The girl stopped, her cheeks red from running but her grumpy expression firm.

"Come no further, *little girl*, for I am the Great Cecil and I will vanquish you with the help of my coven!" the boy yelled. I rolled my eyes.

"No! You cannot leave me alone! Mother said you had to take me with you today!" the girl cried, and my heart ached for her.

"We have no mothers! We are great sorcerers here to banish monsters! Are you a monster?" a boy in a red shirt called. The girl stood, mouth agape in confusion. She stepped back from the boys, unsure of what to do.

"N-no," she stammered.

"That is exactly what a monster would say!" one of the boys shouted.

"Get her!"

"No!" the girl screamed, taking off running. The boys chuckled and began their chase. A molten rage bloomed in my heart as they all came racing towards my hiding spot. Without much time to think, I stood up, revealing myself and startling all the children. They screamed, the little girl running to who I assumed was her elder brother.

"Oh no! No, no. It is alright. I will not hurt you. I only wanted you to stop chasing her with your sticks – uhm, wands?" I finished meekly, looking hopefully at the little girl. Her eyes were filled with terror as she clung to her brother. He held her with one arm and defended her with the same stick he had just attempted to attack her with.

"Who are you? What are you?" a brave boy with a black jacket asked in a demanding tone, brandishing his stick like a spear. I raised my hands in defense and the children moved back.

"My name is not important, I am a…" I trailed off. Master Wais had hammered into my memory the importance of never giving away our real names, and I could not tell these children that I was a fairy. After all, I could not prove it to them with magic or anything else.

"A traveler." Their eyes were still wild and uneasy. I looked to the little girl for solidarity, but only found pure horror.

"Thomas, does she have the plague?" she asked, frightened. Panicking, I reached forwards to reassure her, but that scared them all into running away. They disappeared through the trees like a herd of deer. When I followed them, I learned quickly that the children had called for their parents. Adults were running about, screaming about the plague. I slid back into the forest while the village whipped itself into a frenzy.

This is all my fault. I could not help but think that, at least. My mind was stuck on the portion of the Solarisian guard's instructions where he told me someone here might help me. *I ruined my only chance at help. What do I do now?* There was no reason to stay hidden on the outskirts of this village any longer. I chose a direction and walked, letting every stone I felt be my punishment for the discord I had sowed in that helpless village.

I came across an actual cart road after a while, when the sun was descending from the sky. *I need to find shelter before it gets too dark to see – it is not like I can conjure light or even a fire.* This cart road was all dirt with wheel ruts carved into the middle. I walked along the right shoulder, avoiding any large obstacles like sticks and stones. I came to a smaller path, a footpath, that snaked up into the trees.

Now I had to make a decision: stay on the wider, more traveled path or explore what the smaller path had to offer. One would certainly lead to a civilization of some kind, but after how long? The other path was made off of the larger path for a purpose, one great enough to wear into the ground and create a new road. Something in my chest told me the smaller path would be fun. *Why am I concerned about entertainment right now?* Shaking my head, I ventured up the second, smaller path in hopes that it led to shelter of some kind quicker than the other.

Once I find shelter, I can start looking for food. I have not eaten anything all day. I hope food is not too hard to find around here. My anxiety spiked, and I began to worry about what types of food were available and if I could remember not to eat anything poisonous. I was surprised my stomach had not grumbled at me. My bare feet crunched up the dirt path littered with leaves fallen from the sleeping trees. There were barely any stones in the way on this path, which I was grateful for. I took one long look behind me before turning the bend into the trees.

The forest enveloped me on both sides as I continued. I saw the path had one more turn into the trees. Hopefully, there were no more hidden turns, or I may eventually get lost in the woods. *It is not like I can soar above the tree crowns to find my way.* I turned the bend and was pleased to find a quaint, one-story cottage set into the far side of a small clearing. There was a stump with an axe buried in it out front for cutting firewood. It was still and eerie from how empty it felt.

The door to the cottage was on the farthest right corner of the front, and a medium-sized window with dusty brown shutters took up the rest of the face of the house. I approached carefully, glancing around before gingerly knocking on the wooden door. I heard nothing while I waited – not even the shuffling of shoes on the floor. I knocked again and heard nothing in response. Gnawing on my lower lip, I fought myself on whether or not to try and open the door. Curiosity and impending darkness moved me forward, twisting the knob of the door. It slid open freely – unlocked. A small flame of hope flickered to life as I entered the one-room cottage.

Inside the cottage was a table with benches to my left, a bed in the far left corner, and two tall storage cabinets. I closed the door behind me, feeling unwelcome and safe at the same time. I was thankful that I would not be out in the darkness tonight. The floor of the cottage was all dirt, but it was all soft dirt with no rocks. A circular fireplace was carved out of the wall to the right of the door. The bed was wedged into the far corner between the fireplace and the rear wall. I noticed a large chest at the foot of the bed. When I walked over to inspect the chest, it was clear no one had been there in a while. A thin layer of dust coated the bed, the chest, and the table. I swiped a finger across the table and came back with a smudge of dust, which I rubbed on my dress before facing the chest.

I pulled at the chest to open it, but it was not locked either. The lid swung up, displacing the dust that sat on top of it. Inside the chest were two blankets – one green and one brown – a worn leather satchel, a pair of worn leather gloves, candles, and a small purse of coins. I took out a candle and went to the fireplace for a striker or matchstick. I found the striker and lit the wick of the candle. The added light helped me see a candle holder at the edge of the hearth near the bed. It had a mostly melted candle still in it. Using my free hand, I dug out as much of the old candle as I could, then stuck the new one in with a dab of melted wax that I dripped from the top.

I took the candle over to the cabinets and used the light to look for food. I found mostly cutlery and linens in the first. In the second, I found salt-covered dried meat and several liquid and vegetable-filled jars. I gave the jars a suspicious flick, with which the glass answered with a *ting* and a little bubble floating up from the bottom. Forgoing the jars, I took the dried meat and closed the cabinets. My eyes fell on the bed; I very much wanted to crawl into the covers and fall asleep. *It will be nice to sleep in a real bed again, not in some straw box.*

The covers were dusty, but I did not mind. I took one edge and – after setting the candle down – the other, shaking out the covers. As the covers flew up, my eyes fell on the skeletal remains of someone. I screamed and immediately dropped the covers, running to the opposite corner of the cottage. Crouching behind the chest at the foot of the now unusable bed, I saw the candle I had left on the hearth and shivered. I would have to retrieve it.

I stood on shaking legs before dashing to the hearth. Grabbing the candle filled me with a rare type of bravery. I looked back at the bed and a chill ran up my spine as I looked into the hollow eyes of the cottage owner's skull. I flew to my refuge in the corner as quickly as I could without extinguishing the candle. I set the candle on the table to my right and opened the chest again, mostly to block my view of the corpse. I pulled out the extra blanket, gloves, satchel, and coin purse. The gloves fit nicely over my blackened fingers, if only a little bit. I put the coin purse in the satchel and closed it. The bag became my pillow as I bedded down for the night.

I was uneasy about sleeping mere feet from a corpse and taking things that did not belong to me, but it was a small burden to bear for shelter, and it was not like the cottage owner would be needing these things anymore.

Chapter Twenty-Five

In the morning, I woke confused, at least until I sat up and saw the hollow eyes of the corpse again. I returned the blankets to their chest and left the cottage in a hurry with my new bag and returned to the main road, still barefoot. I was not checking the body for shoes. I would adjust the need to acquire a pair some other way.

The sun rose as I walked along the road. It was nothing like Florence, but it had its own majestic vibrance. Carts and other travelers passed me going in the opposite direction. Some saw my bare feet and moved on, while others would stop me to question where my shoes had gone.

"They were taken," I would say.

"By who?" they would ask.

"I do not know," I would answer. *At least they were not assuming I had the plague, hopefully they thought my feet were just dirty.*

No one offered me a spare set of shoes though –they only wanted to know why I traveled this way. I soon began ignoring requests to stop and converse about my lack of footwear. Not long after that, I removed myself from the main road entirely. Instead, I wandered back into the forest to walk next to the path inside the treeline. I was quickly rewarded for my adventuring.

I stumbled upon a grove of apple trees. In awe of my find, I expressed gratitude to each one as I picked them from their branches. I could only reach a few branches, while some I had to jump and pull down, but the reward was juicy, fresh fruit that had grown in the shade of surrounding trees. A handful were picked by insects. I tossed those away, but the good ripe ones went into my new bag. Soon, the bag was bulging with a bushel. I wandered over to another type of tree – one that did not have rotting fruit at its base – and settled down to enjoy my feast.

The apples were crisp and juicy; I had picked them just in time. After my second bite, I half-wished that I'd taken more of these delicious apples. The flavor was so rich that it quelled my hunger from the day before. Once full, I rested against the tree. The air was cool and my stomach was full, I could almost take a nap, but refrained. Sleeping out in the open like this would be arrogant and foolish. I could be attacked, or worse. I thought of the coin purse in my satchel.

I reached in, displacing some of the apples as I dug to the bottom in search of the coin purse. It lay trapped at the bottom. A tug got it free while tossing a few more apples from the bag onto the ground around me. I cradled the pouch in my lap and worked to return the apples back into the bag. Then, I took the coins out of the purse and organized them by size and color. There were two sizes of silver coin and one gold coin the size of the largest silver. If I was right, Master Wais had had me memorize a few mints of coins from various close human regions. These were pennies, groats, and a half noble. It was not a rich collection, but it could help me get something in the future. The half-noble piece might get me a room somewhere, but would six pennies get me a pair of shoes?

I decided it was time to get up and venture onward to find a new village for assistance, but when I stood, I noticed something odd. My hair was standing up, lazily floating around me like a silent wind had whipped it into a frenzy. *Perhaps there is static nearby? It would be strange to react to magic now after my connection had been severed.* I shrugged it off and left the apple grove, following the road through the trees again. That was until I saw a glint of metal in the forest.

I picked my way through the foliage, following the shimmering light further into the forest. Passing through a thin sapling group, I spotted my target more clearly. In a ditch by a stream, maybe even the same one from before, lay a white horse and a little girl with flaming red hair. She rested her head on the horse's belly, clutching a spear with tight fingers.

I quietly approached, the glint of the spear beckoning to me. *If I could get something like that, I could hunt for food.* The thought made me feel dirty, plotting to steal from a little girl. But the idea of food made me hungry for another apple, so I drew one out and bit into it, forgetting how loud the crunch of a good, crisp apple could be. My eyes went wide as the little girl and her horse both startled awake. *Shit.* I tried to be sly and reach for the spear while she was still drowsy, hoping that I was startling enough to be able to run away with it. However, the horse made a soft whickering sound, and the little girl's hazel eyes flashed open. She pulled away the spear immediately.

"This is mine!" she proclaimed.

"Fair," I responded, sitting back on my heels. She inched back, burrowing farther against her horse. I reached into my bag and offered her an apple.

"Trade?" I tried. She shook her head firmly. I shrugged and returned it to my satchel. I saw she wore the tiny cloak of a tooth fairy around her neck on a string. It jostled and moved almost imperceptibly. To a human, it might not have moved at all, but I saw it. That must be where the lingering magic essence was coming from – the reason my hair was on end. The girl noticed me staring and tucked it inside her oversized shirt, then tightened her grip on the spear.

"What is a little star like you doing out here?" I asked, worried.

"I am not supposed to talk to strangers," she replied. *Smart girl.* I wanted to test her, to see if she was even ready to meet a tooth fairy. They were vindictive, evil little rats. If she had a cloak, it was for a reason, and I was willing to bet it was not a good one.

"I see...what do they call you where you are from, little star?" I asked. Her gaze shifted all around us, scared. I tried to look as unthreatening as possible so she might settle down and answer me. Then her face set into determination.

"Annette. Annie is what you can call me," she declared. I crossed my legs and sat in the dirt.

"Clever little girl, Annie," I chirped. She would be fine in the fae realm. I could tell that was not her true name, but one that she had learned.

"What do they call you?" Annie asked. I hummed and allowed my eyes to wander as I searched for some fake name to trade.

"Raven is fine, for now," I responded and moved closer. "Now we are no longer strangers, so tell me, Annie... Why are you in the woods with a cursed object?"

Annie blinked at me in confusion.

"I do not catch your meaning." She was stoic.

"You stink of a curse. I could sense it from far away. Have you come to rid yourself of it?"I prodded.

"In a way... I am trying to find the doer of the curse, to make him undo it," she said. I took in her appearance, looking at her soft leather shoes, and grinned.

"I see, I see," I replied. Annie nodded, then glanced at her horse. It had its ears back and nostrils flared at me.

"I may have a solution for both our problems, little Annie. If you are willing?" I tried. She was hesitant, but finally answered.

"I will hear what you have to say before I agree to anything." Annie spoke. I laughed and fell into the dirt on my back.

"Very well, bright star. I will trade you information for your shoes. I will tell you where you would like to go in exchange for your feet coverings," I said. Annie looked at me with her face full of confusion. Her hold on the spear wavered.

"Your suggestion is to tell me directions and I give you my shoes?" Annie repeated to me.

"Yes, but no. I know not where you come from, little star, but where I hail from, we only trade. Do we have a bargain?" my voice had an edge, as I was getting tired of this exchange. Annie chewed her lip, a gesture that made me fond of her instantly.

"I will take this bargain, but I will only give you my shoes after I write down the directions." She had a stern air about her.

"How do I know you will not take my information and leave?" I asked, looking at her from the dirt.

"My Na – My horse cannot get up fast. I will take off the shoes and then throw them to you after I have finished writing," she offered.

"You will take them off, then I will tell you where you want to go, and then you will throw your shoes at me?" I repeated back to her.

"That's the idea. I thought since we are not strangers we might trust each other a bit?"

"This is agreeable. Notify me when you are ready to proceed," I said, resting my hands on my stomach. I watched my hair float at the mercy of the light magic puddle this girl had around her as she pulled out her writing material. Annie took one more moment to unlace her shoes and take them off, setting them beside her. They looked well-worn and old. Annie tied the lacings together and nestled into her steed, using her knee as a writing surface.

"Raven? I am ready for that information now." I stilled and thought back to Mythenia and how to get there. In the human realm, you had to know where to go or get very lucky. Suddenly, I felt the warmth of a hug through my entire body. Looking up, it was like I could see the stars move, making a map.

"To find the one who snuck inside your home. For he will face the King upon the throne, only then will you escape the Pit of Bones. You pass through the bark of a twisted hawthorn, shadow fast run to the hills once you are alone," I enunciated as much as I could while speaking slowly. I had not tried speaking while having a vision before.

"Watch out," Annie called as she tossed her footwear to me. I watched the shoes soar across the ditch and land in the foliage next to me. Annie packed up her things and picked up her spear once more. She watched as I untied the knot in the laces and slipped my feet into the small worn shoes. They were a bit tight.

I had a theory that I wanted to try. Carefully, and with my hands covered, I imagined the shoes growing slightly, collecting energy from around me and slapping the shoes with all the magic I could muster. The shoes grew, and the searing pain in my hands and feet told me that the black scar had grown.

"This is where I leave you. Goodbye, Annie." I stood and brushed off the dirt from my bottom. I began to walk away when Annie spoke again, making me turn back.

"Goodbye Raven, tha–" she started. I cut her off by closing the distance and holding a gloved hand across her mouth.

"Shh, shh, shh, bright star. You are *never* to thank your equals for a trade. You would not want to owe them something later," I lectured. Annie nodded her head in understanding, and I removed my hand and bolted to the trees.

I pulled the gloves off to see that the blackness had grown up to my wrists. Soon the gloves would not cover the scarring. I walked fast through the forest until I burst through a trimmed tree line on the outskirts of a walled city. There was a stone road leading up into the city, which looked like it was heavily guarded with knights in shining armor. I was not going to mess with that. If someone thought I had the plague, they would do a lot worse than run away and lock the town down.

I chose to stay at the tree line again and followed the road heading north, if the sun was any indication. The sun was passing overhead at high noon, meaning west was to my left and east was to my right. If I was right, south was at my back and north was in front of me. The trees provided me with shade as I walked along the edge of the woods, watching travelers as they sped by me on the road with their horses and carts. It was not so bad now – walking in the woods with shoes on was far easier than avoiding every little obstacle. *What if I just stay in the woods? I do not need to find a town. It is unlikely anyone would help me with these scars.* I looked at the burned skin poking out of the gloves.

I let my mind wander as I did on the edge of the woods. I thought about finding a cave or even building a shelter. However, I was stopped by the hard truth that I lacked the tools to do any of the necessary work to accomplish any of those things. I had no axe or spear, not even a striker to light a fire with. Now I found myself missing the creepy corpse cottage and lamenting that I had not taken the axe with me. At least I had food for a while. Apples were not much, but I also had the salted meat jerky.

Before long, I realized I was approaching a new village. I noticed several stumps which were an indication of housing or firewood harvesting. This prompted me to fall deeper into the woods. Searching for some type of shelter, I found a rocky outcropping on the side of a hill. It was dry and flat. If I could manage to build one, I could have a fire.

I began looking for kindling the way Master Wais had described. Twigs and branches that I could easily break open, nothing green or damp. I found a decent armful of fallen branches from an oak, picking the ground clean. I needed another pocket of kindling but had to find another spot to search. Just a bit further, I found a bunch of broken-off twigs and fallen branches under an unfamiliar tree. I was weaving a bundle of the kindling I had found when a wet drop hit my skin. I looked up and saw the sky becoming increasingly grey as clouds gathered above.

The weather rapidly changed from a cheery afternoon sun to dreary, gloomy drizzle. I rushed under the tree to avoid getting my kindling damp, but I had failed. Many of the branches and twigs were already wet. The rain permeated the tree, dripping down onto me. My only chance was to run for it and hope some of the kindling on the inside of the bushel would stay dry. I pushed off the tree and ran for the outcropping I had chosen.

Arriving at the outcropping, damp from the cold rain, I flung the bundle onto the stone to check for usable kindling, but it was no use. Every stick, twig, and branch was wet. I had no way to dry them to make a fire. I fell to my knees in despair, the hard surface jarring a cry from me. Then I could not stop crying. Huge, salty tears ran down my face to drip off of my chin onto the dry stone. I slipped the satchel off my body and placed it next to me. Pressing my back against the stoney flat rock behind me, I drew my knees to my chest and let the sobs take me. I prayed that if anyone heard me, they would leave me be or come to help me. I could not handle any more issues.

Chapter Twenty-Six

From my perch in the rocks, I could see the warm glow of fires in a village below, once my eyes dried of tears. I watched the subtle pulse their hearths radiated. The outcropping stayed dry, my kindling still wet. Shivering against the cold, I watched the sky grow darker as the sun went down behind the clouds. The night was here and I feared the increased cold. *Why did I not take a blanket from that cottage?*

The drizzle continued until the sun fully set and the land was growing dark. A hole in the cloud opened up above the village. I could see a handful of little stars and half of the moon – the other half was obstructed by the remaining clouds. Light from the moon illuminated the chimney smoke from the village fires. It was growing colder by the minute and my clothes were still damp enough to betray me.

My choice dwindled as the light did. I quickly assessed my options, soon coming to the conclusion that the most sane option was to venture towards the village. It was dark now, so anyone who might potentially see me would not get the chance to see my hands. I pulled myself up from the ground and began the slow, gentle descent from my rocky perch.

I was scared to slip and fall and lose my bearings, so I walked and stepped carefully each step down. I did not have natural knowledge of the landscape, as I was not native to this area, but I did pay attention when finding my spot. If I kept straight, I would reach the first building with a fire.

If there was no inn or tavern, I would find some decent place to sleep. Even the stables would do, as it is not like I have not slept on straw before. I felt the rocks and sticks on the ground below. Thankfully none had slid out from under me. Before long, I reached the edge of the trees. The little house lights illuminated only a small portion of the nearest trees, but it helped me pick my way over to the cobblestone pathway.

I snuck by the cottage to the stone path leading into the town proper. The stone was still slick from the rain, but the grit from the mud helped me keep my footing. Following the path into town, I passed a sign attached to a fire-lit home that read: Penfro Port Customs Office. *Strange, I do not feel the tell-tale signs of a seaport... this does not feel like any of the human or fae ports I have visited before.* I looked around in the dark and could not tell a house from a barn, but there was surely no ocean. The sound would be obvious, and there was no salt in the air – no crashing waves. *Do humans make land ports?* I shook my head, dislodging the thought, deciding that now was not the time, and instead moved further into the port city. Several buildings built shoulder-to-shoulder were lit up with internal fires. Some had empty flower boxes, leading me to imagine they were homes.

Ahead, I saw a building with multiple windows with multiple fires. Drawing more wisdom from Master Wais, I knew only two buildings in rural towns had multiple fires: Manor Homes for the Aristocracy and Inns. I headed towards the building, praying to the stars above that it would be someplace I could sleep. As I drew closer, I could see the outline of a fence and gate. *Damn, a manor house.*

I shifted my gaze to skirt the fence until I could find an opening or a stable house. Anything would do at this point; it was getting cold.

The fencing ran quite a ways with no defects, and as far as I could see, no stables. *What kind of manor has no stables?* I stopped to press my face into the darkness once more. If I could stare long enough, maybe my eyes would adjust and I could see something new.

"Oi! What are you doing over there?" a nasally male voice demanded. I turned around to see a lightly armored man in a little pool of light from a torch that he held in front of him.

"Oh! I was – I am…looking for a place to stay, I suppose," I finally spit out. He rolled his dark eyes at me.

"Sure. The tavern is up the road 'bout a mile.' He pointed with his free hand to his right – my left.

"I appreciate your assistance. Thank you," I said, then quickly reached for an apple. It slipped out of my fingers, and I fumbled trying to catch it. It fell and the man grunted. His torchlight began to disappear while I fished for another. By the time I was able to retrieve one, he was gone. *Shit! That is going to bother me for a long time.*

With a deep sigh, I picked up the fallen apple and tossed it between my hands as I walked up the road the man had pointed towards. I found there were more homes, but this time with more space in between the buildings and some patches of dirt out front. Some of the homes had made use of their space by hanging a clothesline or tilling a garden. The alleys between them became eerie in the darkness.

The next few buildings must have been the start of the business district. I saw several braziers that were extinguished by the rain. I ventured into the darkened streets and began to feel a thousand tiny fingers crawl across my back and the backs of my legs. They were not real, but they felt creepy and invasive, like the shadows were chasing me, hunting me down. My heart jumped and jumped again like it was running out of my chest, taking my mind with it. I fought the urge to run with all my strength. Then, for some reason or another, I thought of Lord Caligo and his ability to float through shadows. *What if he came to get rid of me as an act of the Queen? I have to find a place to hide!*

I searched the alley as I passed by, keeping my head forward and back straight. Every deep shadow held the possibility of him. I quickened my pace, hoping to reach some pool of light soon, but so far, I only found a few in the distance. If I had my wings, I would not be walking or scared stiff. I would soar above the buildings and my wings would cover me in my pool of silver light. I would have also been able to cast some type of light spell. Never again would I be able to cast any spells. Never again would I feel the wind in my hair or the pure joy of soaring above clouds.

Tears pricked my eyes, falling slowly down my cheek and off my chin. I sniffed them back and had to fight the urge to dive into a corner and sob myself to sleep. *I want to sleep in a bed if possible, so do not give up now.* Finally, a pool of light from an alley window appeared! I turned fast and went straight to it. Like a moth to a flame, I hovered over the edge of the window. Looking in carefully, I was able to see a woman cradling her child. Through the thin planks of the window, I heard her say something in a sweet soothing voice.

"It was only a night terror. You are fine. We are here for you, though your family sleeps soundly. I envy his ability to lay his head down and fall asleep. You are like me – imagination galore! It can be a heavy burden to bear, but also a lovely gift. Be still and let me put you back to sleep."

"Ok mama," the little girl said. I barely heard her over the rustling of the sheets. The sweet exchange brought me to tears, not because of the heartwarming mental image, but because when my mother heard of my night terrors, she told me it was possible that someone from Obscurum was trying to manipulate me and told me to use a light spell to ward them off. There was no comfort in that. Sure, it was practical, but I needed the emotional connection. She was only ever emotional when she got mad. Tears threatened me again.

I ran into the darkness again; the fear of being caught outweighed my fear of the dark. I sniffled and hiccuped as I walked up the street. Finally, I spied the building that was the Inn. Multiple fires burned in multiple windows, as well as freshly lit torches burning brightly near the doorway. There had been several outdoor torches and braziers that had been extinguished by the rain – I saw hazy smoke wisps coming off of a few. The tavern had put fresh wood in the braziers and a door was propped open with a rock. Through the door, I heard the faint sound of sweet music drifting onto the street. A couple of people lingered out front, happily engaged in conversation while smoking from pipes.

Ducking into an alley, I tried to calm my nerves. I knew my eyes were puffy and my nose red from crying, so I hoped no one would notice. I took in several deep breaths, letting them out slowly like Aurora taught me. *Oh gods, Aurora.* It had been a while since I had thought of her. The tears flooded out, and I could only turn a few sobs into breaths. Then, with a deep breath that I held and released slowly, I stepped out to the street again.

"H-hey-y there… pretty la-ady?" a sandy-haired man asked. He wobbled on his legs and stank of beer. He was on the pudgy side but not unattractive – except for his manners.

"Hello," I replied with an uncontrolled sob. *Aurora would have run this man off by now.*

"Oh – I, Uhm. Go-good night." He turned and walked away. *At least looking like a mess kept me from being harassed.* With more confidence, I approached the tavern, excusing my way through the group standing near the entrance.

Inside the wood frame building was a central hearth surrounded by nice wooden tables that were mostly filled with people. Several wooden stools and benches lined the walls under torches, also mostly filled with bodies. No one paid me a single glance. The bard whose song I heard in the street sat in the farthest right corner. The leftmost wall had a counter with a few empty stools where a beefy bearded man with mud-brown hair whistled his cheery tone while he cleaned his space. The tavern walls were broken up with doors that I assumed led to rooms along the front and back walls. As I approached the bar, I saw a hallway that led to more rooms.

"Hullo traveler! Oh – what has happened to you?" I noticed his voice was oddly melodic. He gestured to the empty stools for me to sit.

"I– uhm. I would like a warm drink if you have any. I do not have much coin, but I could work for my meal if you like." I pulled the stool at the end of the counter out and sat down after wiggling some to get on. The wooden counter was smooth, clean, and decorated with preserved flowers.

"I do have a hot drink, but no work. I have a stack of tasks for around the village if that is of interest to you?" he asked. I shook my head.

"I am not an adventurer. I do not really know what I am, if I am honest..." I trailed off.

"Oh dear... Well, have you got anything to sell?"

"Just a bunch of apples," I sighed.

"Apples! Yes! I would love to buy some of your apples. How many have you got? Make sure to keep some for yourself." He was very animated, talking with his hands. I pulled my satchel into my lap and began to remove apples from it one at a time until there were six in a row. The barkeep's eyes were as wide as his smile.

"No one wants to collect food anymore. I have to go to the market every day for anything fresh! Thank you!" His appreciation sparked the fae contract in me. I could not jeopardize this interaction with a contract though... "I will give you two pennies a piece. Does that sound fair? A hot ale is four." He pointed to a written sign that I could not read. Master Wais did not care much for human language, so I did not learn much of it.

"Yes, that sounds fair to me. A hot ale sounds nice." The spark of a social contract withered as we agreed. Humans use 'thank you' too much.

"Let me get that for you and your change." He collected the apples from the counter and disappeared behind a door that I assumed led to a kitchen. I was left alone with the sounds of the tavern, but soon enough, the barkeep came back with a steaming mug of ale. I gratefully took it and then noticed he held his hand out to me with two pennies. I extended my hand to take them and he dropped them into my palm.

"One more thing, please."

"Yes?"

"How much is a room? I uh... cannot read," I said. Technically, I could read fae, but human numbers were another beast entirely.

"Oh sure! Two nobles. Cheapest in the port!" he chuckled, wandering over to more customers who had approached the counter. I knew I did not have enough, only having a half noble and a handful of pennies...and now six apples down from my stash. *Ale it is then*. I put the mug to my lips and drank deeply. The hot ale burned my tongue but slowly began to warm me from the inside out. After a couple of good swigs, I could feel my senses dulling. The hole in my chest no longer ached, and the thought of aurora brought a happy feeling, not melancholia.

The barkeep returned and asked if I wanted the room or not. I told him that I could not afford it, but ordered another ale. He reminded me of the task billets for the town.

"I am no adventurer," I repeated. He chuckledled and left to retrieve a second mug. I took out two more pennies from my coin purse, placing the four on the counter for him when he returned.

"Good ale, right?" he joked as he set down the new steaming mug, then slid the coins off the counter into his hands and took the empty mug away. I had not noticed he returned.

"Yesss," I responded, unable to keep from sounding strange.

"Best in the port!"

"What kind of port is-s this-s, anyway? I saw no ocean nor did I sm-smell salt air," I questioned. The barkeep chuckled again, which annoyed me since I was being serious.

"We are the final port inland. All the rivers empty here into a lake that drains into the sea. We are leagues away from the ocean proper."

"Ah. th-that clears up my... my confusion. My app-app-reciation to you, kind s-sir." I raised the new mug and began to drink deeply. All my fears and worries melted away as the ale fell into my stomach. The feeling was almost as freeing as flying. Almost. More like swimming, I supposed.

I finished the mug in a few gulps with my head tilted back, desperately seeking any warmth of any kind. I coughed, the taste of bile rising in my throat. I looked around for a place to spit it out but the room spun like I was falling from the sky. I had to lay my head down. I folded my arms on the counter and rested my head. My arms made the worst pillow. I could see the world spin around me, but my head was too heavy to lift and see. My mouth felt fuzzy and my ears were being bombarded with noise. The bard's soft music had stopped and someone was speaking close to me.

"Are you okay?" A gentle, warm touch found me.

Chapter Twenty-Seven

I was falling...or was it flying? No, definitely falling. My mouth opened, but the scream I expected never came. I fell through the darkness, the chill of icy fingers brushing my face and hair, causing a shiver to run down my spine that exploded in my bones. The falling continued through darkness, the cold hands brushing me as I passed. I asked them to stop, but again, no sound would escape my mouth. Then, before my eyes could deceive me, a pinhole of light opened beneath me. I would have missed it had I blinked. I was sure it was a trick, that there was no real light, but it grew like it was coming up to meet me. Scared, I tried to scream, but the hollow sounds of nothing only added to the terror of the impending, engulfing light.

It was not as they said, going into the light. It was not the end. I continued to fall, and the sensation of air passing me by was the only familiar feeling that I could place. I looked above me and witnessed the darkness leaving in a cloud. I screamed in earnest because where there was light, there should be...things! Everything! This was a vast emptiness, an entire blank, never-ending canvas. Warm sensations, like a gentle caress, came from the nothingness. I flinched away from them, only to have my cheek cupped by another. Liquid filled my mouth as though I had landed in unseen water.

Is this what it is like to go blind? Is that what has happened? I spit the water out and flailed about, hoping to splash whatever water was around me. Nothing happened. I touched nothing except warm, firm hands on my forearms. They were strangely familiar.

"Hey," someone whispered. I jumped and the hands came back to my arms gently. There was no one to see, but the soothing voice came again.

"Shh, it is alright. Shh." The words were familiar, just like the mother's comfort I had seen and heard from the alleyway the night before. I opened my eyes and saw an effeminate, thin, pale man with vibrant purple hair and a long nose gently shaking me awake. His hazel eyes were wide with concern. Shocked, I tried to scoot away from his touch, only to find I had little room to do so. My hand slipped off the surface I was resting on and I fell to the floor. I saw that I had been resting on a bed and now was wedged between the bed and the wall.

"Oww," I moaned. Sunlight pierced through a window across the room.

"Niv! Hey, someone!" the man's nasally, melodic voice called. A very loud door opened with a creak and footsteps came rushing in. A woman with the complexion of wheat grain covered head to toe in a large, ruby red wrapping bent over me, her brown, doe eyes showing similar concern.

"Oh, let me help you." She clicked her tongue at me and extended a hand. I took it slowly, but she was fast and firm in pulling me up. Once on my feet, I was immediately nauseous. I think she noticed because she brought me to the bed again, helping me sit on the edge. I sat gingerly and she retreated to a small table in the corner under the window. She brought me a simple ceramic mug with the look of a stern caretaker, similar to that of my nursemaid and Mrs. Sykes. I sipped from the mug and found it was cool water with mint. I drank deeply, the cool mint water soothing my throat and cooling my stomach.

"Steady, you were quite ill last night. I hope you do not mind, but we thought you could use some help." She spoke with an accent I could not place, but her 'w's sounded like 'v's and she could not pronounce the 'th' sound without it sounding like a hard 't'. I had to concentrate more than I was able to understand her. I nodded after decoding her speech.

"I am Nivedita Thapa of the Vaishyas." She extended her hand again and I tentatively took it with my still gloved hand, half expecting her to pull me into a hug. Instead, she shook my hand firmly with both of hers.

"This is Nicol. The bard you might have heard last night." She stepped aside and swung her arm in a flourish towards her purple haired companion. He leaned against the wall watching us and gave a small wave when Nivedita introduced him, but he did not come close again.

"Bon matin," he said. I felt my face scrunch in confusion, as his accent and speech were foreign to me. I sipped at the remainder of the cool mint water while the two blinked and stared at me. *They want me to introduce myself, but how can I with no home nor a name?*

"Ahem," Nicol cleared his throat. I looked up and saw they were continuing to earnestly watch me.

"I – uh – I do not know who I am..." I replied meekly, looking at them both. Nivedita turned to Nicol. His face was the only one I could read and it was pained in confusion.

"Well, how about we get some food in you? Maybe you will remember then." Nivedita coaxed me off of the bed, then took the ceramic mug from me and set it on the table. With her blocking the sun, I could see the rest of what was set on the table: vials and jars filled with various herbs and liquids next to a box with a strap and my satchel.

"My bag!" I exclaimed. Nicol scooped it up and slid it over my head.

"There you go, no need to lose your cap."

"I appreciate you returning my meager belongings," I whimpered, "and for taking care of me, even though I am a stranger to you."

"Well, of course. Caring for others is the mark of a compassionate soul. It was our friend Catherine that insisted, and she is one of the most compassionate people we know."

"Catherine?" I asked, taken aback.

"Yes! One of our other companions. We will meet them downstairs." Nivedita led me gently from the bed to the door. Nicol opened the door for us and we left the sunny room behind.

Through the stone and wood hallway, we re-entered the tavern from the doorway behind the counter. A blonde woman with an oval face stood, waving at us. We changed directions to meet her. *She must be Catherine*. She stood next to a muscular man with bronze skin who sat with his arms crossed over his chest. He watched our approach with keen eyes. As we approached the table, the blonde woman's green eyes caught mine – she inspected me from head to toe and back up.

"Glad to see you are still with us." Her voice was almost as lilted as Nicols, but her accent was different. Nicol sat next to the other man, lute in hand. Nivedita pulled out a chair for me next to Nicol before settling herself in the seat next to Catherine.

"I am, and I appreciate your kindness. I am afraid I do not have much to repay you with –"

"Nonsense," Catherine interrupted. "We did not help you in hopes of repayment. I saw you and you seemed unwell. Luckily, we approached you before you fell off your stool! Viçente caught you, thankfully. We all decided you would be safer with us." Her companions murmured in agreement. Nivedita gently placed a hand over my left hand that rested on the table.

My heart sank just a little deeper into the pit of despair in my chest. *These folks do not know who I am. Hellfire, I do not even know who I am, and yet they brought me into their rooms and took care of me.*

"So, where are you headed?" Catherine chimed in, kicking me out of my ruthless thoughts. I had no answer.

"I do not know. Wherever I can I suppose." It was clear that my response was not satisfactory. Catherine and Nivedita shared a smirk. Catherine leaned over to the man with bronze skin and whispered something in his ear. The man she called Viçente nodded and waved Nicol over to him. They whispered to each other while glancing at me and came to an agreement.

"We have a proposition for you, if you are prepared to listen?" Nicol turned to me.

" I suppose. What is going on?"

"You have nowhere to go, no?"

"Correct," I answered hesitantly.

"Bon! You also have no supplies?" he continued.

"Correct again." I felt my shame burn into my cheeks and up into my ears.

"This is what we are thinking… You come travel with us!" My stomach dropped, now a cool cavity in its place. I looked around the table; the entire group had matching looks of determined anticipation.

"No, you cannot be serious. I do not possess any skills. Es-especially not any that might assist you," I stammered. I was sure that they were only being kind and not insisting I join them.

"S'il vous plaît. You do not even know what we do! How can you be sure you are not helpful?" Nicol leaned on the back of his chair. We sat, locked in a staring contest of wits for a time. He stared unwaveringly, me timidly blinking occasionally.

"What is it that you do?" I tried to ask, shy in my approach.

"Many a things! Mostly, we follow the whim of mademoiselle Nivedita." He gestured to her kindly.

"Why?" I asked before thinking. The group exchanged looks of surprise, and I felt my blush return.

"You are entertaining," Nicol chortled. "Niv had the coin at first, but now we go where she can train or sell her tinctures."

"I still do not see how I can be of use to you," I said seriously.

"Ah, yes. That. Well, who could not use a fairy on their side?" Nicol laughed. I glanced around the table, noticing how everyone looked at me with an expectant smile.

"You know?" I looked back to Nicol. He nodded, and the cold pit in my stomach expanded. *They will want me to do magic for them. How long will it take for them to leave me when I tell them I have none.*

"Your ears, darling," Nivedita spoke softly and squeezed my hand. I looked at her and her smile was genuine, welcoming. I took a moment to look at each of them and found that they all continued to look at me with genuine happiness and excitement.

"Alright. I will accept your offer to accompany you, but I must tell you something first. I hope it will not change your minds."

"Go on," Catherine urged.

"I can no longer perform magic of any kind. Not without a great deal of pain." I looked at the space between Catherine and Viçente as I spoke, the pit in my stomach contracting and filling with warmth. The group exchanged looks and shrugged in turn.

"That does not seem to be an issue. You have hands, no?" Nicol asked. That got me to let out a small, single breath laugh.

"Yes! And I consider myself a quick study. I will aim to learn whatever tasks you give me."

"Bon! Then it is settled. You will join us and we will make sure that you eat when we eat." Nicol extended a hand to me, which I took with mine. We shook on the bargain. I looked at the group and questions began to bubble up in my mind. *They all seem to come from different places... How did they end up together?*

"If it is not too invasive, might I ask what you study?" I asked Nivedita.

"You may! I am a student of apothecaries, medicines, and chemistry. We came to Penfro as a stop on our way to Llawer-enni and maybe farther. There are a plethora of mentors in this region that could teach me more about elixirs and remedies," she explained. I nodded. *A noble endeavor...*

"What of the rest of you?" I asked, looking to Nicol. The pit in my stomach was still there, but it was not as painful. Nicol held up his lute. I nodded, then turned to the muscled boulder of a man – Viçente. He watched me with steady, brown eyes.

"I am escorting the lady Catherine," he said succinctly.

"Alright, uhm, then what is your goal, Catherine?" I looked at her. She leaned on the table with her elbows to speak to me.

"Anything." She wiggled her eyebrows deviously. Nivedita's head whipped around to stare at Catherine. I imagined she scowled, but I could not see her face. Catherine smiled and returned to her seat.

"No. Not *anything*." Nivedita corrected.

"Okay – yes. My goal is to do anything but get married!" she laughed, leaning back into her chair. Nivedita let our a sigh and Viçente rolled his eyes.

"Oh, I see. So everyone follows you around while you look for opportunities to learn. You must all know each other from childhood or something of the like?" I addressed Nivedita.

"Well yes, they do follow my whims. However, I do not always choose where we go. There are other areas of study that I am curious about. As to the childhood friends – no. We have all met along the way" she explained nonchalantly. I nodded. *They must have met by chance.*

"So... what is your story?" Nicol redirected. I turned my head to look at him and clasped my hands in my lap. He smirked while he mindlessly braided his long, purple hair.

"My story?" I asked.

"Yes, how did you get to be here, and why were you getting so drunk?"

"Drinks were all I could afford and it was cold out. I came through the portals – do you not know of the portals?" I questioned in return.

"Yes we do, but there is no record of one near Port Penfro," Viçente interjected gruffly.

"Interesting... you plot and track portals?"

"Yes?" Catherine asked cautiously. I swallowed a laugh.

"Humans are so interesting. The portals in the Human Realm are random at best. Plotting them is like trying to make a cloud chart. The only way to find a portal is to find a liminal space, and that shifts with the day's light," I explained with a giggle lodged in the back of my throat.

"Oh. Well, thank you," Catherine said. The words lit that spark of social contract in me again. I felt the pull of my childhood lessons begin. *Thank you means I owe you.* Catherine turned to Viçente and gestured for him to give her something. He dug into his bag and pulled out a worn, ratty map, not unlike my clothing. Catherine began crossing off question marks and asking me for the area I remembered. I did my best to explain the village I had passed by first, careful not to mention the creepy cottage.

"That was almost clever," Nicol said coolly. I returned my gaze to him. "We would still be grateful to learn more about you. Who are you and where have you come from?" he redirected again. *He must have dealt with some tricky fairies before. I am not deliberately trying to not answer, I simply cannot.*

"I—I did not mean to. I-I am from Mythénia, the realm of fairies," I stammered.

"And your name?" Catherine pressed.

"I-I do not know," I said quietly, picking at my gloves.

"What do you mean you do not know. Have you lost your memory or something?" she pressed again.

"Or something..." I repeated with shame. I caught her eyes and we stared at each other for a moment.

"Alright, alright. For now, what can we call you?" Nicol smoothed over the conversation. I looked around the table; four sets of eyes watched me mull over my options.

"I do not mean to make this difficult, but you may call me anything – anything respectable that is." I chose my words carefully.

"Alright, well… we can work on that later," Nivedita intervened with a hand on my shoulder. I gave her a grateful smile.

"How about a round of breakfast and ale before we hit the road again?" Nicol suggested, taking the hint. Nivedita and Catherine took suggestions from everyone, but came back with plates of eggs, hot buns, and dark gravy. The guys dug in eagerly and the ladies ate politely while making light conversation.

"Nicol, could you go collect my box?" Nivedita spoke up after a moment. He nodded and carefully left the table, returning down the hall to the room we had come from.

I stared at my steaming roll in the gravy and grimaced. Picking it up, I tried a bite. It was tart and thick, not how I enjoyed my food. I swallowed my regretful bite and offered my gravy and roll to the table. I ate only the eggs, as they were untouched by the strange gravy. Soon, Nicol came back from the room with a large box that rattled and clinked with every move. He set it on the table and noticed my plate.

"You do not like gravy?" he asked. I shook my head. With a chuckle, he took my plate and flooded his own with my remaining breakfast. He gave me a grateful smile and I felt the pit in my stomach close.

Chapter Twenty-Eight

As soon as everyone finished eating, Viçente scooped up the plates and mugs and returned them to the bar. When he came back, he shrugged his bag onto his back. I saw that he also had a long sword on his hip.

"Let us get to the river," Viçente commanded. Catherine followed, shouldering a large pack herself. Nicol carried a medium bag, stuffed full, and his lute. Nivedita carried the small box – trunk, now that I got a better look at it. I followed behind everyone as we filed out of the front door of the tavern onto the sunlit street.

"Where is the rest of your gear?" Catherine asked me. I turned to her, holding a hand up to shield my face from the sun.

"Right here." I patted the sachet that hung across my body.

"Very funny. Seriously, where did you stash your gear?"

"I have nothing else," I said softly, looking away. A pang of sadness hit me in the gut.

"Oh dear... I am so sorry. We will help you. I can give you one of my dresses so you have more than ... this." She pulled at the sleeve of my current tunic dress. This one was still blood-stained and dirty. She looped her arm in mine and gave me a pained, sympathetic smile. Catherine guided me behind the others as we ventured on through the town, Viçente leading the way towards where – I assumed – were the docks. Nivedita and Nicol walked behind Viçente, locked in vigorous conversation, flailing their hands around as they spoke.

"This is not the ocean, Niv! You will be fine!" Nicol encouraged Nivedita. I turned to Catherine for answers.

"Niv is from far inland India – do you know of India?" she asked, and I shook my head. "Ah, well," she clicked her tongue and continued, " in India, they get massive floods called monsoons. Because she lived inland, she never had experience with the ocean, but being around the monsoon waters has given her a fear of deep water. Nicol said she passed out from sheer panic during their voyage from France – do you know of France?" I nodded. Catherine smiled, which encouraged me to explain further.

"I spent a year in Italy, just a few months ago. It was pleasant and there were occasional talks of France, but what I know about it is very little." She nodded and faced forward again.

We approached the docks where many beautiful boats sat, awaiting their cargo. Shipmen and dock workers loaded crates and barrels on and off ships with diligent precision. Viçente set down his belongings, quickly asking Nicol to look after them before going off alone to speak with some official-looking men. Nicol plopped down on the ground. Nivedita followed, but sat as far as she could from the water. Nicol twisted his lute around and began to strum lightly as Catherine and I joined them on the ground. He played a lively tune that accentuated the sounds of the docks, like a sea shanty, but more relaxed.

We waited for Viçente's return. He came trotting up the boardwalk with a happy grin.

"I got us a lift to Llawer-enni! There is a bargeman up the docks ready to leave with room for passengers. He says we can have passage for one gout potion." He looked to Nivedita.

"They are not potions! They are tinctures or salves! Potions make me sound like a witch! Do not get me in trouble, Viçente," Nivedita growled. Viçente raised his hands in defense and apologized. Nivedita accepted and we collected ourselves and our belongings to follow Viçente to the barge. While we walked, Nicol broke away from Nivedita and linked his arm in mine, leaning close to whisper in my ear.

"Will you do me a favor?"

"That depends. What is it?" I responded.

"Will you sit on Niv's other side, to block her view of the water? I will be to her right. She will need to concentrate on her alchemy or whatever," he explained, waving his hands.

"Yes, I can do that," I agreed with a smile. *The first thing I could do to be of use!*

"Merci." He dipped his head and returned to Nivedita's side.

Viçente helped Catherine onto the barge, where a greasy man stood near the single sail. He gave Catherine directions that I could not hear, but I saw him point. Nicol stepped onto the barge without issue, then turned back to take Nivedita's trunk. She wavered and cautiously approached the small gap. I could see her face set with determination as she thrust her trunk at Nicol. It smacked him square in the chest, making him suddenly gasp for air. Viçente witnessed the scene and laughed heartily. His voice was deep and carried. Nicol gave him a partially dirty look and thrust the chest to him. He caught it deftly.

"Hey! Be careful! The glass vials!" Nivedita yelled at them. Nicol gasped dramatically, causing more laughter to erupt from Viçente. Nivedita turned to Viçente to scold him, but Nicol took his chance to lift her onto the barge quickly. She barely had a moment to realize what had happened before her body tensed up and she was forced to sit down.

I was also wary of the water, but no one was going to pull me up onto the barge, and I did not want to be a burden so soon. I readied myself by choosing a spot where my feet should land. Viçente offered me one of his rough square hands, so I took it and, with his assistance, was able to board the barge.

"Thank you," I said, then froze. If he acknowledged my gratitude, I may be in debt to him for however long it took to get one in return. I watched Viçente closely. He nodded once and began arranging the bags near our seating area. Everyone sat just below the sail deck on the bench, the bags piled along the right side. Viçente sat and Nicol caught my attention by waving. He gestured to the open space beside Nivedita furiously. I quickly made my way to the open seat. Nivedita gave me a queasy smile then returned to staring intently at the contents of her trunk. Nicol rubbed her shoulders with a flat hand and encouraged her to work on the gout remedy. She nodded and Nicol helped her gather the ingredients, holding them in his arms for her.

Inside her trunk were vials of powders to the right and liquids to the left. She carefully collected a vial with lilac-colored flower petals and a large vial of a viscous liquid.

"An' we're off!" a croaking male voice came from behind us. I stifled a gasp, as I had forgotten we were on someone else's barge. I turned around to look at him as he spoke. He was hunched over and I could see his skin was as oily as his hair.

"Name's Lardwick. Y'all are on my lovely barge the Lady Adelpha. We'll be dockin' next in Llawer-enni." He used a large pole to push the barge away from the docks before catching the sail. "I is not used to havin' guests. Please do mind ma' things."

I became focused on Nivedita's salve making, effectively drawing out the bargeman's ramblings. She pulverized the flower petals into the liquid, making a paste. She did not look up from her work at all. Her hands were steady and practiced with each item she grabbed. I watched as she picked a clay jar from its spot and scraped the lilac-pigmented salve into it, finishing by placing a lid on top. She then gave it to Nicol – without looking up – and worked on putting away her ingredients. I watched him pass it to Catherine, who then gave the jar to Lardwick.

"Thank ye."

"Is that what you gave me?" I asked Nivedita. She looked up at me, but her gaze drifted over to the water and she quickly looked down, returning to organizing her trunk.

"No. You did not, and still do not, have gout. You got a little too drunk, so I fed you a charcoal slurry to keep you from feeling too bad when you woke up," she explained. I nodded like I understood. We rode upstream through a man-made canal, I could see the ductwork and supports. I watched people travel on the banks, but we surpassed them after a time. Nicol pulled out his lute with Lardwick's permission and played some song that Lardwick requested. The tune was more strumming than Nicol's previous performances, which were melodic and sweet. This was bouncy and had a faster pace. Catherine and Viçente began to clap along, creating an accompanying beat. I turned to Nivedita, who was intently staring at the floor.

"You must think I am incredibly ridiculous," she laughed. I blinked a couple of times, surprised.

"No. The opposite, in fact. I, too, am terrified of water. I cannot swim. You have a lovely group of friends to take care of you while you face this fear. They help you board and care about how you feel. I think you are ridiculously loved."

"I am. I am very lucky. You also have this same lovely group to assist you, too." She closed her eyes and turned her face to smile at me. I smiled back before I realized she could not see. I stopped feeling embarrassed.

It was not long before we reached the end of the canal. I saw a small sign but could not read what it said. I reached over and poked Nicol.

"What does that sign say?"

"Llawer-enni docks," he answered.

Lardwick expertly guided his barge to an open dock where a well-dressed man came to meet us. Lardwick threw a rope to the man on the dock and tied the barge down. The barge knocked on the dock a couple of times as it lulled to a stop.

"Pleasure to have you in Llawer-enni! Sir, your papers?" the dockman called to Lardwick as Viçente helped Catherine off the barge. The dock man and Lardwick engaged in their own conversation while we regrouped and disembarked in the same order we boarded. I followed our group off the docks, where Catherine took charge leading us down the road, northeast. We quickly happened upon a busy market with women and men hurrying from the docks to stalls to baskets and away. Viçente stayed close to Catherine, but Nicol and Nivedita stayed on the outskirts of the market, inspecting stalls.

"What are they doing?" I asked nervously.

"Catherine is inquiring about medicines and remedies. We learned that people are wary of my asking. When Nicol and I first landed here, we connected with someone we had to pry to get any information from, well, other than where the nearest tavern was. Anywhere Catherine goes, so does Viçente. It has always been that way," Nivedita explained. We watched from afar as Catherine wove in and out of the flow of people, stopping at stalls to ask questions. I watched as she began arguing with a man behind a stall of glass vials. Viçente urged her to move on, hand on his sword. She did after a threatening gesture was made to the merchant. The pair returned to us forcefully. Catherine stopped in front of us with a huff, Viçente on her heels.

"The nerve of some people! I swear –"

"Catherine…" Viçente stopped her. She rolled her eyes, but I could tell she finished the sentence in her head.

"That man, however rude, was quite helpful. Apparently, there is an herbalist north of here, halfway to Hulfford." Catherine pulled out her map and pointed to a general area with her finger.

"We will check here," Viçente suggested, tapping the paper.

"Not a physician or apothecary, but herbalists have their own unique recipes that I know will be helpful. Shall we go then?" Nivedita turned to everyone, and in turn, me last. We all agreed. She took my arm in hers and we deferred to Catherine for directions.

"Wait, we should check our supplies. We may not have enough to make it to Hulfford," Nivedita spoke up after we passed the mark and could see the edge of town.

"We are prepared," Viçente proclaimed, gesturing to himself and Catherine. Nivedita and Nicol lowered their shared food bag off of Nicol's back. They checked together and ruled that they were also set. All eyes were on me then. I pulled my satchel open and counted the three remaining apples.

" I have three apples, will that be enough?" I asked. Nicol and Viçente exchanged a fleeting glance of pity. Nivedita handed off her trunk to Nicol and took me aside. We began walking towards the market.

"My dear, please do not take offense, but unless fairies eat less than humans, that will not get you through today and Hulfford looks to be two, if not more, days away. Let us find you some more rations at the market. Do not worry, we all pool our rations for meals so that no one goes hungry. Do you still have some coin?" she asked. I nodded and dug through my satchel for the coin purse. Pulling it out, I handed it to her gingerly. She opened the small bag and counted my coins.

"You should have enough for bread and cheese. That will help you keep your apples longer. Take these." She handed me two coins and closed my coin bag. "Now, go to that woman in the blue dress standing behind the bread. I will be right behind you."

I took a deep breath and approached the woman at the bread stand. She wore a dirty blue cotton dress with a waist apron. Her attitude was cheery, though also tired.

"Hello. Could I get a bit of bread and cheese?"

"Well, sure! Any type in particular?" She gestured to her assortment on the table. I pointed to the pale cheese and golden bread. She wrapped them in a cloth and explained the price. Nivedita nudged me again, I handed over the coins she set aside and in return, I got the bread and cheese.

"Thank you for your patronage!" The woman ended our transaction with a cheery smile before engaging her next customer. Nivedita and I returned to the others, now ready to venture into the forest to find this hermetic herbalist, somewhere in the woods.

Chapter Twenty-Nine

The forest was in the late stages of autumn, where the leaves had fallen off their branches, for the most part, coating the ground in a crunchy layer of debris. The trees looked like creepy, gnarled hands reaching for the sky. Viçente had broken away from the ground to scout ahead for any signs of the hermetic herbalist. When the road had thinned out, Catherine had directed us to follow the river. Her map showed Hulfford was at the end of the waterway, leading her to assume the best way to travel was nearest the river. We walked in relative silence, except for our feet crunching through the leaves.

Ahead, I saw Viçente jogging back to us, his hair bouncing like a dog's ears. We collectively stopped and waited for him to rejoin us.

"Up the road – about a mile – there is a cottage – with smoke – coming out of – the chimney!" he informed us between gasps. Catherine folded her map away and stowed it in her pack. Now it was Nivedita's turn to lead the way. Viçente pointed in the general direction of the cottage and she began slowly walking north. Nicol hung back to walk with me. At first, he was silent, but the closer we got to finishing the mile walk, he broke and asked a question.

"Where are your wings?" he asked with confusion. My heart sank at the unprovoked reminder.

"What do you mean?" I tried to avoid the question.

"Well, is it not true that most fairies have wings?" he poked.

"Some do, yes, but not all. For instance, flower fairies and sprites *will* have wings, unless there is a birth defect or one parent does not have wings. Tree folk, or dryads, do not have wings. Most would need a wingspan half the continent to even try and fly. Does that answer your question?" I tried to be relaxed with my answer.

"No. I asked about *your* wings. Were you not born with any?" he continued, oblivious to the pain this subject inflicted.

"Not anymore," I answered quietly.

"Sacré bleu! Is that what this dark stain is? I thought maybe it was some other kind... my deepest apologies." he said, rushing to correct his mistake.

"Yes, that is what the stain is from... though you do not need to apologize," I said, though the wound was already open.

"Please forgive me," he begged with a wounded look on his face, "S'it te plaît."

"I do, I do. What is that you are saying? I do not understand it. Is it not English?'

"Non, non. I am French, do you not know of France? It is across the channel." He waved his hands south with a gleeful smile.

"Where is French?"

"France," he enunciated the '*a*' sound, making it more round, almost like an '*o*'. "The country is *France*, where we speak French," he laughed.

"Why did you leave France?" *Now I am the nosy one.* Nicol did not flinch or freeze. Instead, his face grew hard, and he would not meet my gaze. He stared forward as he walked through the crunchy leaves.

"My father," he said. It was all he said at first. But then he went on. "When my mother passed, he became a slave to alcohol. He would work, then pass out at the tavern, or come home and take his frustrations out on me." He had a distant look in his eyes as he spoke.

"Nicol, I am so sorry–" I started, but he stopped me by raising a hand. He wanted to say more.

"One day I got so fed up, I fought back. That was a mistake. He pulled a knife and threatened to '*gut me like the fish I was*'. After that, how could I stay?" he said it like a question, but I knew he did not want a response.

"I spent some time on the street until Niv found me. We have been inseparable, and my hair colored, ever since," he concluded with a more jovial tone.

"Your hair turned purple when you met Nivedita?" I was confused. Nicol laughed with his whole body before he could answer.

"Non, non. She offered to pay me to experiment with my hair, and I told her she could just have it. Once we knew it worked, I started to like the color. Now most of southern England knows of the lavender-haired, lute-playing bard!" he winked.

Ahead of us, Nivedita and Catherine turned into the forest, towards puffs of smoke I could see through the trees. Viçente waited for Nicole and me, then navigated us to a fallen tree near the house. We watched as Catherine approached the door for Nivedita. She knocked, and there was a long pause that followed. But then, the door creaked open slowly, and a white-haired woman bent over with age answered the door, wearing a green robe dress.

"Hello, I am Catherine Wilcott, and this is my companion Nivedita Thapa. She has come from India to study English medicines. We heard there was an herbalist living between Llawer-enni and Hulfford. Might you be her?"

"Who are they?" the woman asked, ignoring Catherine's question.

"Our other party members. They will not bother you." Nivedita responded.

"I am a herbalist, but I cannot say for sure if I am the one you seek. You may call me Merona." she beckoned Nivedita and Catherine inside and left the doorway. Nicol, Viçente, and I remained outside. Viçente leaned back to rest against the stump of the fallen tree. Nicol attended to his lute, wiping it down with a cloth and plucking, not playing, the strings.

I watched the trees like I used to at home. The sun rays that broke up the bare branches became brilliant pools of light on the ground. One large pool of light caught my eye. I slid off the log and walked past the cottage to the pool of light shining so bright against the leaves that I thought it was maybe a puddle, but no. It was a pile of yellow leaves reflecting the light outwards again. I wanted to feel the human sun on the skin of my hands, to test it to see how badly it hurt. Carefully, one finger at a time, I pulled the glove off of my right hand.

Holding it up, I passed it through the sun beam. It did not burn or sting. I passed through again slower, pausing in the middle. My hand obscured the light from the golden leaves. I wiggled my fingers, watching the shadow until my hand began to sting.

"Not again!" Nicol sighed. I turned back in the direction of his voice to see that he had crept up behind me and was fixated on my blackened hand.

"What?" groaned Viçente.

"The plague," Nicol exhaled. Viçente jumped to his feet and backed farther away from me. Nicol retreated farther away. I hurriedly replaced my glove.

"No, no. I do not have the plague," I whispered. "Fae cannot contract the plague. These are... burns." Viçente approached me cautiously.

"Show me?" he encouraged. I obliged and pulled off both gloves. At first, he only inspected them virtually, but then he used the sleeve of his tunic to flip my hands over. Very gently, he touched my skin with his rough hands.

"Does it hurt?" he asked.

"Not anymore."

I looked to Nicol, who had moved closer to watch Viçente, but he would not look at me. He held a confused scowl as he fixated on Viçente's inspection of me.

"It is alright. There are no pustules or lesions. She tells the truth," Viçente called. Nicol, still skeptical, shook his head and did not come closer. He waved us off like a pair of flies.

"How did this happen?" Viçente asked, his changing to something softer Was it sympathy? I could not be sure.

"I... I cannot say until we are with the others. I would like to say it only once. That part is painful." I looked at him, pleading with my eyes. He nodded in understanding and gestured for us to return together to the log. Nicol removed himself from the area to sit alone on the ground away from us, tapping on his lute.

Just then, the three women came out from the cottage, determination etched on all three faces. They marched a few paces before Catherine and Nivedita realized something was wrong. The old woman, however, did not. Catherine urged Nivedita to go on, but Nivedita protested until Catherine insisted she would catch up.

"What is going on out here?" She scolded us. Nicol looked towards Viçente and me. She gave us a matronly state and I broke. Taking off my right glove again, I showed her what the issue was. She gasped and stepped back, covering her face. It was Viçente who stood to defend me. He reached a hand to Catherine.

"It is ok, it is not the plague," he exclaimed, urging her to come back. She took his outstretched hand and allowed herself to be led back. She looked unsure but inspected my hand her own way. Once she was satisfied, she looked me very seriously in the eye.

"What happened?" her tone held an edge.

"She would like to tell us all later," Viçente answered for me. "Go, Nivedita may need you." Catherine nodded and jogged off loudly to rejoin Nivedita and Merona, her pack jostling as she went. I replaced my glove again and stared at the leaves on the ground. It was not until evening, when the sun began to fall behind the trees, that the women returned from the woods. Catherine took up the rear while Merona held onto Nivedita's arm.

"She will be right back out. I have one more thing to show you," Merona croaked. Catherine decided to wait outside with the rest of us, dropping her pack on the ground next to Viçente's feet. She plopped down on the fallen tree between Viçente and me, leaning her head against him and releasing a heavy sigh.

"What ails you, my friend?" Viçente queried, giving her a curious grin. She opened her eyelid the slightest bit to catch his expression.

"My feet, dear, they ache. We did not stop! That woman has some feet on her!" Catherine exclaimed. Viçente and Nicol both snorted at her response. Viçente nudged her off and patted her back.

"We should have beds tonight," she said.

"And a story from our fairy, right?" I looked up at Catherine's use of my race. She was studying me. I hoped it was just for my reaction, but I could not shake the feeling that she resented me now.

"Yes. I will answer as many questions as I can," I replied softly, trying not to make eye contact. Unsuccessful, I caught Viçente's eye, and he gave me a supportive pat on the shoulder.

Nivedita stepped out of the cottage, finishing a conversation with Merona before firmly shutting the door. She walked to those of us on the fallen tree, stopping in front of me with her hands on her hips.

"What on earth is going on?" she lashed out at me. I looked to her to speak while looking her in the eye, but her strong scowl deflected my stare expertly. Staring at her chin was as close as I could raise my eyes to speak.

"My skin is blackened, but not from the plague. I asked everyone if I could explain once we were all together – at a later time," I rushed my response. Springing a single glance upward, I saw Nivedita's fierce brown eyes fixed on me.

"Show me." She was firm but gentle. I nodded and took my left glove off, setting it on the tree next to me. Nivedita knelt on the ground to inspect my hand.

"May I touch you?" she asked me. I nodded, and she gently touched my hand where it was blackened. "Does it hurt?" she asked, brushing my knuckles.

"No." I could barely feel anything from my hands. It was odd to have once felt so much and now so little.

"Hmm." She stopped and looked up at me. "Well, we need to get to the next town before it gets dark. Nicol?" She turned away from me to collect Nicol. He and Nivedita spoke privately away from the rest of us. She seemed to convince him that it was safe to travel with me. They led the way north toward our next destination. Catherine shouldered her pack and followed, stopping only to call to Viçente and me.

"Are you coming?" Viçente stood off the log and offered me a hand, urging me to come with them still. I thought for a moment about leaving silently into the woods to live off of what I had on hand until I could forage. I would not be welcome in any town so long as my hands were black. With no other reasonable choice and a heavy heart, I allowed myself to be pulled from the log and guided towards a path in the forest. Nicol stood the farthest away from me. Everyone else had waited for Viçente and me to rejoin them. They began walking as soon as we were close.

We went northwest towards Hulfford, which Catherine notified us was half a day away. The night almost beat us there. We had just enough dusk light to find the tavern. Catherine called Viçente up to the front to muscle our way in past the crowd of sweaty residents. I watched the local patrons shoot us all vicious glares, but stuck to my group anxiously. We snaked our way to the barkeep counter where a tall lanky woman with red hair was taking orders.

Viçente and Nicol shouldered their way to the front to speak to the barkeep. Nivedita, Catherine, and I stayed behind them, waiting. The barkeep was annoyed that they had interrupted more paying customers on such a busy night, but quickly changed her demeanor when Nicol flashed his lute. She flapped her hands past them towards the hearth. Nicol bowed at the wait several times, thanking her before pushing us to the hearth pit in the middle of the room. Nicol spoke quickly to Viçente and Catherine before moving to a table very close to the fire. Catherine threw down her pack, and Viçente disappeared back outside. I suddenly felt so alone. He was the only one who had not looked at me like I was infected. *Maybe it would be better if I slipped out and let them be.*

Nivedita waited for me and reached out a hand to me. I studied her face. *Does she think I have the plague? No, surely not if she offers me her hand.* I decided against myself and took her offered hand. We joined the others as Nicol began a slow melancholic tune. The patrons of the tavern became less chatty and soon settled into their seats to create a quiet and respectful night.

Chapter Thirty

Nicol began to draw a crowd of content patrons that hovered nearby to make requests. The crowd overtook the table we had chosen, and they did so quickly. Nicol switched tunes and began a soft promenade around the fire pit. Catherine and Nivedita stared at me, creating an air of awkward attention. One that only increased when Viçente returned, sweaty and carrying an armful of firewood, which he put to the side of the fire pit. Once it was all put down, he returned to us.

All three sat staring at me, anticipating my explanation. I closed my eyes and took a deep breath. The fire was strong, Nicol's music flowed into my heart, and I released the breath slowly. One finger at a time, I removed my gloves, setting them on the table.

"It is not the plague, I hope Nivedita can confirm that for you all," I started, looking at Nivedita's gentle face for reassurance. She nodded, and in turn, I gave the others a regretful half-smile that I hoped would portray my truthfulness. I looked around before laying my hand on the table for the other two to examine. Viçente and Nivedita were content – it was only Catherine who I now needed to convince.

"Nicol will be busy for quite some time, friend. You should tell us now. I will help you explain it to him later," Nivedita prompted.

"Of course, I am sorry. Before I begin, I have to ask what you know of the Fairy Realm?" I asked quietly. Catherine rolled her eyes to

Viçente, who looked to Nivedita for assistance. They shared a look of impatience and I could feel shame eating away at my gut.

"Enough to have stories read to us as children, but none of us have been there, if that is what you are asking," Catherine snapped in reply. Nivedita laid a hand softly on Catherine's arm.

"No one I know of has been, but the open trade is known," Nivedita replied. She and I turned to Viçente, who nodded silently, leaning an arm on the table.

"Yes, I, too, know of fairies, but you would be the first that I have met. I have my suspicions that some of the folk I have met before might have been, but never asked," he said. Now it was on me to explain the best I could about my burns.

"Where I come from, think of it like a country, I suppose. We called our region Effection, because most of the effectually talented clans originated from our region," I began, but I noticed some other patrons began to listen in. I hunched over our table, beckoning to the others to lean in with me. Catherine, Nivedita, and Viçente hunched over the table as well, leaning on the table to hear me. Catherine waved her hand in a circular motion, urging me to continue.

"My parents were forced to marry to solidify a treaty. I am their first child." Catherine nodded furiously with a look in her eye that told me she understood the burden. "I was asked to marry, and when the moment arrived, I could not go through with it. There was nothing wrong with the lord by any means, save a few pompous opinions. I only wanted to serve my people with knowledge and true acts, " I lamented. Tears pricked my eyes, threatening to fall. I dared not let them, fearing that the group would see it as an attempt for sympathy. I did not want to be seen as something to be pitied. Catherine reached a hand to me, and when I went to take it, she flinched away for a second before taking my hand.

"You would not marry the lord, so they did this? Is that common punishment among the fae?" she asked, squeezing my hand gently. Her face was covered in sympathy.

"Yes and no. As far as I know, it was an accident. I believe the Queen lost her temper and lashed out at me, but for all I truly know, it could have been my mother that maimed me. The trial they forced me to participate in was like rubbing dirt into the wound, though."

"Trial?" Nivedita exclaimed. I looked at her in surprise. A few patrons from surrounding tables looked over at us. Nicol switched to the first song I had ever heard him play. I lowered my gaze, remembering the trial, but I had to continue. I made a promise.

"My refusal to marry the Lord resulted in my Queen – or mother – firing a beam of light at me, burning me, and catching my gown on fire. Luckily, I was saved by my father and my lady-in-waiting, but the damage was done. A monarch has not attacked one of their subjects before, so a trial was called for by the other rulers of the other three regions and my father. I learned during the trial that she wanted to execute me. I was held in the Queen's tower for several days where I learned I had lost my connection to the essence – magic. Any attempt to cast a spell or even draw from the essence resulted in a burning sensation that I later realized was this." I displayed my hands to everyone at the table. *It is almost funny how horrible this all sounds now.*

"What was the outcome of the trial?" Catherine asked. I locked eyes with Catherine. She still held my hand firmly, her green eyes furiously holding my gaze. I nodded and continued.

"The outcome was exile. I am never to return home, well, I have no home now. No family either. That is why I cannot give you a name to call me. They took away the name my parents gave me," I choked out. Catherine rubbed my hand with hers, her face contorting in anguish. Nivedita reached over and took my other hand. She prodded the blackened skin and gave a quick look around the room.

"You can do no magic at all?" Nivedita asked.

"I can perform small acts of magic, like transforming the size of these shoes," I poked my foot over the edge of the table, "but anything that resembles my former abilities results in pain," I finished, a quiver sneaking into my voice as I tried to hold back the tears. I was unable to hold them back and they rolled down my cheeks. Catherine and Nivedita squeezed my hands in support.

"Pain?" Nivedita asked. I laughed against my will. A small giggle, but it broke the tension enough for Viçente to chuckle back. Catherine snorted, but took my attention back seriously by tapping my hand gently with a finger. I cleared my throat to stop the laughter.

"Yes, when I woke up in custody in the Queen's tower, it was nightfall. I attempted a simple spell from my bloodline and my hands and feet burned in immense pain. I have not been brave enough to try any other bloodline magic, but I can perform the infant magic of simple transformations, probably even levitation, but I do not know how much essence I have in reserve. The human realm has little to no magic, and I do not know what happens when a fairy runs out of essence."

"What is your bloodline magic – was–?" Viçente interjected. Catherine smacked him with the back of her hand on his chest. He continued to stare at me, unbothered by the assault.

"My mother was of the light clan, my father of the darkness clan. They called me The First Star. Now I suppose that title would go to my sister. I used to be able to conjure magnificent stars and willed them to do wonderful things."

"Oh, honey…" Catherine comforted me. She gave Viçente a dangerous look. "I hope you can forgive our worries. The plague has ravaged all of Europe. We all have a story of our escape from the plague. Viçente and I ran into Niv and Nic in much the same way. No one would touch me, let alone some near enough to learn I did not have the plague!" she laughed sadly.

"My gods, you are right. I had mostly forgotten about that. Go on! Tell her!" Nivedita encouraged, and a small giggle escaped her. She smiled ear to ear at Catherine, like a mischievous cat. Catherine rolled her eyes and faced me.

"Viçente and I had just barely gotten comfortable with one another when I caught the fever. The chills made it impossible to walk, and this poor gentleman carried me from village to village until he could not. We used all of our coin on a room at the inn where I was either too cold or too hot. A mess, if you will."

"I will! I had no idea how to cure you! I thought surely she would die!" Viçente told me. Catherine patted his arm comfortingly.

"Nivedita was accompanying a rural physician that we had called. She knew immediately that it was some manageable fever but the physician thought *he* knew better. Nivedita ended her apprenticeship immediately and attended to me. For days, she sat by my bedside nursing me through each hot flash or cold chill, keeping me alive. I swear to it!" Catherine concluded enthusiastically. I swore I saw Nivedita blush.

"Nicol and Viçente worked to pay for the room and after a week or so we came to realize we were all a great team. When Catherine regained her strength, we told her what our plans were. We were – are – aligned. Thus we are the group you see before you today!" Nivedita laughed.

"What were your plans?" I asked. Catherine fixed me with a sympathetic look.

"The truth of it all is that I am like you," she started like a theatrical performer, speaking dramatically with her hands. "My father arranged a marriage to a wealthy lord – twice my age – to settle his debts! I ran away the night before and just *barely* escaped. Lucky for me, my father had never been much of a huntsman and could not afford to send one after me," she explained. Viçente and Nivedita nodded along like they had heard this every day.

"I am so sorry Catherine. That sounds horrible." I replied, trying to be sympathetic.

"Oh no! My escape is nowhere near as tragic as yours. We are sorry for *you*. *Exile* explains why you do not have any supplies!"

"And the drinking," Viçente yawned, earning a jab with Catherine's elbow into his ribs. That one got through his tough exterior. He gave Catherine the glare of an angry brother unable to tussle with his sister while he rubbed the spot.

"You are right. I was attempting to feel numb. It would have been better than the horrible feelings I was drowning in," I caved and explained further.

"Of course." Nivedita was much better at sympathy.

"I think I remember the innkeeper saying we could have hot meals for working, along with a room. I am going to check on that, Viçente excused himself.

"Do not worry. We will help you get back on your feet, and then it will be your choice to stay with us or not," Nivedita assured. Viçente returned with two plates of hot food. He set them in the middle of the table and I saw that one was sliced pork and the other was a half loaf of bread along with three extra empty plates. Catherine caught my look of confusion and explained.

"We usually do not get much to eat unless we have coin to buy it with. We are lucky that we can get some extra plates. Now we each add something to the table and share. I am going to add my remaining berries before they turn sour." she fished out a handkerchief of pink raspberries. Not the most fancy of dinners but surely enough to help us sleep. I brought out two apples and added them to the feast.

"If I had a knife, I would divvy them up, but this is what I can offer. Nicol will need something more after singing so much, and Viçente after chopping the firewood," I said sheepishly. Viçente looked at me with an expression I could not place. He quietly took the apples and sliced them up into ten pieces. Catherine and Nivedita worked in tandem to separate the food onto each plate as evenly as possible.

"Nivedita chose the two plates closest to her and took them both to where Nicol had sat to play his melody. He continued to strum as she and Nivedita began to talk. He even strummed while he ate! He looked at me a couple of times and I surmised that Nivedita was explaining my burns to him. I ate from my plate, occasionally looking over to them in hopes that I would see him relax in understanding, but I ended up catching his eye. His hazel eyes had a passionate fire in them, mirrored by the fire he sat next to. I looked down at my plate quickly and became self-conscious of my blackened hands. I slipped on my purple leather gloves once again and returned to my meager meal. Catherine and Viçente dissolved into their own world, chatting about old adventures. I listened politely like I used to at home.

When the bottoms of the plates were visible, it was Catherine who yawned and stretched before gathering the plates to return to the innkeeper. When she returned, she waved a brass key attached to a bit of parchment with a string.

"Our room awaits! She said there are *three* beds! How lucky!" Catherine proclaimed while shouldering her pack. Nivedita rejoined us as Nicol began to sing a new ballad – this one about bears.

Together, the three of us followed Catherine through a short hallway to a staircase. We ascended the stairs and at the top, Catherine found the room matching the symbol on the parchment. She inserted the key and turned the lock, opening the door for us. We filed in one after another, Catherine being last.

The room was sizable – I would guess ten paces by ten paces. There were indeed three beds, but I was unsure how that was considered fortunate to Catherine when there were five of us.

"Usually the gentlemen give us ladies the beds, while they take the floor. Then we sacrifice our pillows to the gentlemen so that the floor might be more bearable. The mattresses and pillows are all straw anyway, so the comfort can be shared." Catherine laughed, throwing her bag onto the only bed on the same wall as the door. The other two sat under the window and against the opposing wall to the left. Nivedita took that bed, leaving me with the one under the window. I took the two pillows from my bed and gave them to Viçente. He laid out a cloak or blanket of some kind before laying the pillows down. He had three in total; the other three rested near the door for Nicol.

I could still hear Nicol's sweet voice and beautiful chords from our room. It drove me to make a decision. That decision was to go down and speak with him, under the guise of sharing the room key.

"May I take the key to Nicol?" I asked. Catherine exchanged a look with Nivedita, then they shrugged and Catherine tossed me the key. I caught it and quietly left the room, smiling at Nivedita as I closed the door.

Nicol was sitting atop an empty table near the hallway entrance. Other patrons were leaving to settle in for the night. I saw a couple leave some copper coins on the table for Nicol as they left the main hall. I waved to catch Nicol's attention. When I did, he nodded, allowing me to approach him, but he did not stop singing. I held up the room key and he urged me to sit down by gesturing with his head. I sat slowly, being careful not to disturb anyone generously gifting him coins.

I chose a chair near his feet and sat down, as the coins were being tossed to his other side, then I set the key down.

"Everything is ready, and I thought I would bring the key to you so that I may have a chance to apologize," I started. Nicol continued to sing, but watched me intently. "I am sorry to have kept this from you all. It was wrong," I said as loudly as I dared, not wanting to overtake his music while the few stragglers moved past. Nicol nodded, either in agreement or encouragement to continue. I did not know which.

"I understand if you would no longer like to travel with me. However, I do feel indebted to you and Nivedita for nursing me back to health. I would like to stay until that debt is repaid."

"You do not owe us. As Catherine said before, this is just what good people do. They take care of one another, regardless of the chance that it will be 'paid back'," Nicol said, breaking from his lyrics to speak to me. "Wait a moment and we will speak." So, I did. The song seemed to go on forever, but in truth, it was just enough time to let all the remaining patrons filter out of the main room into the hallway where our room was or out the front door. The innkeeper slapped the lockdown on the door for the night with an exhausted sigh.

"Thank you for your lovely music! Enjoy your stay!" she called to us as she wandered into the backrooms. Nicol placed his lute between us on the table and then gathered the copper pennies from his other side.

"Thank you for the apple slices. They added the perfect sweetness to Catherine's tart berries." He smiled genuinely down at me. I tried to smile back, but it was not as genuine. I still had some sadness in my heart and was worried about what he might say next.

"Why are you so melancholic?" His brows turned up in question.

"Excuse me?" I responded. *How else am I supposed to feel?* He readjusted to face me better, still looking down.

"You have improved your situation overnight. How are you so sad when your fortune has changed?" His words struck a chord in me. *He is right, I could be worse off. There were far worse places to be than in a warm inn with genuinely nice people.*

"You are right. I suppose I am still sad at the loss of my family," I thought out loud.

"Even after they threw you out?" he snorted. I dropped my jaw in surprise at his forwardness.

"Yes, I suppose."

"They do not *deserve* you." Nicol's words caught me off guard. A sob lodged in my throat, choking me.

"If loving you was as easy as throwing you away, they would not have done it," he added. Almost tearing the sob from me, the truth cut deep.

"I am sorry for how I have treated you today. That is not who I am, and I hope you will give me another chance to behave more appropriately. I lost my mother to the plague. The plague has always threatened my life. I could not bear to lose my friends to that pain," he explained. I started to respond, but he held up a hand. "No need to explain further. I believe what you told Niv was the truth. She vouched for you."

I shamefully looked away, trying to get my mind to soak up this moment. Nicol slid from the table and scooped up his lute, as well as the key, with one hand. He flung his purple braid over his shoulder and offered me his free hand. I took it, and he pulled me up off the seat.

"So... no more magic eh? What a tragedy," he joked as we left the main hall. I directed him towards the room. Maybe it was because I was tense, or let some small gasp out, but Nicol suddenly stopped. He then turned to face me, and that was when I realized why: I had walked right into him!

"Ooph," I gasped. Nicol had the most annoying smile cracking his face. The kind that I had seen many times on Castor's face. He wanted something, and it involved me performing like a stage actor.

"What is it?" I asked cautiously. His smile grew.

"You are holding something back! I can tell," he accused. He was not wrong, but I could not admit it.

"What? No!"

"Oh yes! I did not spend a decade on the streets of Paris without learning how to spot concealment. Tell me!" He was stern, but giddy. The way he held his hands on his hips made me feel like a scolded child. I hesitated, but his stance only grew more impatient as he crossed his arms over his chest and began to tap his fingers slowly.

"Promise not to laugh," I said. He nodded, so I continued. "When I first came to the Human Realm, I learned I could see the stars move."

"Yes, they do that. Many astronomers have proven this. Do they not move in the Faerie Realm?"

"Yes they do, but no not like that. They come together to make shapes and scenes, like in a theater. They make up people and things, and move in ways that show me visions of what is to come."

Nicol's expression softened, and his eyes bored into mine softly. He was studying me, my face, to sense if I was lying, or perhaps joking.

"You do not have to believe me, but that is my 'concealment'," I spoke softly, a little wounded.

"No! I do believe you! It is a type of, how you say... *Divination*?" he asked. I shrugged, because I had never heard the word. *Must be French.*

"Come, tell me all about it, and I will try to explain what I know of the other ways. The other forms of divination. In Italy, they play cards to read fortunes! In the north, I hear they throw bones and stones with figures on them. I have heard of so many, but never of someone seeing fortunes in the stars! You must be an astronomer!" Nicol looped his arm through mine and led the way to the room we shared with everyone else, where he did indeed ask me more questions.

Chapter Thirty-One

When morning came, I was gently woken by Catherine shaking my arm.

"Good morning sunshine!" she cheered. I looked around to see Nicol putting his pillows back on the beds. I sat up slowly, yawning. Nicol gave me a small wave and smile before exiting the room. I slid off the bed to rearrange it before I also left, but Catherine already had two pillows in hand.

"Do you remember earlier when I said I would give you one of my dresses? Here it is." She handed me the two pillows and then a neatly wrapped bundle of dark blue linen. I took it, but instead of putting it on, I just stared at her. I did remember her saying something about a dress, but I did not expect her to follow through.

"I do not know what to say... thank you Catherine," I blurted. She exhaled a laugh, shaking her head.

"Thanking me is enough. I will wait for you on the landing. It may be uncomfortable but at least it will not have that massive bloodstain on the back. We will find a way to wash it so that you can have two," she said with a grimace. Then she let herself out of the room, closing the door quietly.

I studied the garment once I was alone in the room. It seemed to be a simple linen gown – not anything fancy like my mother would have liked, but more like the peasant garments she hated. The sides of the gown had lacing to adjust the fit. The long sleeves were my only concern; I was worried that they may be too long. *At least I can dress myself with this.*

Taking the bloodstained dress off was difficult in its own way. The ruddy brown stains on the back had grown as my wounds had reopened. I sighed and tossed the dress onto the bed before slipping on the blue dress. It was surprisingly soft, and the feeling of a clean outfit almost made me cry. I adjusted the lacing on the sides while I held the tears back. The sleeves were a few inches past my fingertips. *No problem, I will simply roll them up.* I began to cuff the sleeves of the dress. The only thing I was missing now was a bath.

I rolled up the dirty dress and stuffed it in my satchel. Opening the door, I found Catherine leaning on the railing. Her eyes went wide once she saw me.

"My dear! You look so lovely!" she gasped. I readjusted my satchel to divert some of the awkwardness I felt. Catherine took my hand and encouraged me to spin around, and when I did, she let out an appreciative sound.

"Ooh! Just as I thought! This color suits your eyes!" After her compliments were finished, she nodded to the stairs for me to follow, then started to descend. I followed her down, and as we came into the main room, I saw the others at a new table in the far back left corner. There was a plate of fruit on the table that they were picking off of. Catherine caught their attention and graciously gestured to show off my new dress. Nivedita and Nicol both gasped in awe.

"Your eyes!"

"C'est magnifique!" they said respectively. I felt my cheeks warm and I knew they were bright red. Viçente gave me a small smile while he continued to eat. Catherine and I sat down, and she tapped me on the shoulder to show me her addition to the breakfast: a few strange, leafy greens. I took that as my cue to add my portion. I rummaged in my satchel and decided on the portion of bread I had purchased the other day.

"Thank you," said Catherine, giving me a large portion of fruits and the greens. She broke the bread into pieces of five, giving me the first before serving the others. Nicol caught my eye from across the table; a sweet smile and a look of camaraderie glowed back at me. I smiled in return, thankful for everything. Things appeared to be mended betwixt us, and he winked before returning his focus to Nivedita's intense mixing. I, too, became transfixed by her fluid movements as she multitasked between two bowls of a similar mixture and her portion of breakfast. The mixtures were different only in color – one was a waxy green and the other a more clear green. She used her left hand to pick at food while her right did most of the work mixing and choosing ingredients.

We ate slowly, but Viçente finished before us all and began packing up. Nivedita took the hint and began to gather her things as well. Nicol helped her store the jars that were now filled with the two liquids. Catherine packed up the leftovers, so I did the same. The innkeeper stopped by to collect the singular plate and to thank Viçente and Nicol for their work the night before. With Viçente at the front and myself at the back, we filed out of the tavern into the warm morning air, Viçente holding the door for us.

People were out in droves, most of them funneling north. Nivedita joined Viçente at the held of our crowd, directing us with the flow of Hulfford's citizens. They led us to quite a busy marketplace, rows of market stalls buzzing with patrons haggling prices. Nicol drifted to the back where I was lagging. He lightly gripped my elbow and guided me to stay with the group as I ogled at the foreign goods. If I were to close my eyes, I could have pretended I was home, in Inanis. The sounds and smells were so similar. Nicol kept pace with the others until we reached a small water fountain topped with a statue of a woman in a flowing gown. Nivedita picked a spot of shade under the fountain, then began to unpack her jars of liquids.

"We are going to brave the shops." Catherine dumped her bag next to Nivedita, who was setting up her tinctures, before heading down an alley with Viçente. Nicol shrugged and perched on the lip of the fountain with his lute on his knee. I thought for a moment about following Catherine, but my curiosity about Nivedita's potions won me over. I sat next to Catherine's bag, next to Nivedita's right side, the trunk on her left. She set the jars in neat rows in front of herself on a small cloth she had laid out.

"If you do not mind my asking, what are these?" I asked. Nivedita looked up at me with a sparkling smile.

"This is a tincture made with boiled water and the herbs I harvested yesterday with Merona. One drinks this to help with a stomach ache." She held up the clear green jar. "This is a salve or ointment for burns or rashes," she cheerily explained.

A curious woman wandered over to inspect Nivedita's wares. She made various sounds of thought before she asked Nivedita what they were. Nivedita was animated, speaking with her hands as she explained the tinctures again with a more theatrical flair.

"Oh! My husband burned his hands on rope just yesterday! This is just the thing! How much?"

"Four pence," Nivedita said firmly with a delicate smile.

"Four pence? I shall give you three!" the woman bartered. I looked to Nicol for guidance. He caught my worried look and nodded slowly, then mimicked taking a deep breath, urging me to take one as well. I did, inhaling deeply and exhaling slowly. Nicol began a soft, slow melody, reminding me of the waltz from home.

"Five pence!" Nivedita increased the price, and the woman gasped.

"I've three pence. That is my final offer. I have to feed ma family," she whined. Nivedita looked to Nicol, who shrugged, then gave in with a regretful nod.

"Deal." Nivedita stuck out her left hand for the coins, holding a jar in her right. They made their exchange and the woman went on her way.

The next several sales were much the same. I watched with awe as she dealt with each customer. Another mother purchased both the tincture and the salve and somehow haggled the prize down to one groat. A man with his arms quite full knocked over two jars but Nivedita only made him pay for one. A woman with six obnoxious children was our last customer before Nivedita was out of stock. She stood, groaning and stretching, then engaged Nicol with a touch. He stopped playing and looked at her.

"Would you two go to the forest and find all you can of these two flowers?" She handed us each a white flower; mine had multiple minuscule flowers that made up the larger flower. "Yarrow," Nivedita said. Nicol received a flower she called 'chamomile', then pointed us west.

Nicol led the way, working our way through the buildings until the dense tops of trees were visible. We found that there was a small stone wall we had to go over, but otherwise, we easily arrived at the forest, where we began to look for our respective herbs. Nicol held his flower in front of him as a guide, so I copied him and compared every white flower to mine.

"Have you found any?" Nicol broke the silence.

"What? Oh, the flowers. No, not yet. Have you?"

"Yes! My hands are getting full. May I put my bundle in your satchel?" he asked nicely. I pulled open the top of the bag and allowed him to dump his handful in.

"Thank you! Now let us find some more of this 'yarrow' she wanted. The faster we get back the more Niv can make." Nicol prepared to look for my herb, stopping to study the bloom in my hand.

"Really? She has sold everything for fair prices. Should we not have enough for a room tonight?" I asked. Nicol stopped, turned around, and plucked the flower from my hands.

"Yes, we do potentially have enough for one night, but we are trying to save enough coin for the winter." He gave me a stern look, as though I should have known.

"Oh. My apologies." I lowered my eyes and attempted to continue looking for Yarrow, but Nicol was not. He tilted his head to catch my eyes.

"You do not need to apologize. You do not know these things. Is the fairyland always warm then?" he asked, encouraging me to take his hand and follow him.

"No, the seasons do change, but as far as I know, everyone has someplace to stay when the snow arrives." I took his hand.

"As far as you know? Were you a hermit or too poor to peek into taverns?" He aided me in getting over a fallen tree.

"No, my place in society was quite high as I understand it. My parents were a duke and a duchess. If those mean anything to you."

"A duke?" he gasped, and I nodded. "Mon Dieu! That explains everything!"

"Explains what?"

"You know next to nothing of the wider world on your own. We have been curious as to why everything is new to you, but being the daughter of a duke... well, that would explain it," he snorted. I wrinkled my brows in confusion and stopped walking, forcing Nicol to stop, too.

"Former," I corrected. He gave me a look of utter confusion, and then his face melted like candle wax in a fire when the realization set in.

"Right... I am so sorry. Might we start again?"

"What do you mean?"

"I apologize, and we change the subject to anything you like. Let us be friends. I am sorry for the inconsiderate comment about your past. Please, ask me anything." He bowed his head, offering me his hand again, so I took it as we continued to search for the yarrow. I worked on a response, lost in thought.

"It is alright. I am not offended. I can only experience some pain from memories. I miss my father and my siblings. Do you miss anyone?"

"My mother." Nicol looked to me. I offered a sympathetic smile. We continued to search for more yarrow, occasionally finding something similar but with less fuzz and an off assortment of flowers. Nicol wanted to take them anyway, but I insisted we return with only what we needed.

"We do not know what these plants do." I gently laid a bundle of the wrong flowers Nicol had picked in the tall grass.

"You are very precise, uh.. Miss Fée?" I was stunned for a moment, and he waited until I shook my head.

"I would only like to please Nivedita. She has been so kind, and I am still in awe of her looking after me that night." I giggled a little. Nicol nodded in understanding.

"I promise you do not need to impress her. Well, there is one thing..."

"One thing? What do you mean?"

"You require a name, Mademoiselle. We cannot keep calling you 'fairy' or 'you'. Simply put, it is rude." I pondered what he said for a moment as we continued to walk and collect yarrow. My satchel became full, not heavy, but the herbs began to fall out. We held the extra and turned around to head back to town.

"I understand what you mean, but I cannot help you. My banishment severed my connection to my family. I have no name now. Anything respectable will be fine."

"Yes! Respectable! We must find one for you!" Nicol exclaimed. I spun my head around fast to catch his expression, thoroughly confused. He looked giddy like a kid getting a sweet treat on market day. *What on earth is happening? These people are exceedingly generous, but why?*

"Mon amie, what is that face for?" He helped me swing my leg over the short stone wall. I chewed my lip, thinking of how to respond.

"I am appreciative of everyone's generosity, but where does it end?"

"Kindness and generosity should never end, mon amie."

"What is that, 'mon amie'? You could call me that!"

"Aha! I do! 'Mon Amie' is French for 'my friend'. You are my friend, are you not?" he laughed as we walked the alleyways back to the water fountain. I was surprised at his ability to remember the way, because I was hopelessly lost.

"Oh," I stopped, surprised. "Yes, I would like to be."

"You are! Now come on, let us get these to Niv. Maybe she will have some ideas." He nodded his head in the direction we were meant to go. When we found the fountain again, Nivedita, Viçente, and Catherine were lounging as they'd waited for our return. Nivedita appeared completely packed and utterly bored. She noticed us as we came out of the final alley, waving in big, animated arcs. Nicol left me to rush to Nivedita and tackle her with a long-armed hug. He squeezed her tight yelling, *'I missed you! I missed you!'* over and over in the most theatrically pitiful whine. I approached slowly, pulling out the herbs in handfuls from my satchel. Attempting to separate the two from each other, I was fully engrossed in the task and did not see that Nivedita had begun to unpack until I knelt on a plate of gooey substance.

"Eehw," I mumbled as I readjusted. I looked down and saw I had knelt in something that Nivedita had placed on the ground.

"I am so sorry!" I exclaimed before I could stop myself. This time, there was no pit that opened under the social construct.

"It is alright. This we can get more of easily, I am sure," Nivedita said. The tension of a social contract from the apology would have bored into me in Mythénia, but now it was like it never existed. Handing over the herbs, I caught Nivedita smiling at me, and then at Catherine and Viçente.

"What?" I asked. Nicol took my hand, grinning from ear to ear.

"We have all agreed that we cannot call you 'friend' until we have a name to call you by!" he chuckled.

Chapter Thirty-Two

Everyone collected their belongings and followed Catherine north, and then northeast. She and Nivedita made up the front while Nicol and Viçente took up the rear, putting me in the middle.

"The parchment shopkeeper told us there is for sure an herbalist in Treamlod. We will get there about mid-afternoon to early evening," Catherine explained.

"We will miss the remaining daylight for sales. I did not make enough coin for new jars *and* a room tonight," Nivedita lamented.

"We shall find a way. Let us get there first," Catherine reassured, patting Nivedita on the back.

"I could pass the time with a song!" Nicol chimed from behind me. I turned my head back to catch Nicol's cheeky green and Viçente's annoyed eye roll. I chuckled and faced forward again.

"We could pass a few more suggestions for your new name," Catherine suggested. I made an attempt to look entranced by the surrounding wood, as if I did not hear her. In truth, I had seen so many ash, birch, rowans, and black alder in my life that I was not impressed by the collection around me. Catherine caught me checking the path ahead and raised a quizzical brow. I smiled sheepishly and she gave me a stern glare in return.

"I suppose that is alright, but you do not have to. 'Fairy' is fine." I stated. Nicol scoffed loudly.

"You deserve to be called something more than your race. You had a name before, and you shall have one again. I am more than a Spaniard and he is more than a Frenchman," Viçente insisted.

"You should all think of a few. We have a ways to go before we reach Treamlod. I will keep us on track if Catherine will give me the map. Then you all can discuss names. I will not have much to add. Surely, you do not want an Indian name," Nivedita said with an edge to her voice. Catherine did not in fact hand over her map. She instead put it away.

"Nonsense. We are on a road, it will take us there. Why should a fairy not want an Indian name?" Catherine fixed her with a drilling stare. Nivedita did not shy away, but her walk became much faster. We all kept pace, but with much effort.

"Well, what do you say?" Catherine shot at me with her piercing, green eyes. I blanched at the direct question.

"I would not mind. I will listen to all your suggestions." I tried to be kind, though I doubted they would find something that really fit me. There was no harm in letting them try.

"Truthfully?" Nivedita stopped, bringing us all to a halt. Everyone was looking at me again. I nodded, but we did not continue walking.

"Yes. If we can find something suitable, I do not mind what region it comes from." I shrugged. Nivedita pulled me into a tight hug, squeezing all the air from my lungs.

When she released me, we all began to walk again. This time, Nivedita walked with me, taking my arm and studying my face. Her eyes rolled over my entire body, always coming back to my face.

"Will you tell us anything about your former name?" Nivedita asked.

"No, it does not feel right. I am no longer her." I did my best to appear confident and firm, but inside I was crumbling. With a shared inhale, Nivedita accepted my answer.

"Right then. I will start." She gave me another glance. "Maya?" I felt nothing, so I shook my head.

"Viçente's turn, then Nicol, and then you, Catherine. Then we shall start over," Nivedita directed.

"I knew quite a few Cecilias?" he tried. But again, I felt nothing, forcing me to respond with another shake of my head 'no'.

"My mother's name was Colette – do you like the sound of that?" Nicol asked. I felt sad that the name felt so hollow to me. I could have said, '*it is lovely, please call me Colette*', but I could not be disingenuous to them while they were the example of genuine.

"It is a lovely name, but I cannot accept it. It is not a fit." I did my best to speak up, looking behind me to reassure Nicol I was grateful. He did not look upset.

"My turn! What about Agnes?" she giggled, I laughed a little, then thought about the name. I could not feel any connection to being called Agnes.

"No thank you," I chortled.

"I have a cousin named Jiya... Do you think that could be a good fit?" Nivedita threw out.

"No, she needs her own name, not a borrowed one," Viçente interjected. It was no match either, so I did not speak up.

"Isabel?" he tried. I looked back to see his relaxed but curious expression, and I shook my head again.

"Johanna?" Nicol tried.

"No, thank you."

"Johanne!" Catherine chimed from the front.

"I am still going to have to say no," I said, feeling no connection.

"What about Navya?" Nivedita asked. I mulled it over for a few paces. It had a nice sound, but gave me no feeling of connection.

"I am sorry. It is a nice name, but I feel no connection." I squeezed Nivedita's arm.

"Gloria?" Viçente tried. I let it sit with me, but no connection formed.

"No, I am sorry."

"Eloise?" Nicol suggested. There was almost a tingle in my heart, but the strong connection I was looking for did not appear.

"I am sorry, again, but no."

"What kind of a connection are you hoping for? Should we have you list fairy names to help you choose?" Nicol asked.

"You came close just now. The connection is just a feeling I have. I cannot explain it. Please continue, as I doubt any fairy names will be fitting," I reassured him. The brittle feeling of my loss still hung in my chest.

"Mary!" Catherine exclaimed from the front.

"No, sorry." I already had my own feelings of the name Mary.

"How about you tell us a couple fairy names so we can come up with something similar?" Catherine suggested. The rest of the group murmured in agreement, folding me into submission.

"Alright… let me see. I once met an air fairy named Susurri, a plant fairy named Hedera, and a moth fairy named Tinea. Does that help?" I asked.

"Mhmm", "Yes", and "Oui" were all said in tandem by Catherine, Nivedita, and Nicol respectively. They were quiet for a while, but eventually picked up again. The sun was beginning its descent to the trees and the hills again.

"The last name I can think of is Priyanka," Nivedita suggested. I took my time assessing the name. A feeling of reverence appeared but not the warm, soft connection of a name.

"It feels regal, but not for me," I answered.

"This one may be too odd, but Paloma?" Viçente tried. It was unique, I gave him that, but the feeling I sought did not show. I shook my head with a mumble.

"Sibyl!" Nicol blurted. A pang like a bell rang in my chest. I thought this was it, but was curious of Catherine's suggestion, too.

"Mmmm… Catherine?" I urged. Nicol sighed behind me.

"Hmm. What do you have to say about Matilda?" Catherine mused. A similar – but lighter – chime rang out in my body. I was filled with the soft warm feeling I was looking for.

"I feel a strong connection between both of those suggestions. I have no idea how to choose between them. How does one choose between two names when they both call to you?" I asked. Catherine threw her head back laughing.

"You do not, in fact, have to choose between them. You can have one as your given name and the other as your second name. Where I am from, we call it a baptismal name, usually after a saint. Mine is Hilda for Saint Hilda, the saint of learning, culture, and poetry, " Catherine explained.

"How do I choose which one is first?"

"Probably the same way you chose them individually. Do you prefer Sibyl Matilda or Matilda Sibyl?" Nicol asked in return. I thought for a moment, allowing both to have space. They chimed and rang out like bells as I repeated them over in my mind. *Matilda Sibyl*. The tinkling of the bells was loud. *Sibyl Matilda*. The sound resonated, filling my body with a warmth of the homecoming I never received.

"Sibyl Matilda," I said finally. The group hummed and mulled over their own thoughts aloud.

"It suits you." Niveidta said, breaking the silence first. I smiled, feeling lighter than I had before. *I am no longer nameless.*

"I agree! There is a saint Matilda; she is the saint of large families! Maybe she will help you rebuild a new family!" Catherine cheered. I laughed to keep the pain at bay. I could never dream of replacing my siblings.

"Thank you everyone. Wait, what about a surname?" I had almost forgotten. "Will I need one?"

"I rarely give mine to anyone. It only denotes where I come from," Nicol stated.

"Mine is a title of pride. Everyone in our region of Spain knows of the noble Çerons. We are known for our community service," Viçente said with pride.

"I give mine out when I am trying to get in someone's good graces. There are no Wilcott lords, so no one will assume I am collecting taxes." Catherine stopped to study her map when we came to a fork in the road.

"It is already clear to most that I am from India, so there is usually no reason to give my family name, but for the same reason as Catherine." Nivedita shrugged.

"How does one acquire a new surname?' I asked, half-knowing the answer, half-hoping I was wrong.

"Usually by marriage," Catherine said.

"There is another way. In some cases people, will change their surnames when they move to a new place. Something like 'Greystone' if their home is called something like 'The Greystone Manor'. You could always name yourself after the place you settle in." Niveidta explained.

"Great! I like that option more! I will take it," I said excitedly.

"Then we will need to help you find someplace permanent," Nicol said. The idea of a home warmed my heart even more than the new names had.

"How much farther?" Nicol complained. The sun was touching the tops of the bare trees. We had more shade, but we would not have time to do much besides looking for a place to sleep.

"The map shows one more bend in the road, then we should see a tavern called 'The Wagon'," Catherine answered.

"Dieu Merci!" Nicol exhaled. I also heard Viçente sigh. Nivedita had a firm grip on my arm that was a comfort to me as I was drawn to the fiery colors of the remaining leaves. I could almost pretend I was still in Mythénia if I closed my eyes a little and let my mind wonder.

"Do not celebrate too much. You will accompany Sibyl on her first attempt to acquire us a room." Nivedita jostled my arm, keeping me from my day dream. Nicol groaned, making me feel guilty, but I was grateful for the company. I meant it, I would do whatever I could to help my new friends. I looked around to see each of them in various stages of contentment, aside from Catherine, who I could not see. I gave Nivedita a friendly pat on her hand and she released me from her grasp.

I walked a little faster to join Catherine at the head of our party. She greeted me with a pleased smile.

A tall wooden building came into view on the right side of the road. I pointed to a sign with the letter markings on it.

"The Wagon," Catherine explained, waving Nicol up from the back. Catherine melted into my previous spot next to Nivedita and slowed the group to a halt as we approached the door. Nicol took a measured look of the place before opening the door for me.

"Ladies first." He smiled. I scrunched my nose in fake annoyance, but went in first. The inside of the tavern was quite noisy and chaotic. Men were heavy in their cups and tossing objects about the room. I searched for anyone taking orders and found a man not much older than Nicol by the looks of him. He wore a tan tunic, worn leather boots, and a vest made of patches. With a wave, I approached and hurriedly thought of what to say.

"Hello, welcome to The Wagon! Can I get you a flagon?" he jovially greeted us.

"Not at this time. We have come to request a room for us and our three companions." I had to raise my voice to be heard above the ruckus.

"Ah! I may have just the thing!" he waved us over to the desk set in a nook in the wall. He flipped open a tattered book and frowned.

"Sorry. No rooms tonight. I am afraid I am all full." He shrugged.

"Perhaps a shed or storage building?" I asked quickly. He shook his head.

"Try up the road a few miles," He said with a frown. I looked at Nicol, who shrugged.

"Sometimes this happens," he leaned down and whispered in my ear, patting me on the shoulder. "Let us tell the others." He nodded towards the door and we left, picking our way through the crowd of lively patrons. I tried to keep my head up, but felt like I had failed them already. When we got outside, Catherine and Viçente were lounging on a patch of clover and leaves under an alder tree. Nivedita was nowhere in sight.

"Where is Niv?" Nicol asked.

"She went to look for ingredients," Catherine answered, looking to me for details on our sleeping arrangements.

"They are full and do not have a place to put us. Not even a storage building. I asked," I blubbered, my heart becoming heavy with disappointment in myself. Tears formed in my eyes.

"Alright. Let us catch up with Niv then," Catherine said.

"Wait," Viçente stopped us, "there she is." He pointed to the red robed figure of Nivedita, who was strolling toward us.

"Do we have a room?" she asked as she rejoined us. I hung my head and informed her that I had failed to secure a room.

"It happens sometimes. Viçente, you and Catherine go back in for food and clear directions to the next inn, please," Nivedita urged.

She handed Viçente a few copper coins. They left their bags with us as they entered the tavern. Nivedita set up her workstation under the alder tree and began mixing ingredients.

Catherine and Viçente returned shortly, even more disgruntled than we had been. Catherine was red faced and bursting at the seams. Viçente carried a load of burnt bread. Nicol stared at the bread with disgust, and Nivedita waved Catherine over to her.

"What happened?" Nivedita asked, but Catherine did not answer. Instead, she plopped down on the ground with a pout.

"The innkeeper insinuated Catherine could 'work' for her room, but her 'knight' was not welcome. He then gave her the most unserious directions, straight to his bedchamber. He must have taken the rejection badly, as this was the only loaf he would sell us," Viçente informed us. Catherine huffed and continued to pout while Nivedita rubbed her back.

"No sense in sticking around here then. Let us go," Nivedita proclaimed. Viçente and Catherine donned their packs again and we walked into the small town of Treamlod. The shops were closing and people were meandering home. We followed a small crowd to what must have been their housing district. As the sun went down, the road took us past homes with fires glowing in them and back out into the forest. We continued northeast until Nicol forced us to stop by sitting on a boulder to massage his feet.

"My feet are killing me," he complained. I had to admit mine hurt too, but I would not have said anything for some time.

"We need to find shelter," Catherine insisted.

"I simply cannot walk another step," Nicol whined. Catherine sighed. We all watched Nicol to see what he would do.

"Can we not build a camp?" he tried.

"Do you see a shelter?" She waved her hand around us, and a triangular shape caught my eye. "We cannot make camp out in the open without one of us staying awake to guard against marauders."

"I do." I said. Everyone looked at me. I pointed to a thatched room peeking out of the underbrush a little ways off the path.

"Astounding!" Catherine rejoiced, heading towards the building. As we approached, I saw it was more of a shack than a shelter, but I supposed it would do. After all, I have slept in a crypt cottage, so as long as there were no mummified remains, I should be fine. We fought the overgrown shrubs to find a door, and once we found one, we pried it open.

Inside was a dirt floor and high rafters. Viçente went to work building us a fire while Nivedita began taking collections for dinner. A draft blew through the cracks in the door, but otherwise, it was cozy. I looked around the small room in awe. I felt warm and safe with these people. They had been nothing but kind and generous to a stranger. *I would have to work my hardest to repay them, but how?* We had our dinner and curled up by the fire to sleep. Viçente slept closest to the door, hand on his sword. I fell asleep with ease for the first time in what felt like ages.

Chapter Thirty-Three

"Help attract customers. This one is for burns." Nivedita handed me a jar of the tallow and yarrow mixture, then sent me on my way towards Catherine. Nicol was playing an exciting, lively tune while Catherine worked to persuade those passing by to purchase Nivedita's wares. We had set up in a vacant square on a half-abandoned corner of the road. There had been several dusty crates that we repurposed for a makeshift merchant stall. I looked at the crowd of people funneling out of their houses and picked a woman who did not seem to be in a hurry.

"Hello, can I interest you in an ointment for burns?" I engaged the woman. Her blonde hair was pushed back with a head scarf, which matched her dark red dress. Her hazel eyes raked me up and down, then away. She was gone with no answer. I sighed. Catherine and I did our best to divert the passers-by towards our setup, but only a few people stopped, mainly because of Nicol's performance. By the time the crowd had thinned, we had sold only two jars, one of each for a total of eight pennies – so I was told.

"How about we make for Aberteifi?" Catherine suggested, displaying her map and pointing to a Northern coastal dot. Nivedita and Nicol shared a look, then shrugged.

"Why not?" Nivedita agreed and began to pack her trunk.

"It will take us the better part of the day to get there," Catherine advised.

"That is ok. We cannot stay here." Nivedita looked around, waving her hand to exaggerate the lack of customers. "There is no money to be made here. Not with an herbalist established in the town." With her truck packed, she stood and joined Catherine on the path out of town. I pushed off the wall and fell into step with Nicol. Viçente followed behind.

"It is too bad there is not someone among us with a novel talent. Something people *would* pay for." Nicol looked down at me with a sly smile. I stared at him, confused. He returned my quizzical stare, making me feel as though I had missed some important piece of information. I faced forward to watch where I walked as we reentered the forest.

Fall had truly set in on this land. The trees were bare, the air was chilly, and our every step echoed with a crunch from the fallen leaves. No one uttered a word as we started our late morning. The sun was rising, steadily warming the air as we passed by the spot where I had discovered our previous night's shelter. I looked at it as we passed, catching Viçente also watching. He, however, looked away first. His eyes caught mine when he faced forward. I looked away before my cheeks could betray my embarrassment.

"We will get to Aberteifi by the evening, which means if we are lucky, we can catch the crowd going home for the evening. What kind of potions do you have ready?" Catherine asked Nivedita. I listened to their conversation.

"They are *not* potions," Nivedita corrected. "They are *remedies*. I still have about half of what I had this morning. Burn ointment and stomach pain relief."

"Is there anything else?" Catherine inquired. Nivedita looked back to Nicol. They seemed to share some unspoken mental conversation before Nivedita responded.

"Hair dye, but not much. We could try to sell it as a wool dye, but it is not made with indigo." I caught Nicol staring at me intently again.

"What?" I mouthed to him. He shook his head and rolled his eyes back to his lute.

More pedestrians joined us on the road, driving us to silence for a time. We were surpassed by carts pulled by oxen and mules. A few single riders astride beautiful horses and a pair of riders with a pack mule also passed by us. I watched them go, careful to avoid Nicol's eye. I was unsure what he wanted, but I could not ask without the others listening in.

I got minorly excited when I saw the riders pull off to one side of the road. Even *I* knew horses and riders stopped for only a handful of things. As we passed, I became inexplicably happy. I saw the sparkle of water.

"Catherine!" I exclaimed, stopping in my tracks and causing Viçente to run into me.

"Yes?" she responded matronly as she turned around to see the collision. I saw everyone looking at me again and immediately became embarrassed.

"The water..." I mumbled. Thankfully, I believe she heard me. She looked where I had pointed and nodded.

"Ah yes. We should stop for a wash," Catherine insisted. Viçente started to argue but was cut off by a deliberate stare from Catherine.

"Well? Come along." Nivedita took my hand and led me to the water. The water that we could see from the road was where the horses were drinking and the other pedestrians had stopped. Catherine took us to the river bed and up the stream until we found a bend that created some idea of privacy. I looked around and saw that Viçente and Nicol had followed us. They bowed away behind a thicket of shrubs, turning their backs and sitting down.

Nivedita and Catherine removed their outer garments and waded into the river shallows. I had no luxury, so I decided that my whole person should be washed, including the clothes I wore. I took off my gloves and shoes, placing them next to my satchel and the other girls' bags. I took out my first dress, the one with the blood stain, and took it with me to the river.

Stepping into the cool river brought an energetic thrum through my body. The water came up to my ankles, my blackened feet and ankles fully hidden. My dress became damp, the moisture creeping up the fabric. Though the water was cold, I found a deeper part of the shallows, picked a section of the rocky river bed, and sat down, making Catherine gasp and Nivedita laugh.

"What did you do that for?" Nivedita giggled. Catherine began to hiccup and we both looked at her. She was doubled over at the waist laughing and hiccuping, causing Nivedita and I to erupt in laughter at her.

"To wash everything!" I responded, chuckling. Still sitting in the water, I tossed myself backward gently into the stream, drenching my hair and clothes. I came back up with a gasp, the other two still laughing uproariously.

"Use this." Nivedita handed me something solid that smelled of lavender. I looked at the odd, misshapen, stone-like lump. It was a milky white with flecks of black and green.

"What is this?" I asked.

"Lye soap. Use it on your skin and clothes, but do not drop it! The gentlemen will need it eventually, too," Nivedita explained. I held it carefully and did as she said, washing my skin and the dress. I pulled the dirty shift over my lap and began to scrub at the blood stain. Catherine was washing her extra dress against the rocks, so I followed her movements and used a large rock to push the soap into the garment. The stain lifted, but not fully. There was still a noticeable stain on the back. *Maybe in the future, I can dye it with Nivedita's help.*

"May I have the soap, please?" Catherine asked.

"Let me rinse my hair and I will bring it to you!" I called, then laid back into the water one more time. Pulling myself up was hard with one hand, but I did not dare use the hand that held the precious soap. My old dress was still soaking wet and heavy but I pulled it out of the river and flung it over my shoulder. In doing so, I accidentally sprayed Catherine with droplets of water. She looked up at me fiercely, but then broke into laughter again. Her laugh, ever contagious, got me laughing too. Soon, Nivedita was laughing with us and we were surely catching attention. I carefully handed off the soap to Catherine and found a low tree branch to hand my shift for the time being.

"So, what was Nicol saying back there?" Catherine asked as I handed her the soap. I looked at her, hoping to hide the fear in my eyes, but she was busy scrubbing her garments.

"I do not know what you speak of," I responded, watching her carefully, knowing she could easily remove me from this party. I returned to my satchel picking up my gloves and shoes.

"Yes, you do. He said, 'Too bad there is not one among us with a novel talent with which we could make money' or something. Right?" I hung my spare dress on a tree to dry, carefully sitting on the ground below.

"Oh yes, I did hear that, but I do not know to what he was referring," I attempted to respond, but it was half a lie. I had one idea of what he was inferring. Nivedita waded out of the water and took up her wrap again. She watched me as she re-wrapped herself and then came to sit next to me.

"As you were the one walking next to him, we thought you might have seen whom he was looking at or if he was preening," Nivedita added. Her gaze was now fixed on me. I felt a light pressure in my heart. I looked to Catherine, who had finished her washing and collected everything of ours that was by the water. She walked to us, handing Nivedita the soap. She sat in a heap after hanging her wet garments near my extra dress.

They both stared at me, giving me all the space to answer. I had no way of fully knowing who Nicol was truly speaking of, but in my painfully broken heart, I knew he meant me and my secret ability. *How would they react to being lied to again? I told them I could not perform any magic.* After a few moments of locking in a mental debate with myself, I took a deep breath and answered.

"Me. He was speaking of me," I said. Their eyes widened and their heads tilted to the right with curiosity. I knew the next question. "I have a...skill that might get us more income, but that is if we do not get run out of the town."

"Well spit it out already!" Catherine barked, causing me to flinch.

"I-I can see the stars m-move in senses that predict the future." I squeezed my eyes shut, awaiting the disbelief and scolding. They did not come, nothing but a soft *ooh* from Catherine was uttered.

I opened my eyes to see a glittering awe in their eyes. Catherine was smiling, mouth wide from her gasp. Nivedita seemed to be sorting facts with a quizzical, far-off stare.

"How does it work exactly?" Nivedita inquired, her expression still puzzled.

"When the sky is clear and I can see the stars, they will move from their fixed positions to make shapes of people and things. Then they sometimes act out scenes the way theater performers do," I explained. Nivedita nodded as I did.

"Nicol is right. That could be profitable, but you are also right, we could be run out of town, and a coastal port is a far better place to be in the winter than the middle of nowhere." Nivedita responded. Catherine nodded along.

"If that is what you would like. You by no means have any obligation to perform this magic of yours. Can you read on command?" Nivedita asked. I shrugged.

"I had not thought to try, to be honest," She continued to nod, and Nivedita pressed a hand to Catherine's shoulder to calm her, finally getting her to stop.

"Are you all done giggling and playing in the water?" Viçente called from around the bend.

"Yes!" Catherine bellowed and the gentlemen came around to where we were sitting.

"Shall we continue to Aberteifi?" Viçente asked. We ladies looked at each other like we agreed in an unspoken conversation that we would. We gathered our garments, and I slipped on my gloves and shoes, before following Catherine as she walked to where the gentlemen were waiting – on the other side of the underbrush.

"Sibyl was just enlightening us on her extraordinary talent of prophecy. Do you think we could sell that? A port city has surely seen its fair share of outlandish performances," Catherine pitched. Viçente chewed his lower lip and shrugged, looking to me for my thoughts.

"I do not know. The decision will be up to her when we reach Aberteifi," he responded, gesturing for us to hurry along back onto the road. Nicol wiggled his eyebrows at me with the same ear-to-ear grin as before. I was beginning to learn what it all meant. He strummed up a lively tune I would have placed at a seaside picnic, leading us out of the trees and back to the road. Nicol and Nivedita led the way, while Catherine and I took the middle. Viçente took up the rear as he always did, hand on his sword hilt.

The sun was nearly overhead. This would normally be the time for a midday meal, but I dared to not ask to stop for a second time. Catherine nudged me, offering a tear off of her bread. I accepted graciously. With music and food, this could almost be a picnic. *A walking picnic.* With the stop, we would probably miss all potential time to sell any of Nivedita's remedies. My heart began to beat to the tune of Nicol's strumming, and my mind began to run wild.

What if I cannot do it anymore? What if they do not believe me? What if I see something horrible? What if I see something good and it does not come true?

Catherine jostled me from my anxious spiral, pointing out some little animals here and there. A squirrel in a tree, two birds building a nest, and a deer with her fawn. I saw some of the other travelers had pulled away from the road to have their midday meals in the shade. I prayed we would not stop for the same reason, for the conversations would surely gravitate towards the newly revealed bit of information on me.

Nicol ceased his upbeat strumming, making me grow even more nervous of an impending serious conversation. It did not come, but my heart would not let it rest. We continued on in silence, and Nicol's lute returned to his back, resting on the strap. Catherine closely examined the map while I had my silent panic attack.

We trekked the remainder of the day until the sun began its descent behind the gnarled tops of the trees, creating long shadows and cool breezes. Ahead, I spotted the roofs of several tall houses sprinkled in the trees. The thatched roofs blended into the bare tree tops. I pointed out the buildings with excitement.

"Catherine look! The town!" Catherine looked back to me with a less than enthusiastic, dull expression.

"We will have missed the last crowd. Drunkards do not pay for ointments. Let us find a place to sleep for the night," Nivedita spoke. There was a heaviness in her tone. I instantly felt horrible for our unplanned washing stop.

Catherine directed us to a tavern on the outskirts of the large port city. They were adamant that we would not be able to afford the room, even if Viçente and Nicol pitched in with some labor. We turned around and made camp just outside the town wall.

"Not the most desirable place to sleep, but now maybe Sibyl can show us her prophetic ability, eh?" Viçente grunted.

Chapter Thirty-Four

They hounded me to pick one of them to demonstrate with. I gave in and chose Viçente because of his lack of interest. Catherine wanted to be chosen, but I could not risk her amiability. Viçente, on the other hand, seemed disinterested in me as a whole. When he looked at me, I felt as though he were reading a complete list of my inadequacies and failures. If he was unsatisfied, I would feel only minimal rejection. I was able to convince them that I would perform better after our dinner, when the sun was fully gone and the stars had ample room to glimmer.

I ate my portion of bread, cheese, and beans as slowly as I could manage on my empty stomach. Before I knew it, my meal was devoured and my new companions were staring at me intently.

"What do you need to begin? Do we need to chant something in fairy language?" Catherine asked. I looked at her in confusion.

"Do you know any *fairy words*?" I repeated back to her. She shook her head. I thought to myself for a serious moment. *A table would be nice, but for now, the ground should work*. I gestured to Viçente that he should come sit next to me on the ground. I made sure that I was under a clear patch of sky, unobstructed by tree branches or clouds, and away from the campfire.

Away from the fire was cool, and a shiver began to race through my body, leaving me shaking. I adjusted myself, waiting for Viçente to let me know that he was ready. I awkwardly crossed my legs as soon as Viçente did. I leaned forward, intending to hold his hands, but stopped.

"May I hold your hands?" I asked. He held out his hands, palm up to me. Carefully, I removed my gloves in hopes that the physical contact would enhance my chances of receiving a vision about Viçente. Taking his rough hands in my blackened ones felt odd, but I persevered. I took a deep breath in through my mouth, held it, and released it slowly.

"Do you have a question or something I can focus on?" I asked Viçente. He thought for a moment.

"Will I make my family proud?" he finally asked. One more deep breath, and I focused upon the stars. The constellations above me were unlike the Mythénian sky, but the stars would always be stars. I watched as they moved, feeling my hair rise like it had when I met little Annie in the woods. *It is working!* I was amazed that I could see some wisp of the magic working. The stars danced into a new position, clustering to make the broad muscular outline of Viçente surrounded by a group of people I could not discern. I saw him laugh heartily, throwing his head back in a new rush of laughter before making a toast and drinking his mug completely gone. With the swish of his cup, the vision was gone, the stars back in their places in the heavens.

I lowered my head, shaking off the feeling of the vision. Everyone waited eagerly with their eyes bulging out of their heads.

"Well?" Catherine asked.

"What did you see?" Viçente added. I took a quick look around to solidify this scene of everyone still caring for me.

"Would you like the simple answer or all of what I saw?" I returned to Viçente. He thought quietly for a moment.

"Tell me all of what you saw," he decided.

"Let us move back to the fire, I am cold," I said, slowly pulling myself from the ground and picking up my gloves. Viçente sprung up and offered me his hand again. Surprised, I took it. He hailed me onto my feet and we rejoined everyone by the fire. Checking to see if Viçente was ready, I nodded at him. He nodded back.

"I saw you, surrounded by people. I could not see their faces, but they all raised a mug to toast you. You laughed deeply and drank with them," I told Viçente. He nodded and looked around the fire at his companions. I replaced my gloves on my hands.

Catherine was wide-eyed and focused on me. Nivedita and Nicol were whispering to one another behind a wall of their hands. I felt the nervous monster climb up my back and perch on my shoulder, whispering doubts in my ear. It whispered damning things. *They are displaced with your demonstration.* I tried to ignore it, but it was much louder than my own thoughts while no one talked aloud.

"That answers my question quite beautifully. What do you say?" Viçente addressed the others.

"Results are results, but as far as getting people to pay, we may have to dress it up a little. I could play music for customers," Nicol suggested.

"Yes, we would need to up the performance aspect, to catch people's attention. Do you think we could make a sign?" Catherine asked. Nivedita nodded at the suggestion. They looked at me now.

"Would you want to try and read for more people?" Nivedita asked. I thought hard for what felt like an age. I stared into the fire as I thought of what else I would need to read for others – strangers.

"If we were to make a sign, what would it say?" I asked. There was a long silence until Catherine spoke up.

"We would need to paint your name and whatever you call this, and how much you would charge. What *do* you call it?" she asked.

"How much would you charge?" Nicol chimed in. I looked between the two, attempting to decide how to answer, but came up empty-handed.

"I am unsure. I never got to explore it before – well – you know," I admitted.

"Well from what you have said. It sounds like astrology. How does that sound? Sibyl the Astrologer?" Nivedita asked. I liked it very much. Having a name for my talent made me feel more real than I had in weeks. My heart grew lighter, and for once, I had hope.

"I think it is perfect. Thank you. How will we make a sign?" I inquired. The group was silent again as we thought.

"We may be able to trade for ink, and then we would need a board. We may even be able to find some scrap wood by the docks," Catherine thought aloud.

"That is a very good idea," Nivedita responded. Everyone nodded in agreement.

We devolved into our own conversations about the journey, plans for tomorrow, and our hopes for the future now that we have another idea for income. I laid my satchel on the ground as my pillow, then rested my head on it. A wave of exhaustion hit me at once and I had to fight to stay awake. The sound of my companions chatting lulled me to sleep, and the last thing I saw was Viçente's warm smile as he talked about his hopes from my vision.

In the morning, we ate the last of our combined food, then split into two groups. Catherine and Viçente went to the docks to scavenge for any discarded wood. Nicol, Nivedita, and I returned to the town proper to see about getting some ink. Nivedita counted my coins and let me know we could use it all for the ink. I had forgotten that she still had my coin purse. I was at ease knowing that my frugal friend held onto it.

Finding a shop was the hard part. The buildings were all the same rocky-bottomed, wooden structures with thatched roofs. Somewhere in the heart of the busy port city, Nicol spotted a sign with a quill. He held the door for us ladies as we entered the neat and organized shop. I looked around, astounded at the sheer amount of writing supplies. There were parchment rolls, piles of flat parchment, and a whole display of ink, blue, black, and green! A clean-shaven man stood behind the counter of the shop, a flat cap covering his grey hair. He argued the price of parchment with a well-dressed woman in red with blonde hair. Nivedita began inspecting rolls of parchment and a collection of quill feathers. I followed suit, admiring the shop's wares, putting every item back the way she did. Nicol wandered through the shop, not touching anything.

"How may I help you?" the man called from behind the counter. The blonde woman had left, and now we were alone in the shop. Nicol approached the counter, leaning on it. Nivedita and I followed, but stayed back. I wanted to hang back in the event that the man became upset and we needed to flee the shop, hiding my hands to hopefully keep him from crying 'plague' too.

"A bottle of ink please," Nicol asked.

"10 pence," the man said firmly. Nivedita handed over our coins without argument. He seemed surprised that we did not haggle. The corners of his mouth turned down, but he handed us the bottle of ink.

"Thank you," Nivedita said with a bow of her head. Taking the ink, Nicol dipped his head and they turned to leave. Nivedita turned me around and led me out of the shop. We walked quite a ways before they stopped me.

"What was that?" Nicol asked. I looked up at him, thoroughly confused. He waved a hand dismissively.

"Shall we go find our friends?" Nivedita asked. I nodded furiously. They were supposed to be along the river or at the docks. We made our way to the bridge near the town gates. Looking down each side of the river, we collectively chose to go west, towards the only docks we could see.

Walking along the river could have been comforting if there were not piles of people's refuse strewn about. The town clearly used the river as a means of disposal. We encountered a few other pedestrians as we crept up the banks. Nicol and Nivedita were more outgoing in reaching out to people for help.

"Have you seen a tall Spaniard with a broad sword accompanying a short, blonde English woman?" Nicol asked a man. He answered no. Nivedita asked a young man the same. No one had seen them come this way, so we turned around and made our way back to the bridge. When we arrived, we saw a man with four crates ambling towards the entrance to the river.

"Excuse me, sir? What are your plans for those crates?" I asked boldly. He stopped and narrowed his eyes at me. I stayed put, straightening my shoulders.

"What's it to you, eh?" he grumbled back to me. I stiffened, but Nicol placed a hand on my shoulder. His support emboldened me.

"If you planned to dispose of them, might my companions and I take them off your hands?"

"What for?" he inquired.

"I will be performing astrological readings tonight, so having something for people to sit on would be nice," I answered. His eyes widened, and his face broke into a bright smile.

"Of course! If you promise me a reading!" he chuckled, setting down four crates. Nicol picked up two, handing them off to me and Nivedita. The man waved to us as he returned the way he came. Nicol picked up the last two and carried them. We decided to search the east banks for our friends.

The first person we saw we mistook for Catherine until she was closer. She had the same golden blonde hair and a small frame, but sadly was not our friend.

"What do you have the crates for?" she asked us.

"Our friend here will be doing astrological readings tonight near the docks, come find us! You will know it is us when you hear the lovely French music!" Nicol stepped in, lively to pitch our services.

"Oh really? How exciting!" she smiled and scurried away to join a group of young ladies. We continued on and soon enough found Catherine and Viçente. They had a large plank of wood that Viçente carted up the bank.

"Catherine!" I called, waving with my free hand. She saw us and pulled Viçente in the right direction by his shirt. They rejoined us with a flourish from Catherine to show off the plank they had found. It was nearly as tall as her, weathered and warped. I imagined that maybe it had come from a shipwrecked vessel. Viçente noticed me examining the large plank of wood.

"We found this in an abandoned old barn north of town," he explained.

"How are you certain it is abandoned?" I asked, looking at the warping and how the edges appeared like a tattered map.

"We walked around a bit and inquired the folks we saw pass by. As far as we are aware, the owner has passed with no kin and the neighbors have just built around the building." Catherine answered. I nodded.

"A delightful find indeed!" Nicol added.

"You got the ink?" Catherine asked. Nivedita brought the ink out of her trunk and offered it to Catherine. She took and examined it, then began to look around her feet with a stern look on her face.

"What is the matter?" I asked.

"What will we use to paint the letters?" she asked. We thought for a moment.

"I could use my finger?" I offered. *It is not like the black ink will stain my hands.* She shook her head.

"You could get some on customers. Let us think of something else." We had another moment of silence as we all thought to ourselves. I thought about suggesting my gloves since they would not touch anyone but me.

"Use this." Nicol handed over a scrap of fabric. Catherine received it like it was the most precious shred of silk.

"Viçente, can you brace it so that I might write? What do I put on the sign?" Catherine asked. Viçente angled the plank of wood like a writing desk, but lower for Catherine.

"Astrology readings," I said decisively. Catherine dipped the fabric into the ink and began writing in big scrawling letters as if the fabric and her finger were a quill.

"How much will you charge?" she asked again. I shrugged, unsure of the values of the coins or my ability. Catherine looked to Nivedita for answers.

"Ten pence?" Nivedita suggested.

"Certainly not! This is a *rare* talent!" Nicol screeched from my left.

"What do you suggest then?" Nivedita retorted.

"I say a crown!" Nicol exclaimed.

"Being a port town does not simply mean that the wealthy few are here and dare to spend coin below their stations. We need something more manageable for the average citizen. How about a shilling?" Catherine looked to me for confirmation. I nodded, as did Nicol and Nivedita. Catherine added the price and a splotch in the middle.

"What is that?" I asked, pointing to the splotch in the middle.

"A star of course!" she explained. I moved forward, taking the swatch of fabric from her. Now I could see the five points, but I evened them out and added some decorative swirls to the sides to fill the space. I stepped back to admire our work. *I might make it out of this after all.*

Chapter Thirty-Five

We set up our reading stand, with a few lit tallow candles, by the docks like Nicol had said. We used all four crates, two to sit on and the other two as a makeshift table. Viçente leaned the large 'astrology readings' sign against a building closer to the road, then he hid himself away in the corner, ever watchful. Nicol and Catherine attracted customers at the end of the road where the sign faced. We could only attract the evening crowd and those who did not have something to rush home for. Nivedita and I set up the crates, ready for customers.

Nicol played a tune Catherine knew. She sang the words sweetly, but I could not place them. The music attracted our first customer, a tavern owner. The woman was on her way back from the bakery when she stopped, hands full of bread.

"What have you got here?" she asked Nivedita.

"A tincture for stomach ailments and an ointment that helps a burn to heal," Nivedita answered. The woman purchased a jar of the burn ointment from Nivedita and then turned to address me. I felt my body freeze and a wave of dizziness fell over me as her eyes found mine.

"You must be the astrologer?"

"Yes, ma'am. Would you like me to read your fortune?" I asked in return, standing to offer my seat. She smiled at me and took the offered seat. She blinked at me, waiting for instruction.

"Oh! I will need to hold your hands. Is that alright?" I began to remove my gloves, but waited for her consent.

"Yes!" she said excitedly. I removed my gloves and her excitement waned.

"I promise I am not sick. It is a scar, a burn scar," I explained. She was uneasy, but held her hands out to me anyway. "Do you have a question about some issue you would like clarification for?" She shook her head and I began.

Taking a deep breath through my nose, and exhaling slowly through my mouth, I tilted my head to the sky. The stars were just beginning to shine. Nicol's music filled my ears and heart, and the stars began to move. I saw the shape of this woman, and her belly grew and grew until the image exploded into a million stars. When the sky reformed, there was a still image of a mother cradling a baby. Then the stars slipped away, back into their fixed positions. Looking at the woman, her eyes bulged from their sockets.

"Your hair!" she exclaimed. I quickly ran my hands through my locks, taming them down. "It was floating as if a breeze had blown through!"

"Oh yes, it does that. I was able to see a vision. Let me tell you of it," I said, slipping my gloves back on. She remained frozen in awe. "I watched as you grew until you had a beautiful, happy baby." The woman's blue eyes welled with tears. She sputtered as she reached forward to hug me.

"Thank you, oh thank you!" She squeezed me tight. She laid a shilling on the makeshift table and ran off her bags of bread, tears streaming down her face. Nivedita and I looked at each other. I was a bit worried for the woman, but Nivedita gave me a reassuring smile that put me at ease. Catherine was no longer singing, but instead urging the slow stream of people to divert and see our miniature market set up. Nicol came over to see how we were in between songs and to give his fingers a break.

Just as Nicol was returning to his post, three burly men appeared at the road and came directly to me with gruff, decisive steps. Viçente stepped out of the shadows and prepared for an altercation, hand on the hilt of his sword. I recognized one of them in the dim lighting. It was the gentleman that we had recovered the crates from.

"See lads? What did I tell you? I found an astrologer!" he exclaimed. I impulsively extended my hand to greet him. Viçente jerked his sword out of its sheath a bit, but I caught his eye and conveyed all I could to him that it was alright. The man in front of me laughed a quick, 'Ha, ha!'

"Yes, I am Sibyl, the astrologer. You are here for your reading?" I drew up my brave face, looking to Viçente to see he was hanging back, still intently watching the large men.

"Indeed! How does this work?" he asked. I gestured for him to take my seat on the crate. He shrugged to his mates and sat.

"May I hold both of your hands? Mine are burned, but not sickly. I promise." I took off my gloves, the blackened skin almost melting into the shadows.

"I am a seasoned mariner, m'lady, nothing can get to me." He held his hands out to me, so I took them and leaned back to see the stars. I felt my hair rise with the flow of magic, and Nicol's light-hearted strumming had begun again, filling me with a sense of support.

The stars slowly left their seats in the sky, twisting and melding to create the image of this man on a ship in rough waters. The ship approached a bay and the outline of a man was ready to disembark. Once docked, he sprang from the ship towards the glittering outline of a woman. They embraced, and then the vision was over.

"Oh!" I gasped, coming back to the moment. "I saw a man, you, sailing across the ocean to a port where a beautiful woman was waiting for you!" Tears filled my eyes at the romance of it all. The seaman looked at me with awe, his eyes twinkling.

"If what you say is true, my dear Francesca will be waiting for me! Grazie!" he exclaimed, placing a coin on the table before embracing me as he stood. His mates shoved each other in a bid for who would go next. Nivedita slid the coin off the table and added it to my coin purse, which I suppose was *our* coin purse now. No one else seemed to have any coin. When I was released from the manly hug of the first seaman, I chose from his mates for who would go next. I did not even have to ask his permission before he thrust his hands out to me.

Taking his hands and turning my head to the sky, I watched as they moved in beautiful arcs and swirls until they made the shape of this bearded man before me. He was at the helm of a great ship, sparkling even. Using some looking device he spotted something, directing his crew somewhere I could not see.

"You will captain a beautiful ship and lead your men to a lovely reward!" I informed him. He looked to his comrades with a wide, mischievous grin. They slapped him on the back several times in congratulations. He laid a coin on the table.

"Thank you," Nivedita said. The bearded man shook my hand and allowed their last fellow a chance at good fortune. This man was a tall, thinner man with only a mustache.

"May I hold your hands?" I asked nervously. He nodded and produced his hands. They were lanky and long, just like his arms. I took a deep breath and allowed the stars to show me his fortune. The scene before me was this man running away with something valuable. I could not tell if it was his to take or not.

"You will come upon a great treasure very soon," I said, looking back at him. He had a devilish grin on his face and laid an extra coin on the table. His comrades did not seem to notice anything, and they all cheered and thanked us again before leaving in a bustling conversation.

"Where are we now?" Viçente asked Nivedita.

"Four shillings and four pence," she answered. We all looked around at each other, smiles spreading across our faces.

"We almost have enough for everyone to get dinner!" Nicol announced, eliciting a laugh from Catherine and me.

There was a lull in the traffic across the docks. We sat around as a group, talking about the next steps for the night. We decided that when the moon was overhead, we would pack up and find an inn. Nicol was pitching me ideas for songs to accompany my readings when two well-dressed drunken men stumbled into our niche in the walkway. They leaned on one another, chuckling and making jokes I could not decipher.

"Rea-readings, eh?" one said, leaning on his companion. They approached our group.

"Yes, I do the readings," I answered, standing.

"Have you the coin?" Catherine stepped in front of me. The men erupted in laughter, but the second seemed more aware than his friend. He wore a dark cloak that blended with the shadows from the night.

"Yes! I should say that we do!" he chortled. He removed his arm from his companion and helped him to sit on the crate I offered. In the candlelight, I recognized their clothing as the kind my mother would have approved of, the kind befitting lords and ladies. *Nobility*. I made a mental note to treat them like royalty to fatten their egos. I noticed the man who sat wearing a hat with a feather. His cloaked companion fumbled with his coin purse, but successfully retrieved two shillings. Placing them on the makeshift table, he then gestured for me to begin.

"May I hold your hands, sir?" I used my former court voice.

"Why, yes you may! This urchin has *some* manners," the man with the feather in his cap preened, turning his hands over to me. I took off my gloves and then took his hands in mine. He yelped upon seeing my hands.

"I am not sick! I swear, my lords. It is a burn. My companion is a medic, she can assure you." I stepped closer to Nivedita, gesturing to her for her expertise. The man with the feathered cap broke into laughter, and it tinged my heart a little.

"I am – oh I am, I am so very very sorry. I am… well I am afraid I ha-have celebrated too, too much! Please, please … continue." He wiggled his hands at me, stifling more laughter. His drunkenness reminded me of my father. *All I need now is for him to mention a war and I will have found his human counterpart.* Taking his hands again, I tilted my head to the stars and watched the scene they played out. When I was finished, I looked deeply into the man's blue-grey eyes.

"I saw your lordship surrounded by many young children." I knelt to one knee to be more at eye level with the sitting man, and to rest my tired feet.

"That- that is all?" he blubbered. I assured him it was. He nodded and stood, allowing his fellow the crate seat. The caped gentleman sat and offered me his hands. I conducted my ritual and allowed the stars to show me what they would. The vision I received for him was difficult to interpret. He was going to accomplish great things, but at a great cost.

"I see you riding into battle on a steed of bravery. You will be victorious, but upon your return, you hold a limp maiden in your arms. I am sorry to deliver such news." I released his hands and then knelt, bowing my head to the lord. The man laid a gentle hand on my shoulder.

"Rise, my lady, you have done no wrong. Thank you. Now I will know not to take any moments for granted," he told me with a drop of wisdom in his voice. I looked up to see kind and gentle brown eyes blinking softly, like a cat's. With a nod, I stood up and thanked them both for their business.

We were able to keep our excitement to ourselves until the men had stumbled away, but the moment we could not see them anymore, we celebrated with cheers and laughter, all of us hugging one another. *I did it.*

"Now we have six shillings and four pence! Quick, let us find an inn and get a room!" Nivedita exclaimed. Nicol vehemently agreed, speedily breaking down the small setup. Catherine, still laughing, helped Viçente move the sign. I felt so guilty that we did not do more for Nivedita's sales. She had her trunk, my coin purse – which I did not mind her keeping, and one of the crates. I had only my satchel and the last crate. I took it upon myself to use my free hand to take Nivedita's trunk from her.

"You do not need to do that," she protested. I smiled and awkwardly attempted a side hug with my arm.

"I would like to, as my share of the work."

"You are very humorous. You have done enough! You made us six shillings in one night. That is my monthly earnings after the cost of jars and ingredients. You have *overworked* yourself, dear." She patted my arm. I did not believe her.

We walked farther into town until we heard the notable sounds of a tavern. We approached and decided that Nivedita and I should enter to inquire about a room. Nivedita and I went inside and approached a long counter with stools on the side of the patrons. A tall woman with red hair was serving two customers. She glanced over at us and informed us that she would be another moment. I nodded.

"What can I do for you?" she asked in a gravelly voice when she approached. I looked to Nivedita.

"Do you have any rooms available for five people?" she asked.

"Not a room with five beds, but I do not mind if five of you sleep in a chamber with only two beds. I have one available for five shillings."

"How much for five hot suppers?" Nivedita added.

"A shilling, " the woman responded.

"We will take both." Nivedita placed the stack of six shillings on the counter, then looked to me. "Stay here to collect the food. We will set up the room and come back to help you." I nodded. The innkeeper snickered and slid the stack of coins into her palm. I chose a seat to wait while Nivdeita took the room key and left to collect our friends.

Moments later, I watched them return as a group and march cheerfully up the stairs. Each of them waved to me in their own way while carrying the various bits of our astrology reading setup. Just as quickly, they returned down the stairs, unburdened by our absurd baggage. We waited for the meals to be brought out.

I felt the energetic pulse of joy as we all saw the hot meals being brought out to us. We each took one plate and had the same thoughts to retreat to our room to eat. When we arrived at the room up the stairs, I was immediately shocked. They had laid out our crates and the sign as a makeshift table. The crates were the legs and the sign was the table. We all sat on the ground around the makeshift table and dug into the hot meal of salted pork, sweet bread, and half a cob of corn. Nicol raised his bread and proclaimed:

"To Sibyl's amazing prophecies!"

"Hear, hear!" everyone cheered.

Chapter Thirty-Six

The next morning was a mixture of my previous life and my current. I awoke before everyone, but did not get up for fear of waking someone else. We had used the crates and driftwood sign to create a makeshift bed that I chose to take. I was given pillows from the beds and a blanket. I slept soundly while surrounded by my companions. I stayed silent until I heard Catherine rise from her bed. Together, we woke the rest of our friends and collected our belongings.

Out on the street, it was a cool autumn morning with a tinge of frost. Catherine surveyed the traffic and directed us to a nook between two shops to set up. We used the crates to set up a counter and gave Nivedita one to sit on. She set up a beautiful array of her tinctures and began to mix more while awaiting customers. Catherine and I attempted to lure customers her way, while Nicol and Viçente took a seat against the wall of the shop we were next to.

"Have you a burn or singe? Try our ointment! Stomach ache? We have the fix!" we called to people as they passed by. A few stopped and we directed them towards Nivedita.

"Do not forget, there will be astrology readings tonight near here. Listen for the music!" Nivedita said after each of her two sales. Both customers appeared to be quite intrigued by the idea. Nicol took that as a cue to begin playing spritely music and dancing a little jig behind Nivedita to draw in curious passersby.

A short, stockily built man in an apron approached us with his green eyes bulging from his skull and a massive frown affixed to his tanned face.

"Have you a burn or stomach affliction, sir?" I attempted to approach him.

"No! I have a customer affliction! You alley rats are diverting customers from my bakery! I pay my rent to the lord, just as the rest of us *civil* folk do. You could learn to do the same," he spat at me. Catherine came to my side, wrapping her arms protectively around me, even though she was the same height as me. I could not look away from the angry man, but I imagined that Catherine had pinned him with her ferocious stare. Viçente stepped out from behind Nivedita, then moved in between us to face the man, which must have been quite hard considering Viçente was much taller.

"You needed to resort to heated insults, sir. We can be on our way easily if you would only ask nicely," Viçente insisted, resting a hand on the hilt of his sword.

"Ask you nicely to stop practicing theft? Certainly not! Be gone, or I will be calling the constables!" The man puffed up his chest as he looked up at Viçente.

"We do not mind leaving, but I believe you owe my companion ladies an apology." Viçente gripped his sword hilt intentionally – a threat. The little, grumpy man spat on the ground, narrowly missing Catherine's foot. Viçente drew his sword, aiming it at the short man.

"Viçente, no!" I stepped forward, terrified of what he might do. He looked at me for certainty, and I tried to express my worry adequately on my face. He nodded and deftly returned his sword to its sheath at his side. The grumpy baker turned and left. The small crowd that had accumulated now disbursed, and I began to feel overwhelming guilt. Wetness flowed from my eyes in vessels of tears. Nicol noticed and clicked his tongue at me. Catherine assisted in cleaning up Nivedita's items and tearing down our stand.

"Dear, it is not your fault. This happens sometimes. Taxes are higher and people like us who do not have a building like he does must abide by the laws of the land." Nicol reached for my hand, and I gave it. He squeezed my fingers three times, then handed me a crate to carry.

"What if we sit out in front of that old barn? No one is using it!" Catherine suggested. We all looked at each other in turn, checking that we were all on the same page. Catherine led the way, and Viçente took up the rear again with the sign. Nicol attempted to jostle me from my gloomy mood, but I felt it stick. I tried to give him a smile regardless. He seemed satisfied and retracted to walk with Nivedita.

We arrived at the old barn after a few stressful minutes of weaving through the crowds. The building was covered by overgrown plants and surrounded by a short, waist-high wall of stones. We set up on the outside of the short wall, similarly to the way we had in the alley. Viçente set the sign behind the wall and sat atop it to stay out of the way. Catherine and I called to those passing by and Nicol played lively music to draw attention. We did make enough sales for Nivedita to run out of stock. Nicol, Viçente, and I sat and rested as Nivedita and Catherine went to procure more jars and ingredients.

The morning had passed and noon flew by just as quick. Nivedita and Catherine returned soon after with a little food for us all. We then passed the time amiably until the light of the sun diminished. At the first sign of twinkling stars, we set up the small table and seats out of the crates. Nicol began to play an upbeat melody accompanied by his light, tenor singing.

As we waited for customers to appear, I became absorbed in the thought of the barn and what may be inside. It was maybe two stories high, and it had a disheveled thatched roof that was collapsing in on itself. The barn also had two doors, one facing the street and one facing out to the land around it. The left wall was covered in foliage and all the windows were boarded up tight or broken out. The black void where the street door stood open called to me.

"Sibyl?" I heard my new name. I looked around and found Nivedita watching me intently. "I was thinking that perhaps I should sit on the wall with Viçente. That way you are able to sit during your readings?"

"That is very kind of you to offer," I replied. Viçente had propped the sign against the short wall and was holding one side of it for stability.

"I do not mind. I have nothing to sell regardless," she added. My eyes welled with tears.

"I would like that," I answered. Nivedita bowed slightly and hoisted herself up onto the wall on the other side of the sign. Catherine joined Nicol in luring customers in our direction, and before long, we received our first customers. Two well-dressed women in cloaks with lanterns approached us. I appraised them as part of the upper class and adjusted myself to treat them accordingly.

"Is this where we can have our fortunes read?" asked one of the women. From her lamp, I could make out deep auburn hair and a beautiful gown of white lace. I bowed deeply from my waist, gesturing for them to take the other crated seat.

"Thank you," the first woman said, setting the lantern on the makeshift table. Her companion looked to have lighter hair and wore a gown of dark blue with slim-fitting arms and a high collar.

"Tonight, ladies, I will read the stars above to tell you of your futures for one shilling a person," I started. They each placed a shilling on the table in front of the lantern. "Do I have your permission to hold your hands? I will remove my gloves and you will see my scarred flesh, but it is not sickness, I swear to you."

The women exchanged silent words of confirmation, and with a nod, they agreed and removed their own delicate gloves. I removed my leather gloves and stored them in my satchel and then displayed my hands to the lady sitting in front of me. The woman with the auburn hair took my hands and nodded to me that she was ready.

I tilted my head to the stars, taking a moment to glance at the shuttered windows of the old barn. The stars shimmered, moving to new positions of a woman dancing with a man. They danced for a long time and ended with a passionate kiss. I tilted my head back down and blinked away the starry vision.

"You will have a very romantic evening in the near future. One full of dancing and a passionate kiss," I informed her, releasing her hands. She smiled with a tinge of blush on her cheeks, looking back to her companion. She stood and allowed her companion to take the crate seat. I offered my hands to her. She hesitantly took them.

Craning my head back, I watched the stars move and show me the loving scene of a man and a woman watching a child chase a dog.

"You will have every blessing. If you wish to have a family of your own, then it will be coming true. I see a woman and a man watching a child chase a little dog," I said.

"My wish is to give my husband a child." She retracted her hands and replaced her gloves. A single tear ran down her cheek. Then, the strangest thing occurred. When she told me of her wish, a flame of hope sprung to life in the broken cavern that was my heart. It drew me to imagine wonderful, warm thoughts of being whole again.

"Thank you, ah, miss..?" The auburn-haired woman seemed to be asking my name as she took back her lantern.

"Sibyl. You are very welcome. I am most grateful to you for your patronage," I responded with another bow. They collected their lanterns and were on their way. I scooped up their shillings, handing them to Nivedita. Her coin purse had become our vault. My eyes slid past her welcoming face to the dilapidated barn behind.

I was snapped to attention by a young couple drawn in by Nicol's music. This time the woman sat and the gentleman stood behind her, almost as if they were standing for a portrait. I explained my process to them both, including that my hands were safe to touch. They agreed and I indulged my vision to begin. For her, I saw two healthy babies, and for him, I saw a team of hounds fell a magnificent buck. Secretly, I envisioned that buck as Lord Alces. When I told them each their fortunes, they blossomed with joy, hugging each other after each turn. When they ran off laughing with each other, I handed the coins to Nivedita and again became bespelled by the possibilities the old barn might have.

A few more customers visited for readings that night. A round bald man whose fortune was truly fortunate. He was soon to come into money, which seemed to thrill him to no end. He left giddy and with a large, toothy grin. A woman who came dressed in all black with a veil approached next. She removed her mourning gloves and allowed me to hold her hands. The stars moved and twisted, telling me she had lost her husband to the sea, but he had not left her alone. She would have a baby girl and a large home on the coast. The news brought gasping tears from her, and Catherine comforted her as the woman got up to leave.

The last customer was a withered old man who could barely hear. I had to ask Nicol to cease playing for the time being so that I might inform the gentleman of his fortune. The vision I had was of his passing. When I somberly told him, he responded with: "Tell me, do I go peacefully in my sleep or will I have ta use ma knife?" He moved his jacket to reveal a knife fixed to his vest. I told him the truth.

"You will die peacefully in your sleep, but in the dead of winter. They will have to burn your body, and you will not get a proper burial."

"What da I care? I'll be dead!" he laughed and hobbled away.

We blew out our candle and tore down our stand, then made for the inn we had left this morning. Luckily, we were allowed our same room. We joyfully repeated the previous night's events, eating in our room and rebuilding the makeshift bed, which I took again. I fell asleep on the crate bed with a full heart and belly. Whispers of wishes filled my dreams.

Chapter Thirty-Seven

I woke from my dreamy sleep in the early morning. No one else in the room was awake, so I stayed on my makeshift bed, thinking of wishes and dreams. Eventually, I sat up to survey the room – still sound asleep. After a while of the early morning silence, I crept out of the room and out to the tavern floor. The innkeeper was awake and tending to cleaning duties, wiping down tables, and sweeping. Her red hair braided from the crown of her head to inbetween her shoulder blades.

"Excuse me, ma'am?" I spoke softly. As she whipped around fast, eyes wild, I knew I had startled her. She took a deep breath before answering me.

"Yes, miss?" she answered breathlessly. A pit of guilt began to burrow into my chest.

"Is it alright if I leave and come back? My companions are still abed," I asked. She laughed nervously.

"Yes, of course. I will leave the door unlocked." With that, her focus went back to her cleaning duties.

"Thank you," I said cheerily, then slid out the front door into the dewey morning.

The cobblestone street was empty, and a light mist clung to the buildings and street signs. I followed the road back to where we had been last night; the decaying barn. Mist clung to the low wall around the perimeter and the building. I glanced around, and after finding no one there, I drew closer to the barn, the open front door ever so welcoming. It was like the front door of an ancestral home propped open for my return. I peered into the dark opening, but found there were holes in the ceiling, providing a dim ambient light.

My steps were careful as I entered, and I began to poke around, finding large, deteriorating stalls lining one side. A rickety stairway was pinned to the left wall. The stairs led to a loft above that was hanging on by hope. Straw fell through many splinters and holes in the loft flooring; I was not willing to adventure that far. I kicked my feet around the floor, displacing straw and other debris. Then without warning, visions of Twilight Hall flashed through my head.

The grand staircase appeared, and the loft above turned into the nebula cloud that lit the Great Hall. Voices were in the distance, and I followed them through the old hallways of my lost home. The voices grew louder until I was upon them. My parents stood in the ballroom, slinging vile insults at each other. They did not stop as I entered, as they would have in reality. I watched my mother and father argue, seemingly until they noticed me. That is when things became scary. They faced me together and began to insult me in tandem.

"Peasant garb again, Seren?" my mother moaned.

"Leave her be, Eleanor. She does not know any better without her maid!" my father shouted. My mother turned to him and began to insult him again, but he turned to face me again.

"What are you doing here?" he asked.

"I heard voices," I said with a twinge of sadness in my voice. An ache held firm in my chest.

"Seren," he said.

"Yes?" I asked, but he only looked through me.

"Sibyl!" he yelped.

"How do you know that name?" I asked, taken aback.

"Sibyl!" my new name was called again, but this time with a firm hand on my shoulder. I blinked, and the vision of my parents dissipated. I was alone with Viçente gently shaking me.

"What are you doing here?" he asked. I shrugged, having no answer for him. "We were worried you had left for good! You did not tell anyone where you were going!"

"I apologize, that is not the reason. I simply wished to see the barn again – this time up close." I felt a twinge of hope in my heart as I said the word *wish*.

"Listen. Some of us would understand if you wanted to continue without us. All of us would sorely miss you," Viçente admitted. I looked to his eyes for confirmation, and his brown eyes portrayed nothing but honesty.

"No, no. I owe you all too much to abandon you! I wish to stay with you all for as long as possible." As I spoke, an intense warmth flowed from my ore to my extremities, like a hug. I stared at Viçente, hoping for an answer, but instead witnessed a tear fall from Viçente's eye, roll down his cheek, and fall to the ground. Then, he embraced me.

Together, we left the old barn, returning to the inn. Everyone was waiting at the largest table in the room. Nicol and Nivedita were holding each other, their backs to the door. Catherine faced the door, biting her nails. Upon seeing us step through the doorway, Catherine jumped to her feet with a gasp, rousing the other two. They raced to the door with gasps of surprise and sighs of relief, embarrassing me as a group.

"You can have the bed next time!" Catherine sobbed.

"No, no. I asked to sleep on the crates, remember? I am ok, I simply wanted to investigate the old barn," I explained.

"Oh! Yes, you were quite preoccupied with it last night." Nivedita added with a nod. I blushed and she let out one short laugh before ushering me to sit down. Catherine and Nivedita took up the spots next to me on my left and right. Viçente sat the Catherine's left and Nicol to Nivedita's right. An air of solemnity fell across our group. Nicol leaned forward on the table, placing his hand towards me.

"If I can be so abrupt... I think it is time to start planning for the winter. Snow will be upon us soon," Nicol said in a somber tone. Nivedita nodded in agreement and began looking at each of us for confirmation.

"Tinctures and ointments will not sustain us. Not here. My ingredients cost half our earnings. I feel I should sell what I have remaining and keep the coin for food and shelter," she said flatly. Catherine nodded but looked at me and Viçente.

"If we agree on that, Sibyl, you and Nicol will have to carry us through winter. What shall I do for my part?" she asked. Nivedita reached a hand across the table. Catherine took it and allowed Nivedita to comfort her.

"You will do as you have always done – all that we cannot. You care for us, speak for us, and keep us all sane. We will not let you be cold or hungry. Right, Sibyl?" They both looked at me. I was still feeling the warmth in my chest from back at the barn, when I told Viçente that I wanted to stay with them for as long as I could. *They are my friends now. I do not want to see them suffer.*

"No. we will not let you go cold or hungry. Is that not what you promised me?" Catherine looked up at me with a teary smile, nodding. I gave her my hand to hold, so she took it.

"Does this mean you will assist us in solely earning money? We would like you to continue your readings," Nicol asked.

"Your readings do not require ingredients like I do," Nivedita added.

"Of course, the burden will not rest solely upon your shoulders. We will continue to work at the inns we stay at to compensate for the coin," Viçente continued. Nicol nodded, tapping his lute.

"Why, of course. I wish to stay here, with you all, for as long as possible." There it was again – the warmth of a sun washed over me. It grew more potent with the joy I saw springing onto my friend's faces.

"Thank you, Sibyl! We are and will be most grateful. We want you to stay for as long as possible too! Now we have to decide where to stay. We do have some time, but let us not be unmotivated," Catherine said, switching the topic.

"We can stay here if Sibyl's customers stay steady like this," Nicol answered.

"But if the crows should thin during the winter?" Viçente asked. We were all silent then, not sure of how to counteract the severe possibility of the wintery outcome.

"We could find another tavern that is cheaper?" I suggested. Catherine squeezed my hand in support.

"Yes, that is an option, but what about in the worst scenario possible? What then?" Nicol queried.

"You mean if we run out of coins and customers in the dead of winter?"Nivedita clarified.

"Yes... what then?"

"You two men will work!" Nivedita pointed to Viçente and Nicol. Nicol scoffed at the undeniable notion. Catherine and Nivedita giggled, and Nicol smirked, letting me know it was all fun and not serious.

"I wish we had a home from which we could work and live." Catherine said with a sigh. I felt a source of power jolt from her into me, lighting the fire in my chest to a blaze. I knew what I had to do now. I quickly stood up, effectively releasing Catherine's hand. Everyone looked at me with surprise across their faces.

"What is the matter?" Catherine asked, looking up at me, her green eyes etched with worry. I gave her a real smile, from my heart. Her expression changed to curiosity.

"Nothing is the matter, but I do have a solution for our troubles." I said confidently, leading them to the front door of the inn, waving my hands excitedly for them to follow. They collected their things and followed me out the door. I took one of the crates from Catherine with a smile.

"What are we doing?" Nivedita asked.

"Trust me a little, please," I responded, and we continued in silence back to the old barn. Hearing a lofty sigh, I stopped and faced the group.

"Trust me – please," I stated again, leading them into the property, past the rocky wall. I dropped my satchel into the crate I had carried and then set it on the ground. With a little urging, I was able to convince them to join me inside the barn.

"Is it safe in here?" Nicol looked nervously at the crumbling loft and decaying roof.

"Yes. Everything will be ok. Can we all join hands?" I asked, pulling off my gloves. That must have been a sigh, because everyone began to move as I had directed them with no more arguments.

I gave my hands to Nicol and Catherine who stood next to me, and Viçente and Nivedita completed our circle. Taking in a deep, deep breath and letting it out slowly, I provide myself time to think and prepare my next words.

"What do we all wish for?" I asked, keeping the fire in my heart burning.

"Food," Nicol started.

"Fortune," Viçente added.

"A home," Catherine said finally.

"Yes! A home!" I gestured to the old barn around us and everyone looked around the barn with their own versions of disgust.

"You want us to live *here*?" Nicol asked incredulously.

"Not yet. Just listen, please. This will only work if we wish for the same thing, alright?"

"Mmmhmm," they all responded unanimously.

"Great. Now take a deep breath, and think of what makes a home – who makes a home? Close your eyes and fill your mind with visions of a home, right here," I said. They looked unsure, but every one of them closed their eyes.

"Now envision this as *our* home. Keep it simple, but put your heart in it. Keep your eyes closed no matter what," I instructed, watching my companions close their eyes. First Catherine, then Nivedita. Nicol closed his after he rolled them and Viçente waited until I looked at him before closing his eyes. Then after I checked that my friend's eyes were all shut, I pinched my eyes closed too.

I began to envision all the elements of a house: a solid roof, a solid foundation, four walls, windows, and doors. My hair began to float around me with wisps of magic. The inside would have two floors, five bedrooms, storage, and a hearth for cooking and warmth. I imagined that every room was the same size, but reflected each of my friend's unique personalities.

As I brought this image of a real home into my mind, I felt the flame in my heart grow even stronger. Gently, I guided that passionate flame to my creation, willing it to engulf the home and make it whole. I could feel the air shifting around me and hear the wood cracking, but I kept my focus on the mental image of this home I built in my mind, warmed by the passion in my heart fueled by the love of my friends.

A loud snap broke me from my trance. When I opened my eyes, I could not believe them. The barn was transformed. We stood in a large common room flanked by a hearth, a counter, and a wall of doors. I looked behind me to see the second door had disappeared behind the new doors, and the once rickety staircase was now solid, hardy wood. A victorious smile spread across my face.

"Everyone look! Look now! You can open your eyes!" I exclaimed. Their eyes opened to shock, amazement, and wonder. Exclamations of wonder were made as reality set in at what we had accomplished.

"You did this for *us*?" Nivedita began to cry. I walked over to her and embraced her tightly, holding back my own tears.

"We *all* did this for *us*," I said. Catherine broke from the group to run up the stairs.

"There are two bedrooms up here!" she called from the top of the stairs. "One is exactly as I imagined mine to be. The one next to it is painted a dark purple with lavender stars! Might that be yours, Sibyl?" she asked, coming down the stairs with a wide grin and sparkles in her eyes.

"Could be, but I am unsure. Let us all explore. This is *our* home now," I laughed. We disbursed to inspect every inch of the newly refurbished barn together. Nivedita explored the hearth and found a small storage pantry under the stairs with shelves already built in. Viçente explored the first bedroom by the door and found it had its own entrance and exit. He proclaimed it as his so that he could answer the door late at night if anyone called. Nicol remarked that he and Nivedita's bedrooms were next to each other, but vastly different. The only thing they shared was a simple bed against the same wall.

We did, in fact, discover that the starry bedroom was mine. Each of the bedrooms was decorated sparsely with items that were called to the owner. Nicol's had touches of French culture, and Nivedita's was decorated in a style she recognized. Catherine's was similar to my sister's and I's old rooms – elegant and simple. Mine was perfect for me, the colors a subtle reminder of my previous home, with a newer and more whimsical touch.

"Shall we make dinner?" Nivedita suggested, earning a roar of excitement from us all.

"Thank you, Sibyl," Viçente announced as our cheers died down.

"No, no. Truly, I could not have done this without you – all of you. Thank *you*."

Chapter Thirty-Eight

Once we thoroughly searched the new house and assessed where everyone was sleeping, we retrieved the crates and sign from outside and brought them in. Nivedita sat by the hearth, thinking silently about what and how to cook our food.

Like the inside, the outside of the barn had transformed too. What was once a decaying barn was now as beautiful as the two homes on either side. Folks had stopped to gawk at the instant changes of the structure. There were new windows, a front stoop, and a lovely hard wooden door, reinforced with a metal bar from the inside. Viçente found the perfect spot to fix the astrology reading sign – to the right of the door. He had found some nails in the grass and used a rock to hammer each corner to the front of the house while I held it up for him.

"Do you realize we can now find you a surname?" Viçente said to me after hammering the final nail.

"Excuse me?"

"You wanted a surname. If we name the house, we can give you a surname. Unless you like one of our existing surnames, as I am confident any of us would share their own willingly – I know I would."

"Oh, ha." I let a laugh escape my lips as a burning blush crept across my face. I turned away. "I do not think that matters right now." I said, attempting to conclude the conversation.

"If it matters to you, it shall matter to us," he replied, holding the door for me. Our friends milled about the common space, and I leaned against the wall between the hearth and the door, just watching them with joy in my heart. Catherine came down from her room in a new dress I had only seen when she had washed it.

"Hear me, friends." She stood on the second to last step, clapping her hands twice. Nicol lifted himself onto the countertop, while Viçente leaned against the wall near his bedroom door and Nivedita sat on the floor in her doorway. We all lent our attention to Catherine as she spoke from her perch.

"Thank you greatly, Sibyl, for this home. Now, however, I would think we should do as Nivedita suggested and prepare some food. For that, I believe we will need to set up out front to make some sales." Catherine hopped off the stairs and into the storage unit. She came out with the crates and began handing them to everyone except Nivedita. Viçente held the door a second time as we all left to set up outside of our new home, where there were plenty of curious folk awaiting. They stopped to ask us about the new building and the feat they had just witnessed. I knew the magic of what had happened inside, but had no idea what the outward magic looked like to others.

"Our friend is a fairy! she used the *last* of her magic to fix the abandoned barn into a home for us wandering orphans," Nicol began to announce with a performer's flare.

"No! No! That is not it. You must not tell people I have magic, Nicol! They could demand things or raise an issue!" I whispered harshly, pulling Nicol down to me. He pulled away a bit with a sly smile.

"That is why I said you used *the last* of your magic!" I gave him a serious and firm stare. He rolled his eyes and held up his hands in defense. "Fine. what shall I say then?" He looked at the audience of onlookers.

"I do not know. I would have preferred if you had said nothing to them about magic, but now we must have a solution," I hissed. "Try telling them I *used* to be a fairy and we all made a wish together?" Nicol pulled away from my grasp easily, facing the crowd.

"Humble town, folk! I beg your pardon! See, I am a reformed perjurer. I enjoy a tall tale or two. Instead, let me tell you the truth! Oh, how sweet it is! My friends and I used the magic of a wish, together, to transform the old barn. We hope you will allow us to stay!" he tried again, this time strumming his lute after speaking. The crowd did not seem to mind our imposition, and more were drawing closer to see what the fuss was about. Catherine helped to encourage more customers to look our way.

I sat on the stone wall surrounding our new home, next to Viçente and behind Nivedita. She was down to the last of her merchandise already, but we were reminding folks to return later tonight for their star fortunes.

"Who be doin' these fortunes?" called a craggy old voice from inside the crowd.

"Why, our friend, Sibyl! She used to be a fairy!" Nicol lowered his voice, as if conspiring with the villagers for the last part. Various outbursts occurred. I heard a few '*wow*'s, '*ooh*'s, and an '*oh my*!' from the crowd.

Nivedita caught Nicol's attention, indicating to him that she was now out of stock entirely.

"Alright folks, that is all we have today! Please come back after the sun has set to have your fortunes read! We will be in the same spot, just after dark!" he called. There were murmurs of disappointment as the crowd dispersed.

Catherine and Nicol rejoined us against the wall, and Nivedita procured the coin pouch with a winning smile.

"Let us fill our home with good food!" We joined the bustling morning market crowd and very soon figured out where to get the morning fresh fish, salt beef, bread, and fresh produce once it was in season again. Nicol and Catherine were brazen with their advertisement of our early night activities. They were at least mindful enough of others to not mention anything while patronizing stalls or shops.

We purchased a round of salt beef, costing a majority of our coin, and some bread. It was not much, but we would have something. As we headed back to our little house, Catherine and Nicol began to spout off more ideas to increase the show of my abilities.

"You could wear a hat or special headpiece!" Nicol declared. Nivedita reminded him that we had just spent the last of our coin.

"And it would fall off anyhow since I have to look up." I pointed to the sky with a gloved hand.

"You could enact an elaborate ritual!" Catherine suggested.

"Would that not take up too much time? We are doing well for now, and considering we will be staying here, we can all find suitable work for ourselves and let Sibyl conduct her own changes in her own time." Viçente reined in Catherine's spout of ideas.

"I would still appreciate it if most of you could still assist me. Nicol, your music attracts everyone, and having another person to mind the coin is a relief," I interjected. Nicol and Catherine began a new tangent all the way until we returned home.

How serendipitous for me to be able to imagine 'home' without fully falling apart. I found a new home, my own home. My thoughts kept me company while my companions chatted about their plans for the future. We brought in the crates and used them for seats around the common space. Catherine took the salted beef and bread and portioned it out for everyone. Once everyone was served, she took herself to the second stair to sit and eat. We ate together in peaceful silence. The beef was tough, making it very hard to talk as we ate.

"I think I would like to rest a little before I do any readings tonight," I announced at the conclusion of my portion. Catherine and I locked eyes and switched spots without a word, allowing me to freely climb the stairs. I looked behind me to see the friendly, smiling eyes of all my friends. My new family.

"Rest well! Someone will come to wake you at dusk if you are not up by then," Nivedita reassured. My room was the first door, Catherine the second. Inside was a simple straw bed against the right wall and a small nightstand against the outer wall. I pulled back the thin blanket and folded myself into bed. With my satchel on the nightstand and my friends happily conversing below, I fell asleep to the gentle peace of it all.

I had a lovely dream of flying overhead of Aberteifi. I saw endless streets and chimney smoke that melted into the dawn clouds. Ships in the river with goods headed in and out of the bay west of town. The air was cool on my face and the feeling of weightlessness was all-encompassing. I circled the sky above our barn-turned-cottage until I fully descended, landing softly on bare feet. Someone was speaking to me, gently, in words I did not understand. They were distorted by the air around me, but I saw the familiar shape.

"Sibyl," Catherine's voice rang through the air, sounding farther away than the figure before me. "Wake up." My eyes fluttered open to see Catherine sitting on the edge of my bed, her reassuring hand lightly shaking my shoulder.

"'Tis dusk. There are people already waiting by the wall. Will you come down and strategize with us?" she asked calmly. I sat up, and she stood so that I could swing my legs to the floor. I nodded but stopped.

"Let me change first?" I asked. She looked confused, but left my room with a shrug and shut the door behind her. I pulled the blood-stained dress from my imprisonment out of my satchel. I pulled off the gifted dress from Catherine and slipped on the washed, but still stained dress, then replaced the unstained blue dress over top of it. The layers would help keep me warm during the cool night. I removed my gloves, placing them on my bed. This one act made me feel more civilised and put together. I opened the door to find Catherine waiting, a look of confusion still affixed to her face. I pulled the thinner dress out from behind the neckline of the dress. She then immediately understood and pushed off the wall, leading the way down the stairs.

"You said you wanted our assistance; I think we should work in shifts. The first is tonight. Nivedita and Nicol offered to accompany you. Nicol will attend to the crowd, and if there is any trouble, send Nivedita to the house for one of us, " Catherine said, stepping off the stairs. Nicol and Nivedita waited for me by the door with the crates in hand.

"Would anyone object to me conducting the readings closer to the house? That way people can see the sign and we will be closer to help if it is needed?" I asked. Catherine looked around the room, checking with each of our companions in turn. I watched as each of them nodded in agreement. No one was objecting. I smiled at Nivedita and Nicol, signaling to them that I was ready to go, then followed them out.

"Nivedita, I would like you to sit next to me as if we had a bench. Nicol, can you play standing for a while? You can have a crate to sit and stand on while you direct the crowd. That will leave one for the customers to sit directly across from me." I continued to verbally imagine the setup as orderly and precise before I saw the collection of people waiting at the edge of the field – like a cluster of chickens.

"Nicol, will you go down and ask them to form a queue?" I asked. He nodded, as if receiving orders, and left us with one of his crates, marching down the field toward the town folk. Nivedita and I set up our spots as I imagined them. She gave me an encouraging smile as we sat, watching as the line of patrons slowly approached, led by a woman with her child.

"Hello. I am Alice Weaver, and this is Gwen. She has had a cough for quite some time... might you tell us how to cure her?" Alice explained, handing Nivedita a coin, sitting on the crate, and placing her child on her lap.

"May I touch your hands? Mine are safe to touch, just scarred." I displayed my bare hands without my gloves. The girl gave her mother a terrified look, but her mother reassured her with a smile and stroked the young girl's dark hair. The little girl covered her face and coughed a deep, wet cough. She then surrendered her hands, and I cupped them gently between mine.

"I must look up to converse with the stars. Do not be startled by what you see. Everything is just fine," I informed them before looking up. For the first time, I believe I saw a vision from the past. I saw the girl stocking a fire in a small room.

"Your daughter's lungs are compromised by ash from the fires she works on. You must stop immediately. My companion Nivedita may have a remedy to help her clear the cough." I turned to Nivedita, who shook her head. It was not something she knew of. The mother tried to argue that the girl's work was imperative to the family business.

"I saw her stoking flames and coughing," was all I could say.

"Thank you," she said finally. "It will be tough, but I will do anything for my daughter. Your bard informed us that you are in search of a surname. I offer you my maiden name – Jones." Alice smiled wide and escorted her little one away.

As the night went, I worked well past midnight. Luckily, some of our patrons had brought lanterns as well as coins, questions, and surnames. We collected a few notable surnames from our patrons, my selection being Evans, Taylor, Smith, Walker, Green, and Hughes. Catherine explained that we had to dismiss all the names with regional connections, like Robertson, as I did not wish to lay claim to any existing Robert or Robertson titles or lands. Not being born into a family with a clear heritage like that may get me into trouble in the future.

A woman with wild grey hair, tamed by a bonnet, approached me next. I was growing weary of the older folks, as most of their visions were of their deaths, and I grew ever more petrified of having to explain some gruesome end. She agreed to the terms, told me her name, and was very open about her desire.

"I am Louri Howell. I am here for my death story. I must travel to my sister before winter sets in. Will I make it to my destination?" her raspy voice asked me. I tilted my head to the sky and quickly returned with a simple 'no', which she took very well.

"Now young maiden, I hear you will need a surname. I suggest you take mine before it is wiped from history. I have married, and do not have children to pass it onto. If you would take this burden off my bones, I may yet rest in peace." She touched her forehead, chest, then both her shoulders in some kind of ritual.

"I am moved by your generosity, ma'am, I will hear your name, but I cannot promise you whether or not I will choose it."

"My maiden name was Aneurin. Like you, my parents needed a new name and were gifted a name from the land. Aneurin is a name that has been in this area for two lifetimes. Please let it have one more," she begged, but she did not need to, for I had felt that pang of recognition in my bones.

"I will take it. I will be Sibyl Aneurin. Thank you, Miss Howell!" I exclaimed, reaching across the small space between us to embrace her. She hugged me back with a laugh. My heart overflowed with love, as if every crack and break was repaired. Finally, I was whole again.

Chapter Thirty-Nine

My morning was a late one. I slept in until it was almost noon. Not surprising, as I had stayed up well past midnight. I heard the hushed voices of my companions below and roused myself. I dressed only in the blue gifted dress from Catherine, not needing extra layers. I also went without my shoes. I padded down the stairs to see everyone chipper and awaiting me.

"Good morning!" they sang in unison. It brought a wide, unyielding smile to my face. Upon the counter rested a loaf of bread laden with fruit. *A cake.*

"What is this?" I asked with a chuckle.

"This is a birthday cake, silly! Baked with the last berries of the season and topped with honey! We thought you may not want to celebrate your true birthday, but instead, you can celebrate your name day!" Catherine explained.

"We went to the market this morning to stock up on the winter essentials and all agreed we could use a pan. There is no better way to break in a pan than to bake a cake! We hope you like blackberries." Nivedita used a crude knife to slice the cake into five portions, handing me the first. It was sticky with honey and uniquely sweet. The cake began to crumble after the first few bites, forcing me to stuff my face or catch it with my free hand. I looked around to see my friend watching me with either amusement or concern. Nicol snorted, causing Catherine to burst into her contagious laughter, which she tried to hide by covering her mouth. I could not contain my own laughter and sputtered through the cake.

"You do not need to inhale your food!" Nivedita joked, holding her piece of cake in front of her mouth. Her slice looked to be picked at delicately. Her comment elicited a loud boisterous laugh from Viçente, causing me to laugh earnestly. We all laughed from our hearts for quite some time, until Nicol and I were clutching our sides from the hysteria. Nivedita helped us all calm down once I started to cough, handing me her flask of water and patting me on the back.

"What say you about claiming today as your name day? We will make an evening about it, christen the house and you together. After all, this is your house," Nivedita said.

"My house? No, it is *our* house! We built it together," I insisted. I would never allow anyone to say otherwise.

"Yes, my dear, we know, but you are made of magic and we could have never done this without you," she corrected. I felt my cheeks warm and nodded.

"I could not have done it without *you*." I smiled to everyone, catching each of my friend's eyes in turn. "I suppose we can christen the house, together." I agreed, unsure of what my christening was.

"Wonderful. We took the liberty of speaking with the local priest. All we need to do is collect him." Catherine clapped her hands together to remove the crumbs, then gestured for someone to come with her. I held up a finger and returned up the stairs to retrieve my shoes. Running down them afterwards, I followed her outside. No one else followed us when I looked back.

Catherine led the way west through all the streets, past people who noticed my hands and maybe recognized me as their local astrologer. Some even waved as we passed by. I waved back to the last few, surprised at the warm welcome.

"Here we are," Catherine announced, gesturing to a small parish building. I pulled open the door, holding it for Catherine as she passed through. Inside, we found the priest tidying the sanctuary.

"Hello, Father," Catherine called to him. He looked up and waved. He wore a simple cloth robe and sash of white cotton.

"Hello, young lady, uh Catherine, was it?" he responded. I assumed he was no older than four and forty years old.

"Yes! Might you have the time for that christening we spoke about?"

"Indeed! Is this our name day companion?" he addressed me with a friendly look.

"Yes, your holiness." I bent to a curtsy, but he waved me to stand again.

"Please, please. Call me Father, or Father Harris. Let us step over here to conduct your ceremony."

"Wait, no. Can we please go back to our home? Can we do both together, with everyone?" I asked, my heart beating fast in my chest.

Father Harris looked between Catherine and me. After receiving a shrug from Catherine, he looked to me.

"Why not? Let me collect a few things." Catherine took me by the arm and led me outside carefully.

"Are you alright?" she asked me when we returned to the street. "You do not have to do this. It is just a local custom."

"Yes, I am fine, and yes, I would like to do this. Just with everyone together," I responded. She gave me an unconvinced stare, but broke it when the priest joined us outside.

"After you," he called jovially. Catherine nodded, and with her arm looped in mine, she began to walk towards home again. As we walked, Father Harris explained his process and also the payment for his services. He assured us the money goes to his parish and not to his pocket. I looked at Catherine, worried, but she reassured me with a pat on the arm.

When we arrived home, Catherine slipped away to retrieve our companions. She directed us to arrange in the manner of an altar. The priest and I were at the front, my companions on either side.

"This minor ceremony will reflect the views of the church. Are you ready to begin?" Father Harris asked. I nodded and we began. He explained that the water in his flask was prayed over and blessed for christenings only. He also produced a vial of yellow oil that he explained was for anointment.

"You may not understand what I am about to say but I am blessing you in the faith of the church. What is your name, child?

"Sibyl Matilda Aneurin, sir," I replied

"Ego te baptizo in nomine Patris, et Filii et Spiritus Sancti, Sibyl Matilda Aneurin." He drew a figure from my head to my chest, across my shoulders, then dipped his finger in the bottle of oil and made a mark on my forehead. He locked eyes with me and bid me to shut them. As soon as I did, I was splashed with a sprinkling of water across my face. It reminded me of fathers prayers from home, bringing me a warm feeling, despite the chill creeping into my wet skin.

"Now for the house." Father Harris turned to our south-facing wall, the one with the door. "Benedicto Domini nostri Jesu Christi descendat super nanc domum 'Aneurin' et super omnes habitantes in ea. In nomine Patris, et Filii et Spiritus Sancti, amen." he splashed the door with water and drew a symbol on the door frame. I felt a whisper of home in the air.

"Thank you, Father Harris." Catherine approached him, pressing two shillings into his palms. His surprise lifted my heart. Father Harris approached me and took me by my opposing hand, without noticing my burn scars. He gave me a firm handshake.

"Congratulations, Miss Aneurin," he said kindly. Then, with a wave to the others, he ambled off back towards his parish. Nivedita was the next to congratulate me, but with a rib-cracking hug.

"I am so happy for you! How do you feel?" She released me, looking at me.

"Elated!" I responded. Nicol then pushed Nivedita out of his way to wrap me in his own damaging embrace.

"You are now fully blessed. How does that feel to you?"

"I feel well. I am the most happy and grateful I have ever been," I added once I was released from his grasp. He smiled and patted me on the back several times. Looking past Nicol, I saw Catherine and Viçente in a heated argument. They stopped as I approached, but I caught one word.

Leaving.

"Who is leaving?" I asked, my heart jumping into my throat. The two of them froze, staring at me.

"No one." Catherine lied. I fixed them with my hardest elder sister's stern look, even placing a hand on my hip. They exchanged twin looks of guilt that informed me that something was going unsaid. Viçente cleared his throat, gaining my full attention.

"I am only going to be gone for a while. I was sent to learn about the world and I chose to see to it that Catherine would find a safe place to live. That has been done. It is time I return to Spain to tell my family of all I have accomplished."

I gasped. My head began to spin. *Return to Spain? Am I destined to lose everything I work for?* My thoughts began to spiral out of control. I could not contain my tears, so I chose to turn and run back into the house, slamming the door behind me and stomping up the stairs. I threw myself into bed and curled into the fetal position, releasing my sobs fully. *I just do not understand!*

I heard the front door open and several people's footsteps coming inside. Catherine was cajoling Viçente for not waiting until later. They argued until Catherine shouted at him to consider more than his 'ancestral duty' for once, then joined me up the stairs in a huff. She retreated to her room with a swift slam of her door.

After a while, I had no more tears to cry, and a soft knock came at my door. I got up and answered it. Catherine stood there, eyes surely as puffy and red as my own.

"Will you come downstairs with me and let us explain?" Catherine begged. I nodded and let her take me by the hand. We descended the stairs together and headed for Viçente's room. The door was open, and I saw he was lounging across his bed. Catherine knocked, causing him to sit up, his black hair falling around his face.

"May we talk?" Catherine asked. He nodded, gesturing for us to come in. We stood at the foot of his bed while he sat against the headboard.

"Will you please explain to Sibyl your 'ancestral duties'?" she asked, a slight edge in her voice. He sighed, but looked me in the eye.

"I must leave. It is not because of you that I must go, please believe me. The truth is I am *able* to return to my ancestral home to claim my birthright. My challenge was to keep Catherine safe. She now has a home free of any obligation to lead a life that would risk her values. I must return to be knighted in the spring. Then I will come back." His brown eyes radiated honesty, like always. Tears welled in my eyes again.

"You will come back, here, to the Aneurin House?" I approached him.

"Yes, I will return here. To all of you," he said. I looked around to see Nicol and Nivedita looming in the doorway. They smiled as they entered, all of us crowding into the small room.

"Thank you," I whispered, falling to my knees to embrace him. He caught me and embraced me in return. Nivedita and Nicol came closer, adding themselves to the emotional hug. Last was Catherine, who hugged us all aggressively with a grunt. We pulled away with somber smiles stuck to all our faces. Nivedita looked nervous.

"What are you keeping to yourself?" I asked, knowing the look too well.

"Do not concern yourself. Let us enjoy your name day!" she hurried off to the hearth. We all followed closely, and I looked to Nicol for answers, but he had only a blank expression to share.

"Nivedita! What are you hiding?" I asked, following her to the common space. Nicol joined Nivedita by the hearth. She looked like a wounded animal staring out at me, pain in her eyes.

"I do not wish to say until after winter..." She started, but did not finish.

"Tell us now, please," I begged. Catherine and Viçente joined us.

"Is it a bad time to inform you that I would like to return to India for a short while?" she winced, waiting for my reply. I felt my mind spring again, but Catherine's hand gave me the comfort and strength I needed.

"Will you be back?" I asked. She nodded. "Then we better make the best of this winter."

Chapter 40

Given on the Feast of St. Luke, in the 14th year of the reign of King Henry VI, on the 18th day of October, in the year of our Lord 1436.

To our Dearest Vicente,

May this letter find you in good health and in the Grace of Fate. We write to you on this day to update you as to the events of recent days.

Events as of late have been mild, thankfully. Nicol and I have successfully read the fortunes of one hundred head of towns folk. We are more than prepared for this coming winter.

Catherine wishes to inform you that she has taken up the title of School Master for the young children of —

– Aberteifi. I admire her dedication and the admiration the children have for her.

We sorely miss you and Nivedita. We have received a letter from her just last week.

When you return, I must tell you – I will be leaving as well, for but a summer. Nivedita wrote to us of a high scholar in Florence that may very well teach me more of the human stars and constellations. This work will be good for me in order to provide better service to our community.

All the best
Sibyl, Catherine and Nicol